"I have not come to harm you."

His voice was low, almost hypnotic.

That was it. He lured his victims into a trance with his golden eyes and honeyed tone. Shanna shook her head. She could fight this. She would not give in.

He frowned. "You are being difficult."

"You better believe it." She fumbled in her purse and whipped out her .32 caliber Beretta Tomcat. "Surprise, sucker."

No shock or fear registered on his rugged face, only a slight hint of irritation. "Madam, the weapon is unnecessary." He took a step toward her. "Drop the gun, please."

"No!" She gave him her best and meanest glare. "I'll shoot. I'll kill you."

"Easier said than done." He took another step toward her. "I will not harm you. I need your help."

She gasped. "You . . . you're bleeding."

"Can you help me?"

Oh, god, he was gorgeous. Just her luck that the perfect man would waltz into her life two minutes before her death. . . .

KERRELYN SPARKS

How to Marry a Millionaire Vampire

AVON BOOKS

An Imprint of HarperCollinsPublishers

This is a work of fiction. Names, characters, places, and incidents are products of the author's imagination or are used fictitiously and are not to be construed as real. Any resemblance to actual events, locales, organizations, or persons, living or dead, is entirely coincidental.

AVON BOOKS
An Imprint of HarperCollins*Publishers*
10 East 53rd Street
New York, New York 10022-5299

Copyright © 2005 by Kerrelyn Sparks
ISBN: 0-7394-5696-2

Printed in the U.S.A.

*With love and gratitude to my writing pals,
who keep me sane when times are bad
and celebrate when times are good—
MJ Selle, Vicky Dreiling,
Vicky Yelton, and Sandy Weider.*

*Also, my sincerest gratitude
to these brilliant women—
my agent, Michelle Grajkowski,
and my editor, Erika Tsang.*

Acknowledgments

I am indebted to the following people for their assistance: A big thanks to everyone at Dr. Stephanie Troeger's Dental Clinic in Katy, Texas, for helping me to successfully re-implant a vampire's fang. Thanks also to Paul Weider, whose ideas on digital technology opened up a world of exciting possibilities, including a vampire television network. I'd like to thank my husband, Don Sparks, for naming the network. Another round of thanks must go to fellow writers at the West Houston and Northwest Houston chapters of Romance Writers of America, for their unfailing support. And finally, my eternal gratitude to my husband and children, for all their patience and encouragement.

One

Roman Draganesti knew someone had quietly entered his home office. Either a foe or close friend. A friend, he decided. A foe could never make it past the guards at each entrance of his Upper East Side Manhattan townhouse. Or past the guards stationed on each of the five floors.

With his excellent night vision, Roman suspected he could see much better than his uninvited guest. His suspicions were confirmed when the dark silhouette stumbled into a Louis XVI bombé chest and cursed softly.

Gregori Holstein. A friend, but an annoying one. The vice president of marketing for Romatech Industries tackled every problem with tireless enthusiasm. It was enough to make Roman feel old. Really old. "What do you want, Gregori?"

His guest whipped around and squinted in Roman's direction. "Why are you sitting here, all alone in the dark?"

"Hmm. Tough question. I suppose I wanted to be alone. And in the dark. You should try it more often. Your night vision is not what it should be."

"Why bother to practice my night vision when the city's lit up all night?" Gregori groped along the wall till he located the switch. The lights came on with a muted golden glow. "There, that's better."

Roman leaned back into the cool leather of his wingback chair and took a sip from his wineglass. The liquid burned his throat. God-awful stuff. "Is there a purpose for your visit?"

"Of course. You left work too early, and we had something important to show you. You're going to love it."

Roman set his glass on the mahogany desk in front of him. "I have learned that we have plenty of time."

Gregori snorted. "Try to work up some excitement here. We had an amazing development at the lab." He noted Roman's half-empty glass. "I feel like celebrating. What are you drinking?"

"You won't like it."

Gregori strode toward the wet bar. "Why? Are your tastes too refined for me?" He grasped the decanter and sloshed some red liquid into a wineglass. "Color looks good."

"Take my advice and get a new bottle from the fridge."

"Ha! If you can drink it, so can I." Gregori tossed back a good portion before slamming the glass down with a victorious sneer aimed at Roman. Then his eyes widened. His normally pale face turned a purplish red. A strangled sound vibrated deep in his throat, and then the sputtering began. Coughing, followed by choked curses, followed by more coughing. Finally he pressed his palms against the bar and leaned forward to gasp for air.

God-awful stuff, indeed, Roman thought. "Have you recovered?"

Gregori took a deep, shuddering breath. "What was in there?"

"Ten percent garlic juice."

"*What the hell?*" Gregori jerked to an upright position. "Have you gone mad? Are you trying to poison yourself?"

"I thought I'd see if the old legends were true." Roman's mouth curled into a slight smile. "Obviously, some of us are more susceptible than others."

"Obviously, some of us like to live too damned dangerously!"

Roman's attempt at a smile faded into oblivion. "Your observation would have more merit if we weren't already dead."

Gregori stalked toward him. "You're not going to start that 'woe is me, I'm a cursed demon from hell' crap again, are you?"

"Face the facts, Gregori. We have survived for centuries by taking life. We are an abomination before God."

"You're not drinking this." Gregori wrenched the glass from Roman's hand and set it down out of his reach. "Listen to me. No vampire has ever done more than you to protect the living and tame the cravings within us."

"And now we're the most well-behaved pack of demonic creatures on Earth. Bravo. Call the pope. I'm ready for sainthood."

Gregori's impatient look melted into curious speculation. "Is it true what they say, then? You were once a monk?"

"I prefer not to live in the past."

"I'm not so sure about that."

Roman clenched his hands into fists. His past was a subject he would discuss with no one. "I believe you mentioned some sort of development at the lab?"

"Oh, right. Sheesh, I left Laszlo waiting in the hall. I wanted to set the scene, so to speak."

Roman took a deep breath and slowly relaxed his hands. "Then I suggest you begin. There are only so many hours in a night."

"Right. And I'm going out clubbing later. Simone just flew in from Paris, and boy—"

"—are her wings tired. That was old a century ago." Roman's hands fisted once again. "Stay on the subject, Gregori, or I will be forced to send you to your coffin for a time-out."

Gregori gave him an exasperated look. "I only mentioned it in case you wanted to join us. It's a hell of a lot more fun than sitting here alone, drinking poison." He adjusted his silk black tie. "You know, Simone has always been hot for you. In fact, any of the ladies downstairs would love to cheer you up."

"I don't find them particularly cheerful. The last time I looked, they were all dead."

"Well, if you're going to be picky about it, maybe you should try a live one."

"*No*." Roman jumped to his feet, grasped his wineglass, and zoomed with vampire speed to the wet bar in one second. "Not a mortal. Never again."

"Whoa. That hit a nerve."

"End of discussion." Roman poured the blood and garlic concoction down the drain, then emptied the remainder of the poisonous brew from the decanter. He'd learned his lesson long ago. A relationship with a mortal could only lead to heartbreak. Literally. And he'd rather not experience a stake through the heart. What a great choice he had for companionship—a dead female Vamp or a live woman who would want him dead. And it would never change. This heartless existence would stretch on and on for centuries. No wonder he was depressed.

As a scientist, he could usually find something intriguing to occupy his mind. But sometimes, like tonight, it wasn't enough. So what if he was close to a breakthrough on a formula that would enable a vampire to stay awake during the day? What would he do with those extra hours? More work? He had centuries ahead of him for work.

The truth had hit him tonight. If he stayed awake during the day, there would be no one to even talk to. He'd only be adding more hours of loneliness to his so-called life. And that was when he'd given up and come home. To be alone in the dark, listening to the monotonous beat of his cold, lonesome heart. Relief would come at dawn when the rising sun would stop his heart, and once again he would be dead during the day. Unfortunately, he was beginning to feel dead all the time.

"Are you all right, Roman?" Gregori watched him warily. "I've heard that sometimes the really old ones like you get kinda down in the dumps."

"Thanks for reminding me. And since I'm not getting any younger, perhaps you could bring Laszlo in from the hall?"

"Right. Sorry." Gregori tugged on the cuffs of his snowy white evening shirt. "Okay, I wanted to set the scene. Remember the mission statement for Romatech Industries? Make the world safe for vampires and mortals alike."

"I'm aware of it. I believe I wrote it."

"Yes, but the major threat to peace has always been the poor and the Malcontents."

"Yes, I know." Not all modern-day vampires were ridiculously rich like Roman, and even with his company making synthetic blood affordable and accessible, those who were financially challenged would always be tempted to feed off a mortal for free. Roman had tried to convince them that there was no such thing as a free lunch. The victimized mortals tended to take offense. Then they would hire a few Buffy wannabes, and those vicious little killers would destroy every vampire who crossed their path, even the peaceful, law-abiding Vamp who wouldn't bite a flea. The sad truth was that as long as any vampire persisted in attacking mortals, no vampire on Earth would be safe.

Roman ambled back toward his desk. "I believe I put you in charge of the poor problem."

"I'm working on it. I'll have the presentation ready in a few days. Meanwhile, Laszlo had this brilliant idea for handling the Malcontents."

Roman sat heavily in his chair. The Malcontents were

the most dangerous group of vampires in existence. The secret society called themselves the True Ones and spurned the more evolved sensibilities of the modern-day Vamp. The Malcontents could afford to buy the richest blood manufactured by Romatech Industries. They could afford the most exotic, gourmet blood from Roman's popular line of Vampire Fusion Cuisine. They could even afford to drink from the finest crystal. They just didn't want to.

For them, the thrill of drinking blood was not the blood itself. These creatures lived for the bite. They believed nothing could replace the intense pleasure of sinking one's fangs into the warm, pliant skin of a mortal's neck.

In the past year, communication between the Malcontents and modern Vamps had degenerated until an undeclared state of war hovered over them. A war that could result in many deaths—both mortal and vampire.

"Have Laszlo come in."

Gregori zoomed to the door and opened it. "We're ready."

"About time." Laszlo sounded upset. "The guard out here was about to perform a cavity search on our guest of honor."

"Och, ye have a bonnie lass there," the guard murmured in his Scots accent.

"Leave her alone!" Laszlo marched into Roman's office with a female clutched in his arms as if the two of them were doing the tango. Not only was the female taller than the short vampire chemist, she was noticeably naked.

Roman jumped to his feet. "You brought a mortal here?" A *naked* mortal?

"Relax, Roman, she's not real." Gregori leaned toward Laszlo. "The boss is a little nervous about mortal females."

"I am not nervous, Gregori. Every nerve ending in me died over five hundred years ago." Roman could see only the back of the false female, but her long blond hair and rounded derriere certainly looked real.

Laszlo set the female in a wingback chair. Her legs stuck out straight, so he leaned over to bend them. With each adjustment, her knees made a small *pop*.

Gregori squatted beside her. "She's very lifelike, don't you think?"

"Very." Roman eyed the curly hair, trimmed in a narrow, stripper style, between the false female's legs. "Apparently she's a dyed blond."

"Look." With a grin, Gregori nudged her legs apart. "She comes fully equipped. Sweet, huh?"

Roman gulped. "Is this—" He cleared his throat and tried again. "Is this some sort of mortal sex toy?"

"Yes, sir, she is." Laszlo pried open her mouth. "Look. She even has a tongue. The texture is incredibly lifelike." He inserted a short, stubby finger. "And the vacuum causes a very realistic sucking sensation."

Roman glanced down at Gregori, who was kneeling between the female's legs, admiring the view, then at Laszlo, who was slipping his finger in and out of the doll's mouth. God's blood. If he were capable of getting a headache, he'd have a migraine by now. "Shall I leave you three alone?"

"No, sir." The short chemist struggled to free his finger from the doll's greedy mouth. "We just wanted to show you how real she is." His finger was released with a small *pop*, then the doll's mouth relaxed into a frozen smile that seemed to indicate she was enjoying herself.

"She's amazing." Gregori ran an approving hand down her leg. "Laszlo sent for her in the mail."

"It was *your* catalog." Laszlo looked embarrassed. "I don't usually have mortal sex. Too messy."

And too dangerous. Roman dragged his gaze away from the doll's beautifully shaped breasts. Maybe Gregori was right and he should enjoy himself with one of the lady Vamps. If mortals could pretend this doll was alive, maybe he could do the same with a vampire. But how could a dead woman warm his soul?

Gregori lifted one of the doll's feet for a closer look. "This little babe is tempting, though."

Roman sighed. This mortal sex toy was supposed to solve the Malcontent problem? They were wasting his time, not to mention making him feel horny and damned lonely at the same time. "All the Vamps I know prefer brain sex. I assume it's the same with the Malcontents."

"Not possible with this one, I'm afraid." Laszlo tapped the doll's head, producing a ripe-melon echo.

Roman noted the doll was still smiling, though her blue glass eyes gazed straight ahead with a vacant look. "So she has the same IQ as Simone."

"Hey." Gregori scowled as he cradled the doll's foot to his chest. "That's not nice."

"Neither is wasting my time." Roman glared at him. "How can this toy possibly solve the problem with the Malcontents?"

"But she's much more than a toy, sir." Laszlo fiddled with the buttons on his white lab coat. "She's been transformed."

"Into VANNA." Gregori gave the doll's little toe a playful tug. "Sweet little VANNA. Come to Papa."

Roman gritted his teeth, remembering first to make sure his fangs were retracted. Otherwise a Vamp could accidentally pierce his bottom lip. "Enlighten me, please, before I resort to violence."

Gregori laughed, apparently unconcerned by his boss's anger. "VANNA is a Vampire Artificial Nutritional Needs Appliance."

Laszlo twirled a loose button on his lab coat, his brow furrowed with worry. Obviously, he took the boss's temper much more seriously. "She's the perfect solution for the vampire who is still compelled to bite. And she'll be available in whichever race or gender you prefer."

"You're going to make male toys, too?" Roman asked.

"Yes, eventually." The loose button tumbled onto the floor. Laszlo picked it up and stuffed it in a pocket. "Gre-

gori thought we could advertise her on the Digital Vampire
Network. You'd have your choice of VANNA Brown,
VANNA Black—"

"And this would be VANNA White?" Roman grimaced.
"The legal department will love this."

"We could take some promotional photos of her in a
fancy evening gown." Gregori stroked the arch of her foot.
"And some sexy, high-heeled, black sandals."

Roman gave his vice president of marketing a worried
look, then turned to Laszlo. "Are you saying this doll can
be used for the purpose of feeding?"

"Yes!" Laszlo nodded enthusiastically. "Just like a live
female, she's capable of multitasking, satisfying both your
sexual and feeding needs. Here. Let me show you." He
leaned the doll forward and brushed her hair to the side. "I
did the work back here where it wouldn't be so noticeable."

Roman studied the small switch and U-shaped cut. At
the base of the U, a small tube protruded with a clamp on
the end. "You put a tube in her?"

"Yes. It's specifically designed to simulate a real artery.
We developed a circular pattern inside her." Laszlo ran his
finger over her body to show the location of the false artery. "It travels through her chest cavity, then up one side
of her neck and down the other, finally returning to the
chest."

"And you fill it with blood?"

"Yes, sir. She'll come packaged with a free funnel.
Blood and batteries not included."

"They never are," Roman noted dryly.

"She's easy to use." Laszlo pointed at the doll's neck.
"You remove the clamp, insert the small funnel, select two
quarts of your favorite blood from Romatech Industries,
and fill her up."

"I see. Does she light up when she's running low?"

Laszlo frowned. "I suppose I could put in an indicator
light—"

"I was kidding." Roman sighed. "Please continue."

"Yes, sir." Laszlo cleared his throat. "The switch here turns on a small pump inserted inside her chest cavity. A false heart, so to speak. It will cause the blood to flow through the artery and simulate a real pulse."

Roman nodded. "And that's where the batteries come in."

"Mmm," Gregori's voice sounded muffled. "She keeps going and going."

Roman glanced at his vice president and found him raking his teeth over VANNA's big toe. The red glow in Gregori's eyes served as a different sort of indicator light. "Gregori! Back off."

With a low growl, Gregori dropped the doll's foot. "You're no fun anymore."

Roman took a deep breath and wished he could pray for patience. But no self-respecting God would want to hear the supplications of a demon with a mortal sex toy. "Has she been tested yet?"

"No, sir." Laszlo flipped on VANNA's switch. "We thought you should have the honor of being first."

First. Roman's gaze swept over the doll's perfect body, a body that now pulsed inside with life-giving blood. "So at last, a vampire can have his cake and bite it, too."

Gregori smiled as he smoothed out his black dinner jacket. "The taste test challenge. Enjoy."

Roman arched an eyebrow at his vice president of marketing. No doubt, this testing was Gregori's idea. He probably thought his boss needed a little excitement to feel alive. Unfortunately, he was right.

Roman extended a hand to touch VANNA's neck. The skin was cooler than a real human's, but still very soft. Beneath his fingertips, the artery throbbed, strong and constant. At first, he felt the pulse with only his fingers, but then the pounding sensation crept up his arm and into his shoulder. He swallowed hard. How long had it been? Eighteen years?

The pulse spread inside him, filling his empty heart and all his senses. His nostrils flared. He could smell the blood now. Type A Positive. His favorite. His entire body throbbed in sync with the female. His rational thought seeped away, overpowered by a driving sensation he hadn't experienced in years. *Bloodlust.*

A growl vibrated deep in his throat. His groin hardened. He curled his fingers around the doll's neck and dragged her toward him.

"I'll take her." With lightning speed, he tossed her onto a velvet reading chaise. She lay still, her legs still bent and now sagging open at the knees. The erotic sight was almost too much to bear. The small amount of blood in Roman's veins cried out for more. More woman. More blood.

He sat and brushed her blond hair away from her neck. Her dopey grin was a bit disconcerting, but easily ignored. As he leaned over, he caught sight of a reflection in her blank, glass eyes. Not him, for his form could not be mirrored. All he could see were the red, glowing lights of his own eyes. VANNA had turned him on. He turned her face away to expose her neck. The pulsing artery within her sang out, *Take me. Take me.*

With a low growl, he pressed against her body. His fangs sprang out, causing a ripple of pleasure to surge through his body. The scent of blood rushed through him, stripping away the last shreds of self-control. The beast within was unleashed.

He bit her. Too late, his frenzied mind realized an unusual fact. Her skin might feel soft on the surface like a human's, but the inner texture was totally different. Tough, thick, rubbery plastic. If this was relevant, it didn't register, for the smell of blood shattered his thoughts. His instincts claimed victory, howling in his brain like a starving animal. He sank his fangs in deeper and deeper, till at last he felt that sweet popping sensation as he broke through the arterial wall. Heaven. He was swimming in blood.

With a long suck, the blood gushed into his fangs and filled his mouth. He gulped it down and greedily drank more. She was delicious. She was his.

He smoothed a hand down to her breast and squeezed. What a fool he'd been, content to sip blood from a glass. How could that possibly replace the hot rush of blood flowing through one's fangs? By the devil, he'd forgotten how sweet this was. It was a total body experience. He was rock hard. All his senses were on fire. He'd never drink from a glass again.

With another tug on her neck, he realized he'd drained her dry. Good to the last drop. But then a touch of clarity broke through the sensual daze. Bloody hell, he'd lost control. If she were mortal, she'd be dead. And he would have murdered another child of God.

How could this possibly advance the cause of civilized vampire behavior? This doll would remind every vampire how intensely pleasurable it was to bite. No vampire, even the most evolved, modern-day Vamp, could partake of this experience without wanting the real thing. All he could think about now was biting the first live female he came across. VANNA was not the answer to human preservation. She was the death knell to their existence.

With a groan, Roman ripped his mouth away from her neck. Blood splattered onto the doll's white skin, and at first, he thought she'd sprung a leak. But no, he was sure he'd drained her dry. Damn, the blood was coming from him. "What the hell?"

"Oh my God," Laszlo whispered.

"What?" Roman looked at her neck and there, lodged in the tough plastic, was one of his fangs.

"Sheesh!" Gregori stepped closer for a good look. "How'd that happen?"

"The plastic—" More blood dripped from Roman's mouth. Damn, he was losing his lunch. "The plastic is too tough and rubbery inside. Not at all like human skin."

"Oh dear." Laszlo attacked another button with his nervous fingers. "This is terrible. The texture was so real on the outside. I didn't realize . . . I'm so sorry, sir."

"That's the least of our problems." Roman wrenched his tooth from the girl's neck. He'd explain his unfortunate conclusions later. For now, he needed his fang fixed.

"You're still bleeding." Gregori handed him a white handkerchief.

"The feeding vein that connects to the fang is open." Roman pressed the handkerchief against the gaping hole where his right fang should be. "Thit."

"You could use your own healing powers to seal the vein shut," Laszlo suggested.

"It would be clothed permanently. I'd be a one-thided eater for all eternity." Roman removed the bloody handkerchief from his mouth and reinserted his fang into the hole.

Gregori leaned over to look. "I think you got it."

Roman released his hold on the tooth and attempted to retract his fangs. The left fang did as it should, but the right one fell from his mouth and landed on VANNA's stomach. More blood seeped from the wound. "Shit." Roman stuffed the handkerchief back in his mouth.

"Sir, I suggest you go to a dentist." Laszlo picked up the fang and offered it to Roman. "I've heard they can put a lost tooth back."

"Oh, right." Gregori snorted. "What's he supposed to do, waltz into a dental office and say, 'Excuse me, I'm a vampire and I lost a fang in the neck of a sex toy.' They're not going to line up to help him."

"I need a vampire dentitht," Roman announced. "Look in the Black Pageth."

"The Black Pages?" Gregori zoomed to Roman's desk and began opening drawers. "You know, you're starting to lisp."

"I have a bloody rag in my mouth! Look in the bottom drawer."

Gregori located the black phone directory for vampire-owned businesses and flipped it open to reveal the white pages within. "Okay." He ran a finger down the advertisements. "Cemetery plots. Coffin repair. Crypt-keeper services. Custom-made crypts—fifty percent off. Interesting."

"Gregori," Roman growled.

"Right." He turned the page. "Okay. D's. Dance lessons—learn to move like a Latin lover. Dirt deliveries—sleep like a baby in topsoil from the Old Country. Dracula costumes—small to plus sizes."

Roman groaned. "I'm in deep thit." He swallowed hard and grimaced at the taste of stale blood. The meal had tasted better the first time down.

Gregori turned another page. "Draperies—guaranteed to block out that annoying sunlight. Dungeons—your choice of several floor plans." He sighed. "That's it. No dentists."

Roman slumped into a wingback chair. "I'll have to go to a mortal." *Damn.* He'd have to use mind control, then wipe the dentist's memory clean afterward. Otherwise no mortal would be willing to help him.

"We may have trouble finding a mortal dentist who's available in the middle of the night." Laszlo dashed to the wet bar and grabbed a roll of paper towels. Then he proceeded to wipe the blood off VANNA. He gave Roman a worried look. "Sir, it might be best for you to keep the tooth in your mouth."

At the desk, Gregori thumbed through the Yellow Pages. "Sheesh, there's a ton of dentists." He straightened with a jerk and grinned. "I found it! SoHo SoBright Dental Clinic—open twenty-four hours a day for the city that never sleeps. Bingo."

Laszlo let out a deep breath. "What a relief. I'm not sure, since I've never heard of anything like this happening before, but I'm afraid if your fang is not successfully implanted tonight, then it never will be."

Roman sat up. "What do you mean?"

Laszlo threw the bloodied paper towels in a trash can by the desk. "Our injuries are naturally healed while we sleep. If dawn comes and you fall asleep with your fang still missing, your body will close the feeding veins and the wound for good."

Shit. Roman stood. "Then it mutht be done tonight."

"Yes, sir." Laszlo fingered a button on his lab coat. "With any luck, you'll be in perfect shape for the annual conference."

God's blood! Roman gulped. How could he have forgotten the annual spring conference? The Gala Opening Ball was scheduled for two nights from tonight. All the major coven masters from around the world would be there. As master of the largest coven in America, Roman was hosting the big event. If he showed up, missing a fang, he'd be the brunt of jokes for the next century.

Gregori grabbed a piece of paper and scribbled down the address. "Here you go. You want us to come with you?"

Roman removed the handkerchief and tooth from his mouth so his directions would be clear. "Laszlo will drive me. We'll take VANNA with us so everyone will assume we're taking her back to the lab. You, Gregori, will go out with Simone as planned. Nothing will appear out of the ordinary."

"Very well." Gregori zipped over to his boss and handed him the address of the dental clinic. "Good luck. If you need any help, just give me a call."

"I'll be fine." Roman gave his two employees a stern look. "This incident will not be spoken of again, not to anyone. Do you understand?"

"Yes, sir." Laszlo picked VANNA up.

Roman watched the chemist's hand curve around one plump buttock. God's blood, with all that had happened, he was still hard. His body thrummed with desire, craving more blood and more female flesh. He could only hope that this dentist would be male. God help any mortal female who crossed his path right now.

He still had one fang, and he was afraid he'd use it.

Two

𝒥t was another endlessly boring night at the dental clinic. Shanna Whelan leaned back in the squeaky office chair and gazed at the white ceiling tiles. The water stain was still there. What a surprise. It had taken her three nights to conclude that the stain was the exact shape of a dachshund. Such was her life.

With another loud creak, she straightened in her chair and glanced at the clock radio. Two-thirty in the morning. Six hours left on her shift. She turned the radio on. Elevator music droned forth to fill the office, an uninspired, instrumental version of "Strangers in the Night." Yeah, like she was going to meet a tall, dark, handsome stranger and fall in love. Not in her boring life. Last night, the pinnacle of her evening had been when she learned how to make her chair squeak in time with the music.

With a groan, she folded her arms on the desk and pillowed her head. How did the saying go? Be careful what you ask for because you might get it? Well, she had begged for boring, and boy, did she have it. In the six weeks she'd been working at the clinic, she'd had one customer. A young boy with braces. In the middle of the night, a wire had come loose in his mouth. His frantic parents had brought him here so she could reconnect the wire. Otherwise the loose wire could have stabbed the inside of the boy's mouth, resulting in . . . blood.

Shanna shuddered. Just the thought of blood made her woozy. Memories of the Incident swelled in the dark recesses of her brain, gruesome bloody images that taunted her, threatening to come into the light. No, she would not let them ruin her day. Or her new life. They belonged to another life, another person. They belonged to the brave and happy girl she'd been for the first twenty-seven years of her life before all hell had broken loose. Now, thanks to the Witness Protection Program, she was boring Jane Wilson, who lived in a boring loft in a boring neighborhood and spent every night at a boring job.

Boring was good. Boring was safe. Jane Wilson had to remain invisible and disappear into the ocean of countless faces in Manhattan for the sole purpose of staying alive. Unfortunately, it seemed that even boredom could cause stress. There was just too much time to think. Time to remember.

She switched off the music and paced across the empty waiting room. Eighteen chairs, upholstered in alternating hues of dusty blue and green, lined the pale blue walls. A framed copy of Monet's *Water Lilies* hung on one wall in an effort to inject calm serenity into nervous patients. Shanna doubted it worked. She was as edgy as ever.

Usually busy during the day, the clinic was a lonely place at night. Just as well. If anyone came in with a serious problem, Shanna was no longer sure she could deal with it. She'd been a good dentist before the . . . Incident. *Don't think about that.* But what would she do if someone actually came to the clinic with an emergency? Just last week, she'd accidentally nicked herself shaving her legs.

One tiny drop of blood and her knees had shaken so badly, she'd been forced to lie down.

Maybe she should give up dentistry. So what if she lost her career? She'd lost everything else, including her family. The Department of Justice had made it clear. Under no circumstances was she to contact any family members or old friends. Not only would it put her own life back in jeopardy, but it would endanger those she loved.

Boring Jane Wilson had no family or friends. She had one assigned U.S. marshal she could talk to. No wonder she'd gained ten pounds in the last two months. Eating was about the only thrill left to her. That and talking to the handsome young pizza delivery guy. She quickened her pace as she circled the waiting room. If she kept eating pizza every night, she'd puff up like a whale, and then the bad guys might never recognize her. She could be safe and fat for the rest of her life. Shanna groaned. Safe, fat, bored, and lonesome.

A knock at the front door brought her skidding to a stop. Probably the pizza delivery guy, but even so, for a second her heart had lurched in her chest. She took a deep breath and ventured toward the front windows. She peeked through the white mini-blinds she always kept closed at night so no one could see inside.

"It's me, Dr. Wilson," Tommy called. "I've got your pizza."

"All right." She unlocked the door. The clinic might be open for business all night, but she still took precautions. She only unlocked the door for legitimate customers. And pizza.

"Hey, Doc." Tommy sauntered in with a grin. For the last two weeks, the teenager had made a delivery every night, and Shanna enjoyed his adolescent attempts at flirtation as much as the pizza. In fact, this was the highlight of her day. Jeez, she was on the fast track to becoming pathetic.

"Hi, Tommy. How's it going?" She went to the office counter to locate her purse.

"I've got your giant pepperoni right here." Tommy tugged on the waistband of his loose jeans, then let go. The jeans slid slightly down his narrow hips, revealing three inches of silk Scooby Doo boxer shorts.

"But I ordered a small one."

"I wasn't talking about the pizza, Doc." Tommy gave her a big wink and set the pizza box on the counter.

"Right. Well, that was a bit too cheesy for me. And I don't mean the pizza, either."

"Sorry." With pink-tinted cheeks, he gave her a sheepish smile. "A guy's gotta try, you know."

"I suppose so." She paid for the pizza.

"Thanks." Tommy pocketed the money. "You know, we make a jillion kinds of pizza. You ought to try something new."

"Maybe I will. Tomorrow."

He rolled his eyes. "That's what you said last week."

The phone rang, splitting the air with its shrill sound. Shanna jumped.

"Whoa, Doc. Maybe you should switch to decaf."

"I don't think I've heard that phone ring since I started working here." The phone jangled once again. Wow, a pizza guy and a ringing phone at the same time. This was more excitement than she'd seen in weeks.

"I'll let you get to work. See you tomorrow, Dr. Wilson." Tommy waved good-bye and swaggered toward the front door.

"Bye." Shanna admired his low-slung jeans from the back. She was definitely going on a diet. After the pizza. The phone rang again, and she lifted the receiver. "SoHo SoBright Dental Clinic. May I help you?"

"Yes, you may," the man's gruff voice was followed by a heavy breath. Then another.

Oh, great. A pervert to brighten her evening. "I believe

you have the wrong number." She started to lower the receiver when she heard his voice again.

"I believe you have the wrong name, *Shanna.*"

She gasped. It had to be a mistake. *Yeah, and Shanna is such a common name.* People were always calling places, asking for Shanna. Who was she kidding? Should she hang up? No, they already knew who she was.

And *where* she was. Terror jolted through her. Oh my God, they were coming for her.

Calm down! She had to remain calm. "I'm afraid you have the wrong number. This is Dr. Jane Wilson at the SoHo SoBright Dental—"

"Cut the crap! We know where you are, Shanna. It's payback time." *Click.* The call was over, and the nightmare was back.

"Oh no, oh no, oh no." She dropped the receiver in place and realized she was mumbling louder and louder, working her way up to a full-fledged scream. *Get a grip!* She mentally slapped herself and punched in the numbers 911.

"This is Dr. Jane Wilson at the SoHo SoBright Dental Clinic. I . . . we're under attack!" She gave the address, and the dispatcher assured her a squad car was on the way. Right. With an ETA of ten minutes past the time of her murder, no doubt.

With a gasp, she remembered the front door was unlocked. She sprinted to the door and locked it. As she dashed through the clinic to the back door, she grabbed her cell phone from her lab coat pocket and punched the number of her assigned U.S. marshal.

First ring. "Come on, Bob. Pick up." She reached the back door. All the deadbolts were secure. Second ring.

Oh no! What a stupid waste of time. The entire front of the clinic was glass. Locking the door wouldn't keep anyone out. They'd simply shoot through the glass. Then they'd shoot her. She needed to think better than this. She needed to get the hell out of here.

The third ring was followed by a click. "Bob, I need help!"

She was interrupted by a bored voice. "I'm away from my desk at the moment, but leave your name and number and I'll get back to you as soon as possible."

Beep. "This is bullshit, Bob!" She ran back to the office for her purse. "You said you'd always be there. They know where I am, and they're coming for me." She jabbed the END button and dropped the phone back into her pocket. That damned Bob! So much for his saccharine assurances that the government could protect her. She'd show him. Why, she'd . . . she'd stop paying her taxes. Of course, if she was murdered, that would no longer be a problem.

Focus! she reprimanded herself. This sort of jumbled-up thinking would get her killed. She skidded to a stop at the desk and grabbed her purse. She'd escape out the back and run till she found a taxi. Then, she'd go . . . where? If they knew where she worked, they probably also knew where she lived. Oh God, she was so screwed.

"Good evening," a deep voice rumbled across the room.

With a squeal, Shanna jumped. A gorgeous man was standing by the front door. *Gorgeous?* She was really losing it, if she was checking out a hit man. He held something white against his mouth, but she hardly noticed it, for his eyes caught her attention and didn't let go. His gaze swept over her, his eyes a golden brown and tinged with hunger.

A spurt of frigid air jabbed at her head, so sudden and intense, she pressed a hand against her temple. "How . . . how did you get in?"

He continued to stare at her, but with a slight movement of one hand, he motioned toward the door.

"That's not possible," she whispered. The locked door and windows were intact. Had he managed to sneak in earlier? No, she would have noticed this man. Every cell in her body was aware of this man. Was it her imagination, or were his eyes growing more golden, more intense?

His shoulder-length black hair curled slightly on the ends. A black sweater accentuated broad shoulders, and black jeans hugged his hips and long legs. He was a tall, dark, and handsome . . . hit man. My God. He could probably kill a woman just by giving her wildly erratic heart palpitations. In fact, that was probably what he did. He wasn't carrying a weapon of any kind. Of course, those large hands of his—

Cold pain pierced her head once more, reminding her of the times she'd slurped down a frozen Slushee too fast.

"I have not come to harm you." His voice was low, almost hypnotic.

That was it. He lured his victims into a trance with his golden eyes and honeyed voice, then before you knew it— she shook her head. No, she could fight this. She would not give in.

He frowned, dark brows drawing closer together. "You are being difficult."

"You better believe it." She fumbled in her purse and whipped out her .32-caliber Beretta Tomcat. "Surprise, sucker."

No shock or fear registered on his rugged face, only a slight hint of irritation. "Madam, the weapon is unnecessary."

Oh, the safety catch. With trembling fingers, she switched it off, then pointed the gun back at his broad chest. Hopefully, he hadn't noticed her lack of expertise. She widened her stance and used both hands like she'd seen on cop shows. "I've got a full clip with your name on it, scumbag. You're going *down*!"

Something sparked in his eyes. It should have been fear, but she could have sworn it was amusement. He stepped toward her. "Drop the gun, please. And the dramatics."

"No!" She gave him her best and meanest glare. "I'll shoot. I'll kill you."

"Easier said than done." He took another step toward her.

She raised the gun an inch. "I mean it. I don't care how incredibly handsome you are. I'll splatter you all over the room."

His dark brows rose. Now he looked surprised. Slowly, he inspected her once more, his eyes darkening to the color of hot, molten gold.

"Stop looking at me like that." Her hands trembled.

He stepped toward her again. "I will not harm you. I need your help." He lowered the handkerchief from his mouth. Red splotches stained the white cotton. *Blood.*

Shanna gasped. Her hands lowered. Her stomach lurched. "You . . . you're bleeding."

"Put the gun down before you shoot yourself in the foot."

"No." She raised the Beretta again, and tried not to think about blood. After all, if she shot him, there'd be plenty more.

"I need your help. I lost a tooth."

"You—you're a customer?"

"Yes. Can you help me?"

"Oh, sheesh." She dropped her gun into her purse. "Sorry about this."

"You don't normally greet your customers at gunpoint?" His eyes twinkled with more amusement.

Oh, God, he was gorgeous. Just her luck that the perfect man would waltz into her life two minutes before her death. "Look, they'll be here any second. You'd better get out of here. Fast."

His eyes narrowed. "You're in trouble?"

"Yes. And if they catch you here, they'll kill you, too. Come on." She grabbed her purse. "Let's go out the back."

"You are concerned for me?"

She glanced back. He was still hovering by the desk. "Of course. I hate to see innocent people killed."

"I am not what you would call innocent."

She snorted. "Did you come here to kill me?"

"No."

"Innocent enough for me. Come on." She headed across the examining room.

"Is there another clinic where you can help me with my tooth?"

She turned and caught her breath. He was right behind her, though she hadn't heard him move. "How did you—"

He opened his hand, palm up. "This is my tooth."

She flinched. A few drops of blood had pooled in his palm, but with effort, she managed to focus on the tooth. "*What?* Is this some sort of sick joke? That's not a human tooth."

His mouth tightened. "It is *my* tooth. I need you to put it back in."

"No way am I implanting an animal tooth in your mouth. That's just sick. That . . . that thing's from a dog. Or a wolf."

His nostrils flared, and he seemed to grow three inches. His fingers curled around the tooth, forming a fist. "How dare you, madam. I am not a werewolf."

She blinked. Okay, he was weird. A little psycho, maybe. Unless . . . "Oh, I get it. Tommy put you up to this."

"I don't know a Tommy."

"Then who—" Shanna was interrupted by the sound of cars screeching to a halt outside the clinic. Was it the police? Please, God, let it be the police. She edged toward the office door and peeked out. No siren, no flashing lights. Heavy footsteps pounded on the sidewalk.

Her skin crept with cold sweat. She hugged her purse to her chest. "They're here."

The psycho customer wrapped his wolf tooth in the

white handkerchief and stuffed it into a pocket. "Who are they?"

"People who want to kill me." She ran through the examining room to the back door.

"Are you that bad of a dentist?"

"No." She flipped the deadbolt locks with trembling fingers.

"Did you do something wrong?"

"No, I saw something I shouldn't have. And so will you, if you don't get out of here." She grabbed his arm to push him out the back door. A trickle of blood oozed from the corner of his mouth. He quickly wiped it with his hand, but it left a red smudge along his chiseled jaw.

There had been so much blood. So many lifeless faces, coated with blood. And poor Karen. The blood had pooled in her mouth, choking her last words.

"Oh God." Shanna's knees wobbled. Her vision blurred. Not now. Not when she needed to run.

The psycho customer grabbed her. "Are you all right?"

She looked at his hand, firmly gripping her upper arm. A red smear stained her white lab coat. *Blood.* Her eyes flickered shut as she sagged against him. Her purse tumbled to the floor.

He lifted her in his arms.

"No." She was fainting away. She couldn't let this happen. With one last feeble attempt, she opened her eyes.

His face was close. The world was fading away, and still he studied her, his eyes slowly starting to glow.

His eyes were red. Red like blood.

Dead, she would soon be dead. Like Karen. "Save yourself. Please," she whispered. Then all went black.

Unbelievable. If Roman didn't know better, he'd swear she wasn't mortal. In more than five hundred years, he had never met a mortal who could resist his mind control. He'd never met a mortal who wanted to save him instead of kill him. God's blood, she even believed he was innocent. And incredibly handsome—those had been her words.

But she *was* mortal. Her body felt warm and soft in his arms. He dipped his head lower and inhaled deeply through his nose. The rich aroma of fresh, human blood filled his senses. Type A Positive. His favorite. His grip tightened. His groin swelled. She was so vulnerable in his arms, her head dropped back to expose her virginal white neck. And damn if the rest of her didn't look just as tasty.

As much as he craved her body, her mind intrigued him even more. How the hell had she managed to block his mind control? Every time he'd attempted it, she'd slapped it back in his face. The struggle of minds hadn't angered him, though. Quite the contrary. He had still managed to read a few of her thoughts. Apparently she was frightened by the sight of blood. And her last thought before fainting had been about death.

But she was very much alive. She shimmered with heat and vitality, pulsed with vibrant life, and even unconscious, she was giving him one hell of an erection. God's blood. What was he going to do with her?

His extra-sensitive hearing caught the sound of male voices on the front sidewalk.

"Shanna! Don't make this hard on yourself. Let us in."

Shanna? He noted her fair skin, pink mouth, and light sprinkling of freckles across her pert nose. The name suited her. Her soft, brown hair looked dyed. Interesting. Why would a lovely young woman hide her true hair color? One thing was certain. VANNA was a poor substitute for the real thing.

"That's it, bitch! We're coming in." Something crashed through the front of the clinic, splintering glass. The mini-blinds rattled.

God's blood. These men truly meant to hurt her. What

could she have done? He seriously doubted she was some kind of criminal. She'd been too inept with her revolver. And too trusting of him. In fact, she seemed more worried about his safety than her own. Her last words had begged him to save himself. Not her.

The sanest course of action would be to drop her and run. After all, there were other dentists out there, and he rarely involved himself in the mortal world.

He looked down at her face. *Save yourself. Please.*

He couldn't do it. He couldn't leave her to die. She was . . . different. Something in his gut, an instinct that had rested dormant for centuries, flared within him, and he knew. He was cradling a rare treasure in his arms.

More glass shattered in the front office. God's blood. He'd have to move fast. Luckily for him, that wasn't a problem. He hefted her over one shoulder and grabbed her strange handbag with pictures of Marilyn Monroe printed on each side. He cracked open the back door and peered outside.

The buildings across the street were jammed together with metal fire escapes zigzagging up the walls. Most of the businesses were closed. Only a restaurant on the corner was still lit up. Cars dashed along the busier street, but this side street was quiet. Parked cars lined both sides. His extra-sharp senses detected life. Two men behind the parked car across the street. He couldn't see them, but he felt their presence, smelled the blood pumping through their veins.

In an instant, he pushed the door open and swooshed to the end of the block. As he zoomed around the corner, he saw the two mortals just starting to react. They ran toward the open door, their pistols drawn. Roman had moved so fast, they hadn't even seen him. He rounded another corner to the street in front of the clinic. There he hid behind a parked delivery van and watched the scene unfold.

Three black sedans blocked the street. Three, no, four

men were there—two acting as sentries while the other two smashed their way through the glass storefront. *Bloody hell*. Who were these men who wanted Shanna dead?

His arms tightened around her. "Hang on, sweetness. We're going for a ride." He focused on the roof of the ten-story building behind him. A second later, they were there, and he was looking down on the group of thugs.

Shards of glass littered the sidewalk, crunching beneath the shoes of Shanna's would-be killers. Only jagged stalagmites remained of the clinic windows. One of the thugs reached a gloved hand through the broken glass door and unlocked it. The others drew pistols from their coats and entered the clinic.

The door banged shut behind them, causing a shower of glass bits to rain down onto the sidewalk. The mini-blinds swung back and forth with a metallic rustling sound. Soon the scrape and crash of furniture could also be heard.

"Who are these men?" he whispered, but received no answer. Shanna lay still across his shoulder. And he felt stupid, standing there holding a woman's purse.

He spotted some plastic patio furniture on the roof—two green chairs, a small table, and a chaise lounge left in a flat, horizontal position. As he lowered the dentist onto the chaise, his hand glided down her body and knocked into something hard in her pocket. Felt like a cell phone.

He set her purse down and removed the phone from her pocket. He'd call Laszlo and have him return with the car. It was possible to contact other vampires mentally, but telepathic communication didn't always guarantee privacy. Roman was in a dilemma he didn't want accidentally overheard by another vampire. He was short one fang and had just kidnapped a mortal dentist in worse trouble than he.

He zipped back to the building's ledge and peered over. The thugs were leaving the clinic, six of them now, since the four in front of the clinic had been joined by the two from the back. They gestured angrily. Their muttered curses filtered up through the air to his extra-sensitive hearing.

Russian. And they were built like defensive linemen. Roman glanced over his shoulder at Shanna. She'd have a tough time surviving with these gorillas on her trail.

Abruptly, the men halted. Their voices hushed. Out of the shadows, a figure emerged. Damn, so there was a total of seven thugs. How had he missed this one? He could always sense the flowing blood and heated body of a mortal, but this one had completely escaped his notice.

The other six men slowly gravitated toward one another, as if they felt safer in a huddle. Six against one. How could six hefty thugs be afraid of one man? The dark figure moved to the front of the clinic. Stripes of light shot through the ravaged blinds and lit his face.

Bloody hell! Roman stepped back. No wonder he hadn't sensed the seventh man. He was Ivan Petrovsky, coven master of Russian vampires. And one of Roman's oldest enemies.

For the past fifty years, Petrovsky had divided his time between Russia and New York, keeping tight control over Russian vampires worldwide. Roman and his friends always kept themselves up to date on this old enemy. According to the latest reports, Petrovksy was making good money as a paid assassin.

Hiring oneself out as a killer was an age-old tradition among the more violent vampires. Murdering mortals was easy, even enjoyable for them, so why not get paid for the pleasure of going out to eat? The logic obviously appealed to Petrovsky, and he was making his living doing a job he could really love. And no doubt, he excelled at it.

Roman had heard that Petrovsky's preferred employer was the Russian mafia. That would explain the six Russian-speaking, gun-toting mortals in his company. God's blood. The Russian mafia wanted Shanna dead.

Did the Russians know Petrovksy was a vampire? Or did

they merely think he was a hired assassin from the Old Country who preferred to work at night? Either way, they clearly feared him.

They had reason to. No mortal would stand a chance against him. Not even a gutsy young woman with a Beretta hidden in her sequined Marilyn Monroe handbag.

A moan drew his attention to the gutsy young woman. She was wakening. God's blood, if the Russians had hired Ivan Petrovsky to kill Shanna, she wouldn't live through another night.

Unless . . . unless she was under the protection of another vampire. A vampire with enough power and resources to take on the entire coven of Russian vampires. A vampire with a security force already in place. A vampire who had fought Petrovsky before and survived. A vampire who badly needed a dentist.

Roman approached her quietly. With a groan, she lifted a hand to her brow. Her struggles against his mind control had probably given her a headache. Still, just the fact that she could resist him was amazing. And since he couldn't control her, he had no idea what she would do or say next. It made her a dangerous commodity to deal with. It made her . . . fascinating.

Her unbuttoned lab coat had fallen open, revealing a baby-pink T-shirt molded perfectly to her breasts. With each breath of air, her chest expanded. His jeans grew tighter. Her heated blood pumped through her veins, drawing him closer with each pulse. His gaze swept down to her tight, hip-hugging black pants. She was so beautiful, and she'd be so delicious. In more ways than one.

God's blood. He wanted to keep her. She believed he was innocent. She believed he was worth saving. But what if she found out the truth? If she discovered he was demon, she'd want to kill him. He'd learned that too well with Eliza.

Roman straightened. He couldn't make himself vulnerable like that again. But would this one betray him? She seemed different somehow. She'd begged him to save himself. Her heart was pure.

She moaned again. God's blood, she was the vulnerable one. How could he leave her to that monster Petrovsky? Roman was the only one in New York who could protect her. His gaze wandered down her body and back to her pretty face. Oh, he could protect her, all right. But as long as his body howled with hunger and thrummed with desire, there was no way he could guarantee she'd be safe.

Not from him.

Three

Shanna rubbed her brow. In the distance, she heard honking cars and the wail of an ambulance siren. No need for those in the afterlife. She was definitely still alive. But where?

She opened her eyes and beheld a night sky, stars partially hidden with mist. A breeze ruffled her hair against her cheek. She looked to her right. A rooftop? She was stretched out on patio furniture. How did she get here? She looked to her left.

Him. The psycho customer with the wolf tooth. He must have brought her here, and he was coming toward her right now. She scrambled to get off the chaise lounge and gasped when the flimsy furniture started to tip.

"Careful." He was there immediately, startling her when he grabbed her arms. How did he reach her so quickly?

The pain in her head dropped a few degrees colder. His grip on her was firm. Possessive. "Let me go."

"Fine." He released her and straightened to his full height.

Shanna gulped. She hadn't realized he was so tall. And big.

"You may thank me later for saving your life."

That voice again. Low and sexy. So beguiling, but she wasn't in the mood to trust anyone right now. "I'll send you a card."

"You don't trust me."

Perceptive, wasn't he? "Why should I? As far as I can tell, you've abducted me. Without my permission."

His mouth tilted up. "Do you normally give your permission?"

She glared at him. "Where have you taken me?"

"We're across the street from your clinic." He sauntered toward the ledge. "Since you don't trust me, take a look for yourself."

Right, stand on the edge of the roof with a psycho. No way. She'd been stupid enough, fainting in the clinic when she should have been running. She couldn't afford any more moments of weakness like that. The gorgeous man must have carried her out. He really had saved her life. He was tall, dark, handsome, and heroic. Altogether perfect, except for the fact that he wanted a wolf's canine tooth jammed into his mouth. Did he labor under the misconception that he was Wolfman? Was that why her gun hadn't scared him? Only silver bullets could hurt him. She wondered if he was going to howl at the moon.

Get a grip. She rubbed her aching forehead. She needed to stop imagining nonsense and figure out what to do next.

She noticed her purse, sitting by her feet. Hallelujah! She set the purse in her lap and peeked inside. Yes! The Beretta was still there. She could still defend herself. Even against the gorgeous Wolfman if she had to.

"They're still down there if you want to see them." He glanced back at her.

She snapped her purse shut and gave him a wide-eyed Bambi look. "Who?"

His gaze flickered down to her purse, then back to her face. "The men who want to kill you."

"Well, actually, I think I've seen enough of them today. So I'll just be going now." She eased to her feet.

"If you leave now, they'll catch you."

That was probably true. But was she any safer on a roof with a gorgeous escapee from a mental institute? She clutched her purse to her chest. "Okay. I'll stay for a little while."

"Good." His voice softened. "I'll stay with you."

She backed away, putting the patio furniture between them. "Why did you rescue me?"

He smiled slowly. "I need a dentist."

Not with a smile like that. Damn. A smile like that could melt a woman into a puddle of quivering hormones. *I'm melting, I'm melting.* "How . . . how did you get me up here?"

His eyes glimmered in the dark. "I carried you."

She gulped. Obviously a few extra pizza pounds hadn't overly strained the guy. "You carried me all the way to the roof?"

"I . . . used the elevator." He pulled a cell phone from his back pocket. "I'll call someone to pick us up."

Us? Who was he kidding? She didn't trust him any farther than she could spit. But he had saved her from the hit men. And so far, he'd behaved like a gentleman. She ventured toward the edge of the building, keeping a safe distance from the mysterious rescuer.

She glanced down. Wow, he'd been honest with her. They *were* across the street from the clinic. Three black sedans were double-parked in the street, and a group of men stood there, talking. Planning how to kill her. She was so screwed. Maybe she could use an ally. Maybe she should trust the crazy but gorgeous Wolfman.

"Radinka?" He held the cell phone against his cheek. "Can you give me Laszlo's cell phone number?"

Radinka? Laszlo? Were those Russian names? Her skin chilled with goose bumps. Oh God. Big trouble. This guy was probably pretending to be her friend so he could lure her away from the city and—

"Thanks, Radinka." He punched in a new number.

Shanna looked around and located the stairway entrance. Now, if she could just ease over there without him noticing.

"Laszlo." His voice became authoritative. "Bring the car back immediately. We have an emergency situation here."

Shanna moved slowly. Quietly.

"No, you don't have time to go to the lab. Turn around now." A slight pause. "No, I didn't get the tooth fixed. But I have the dentist with me." He glanced her way.

She froze and tried to look bored. Maybe she should hum a tune, but all that came to mind was the one she'd heard earlier in the evening. "Strangers in the Night." Well, that fit.

"Have you turned around yet?" Wolfman sounded irritated. "Good. Now, listen carefully. Do not, I repeat, do not drive past the clinic. Go one block north of the clinic, and we'll meet you there. Do you understand?"

Another pause. He turned to look over the ledge. Shanna resumed her stealthy approach to the stairway.

"I'll explain later. Just follow my directions, and we'll be safe."

She slipped past the patio furniture.

"I know you're just a chemist, but I have full confidence in your abilities. Remember, we don't want anyone else to know about this. And now that I think about it, is our . . . passenger still in the car with you?" Wolfman walked toward the corner of the building, keeping his back to her and his voice low.

So the rascal didn't want her to hear this. *Can you hear me now?* The phrase goaded her. No, she couldn't hear, dammit. Quickly she tiptoed after him. Her old ballet teacher would have been impressed with her speed.

"Look, Laszlo. I'll have the dentist with me, and I don't want to alarm her any more than necessary. So take Vanna out of the backseat and stick her in the trunk."

Shanna halted. Her mouth dropped open. Her throat seized up, making it hard to breathe.

"I don't care how much crap you have in the trunk. We're not driving around with a naked body in the car."

Oh no! She gasped for air. He *was* a hit man.

He whirled around suddenly to face her. With a strangled squeak, she leaped back.

"Shanna?" He turned off the phone and held it out to her.

"Stay away from me." She backed away, fumbling in her purse.

He frowned. "Don't you want your phone back?"

That was *her* phone? He was a murderer *and* a thief. She yanked out her Beretta and pointed it at him. "Don't move."

"Not that again. I can't help you if you keep fighting me."

"Yeah, like you really want to help me." She eased toward the staircase. "I heard you talking to your friend. 'Oh, Laszlo, we have company. Put the dead body in the trunk.'"

"It's not what you think."

"I'm not stupid, Wolfman." She continued to move toward the stairs. At least he was staying put and not making any moves. "I should have shot you the first time."

"Do not fire the weapon. The men below will hear it. They'll come up here, and I'm not sure I can defeat all of them."

"*All* of them? My, don't we think highly of ourselves."

His eyes darkened. "I have some special talents."

"Oh, I bet you do. I bet that poor girl in the trunk could say a lot about your *special talents*."

"She's incapable of speech."

"Well, duh! Once you kill someone, they tend to be lousy conversationalists."

His mouth twitched.

She reached the stairway door. "If you come after me, I'll kill you."

She pulled the door open, but in the blink of an eye, he was there. He slammed the door shut, wrenched the gun from her hand, and tossed it aside. It hit with a *clunk* and skittered across the rooftop. She squirmed, wiggled, kicked at his shins. He grabbed her by the wrists and pinned her against the door.

"By God, woman, you are hard to control."

"You better believe it." She pulled against his grip, but couldn't free her wrists.

He leaned closer. His breath stirred her hair and feathered her brow. "Shanna," he whispered her name like a cool breeze.

She shivered. His hypnotic voice tugged at her, lulling her into a sensation of comfort and security. *False* security. "I won't let you kill me."

"I don't want to kill you."

"Good. Then let me go."

He lowered his head, his breath tickling her throat. "I want you alive. Warm and alive."

Another shiver zigzagged through her body. Oh God, he was going to touch her. Maybe even kiss her. She waited, her heart hammering in her chest.

His voice whispered in her ear, "I need you."

She opened her mouth, then snapped it shut when she realized how close she'd come to saying yes.

He moved back, still gripping her wrists. "I need you to trust me, Shanna. I can protect you."

Her headache returned with a vengeance, cold pain stabbing at her temples. She gathered all her strength, every fiber of resistance, and rammed her knee into his groin.

Breath whooshed out of him, strangling his shout before it could erupt from this throat. Only a few garbled croaks emerged. He doubled over and fell to his knees. His complexion, pale before, turned a mottled red.

Shanna winced. She'd gotten him good. She spotted her gun beneath the patio table and ran to collect it.

"Holy Mother of God!" he gasped, supporting himself on all fours. "That hurts like hell."

"It's supposed to, big guy." She dropped her Beretta back in her purse, then sprinted for the staircase.

"I never—no one's ever done that to me." He gazed up at her, his contorted expression of pain mellowing into a look of stunned wonder. "Why?"

"Just one of *my* special talents." She stopped at the staircase door and grasped the knob. "Don't follow me. Next time, I'll shoot you down there." The door opened with a loud, scraping noise.

She stepped onto the stairway landing and let go of the door. With a loud creak, it started to swing shut. She was halfway down the stairs when it closed with a final bang and left her in total darkness. *Great.* She slowed her pace. The last thing she wanted was to act like one of those girls in the movies, always tripping and twisting her ankle, then lying there helpless and screaming when the bad guy arrived. The banister ended, and she was on the bottom landing. She inched forward with her hands stretched out until she reached the door.

She yanked the door open and was greeted by light. The hallway was empty. Good. She ran to the elevator. A sign dangled in front of the metal doors. *Out of Order.* Damn! She glanced back over her shoulder. So the scumbag had lied to her. He couldn't have brought her up the elevator. She looked around for a service elevator, but couldn't see one. However he'd gotten her on the roof, she didn't have time to worry about it.

She located the central stairwell. Thank God it was lit inside. She rushed down the flights of stairs and reached the ground floor. There was no noise behind her. Thank God. It appeared that Wolfman was not giving chase. She inched open the stairwell door and peered outside. The lobby was dimly lit and empty. The building's main entrance boasted two glass doors. Through them, she could see the black cars and hit men.

She slipped into the lobby, and hugging the walls, she retreated toward the back entrance. The glowing red exit sign called to her like a beacon, promising freedom. Safety. She'd find a taxi, go to some obscure little hotel, and then, in the safety of her room, she'd call Bob Mendoza again. And if the U.S. marshal was still missing, she'd empty her bank account in the morning and take a train somewhere. Anywhere.

She peeked outside, saw no one, then exited the building. Immediately a strong arm encircled her waist and pulled her back against a rock-hard body. A hand smacked across her mouth in an iron grip. She kicked at his shins and stomped on his feet.

"Stop it, Shanna. It's me," a now familiar voice whispered in her ear.

The Wolfman? How could he have beaten her down the stairs? She moaned her frustration against his hand.

"Come on." He pulled her down the street, past a row of empty umbrella tables. A banner fluttered overhead, announcing the name of the bistro. The next shop had a glass storefront, lined with burglar bars. He dragged her into the recessed doorway. The awning overhead shaded them from the street lamps. "Laszlo will be here soon. Just stay quiet until he arrives."

She shook her head, trying to dislodge his hand.

"Can you breathe all right?" He sounded concerned.

She shook her head again.

"You won't scream if I let go? I'm sorry, but I can't have

you making noise with the hit men so close." He loosened his grip.

"I'm not that stupid," she mumbled against his palm.

"I think you're very intelligent, but you're also in deep shit. That kind of stress can cause anyone to make a bad move."

She turned her head to see his face. His jaw was strong and lean. His eyes were focused on the street, no doubt scanning for danger. "Who are you?" she whispered.

He glanced down, and a ghost of a smile haunted his wide mouth. "I'm someone who needs a dentist."

"Don't lie to me. There's a gajillion dentists out there."

"I'm not lying."

"You lied about the elevator. It's out of order. I had to use the stairs."

His mouth tightened, and he resumed his search for danger without bothering to answer.

"How did you get here so fast?"

"Does it matter? I want to protect you."

"Why? Why should you care?"

He paused. "It's complicated." He looked at her, and the pain in his eyes took her breath away. Whoever this man was, he understood suffering.

"You're not going to hurt me?"

"No, sweetness. I've had my fill of causing pain." He smiled sadly. "Besides, if I really wanted to kill you, I could have done it a dozen times by now."

"How reassuring." She shuddered, and his arms tightened around her.

Across the street, a neon sign glowed. The neighborhood psychic was still open for business. Shanna considered making a wild dash across the street and calling the police. Or maybe she should ask about her future. Did she even have one, or had her lifeline run out? Strange, but she didn't feel endangered. The Wolfman's arms were strong.

The chest she was leaning against was broad and solid. And he claimed he wanted to protect her. She'd been so alone lately. She wanted to trust him.

She took a deep breath to calm her nerves and coughed. "Jeez, it stinks here. What is this place?"

"A cigar shop. I gather you don't smoke?"

"No. Do you?"

He smiled wryly. "Only if I'm out in the sun."

Huh? Before she could respond, a dark green car drove past them, and Wolfman started dragging her toward the curb.

"That's Laszlo." He waved to get his friend's attention.

The green Honda Accord pulled over to double-park. The Wolfman strode toward it, pulling Shanna with him.

Should she really trust him? Once she got into a car with him, how could she escape? "Who is this Laszlo? Is he Russian?"

"No."

"His name doesn't sound very American."

Wolfman lifted a brow as if he found her comment annoying. "He's Hungarian, originally."

"And you?"

"American."

"You were born here?"

Now both brows went up. He was definitely annoyed. But he did have a slight accent, and she'd rather be safe than sorry.

The man inside the Honda fumbled around, and the trunk popped open a few inches. Shanna jumped, suddenly remembering there might be a body inside.

"Relax." Wolfman tightened his grip on her.

"Are you kidding?" She tried to jerk away, but her attempt failed miserably. "Don't you have a dead body in there?"

He sighed. "God help me. I suppose I deserve this."

A short man in a white lab coat scrambled out of the green Honda. "Oh, there you are, sir. I came as quickly as I could." He noticed Shanna and fingered a button on his lab coat. "Good evening, miss. You're the dentist?"

"She is." Wolfman glanced over his shoulder. "We're in a hurry, Laszlo."

"Yes, sir." Laszlo opened the back door and leaned inside. "I'll get Vanna out of your way." He straightened, dragging a woman's naked body from the backseat.

Shanna gasped.

Wolfman clapped a hand over her mouth. "She's not real."

Shanna struggled to escape, but he pulled her against his chest and held tight.

"Look at her, Shanna. She's a toy, a human-sized toy."

Laszlo noticed her distress. "He's right, miss. She's not real." He pulled the wig off her head, then plopped it back on.

Oh God. Her Wolfman was not a killer. He was a *pervert*!

She elbowed Wolfman in the stomach, and catching him by surprise, she managed to pull away from his grasp.

"Shanna." He made a grab for her, and she jumped back.

"Stay away from me, you pervert."

"What?"

She pointed at the doll that Laszlo was shoving into the trunk. "Any man with a toy like that has got to be a pervert."

Wolfman blinked. "It . . . it's not *my* car."

"And it's not your toy?"

"No." He glanced back. "Shit!" He seized her and shoved her toward the car. "Get in."

"Why?" She grabbed each side of the doorway and locked her elbows. This was the maneuver that always worked in the cartoons when a cat didn't want to be pushed into a tub of water.

Wolfman moved to her side, blocking her view. "A black car is turning onto this street. We can't let them see you."

A black car? Black sedan or green Honda. Those appeared to be her choices. God help her that she was making the right decision. She climbed into the backseat of the Honda Accord and set her purse on the floor. She looked out the back window, but couldn't see a black car. Laszlo still had the trunk up.

"Hurry, Laszlo! We've got to go." Wolfman got in beside her and shut the door. He glanced out the back window.

Laszlo slammed the trunk shut.

"Shit." Wolfman grabbed Shanna by the shoulders and pushed her down.

"Aagh!" It all happened so fast. A whoosh of air and then, wham, her nose was pressed flat against scratchy black denim. Oh, great, she was facedown in his lap. Her nostrils filled with the scent of he-man and fresh soap. Or was that laundry detergent? She struggled to sit up, but he held her down.

"Sorry, but our windows aren't tinted, and I can't risk them seeing you."

The engine started, and they were on the move. She felt the car vibrating around her, his jeans giving her a full facial massage.

She wiggled until her nose and mouth found a pocket of air. After a few deep breaths, she realized her precious pocket of air was the crevice between his legs. Wonderful. She was doing heavy breathing on his crotch.

"The black car is following us." Laszlo sounded worried.

"I know." Wolfman sounded annoyed. "Take the next right."

Shanna attempted to roll onto her side, but the car made a turn, and she lost her balance. She fell against Wolfman, the back of her head bumping against his zipper. Oops. Maybe he hadn't noticed. She wiggled forward, moving her head away from his groin.

"Is there a purpose for all this activity?"

Oh dear. He had noticed. "I—I couldn't breathe." She squirmed onto her shoulder and curled her legs up so she was lying on her side with her cheek against his thighs.

The car suddenly halted. Shanna slid back and knocked against his zipper once again.

He winced.

"Sorry." Jeez. First she'd given him the knee. Now she was a head banger. How much abuse could a guy take in one evening? She inched her head forward again.

"Sorry, sir," Laszlo said. "The light just turned red all of a sudden."

"I understand." Wolfman laid a hand lightly on Shanna's head. "Could you stop wiggling, please?"

"Sir, they're pulling up beside us!"

"That's all right. Let them take a good look. They'll only see two men."

"What should I do now?" Laszlo asked. "Go straight or turn?"

"Make a left turn at the next intersection. We'll see if they follow us then."

"Yes, sir." Laszlo was beginning to sound ill. "You know, I'm not trained for this sort of thing. Maybe we should call for Connor or Ian."

"You're doing fine. That reminds me." Wolfman lifted his hips.

Shanna gasped and grabbed his knees to keep steady. The muscles in his thighs bunched and rippled beneath her cheek. Oh, Lordy, what a thrill ride.

"Here." He lowered his hips back onto the seat. "I had your damned phone in my back pocket."

"Oh." She shifted onto her back so she could see. The car lurched forward, and she rolled into his groin, nose against his zipper.

"Sorry," she murmured, and scooted away.

"No . . . problem." He dropped the phone on the car seat. "I don't think you should use it. If they know your number, they can trace any call you make and find your location."

He moved his hand to her shoulder, probably hoping to keep her from rolling around.

The car swerved left. Luckily, she slid only a fraction down his thighs this time. "Are they still following us?" she asked.

"I don't see them." Laszlo sounded excited.

"Let's not celebrate just yet." Wolfman looked from side to side. "Drive around a bit more to make sure."

"Yes, sir. Shall we go to your home or the lab?"

"What lab?" Shanna attempted to sit up.

Wolfman tightened his grip on her shoulder and forced her back down. "Stay put. This isn't over yet."

Great. She was beginning to suspect he enjoyed man-handling her. "Okay. What lab?"

He glanced down at her. "Romatech Industries."

"Oh, I've heard of them."

He raised a brow. "You have?"

"Of course. They've saved millions of lives with their artificial b-blood. Is that where you work?"

"Yes, we both work there."

Shanna breathed a sigh of relief. "That's wonderful. Then, you're into saving lives, not . . . destroying them."

"That is our wish, yes."

"You never introduced yourself. I can't keep calling you Wolfman."

His brows shot up. "I told you. I am not a werewolf."

"You have a wolf's tooth in your pocket."

"It's part of an experiment. Like the doll in the trunk."

"Oh." Shanna turned her head toward the front seat. "Is that what you're working on, Laszlo?"

"Yes, miss. The doll is one of my current experiments. Nothing to be alarmed about."

"Well, that's a relief." Shanna smiled. "I'd hate to think I was driving around with a couple of perverts." She turned back to Wolfman, but her nose grazed his zipper. Oops. His pants hadn't stuck out that far before.

She scooted back an inch. "Maybe I should sit up now."

"It's not safe."

Right. And she was safe one inch from his growing crotch. Obviously, her earlier attack on his groin had not caused any lasting damage. Wolfman was well on his way to a full recovery. Very full. "So, what is your name?"

"Roman. Roman Draganesti."

Laszlo spun around a corner too fast.

She slid against Roman. A huge, rock-hard Roman. "Sorry." She tilted her head away from his erection. He was getting bigger by the minute.

"Where do you want to go?" Laszlo asked. "The lab or your home?"

Roman's hand moved from her shoulder to her neck. His fingers gently stroked, drawing little circles on her skin.

She shivered. Her heart started to race.

"We'll take her to my home," he whispered.

Shanna swallowed hard. Somehow, she knew she was taking a turn tonight, a turn that would change the rest of her life.

The car came to an abrupt stop. Her head wobbled with the car's movement, rubbing against the strained denim of Wolfman's beastly-sized erection. He groaned and fixed his eyes on her face.

She gasped. His eyes were red. It couldn't be. It had to be a reflection from the red stoplight.

"Are you sure she'll be safe at your house?" Laszlo asked.

"As long as my mouth stays shut." He smiled slightly. "And my zipper stays up."

Swallowing hard, Shanna turned away. She should have appreciated boredom when she had it. This much excitement could kill a girl.

Four

So much for keeping his raging lust a secret. As far as Roman could tell, the lovely dentist in his lap had finally realized the futility of escaping his erection. Each time she succeeded in putting a little space between her head and his crotch, he rose to the challenge and filled the gap.

He was a bit amazed himself. He hadn't experienced this much desire in more than a hundred years. Now, instead of bumping against him, Shanna was lying very still against his zipper. Her smoky blue eyes were focused on the car's ceiling as if nothing was going on. But the blush on her cheeks and the occasional shudder that rippled down her warm body told him otherwise. She was extremely aware of him. And she knew he wanted her.

Roman didn't have to read her mind to know this. He could read her body instead. The distinction was new to him, and the result was powerful, fueling his lust to a higher degree.

"Roman?" She glanced at him, her blush deepening. "I hate to sound like a nagging kid, but are we there yet?"

He glanced out the window. "We're at Central Park. We're almost there."

"Oh. Uh, do you live alone?"

"No. There are a number of . . . people who live there. And I have security teams on duty day and night. You'll be safe."

"Why do you have so much security?"

He continued to look out the window. "To feel secure."

"From what?"

"You don't want to know."

"Oh, that's informative," she muttered.

Roman couldn't help but smile. The lady Vamps in his coven were too busy trying to seduce him to ever show displeasure with him. Shanna's attitude was a refreshing change. Though he did hope her irritation wouldn't lead to another knee in the groin. Somehow, he'd managed to exist for a total of five hundred and forty-four years without experiencing that particular form of torture. Vampire killers went straight for the heart.

Though to be honest, Shanna was assaulting his heart. The dried-up husk in his chest was beating to an ancient, primeval drum. Possess and protect. He wanted this woman. And he wouldn't allow his old enemy to have her or harm her.

But it went much further than that. He wanted to know why he couldn't control her. She was a challenge that mentally, he couldn't resist. And obviously, given his current condition, he found her physically irresistible, too.

"Here we are, sir." Laszlo slowed to a stop, double-parking next to one of Roman's cars.

Roman opened his door. Lifting Shanna's head a fraction, he slid out from under her. She started to sit up. "No. Stay down until I make sure it's safe."

She heaved a sigh of frustration. "Okay."

Roman climbed out and closed the door while Laszlo did the same. He motioned for the chemist to follow him a few yards from the car. "You did well, Laszlo. Thank you."

"You're welcome, sir. Can I go back to the lab now?"

"Not yet. First, I want to you to go inside and warn everyone that we have a mortal guest. We need to protect her, but at the same time, she must not discover who we really are."

"May I ask why we're doing this, sir?"

Roman surveyed the street for any sign of the Russians. "You've heard of the Russian coven master, Ivan Petrovsky?"

"Oh God." Laszlo clutched at one of the two remaining buttons on his lab coat. "They say he's vicious and ruthless."

"Yes. And for some reason, he wants to kill the dentist. But I need her, too. So we have to keep her safe without Petrovsky figuring out that we're the ones interfering with his plans."

"Oh dear." Laszlo twirled the button furiously. "He would be so angry. He . . . he might declare war on us."

"Exactly. But there's no reason for Shanna to know about that. We'll keep her as ignorant as possible."

"That may be difficult with her living in your house."

"I know, but we have to try. And if she finds out too much, I'll erase her memory." As CEO of a major corporation, Roman was constantly struggling to remain invisible in the mortal world. Mind control and memory wipes made the task much easier. Unfortunately, he wasn't sure he could erase Shanna's memory.

He climbed the front steps to his townhouse and punched in a security code on the keypad by the door. "Explain things as quickly as possible."

"Yes, sir." Laszlo swung open the door and was greeted by a long dagger aimed at his throat. "Eek!" He stumbled back, bumping into Roman, who stopped him from falling down the stairs.

"Begging yer pardon, sir." Connor slid his Highland dirk back into the sheath hanging from his belt. "I wasna expecting you at the front door."

"I'm glad you're vigilant." Roman pushed Laszlo into the entryway. "We have a guest. Laszlo will explain."

Laszlo nodded, his fingers fumbling once again for a button on his lab coat. Connor shut the door.

Roman hurried down the steps to the Honda. He yanked the back door open to find Shanna pointing her Beretta at him.

"Oh, it's you." She blew out a sigh of relief and dropped her gun back into her purse. "You were gone so long. I was beginning to think I'd been abandoned."

"You're under my protection now. I'll keep you safe." He smiled. "At least, you no longer want to shoot me."

"Yeah, that's always a positive sign in any relationship."

Roman laughed, a rusty sound, but a definite laugh. God's blood, how long had it been since his last laugh? He couldn't even remember. And there was beautiful Shanna, returning his smile. The lovely dentist had brought a spark of life back into his godforsaken, endless existence.

Still, he should fight this compulsion to be with her. After all, he was a demon. She was a mortal. Historically, he should be seeing her as lunch, craving her blood, not her company. But he *did* want her company. It was as if his mind was waiting for the next words to come out her mouth, just so he could have the pleasure of responding. And his body was waiting anxiously for the next accidental touch. Hell, accidental wasn't enough.

"I probably shouldn't trust you. But for some reason, I do." She climbed out of the car, and instantly his entire body wakened to her proximity.

"You're right," he whispered, lifting a hand to touch her cheek. "You shouldn't trust me at all."

Her eyes widened. "I . . . I thought you said I was safe."

"There are different kinds of danger." He skimmed his fingers along her jaw.

She stepped back, but not before he felt a shiver run through her. She turned toward his townhouse, shifting her purse to her shoulder. "So, this is where you live? It's very nice. In fact, it's quite lovely. Great neighborhood."

"Thank you."

"Which floor are you on?" She rushed her words, apparently trying to pretend there was nothing going on, that the air between them wasn't sizzling with sexual awareness. Maybe she didn't feel it. Maybe it was just him.

"Which floor would you like?"

She glanced his way, then her gaze locked with his. Her chin lifted slightly, her mouth slowly falling open. Oh yeah, she was feeling it. She sounded breathless. "What do you mean?"

He stepped toward her. "They're all mine."

She retreated a step. "The entire townhouse?"

"Yes. And I will provide you with a new wardrobe."

"What? Wait." She broke from his gaze and squeezed between two cars to step onto the sidewalk. "I'm not going to be your . . . kept woman. I have my own clothes, and I'll gladly pay for room and board."

"Your clothes are in your home, and I doubt it's safe for you to go back there. I will provide you with clothing"—he stepped onto the sidewalk beside her—"unless you'd rather go without."

She gulped. "A few clothes will be fine. I'll reimburse you for them."

"I don't want your money."

"Well, you're not likely to get anything else!"

"Not even a little gratitude for saving your life?"

"I am grateful." She glared at him. "But you can expect all my thank-yous to be extended in a vertical position."

"In that case, let me remind you." He stepped closer. "We are vertical right now."

"I . . . suppose so." Her glare dissolved into a look of wary speculation.

He moved close enough that only a fraction separated

his chest from her breasts. He placed a hand on the small of her back, just in case she tried to step back. She didn't try.

He touched her cheek, so soft and warm. She took a deep breath and closed her eyes. He skimmed his fingers down to her neck. Her pulse throbbed, quickening its pace. When she opened her eyes, there was trust in them. And desire.

He pulled her against his chest and brushed his lips across her temple into her soft hair. He'd seen her shocked expression earlier when his eyes had turned red, so just to be safe, he wanted to avoid eye contact until her eyes were firmly shut and her lips parted, begging for their first kiss.

He smoothed her hair back to expose her neck, then slid his mouth down past her sweet ear to the throbbing pulse.

With a sigh, she tilted her head back. He inhaled her scent, Type A Positive. It was coursing through every cell in her body. He ran the tip of his tongue along the artery and felt her shudder in response. He risked a look at her face. Her eyes were closed. She was ready. He moved in for the kiss just as a block of light suddenly fell on them.

"Oh, bugger," a Scots accent rolled the final *r*. Connor had swung open the front door.

Shanna jumped, then stared at the doorway.

"What's wrong?" Laszlo asked. "Uh, maybe we should shut the door."

"No way!" Gregori's voice piped in. "I want to watch."

Shanna eased back, blushing.

Roman glared at the three men squeezed into the doorway. "Great timing, Connor."

"Aye, sir." Connor's complexion turned a few shades lighter than his red hair. "We're ready for you now."

Maybe it was good timing after all. Now that he thought about it, Roman figured his mouth would taste like blood, and given Shanna's fear of the stuff, the kiss could have been a disaster. He'd have to be more careful in the future.

Future? What future could there be? He'd sworn never to involve himself with a mortal again. Once they figured out who he really was, they invariably wanted to kill him. And who could blame them? He *was* a demonic creature. "Come." He took her by the elbow to escort her up the stairs.

She didn't budge. She was frozen in place, staring at the door.

"Shanna?"

She was staring at Connor. "Roman, there's a man in your doorway wearing a kilt."

"There are a dozen Highlanders in the house. They're my security force."

"Really? How amazing." She proceeded up the stairs without him. Without even glancing his way.

Damn. Had she forgotten their embrace already?

"Welcome, my lady." Connor stepped back to let her pass. Laszlo and Gregori moved back, though she appeared oblivious to their presence.

Smiling, she faced the Scotsman. "My lady? I've never been called that before. It sounds almost . . . medieval."

With good reason. Connor's Old World charm was really *old*. Roman rushed up the stairs. "He's a bit behind the times."

"Well, I like it." She scanned the entry hall with its polished marble floors and sweeping staircase. "And I love this house. Absolutely beautiful."

"Thank you." Roman locked the door and made introductions.

Shanna turned her attention back to Connor. "I love your kilt. Which plaid is that?"

"'Tis the tartan of the clan Buchanan." He bowed slightly.

"And the little tassels on your socks—they match your kilt. That's so cute."

"Och, lassie. Those be flashes to hold up my hose."

"Is that a knife?" She leaned over for a closer look at Connor's socks.

Roman suppressed a growl. Next she'd be telling Connor his hairy knees were cute. "Connor, take our guest to the kitchen. She may be hungry."

"Aye, sir."

"And have your men conduct a full surveillance sweep every half hour."

"Aye, sir." Connor motioned to the back of the entry hall. "This way, miss."

"Go with him, Shanna. I'll come for you shortly."

"Aye, aye, sir." She gave him an annoyed look, then followed Connor to the kitchen, mumbling, "I should have shot him."

Gregori whistled low as the kitchen door swung shut. "Sweet. Your dentist is one feisty little babe."

"Gregori—" Roman gave him a stern look that was ignored.

He adjusted his silk tie. "Yeah, I think I need a check-up. I've got a cavity that needs to be filled."

"Enough!" Roman growled. "You will leave her alone. Understand?"

"Yeah, we know. We saw you drooling on her outside." Gregori strolled toward Roman, his eyes twinkling. "So, you got the hots for a mortal, huh? What happened to the 'never again' speech?"

Roman lifted an eyebrow.

Gregori grinned. "You know, I could tell she really likes those guy skirts. Maybe Connor could loan you one of his."

"They're called kilts," Laszlo said as he fiddled with a button.

"Whatever." Gregori looked Roman over. "So, how sexy are your legs?"

Roman gave him a warning look. "Why are you here, Gregori? I thought you were going out with Simone."

"Oh, I did. I took her to this new club over by Times Square, but then she got mad cause nobody recognized her."

"Why should they?"

"She's a famous model, bro! She was on last month's cover of *Cosmo*. Don't you keep up? Anyway, she was so pissed off, she threw a table across the dance floor."

Roman groaned. Becoming a vampire could vastly increase one's strength and enhance the five senses, but unfortunately, it did nothing to improve one's intelligence.

"I thought it might look suspicious for someone that skinny to be so strong," Gregori continued, "so I took care of it. I erased everybody's memories and brought her back here. She's with your harem now, getting sympathy and a pedicure."

"I would prefer that you not call them my harem." Roman glanced toward the closed parlor doors. "Are they in there?"

"Yeah." Gregori looked amused. "I told them to stay put and be quiet, but who knows if they'll behave?"

Roman sighed. "I don't have time to deal with them. Call your mother and see if she'll keep an eye on them."

Gregori snorted. "She'll love that." He pulled a cell phone from his pocket and stepped away to make the call.

"Laszlo?"

The short chemist jumped. "Yes, sir?"

"Would you go to the kitchen and ask Shanna what she'll need for the . . . uh, procedure?"

Laszlo looked confused for a second, then his expression cleared. "Oh, right! The procedure."

"And tell Connor to come out here for a second."

"Yes, sir." Laszlo scurried to the kitchen.

"Mom's on her way." Gregori slipped the phone back into his pocket. "So the dentist hasn't implanted your tooth yet?"

"No. We ran into a problem. Ivan Petrovsky. It appears the young dentist is on his latest hit list."

"You're kidding! What did she do?"

"I don't know exactly." Roman glanced toward the kitchen. "But I mean to find out."

The kitchen door swung as Connor strode into the foyer. He met them at the base of the stairs. "Can ye tell me why I just made a turkey sandwich for a dentist?"

Roman sighed. He'd have to let his head of security in on the situation. "Earlier tonight, I lost a tooth while conducting an experiment." He removed the bloody hanky from his jeans pocket and displayed the contents.

"Ye lost yer fang? Holy Christ Almighty," Connor whispered. "I've never heard of that happening before."

"Neither have I," Roman confessed sadly. "And I've been a vampire for over five hundred years."

"Wow! Maybe it's old age," Gregori suggested, then winced at the look Roman and Connor gave him.

"The only explanation I can think of is our new diet." Roman wrapped the tooth and stuffed it back into his pocket. "It's the only variable that has changed since we became vampires."

Connor frowned. "But we're still drinking blood, man. I doona see the difference."

"It's how we drink it," Roman explained. "We no longer bite. When's the last time either of you extended your fangs?"

"I don't even remember." Gregori tugged at one end of his black bow tie to unravel the knot. "Who needs fangs when we drink our meals from a glass?"

"Aye," Connor agreed. "And if ye doona keep them retracted, they'll be clinking on the glass, getting in the way."

"Right." Roman didn't like his conclusion, but it was the only explanation he could come up with. "I think it's a case of 'if you don't use them, you'll lose them.' "

"Bugger," Connor muttered. "We need our bloody fangs."

Gregori's eyes widened. "Well, we can't start biting

mortals. I refuse! All the progress we've made would be lost."

"Exactly." Roman nodded. Gregori Holstein was annoying at times, but totally committed to their mission of making the world safe for vampires and mortals alike. "Perhaps we could come up with some sort of exercise program."

"Yeah!" Gregori's eyes sparkled. "I'll get right on it."

Roman smiled. Gregori attacked every problem with unfailing enthusiasm. It was times like this that he knew promoting Gregori had been a wise choice.

The kitchen door swung open, and Laszlo rushed toward them. "There's a problem, sir. The lady insists the implantation procedure is best achieved in a dental office. And she refuses to return to her place of work."

"She's right about her clinic," Roman conceded. "No doubt the police are all over the place by now."

Connor closed a fist over the hilt of his Highland dirk. "Laszlo told us there were some bastards wanting to kill the puir woman. Those bloody whoresons."

"Yes." Roman sighed. He had hoped Shanna could fix his tooth in the safety and privacy of his home. "Gregori, you'll need to locate another dental office, one close by that we can use."

"No problem, bro."

"I'd better watch the lass," Connor grumbled. "We canna have her digging about in our fridge." The Scotsman hurried back to the kitchen.

Laszlo plucked at a loose button on his coat. "Sir, she mentioned a specific product that would greatly increase your chances of a successful reimplantation. She was certain that any dental office would have the product on hand."

"Good." Roman removed the handkerchief-wrapped tooth from his pocket and handed it to Laszlo. "I want you to go with Gregori and take care of my fang until I arrive."

Laszlo gulped and stuffed the fang into his lab coat pocket. "We . . . we'll be breaking and entering, won't we?"

"Don't worry about it." Gregori gripped the small chemist by the shoulder and herded him toward the front door. "The place will be empty, and the mortals will never know what happened."

"Well, okay, I guess." At the door, Laszlo halted and looked back. "I should warn you, sir. Even though the young lady was forthcoming with information, she insists that she will not, under any circumstances, put a wolf's tooth in your mouth."

Gregori laughed. "She thinks it's a wolf's tooth?"

Roman shrugged. "It's a logical misperception on her part."

"Well, yeah." Gregori gave him an exasperated look. "But why didn't you just plant the right perception in her head?"

Roman paused. Laszlo and Gregori watched him, waiting for the reply. God's blood. Hadn't he endured enough humiliation for one night? "I, uh—I was unable to gain control of her mind."

Laszlo's mouth dropped open.

Gregori jolted back. "Snap! You couldn't control one measly mortal?"

Roman clenched his fists. "No."

Gregori slapped a hand against his brow. "Snap!"

"Why the hell are you snapping? Are you a turtle?" It was times like this that firing Gregori seemed to be the wise choice.

"It means I'm floundering in stunned disbelief. Sheesh, bro. You gotta keep up with the latest lingo."

Laszlo frowned, his fingers fiddling even faster with a button. "Begging your pardon, sir, but has this ever happened before?"

"No."

"Maybe you *are* getting old," Gregori suggested.

"Screw you," Roman growled.

"No, no. You gotta sound more modern, bro. Try using

the F-word." Gregori paused, then his face slowly turned pink. "You, uh, were referring to me, weren't you?"

Roman lifted an eyebrow. "The young can be a little slow."

Laszlo paced across the foyer. "This is somewhat beyond my area of expertise, but it seems to me that it is highly likely that you are missing a distinct possibility."

They turned to stare at the small chemist.

He licked his lips and yanked at a button. "Since Mr. Draganesti has never experienced this sort of . . . uh, problem before, the answer may not lie in his abilities or uh, lack thereof." The button tumbled to the floor, and the chemist leaned over to pick it up.

"What are you saying?" Gregori asked.

Laszlo slid the loose button into his coat pocket. "I mean the problem may rest with the mortal."

"She's extremely strong-willed," Roman conceded, "though I've never known a mortal who could resist our power."

"I agree." Laszlo nodded, attacking the last button on his lab coat. "But the fact remains that somehow, she did resist. There is something different about that woman."

There was utter silence while Laszlo's announcement sank in. Roman had already suspected she was different, but to hear one of his smartest scientists reach the same conclusion—it was unnerving.

"This is bad," Gregori murmured. "Really bad. If we can't control her, then she's . . ."

"Fascinating," Roman whispered.

Gregori winced. "I was going to say dangerous."

That, too. But even the thought of danger seemed appealing to Roman tonight. Especially when it involved Shanna.

"We could try to find another dentist," Laszlo suggested.

"No." Roman shook his head. "We have only a few hours of darkness left, and you said it yourself, Laszlo—

the tooth must be fixed tonight. Gregori, take Laszlo to the nearest dental office and secure the premises. You can take his car. It's out front. Laszlo, do what you can to save my fang. Give us thirty minutes, then call my office upstairs."

Laszlo's eyes widened. "You'll use my voice to teleport?"

"Yes." It would be the quickest way to get the procedure over with. But they would never be able to do it unless they had full control of Shanna's mind and could erase her memory afterward. "Gregori, come back as soon as you can. I'll need you and Connor to assist me with the dentist. We have to gain control of her mind."

"No problem." Gregori shrugged. "At the club, I erased a hundred mortal minds all at once. This will be child's play."

By the worried expression on Laszlo's face, it was clear he didn't share Gregori's confidence.

"It should work," Roman said. "Even if she can resist the power of one vampire, she'll be no match for the three of us."

While Gregori and Laszlo hurried out the front door, the words of the chemist echoed in Roman's mind. There was something different about Shanna. What if he couldn't gain control of her mind? She'd never agree to implant his fang as long as she believed it belonged to an animal. He'd spend the rest of eternity as a joke. The one-fanged wonder.

And he didn't dare tell her he was a vampire. She wouldn't want to implant his tooth. She'd react like Eliza and want to bury a stake in his heart.

Five

"Tell me you found Shanna Whelan." Ivan Petrovsky glared at four of the best thugs the Russian mafia had to offer.

They avoided looking him in the eye. Cowards, all of them. Ivan had insisted on staying close to the dental clinic in case Shanna Whelan was hiding nearby. These four men had completed their search of nearby alleys and come up empty-handed.

Three blocks away, police cars screeched to a halt in front of the ransacked clinic. Their flashing lights bounced off nearby buildings, waking the inhabitants. Mortals ventured onto the street, hoping to see something exciting. Like a dead body.

It was a thrill Ivan was usually happy to supply, but tonight, Stesha's thugs had screwed up. Incompetent cowards.

Ivan strode toward the two black sedans they had moved away from the crime scene before the police could arrive. "She couldn't have just disappeared. She's only a mortal."

The four thugs followed him. A blond giant with a square jaw replied, "We didn't see her go out the front or the back."

Ivan breathed in the blond Neanderthal's scent. O positive. Too bland. Too damned stupid. "So, you think she *did* disappear?"

No answer. They watched their feet as they shuffled along.

"We did see the back door swing open," a thug finally confessed, his face stippled with acne scars.

"And?" Ivan waited impatiently.

"I thought I saw two people." Acne Face frowned. "But when we ran to the door, there was no one there."

"I thought I heard something. Like a swoosh," a third thug offered.

"A swoosh?" Ivan clenched his fists. "Is that all you can tell me?" Tension coursed through him, zeroing in on the muscles in his upper spine. With a sudden tilt of his head, he snapped his neck and felt a small measure of relief.

The four mortals winced.

Stesha Bratsk, the local Russian mafia boss, had insisted his own men take part in the Shanna Whelan assignment. A big mistake. Ivan's fingers itched to encircle their thick bull necks and squeeze the life out of them. If only he had used his own vampires. Then the Whelan girl would be dead, and he'd be receiving the bounty money of two hundred and fifty grand.

He was going to get that money one way or another. He thought back, recalling the interior of the dental clinic. No sign of the girl anywhere. The only interesting thing he had found was an uneaten pizza with the name of a deli emblazoned on the box in red and green letters. "Where is Carlo's Deli?"

"Little Italy," the blond thug replied. "Great pizza."

"I like their lasagna better," Acne Face said.

"You idiots!" Ivan glowered at them. "How will you explain your failure to Stesha tonight? His cousin in Boston is serving a life sentence, all because that little bitch testified against him in court."

They shifted from one foot to another.

Ivan took a deep breath. He didn't care what happened to Stesha or his family. They were mortals, after all. But these guys worked for them, so they needed to show more loyalty. And less stupidity. "From now on, I use my own men at night. During the day, you watch the deli and the Whelan girl's apartment. If you find her, follow her. Do you understand?"

"Yes, sir," they mumbled in unison.

Unfortunately, Ivan didn't have much hope for their success. His own vampires would prove much more capable at finding the missing Shanna Whelan. The only problem was they could work only at night. He needed these damned mortals to carry on the mission during the day.

A third black sedan pulled up beside the other two cars, and two more of Stesha's employees got out.

"Well? Did you find her?" Ivan asked.

A bearded thug with a shaved head came forward. "We spotted another car a block north of here. A green Honda. Two men. Pavel thinks he saw a woman."

"I did," Pavel insisted. "They were sticking her in the trunk."

Ivan raised his eyebrows. Had someone else captured the Whelan girl before him? Crap. Someone else wanted the reward money. *His* reward money. "Where did they go?"

Pavel cursed and kicked a car tire. "We lost them."

Ivan snapped his head once more to relieve the building pressure in his neck. "Doesn't anyone train you people? Or does Stesha hire you right off the boat?"

The bald one's face turned red. Red and fully flushed with blood. Ivan's nostrils flared. AB Negative. God, he was hungry. He had planned to feast on the Whelan girl, but now he would have to look elsewhere.

"We did get the license plate number," Pavel offered. "We'll find out who owns the car."

"You do that. And report to me in two hours. I'll be at my home in Brooklyn."

Pavel's face turned pale. "Yes, sir."

No doubt he'd heard the rumors. Sometimes people who entered the home of the Russian coven at night were never seen again. Ivan stepped closer to the six men and stared at each of them in the eye. "If you find her, you will not kill her. That is *my* job. Don't even think about earning the reward money for yourself. You won't live long enough to enjoy it. Understand?"

There was a series of gulps and nods.

"Leave me now. Stesha is waiting to hear from you."

The six thugs climbed into the black sedans and drove away.

Ivan strolled toward the crime scene. Neighbors stood about, huddled in groups while they watched the police. A pretty blond in a pink bathrobe caught his eye. He stared at her. *Come to me.*

She turned and looked him over. Slowly, she smiled. Foolish woman, she thought she was seducing him. He gestured toward a dark alley. She sauntered toward him, swaying her hips, stroking her fluffy pink bathrobe with long pink fingernails.

He stepped into the darkness and waited.

She sailed into her doom as dumbly as a pink poodle bouncing into a grooming parlor, eager to be admired and petted. "Are you new in the neighborhood? I don't recall seeing you before."

Come closer. "Are you wearing anything under that robe?"

She giggled. "Shame on you. Don't you know the police are just a few feet away?"

"Makes it more exciting, doesn't it?"

She laughed again, her voice taking on a huskier tone. "You are a bad boy, aren't you?"

He took her by the shoulders. "You have no idea." In an instant, his fangs sprang out.

She gasped, but before she could react further, his fangs were deep in her neck. Blood flooded his mouth—rich, hot, and with the added risk of the nearby police, it was extra spicy.

At least the evening had not been a complete failure. Not only was he getting a delicious meal, but this girl's dead body would serve to distract the police from the missing dentist.

Ivan just loved mixing business with pleasure.

Shanna paced the kitchen floor. She wasn't going to do it. No way was she sticking a wolf's canine into that man's mouth. Laszlo had just left with the information she'd reluctantly given him, and now, she was alone in the kitchen of Roman Draganesti's house. True, he had saved her life. Also true, he was generously offering her asylum. But she had to wonder why. Was he so determined to have an animal tooth implanted in his mouth that he wanted her in his debt?

She paused at the table for another sip of diet cola. The turkey sandwich that Connor had made for her was still uneaten. She was just too nervous to eat right now. She'd come so close to being murdered. The full impact of that fact was only now sinking in. She owed Roman her life. But that didn't mean she was going to implant his stupid wolf tooth.

Who was this Roman Draganesti, anyway? Sure, he was about the most handsome man she'd ever met, but that didn't guarantee he was sane. He seemed genuinely concerned about protecting her, but why? And why did he have a small army of kilted Highlanders? Where on earth did a person acquire such an army? Did he place an ad in the paper—Wanted: small army of kilted Highlanders?

If he needed this much protection, he must have made some bad enemies. Could she trust someone like that? Well, maybe. She had some bad enemies herself, and through no fault of her own.

With a sigh, Shanna stopped at the table for another drink. The more she tried to understand Roman, the more confused she became. And adding to the confusion was the fact that she'd come darn close to kissing the man. What on earth was she thinking?

Well, duh. She wasn't thinking at all. The car ride had turned her on. Escaping the Russians and bouncing into Roman's swollen manhood had combined to give her one powerful adrenaline rush. It was a mixture of excitement and lust. That was all.

The door swooshed open, and Connor rushed in. He glanced around the room. "Are ye all right, lass?"

"Yeah. Did you tell Roman that I refuse to put that animal tooth in his mouth?"

Connor smiled. "Doona worry yerself. I'm sure Laszlo will be telling Mr. Draganesti how ye feel."

"For all the good that'll do." Shanna sat at the table and dragged the plate holding the sandwich toward her. According to Laszlo, Mr. Draganesti had insisted on her cooperation, and whatever Mr. Draganesti wanted, he was sure to get. What arrogance! The man was obviously used to being in charge.

Romatech. That's where he said he worked. Romatech. Roman. "Oh my God." She sat back in her chair.

Connor raised his eyebrows.

"Roman's the owner of Romatech, isn't he?"

Connor shifted his weight from one foot to another. He watched her with a wary look. "Aye. That he is."

"Then, he's the one who invented the formula for synthetic blood."

"Aye, he did."

"That's amazing!" Shanna stood. "He must be the most gifted scientist alive."

Connor winced. "I wouldna say that exactly, but he's a verra intelligent man."

"He's a genius!" Shanna raised both hands in the air. My God, she'd been rescued by a scientific genius. A man who was responsible for saving millions of lives around the world. And now he'd saved her. She sat down, dazed.

Roman Draganesti. Gorgeous, strong, sexy, mysterious, and possessing one of the most intelligent minds in the world today. Wow. He was perfect.

Too perfect. "I guess he's married."

"Nay." Connor's blue eyes twinkled. "Are ye saying ye like him, lass?"

She shrugged. "Maybe." Her turkey sandwich suddenly looked very appealing, and she picked it up for a big bite. The most incredible, available bachelor had entered her life tonight. As exciting as that was, she had to remind herself of his bizarre reason for coming to the dental clinic. She swallowed. "I'm still not implanting that tooth."

Connor smiled. "Roman is accustomed to getting his way."

"Yeah. Reminds me of my father." That was another point against him. She downed the last of her diet cola. "Do you mind if I have some more? I can get it." She rose.

"No, no, I'll do it." Connor hurried to the fridge and retrieved a two-liter bottle from the bottom shelf. He brought the bottle to the table.

"The sandwich is great. Are you sure you won't join me?"

He filled her glass. "I already ate, but thank ye for asking."

"So, why did Roman hire a bunch of Scotsmen to guard his house? No offense, but it seems kinda unusual."

"I suppose it does." Connor screwed the top back on the diet cola bottle. "We all do what we're best suited for. I'm an old warrior, ye might say. So, working for the MacKay is the best job for me."

"MacKay?" Shanna took a bite of her sandwich and hoped Connor would elaborate.

"MacKay Security and Investigation." Connor sat across from her at the table. "'Tis a large company based in Edinburgh. Run by Angus MacKay himself. Ye havena heard of it?"

She shook her head no, since her mouth was still full.

"'Tis the premier company of its kind in the world," Connor announced proudly. "Ye see, Angus and Roman are old friends. Angus does all the security work for Roman, here and at the corporate office."

A beep sounded at the back door, and Connor jumped to his feet. Next to the door, Shanna spotted a light switch with two indicator lights protruding from it—one red and one green. The red one was lit. Connor whipped the short sword from the sheath on his belt and paced silently toward the door.

Shanna gulped. "What's going on?"

"Doona be alarmed, lass. If the person outside is one of our guards, he'll swipe his ID card and the light will turn green." Just as Connor spoke, the red light went off and the green one came on. Connor eased to the far side of the door, his blade still drawn, his stance like a tiger ready to pounce.

"Then why are you—"

"If an enemy attacks a guard, he could steal the ID card." Connor put a finger to his lips to warn Shanna to remain quiet.

Quiet? Jeez, she was giving considerable thought to getting the hell out of there.

The door slowly opened. "Connor? It's me, Ian."

"Och, good. Come on in." Connor sheathed his sword.

Ian was yet another kilted Highlander, though Shanna

thought he seemed incredibly young for security work. He couldn't be a day over sixteen.

He slipped his ID card back into the leather pouch at his waist, then gave her a shy smile. "Good evening, miss."

"Nice to meet you, Ian." Oh, he was definitely young. The poor boy should be in school, not up all night guarding people from the Russian mob.

Ian turned back to Connor. "We conducted a full surveillance sweep. Everything is clear, sir."

Connor nodded. "Good. Ye should return to yer post."

"Aye. If ye doona mind, sir, after all the running aboot, me and the lads are thirsty. Verra thirsty." Ian glanced nervously at Shanna. "We were hoping for a . . . a wee drink."

"A drink?" Connor glanced at Shanna, a worried look furrowing his brow. "Ye'll need to do yer drinking outside."

It seemed to Shanna that for some reason they were suddenly uncomfortable around her. So she tried her best to appear friendly. With a smile, she grabbed the cola bottle off the table. "Would you like this, Ian? I really don't need any more."

He grimaced with a look of disgust.

She set the bottle down. "Okay. It's diet. But it's not that bad, really."

Ian gave her an apologetic look. "I—I'm sure it's perfectly fine, but the lads and I, we prefer a different sort of drink."

"A protein drink," Connor blurted out.

"Aye." Ian nodded. "'Tis a protein drink, to be sure."

Connor hurried to the fridge, motioning for Ian to follow. With whispered voices, they huddled in front of the open fridge, removing something. They stepped back to let the refrigerator door close. Then they sidestepped together, their backs turned to Shanna and their shoulders connected like Siamese twins as they shuffled over to the microwave on the counter.

Whatever they were doing, it was obvious they didn't want her to see it. How strange was that? Oh well, it was a night for strangeness. Shanna munched on her sandwich and observed the two Scotsmen. It sounded like they were opening bottles. *Click*. Probably the microwave door shutting. A series of little beeps, then sure enough, she heard the whirring sound of the microwave.

The two Scotsmen turned toward her, their backs to the counter and their shoulders pressed together to keep her from seeing behind them. She smiled at them. They smiled back.

"We . . . uh, like our protein drinks warm," Connor said as if he wanted to break the silence.

She nodded. "That's nice."

"So, ye're the lass the Russians are hunting?" Ian asked.

"Afraid so." She pushed back her empty plate. "I'm sorry about dragging you guys into this. You know, I have a contact at the U.S. marshal's office. I could let him handle this. Then you wouldn't have to concern yourselves with me anymore."

"Nay, lass," Connor said. "Ye're to stay here."

"Aye. Roman's orders," Ian added.

Sheesh. The mighty Roman has spoken and all must obey. Well, if he expected her to implant that tooth in his mouth, he was in for a surprise. Thanks to her father, she had become an expert in rebelling against domineering men.

The microwave dinged and the two men whirled around and busied themselves at the counter. They appeared to be screwing the tops back onto the protein drinks and shaking them. Then they stopped and looked at each other. Connor glanced back at Shanna, then rushed over to a cabinet and pulled out an old paper sack. Ian remained huddled over the bottles. When Connor returned, there was a flurry of activity that Shanna couldn't see, accompanied by the crunchy noise of paper.

Then Ian turned with the paper sack in his arms. The top had been rolled down. Inside, no doubt, were the mysterious protein drinks. He walked toward the door, the glass bottles clinking together inside the bag. "I'll be going now."

Connor unlocked the door. "Report again in thirty minutes."

"Aye, sir." Ian glanced at Shanna. "Good evening, miss."

"Bye, Ian. Be careful," she called after him. After Connor locked the door, she smiled at him. "Connor, you rascal. I know what you were doing. Protein drink, my ass."

His eyes widened. "I . . . you canna—"

"You should be ashamed of yourself. Isn't that boy under age?"

"Ian?" Connor looked confused. "Under age for what?"

"Drinking beer. Isn't that what you gave him? Though why anyone would want a *warm* six-pack is beyond me."

"*Beer?*" In Connor's shocked voice, the final *r* seemed to roll for a full thirty seconds. "We have no beer, ma'am. And the guards wouldna ever get drunk while on duty, I assure you."

He looked so offended, Shanna decided her conclusion must have been faulty. "Okay, I'm sorry. I didn't mean to infer that you weren't doing your job well."

He nodded, somewhat mollified.

"In fact, I'm terribly grateful for your protection." She just couldn't leave well enough alone, though. "But I do have to object to using guards as young as Ian. That boy should in bed and going to school in the morning."

Connor frowned. "He's a wee older than he looks."

"What, seventeen?"

Connor folded his arms across his chest. "Older."

"Ninety-two?" Sarcasm crept into her voice, but Connor didn't appear amused. He looked about the kitchen as if he was genuinely stumped on how to answer.

The door to the hallway swung open and a large figure entered the room.

"Thank God," Connor muttered.

Roman Draganesti was back.

Six

Shanna had no doubt Roman ruled his house and corporation with well-assured ease. His dark clothing should have looked drab compared to the colorful kilts of the security team, but it only served to make him look more dangerous. More aloof. More bad-boy, mouth-watering sexy.

She watched as he nodded at Connor, then focused his golden-brown eyes on her. Once again, she felt the power of his gaze, as if it could imprison her and force the rest of the world beyond her reach. She broke the connection and shifted in her chair to gaze at her empty plate. She wouldn't let him affect her. *Liar.* Her heart was pounding. A wave of goose bumps was creeping up her arms. He affected her whether she liked it or not.

"Did you get enough to eat?" his low voice rumbled toward her.

She nodded, refusing to look at him.

"Connor, leave a note for the day shift. They need to keep the kitchen stocked with food for Dr. . . . ?"

Shanna hesitated, then said, "Whelan." After all, they already knew her real first name. And that the Russian mob wanted to kill her. There didn't seem any point in keeping up the pretense of the Jane Wilson identity.

"Dr. Shanna Whelan," he repeated her name as if just saying it would give him control over it. And over her. "Connor, could you wait in my office? Gregori will be back soon, and he'll fill you in on all the details."

"Aye, sir." Connor nodded at Shanna before he left.

She watched the kitchen door swing to and fro. "He seems very nice."

"He is." Roman leaned against the kitchen counter, his arms folded over his broad chest.

An uncomfortable silence ensued. Shanna fiddled with her napkin, aware that he was watching her. He had to be one of the most brilliant scientists in the world. She'd loved to see his lab. No, wait. He worked with blood. She shuddered.

"Are you cold?"

"No. I—I want to thank you for saving my life."

"Are you sure? Your position is not quite vertical."

Surprised, she glanced his way. The corner of his mouth was lifted. His eyes were glimmering with humor. The rascal was teasing her about the fuss she'd made earlier. But even a vertical position had proven dangerous with him. Her cheeks grew warm, remembering their near kiss. "Are you hungry? I could make you a sandwich."

The gleam in his eyes grew more intense. "I'll wait."

"Okay." She rose and took her empty plate and glass to the sink. This might have been a mistake. Now she was only a few feet away from him. What was it about this guy that made her want to throw herself into his arms? She rinsed out her glass. "I—I know who you are."

He moved back a step. "What do you know?"

"I know you're the owner of Romatech Industries. I know you're the one who invented the formula for synthetic blood. You've saved millions of lives around the world." She turned the water off and gripped the edge of the counter. "I think you're absolutely brilliant."

When he didn't respond, she chanced a look at him. He was staring at her with a stunned expression. Good God, didn't he know he was brilliant?

Frowning, he turned away. "I'm not what you think."

She smiled. "You mean you're not intelligent? I admit— wanting to sport a wolf tooth in your gorgeous smile is not the brightest idea I've ever heard."

"It's not a wolf tooth."

"It's not a human tooth." She cocked her head, studying him. "Did you really lose a tooth? Or did you just show up like Prince Valiant to rescue me and whisk me away on your noble steed?"

His mouth twitched. "It's been many years since I owned a noble steed."

"And I suppose your armor is a bit rusty?"

"Yes, it is."

She leaned toward him. "But you're still a hero."

His smile, faint as it was, faded away completely. "No, I'm not. I really do need a dentist. See?" He lifted the corner of his mouth with a forefinger.

There *was* a gap where his right canine should be. "When did you lose it?"

"A few hours ago."

"Then it may not be too late. That is, if you have the real tooth."

"I do. Well, actually, Laszlo has it."

"Oh." She stepped closer and rose up on her toes. "May I?"

"Yes." He lowered his head.

She shifted her gaze from his eyes to his mouth. Her heart pounded in her chest. She touched his cheeks, then lifted her fingertips. "I'm not wearing gloves."

"I don't mind."

Neither do I. Good God, she'd examined a lot of mouths

in the last few years, but it had never felt like this. She lightly touched his lips. Wide, sensual lips. "Open."

He did. She slipped a finger inside and examined the gap. "How did you lose it?"

"Aah."

"Sorry." She smiled. "I have a bad habit of asking questions when the patient can't talk." She started to remove her finger, but his lips closed around it. She glanced at his eyes and instantly felt surrounded by their golden intensity. Slowly, she dragged her finger out. Good God. Her knees weakened. She had a vision of herself sliding down his body to collapse on the floor. She would reach up to him and say, "Take me, you fool."

He touched her face. "Do I get a turn?"

"Hmm?" She could hardly hear with her heart pounding in her ears.

His gaze dropped to her mouth. He skimmed his thumb over her bottom lip.

The kitchen door swung open. "I'm back," Gregori announced. He looked them over and grinned. "Am I interrupting something?"

"Yes. My life." Roman glared at him. "Go to my office. Connor is waiting for you."

"Fine." Gregori headed out the door. "My mom's out here, waiting. And Laszlo's ready."

"I understand." Roman straightened his shoulders and gave Shanna a bland look. "Come."

"Excuse me?" Shanna watched him march out the door. Of all the nerve. So it was back to business, then? He'd opened up a bit, but now, he was back to being the big boss man.

Well, if he thought he could order her around, he was sadly mistaken. She took her time, buttoning her lab coat. Then she grabbed her purse off the table and stalked after him.

He stood at the base of the staircase, talking to an older

woman. She wore an expensive gray business suit and sported a purse that was worth some people's monthly salary. Her hair was mostly black, though a silver streak ran from her left temple to disappear into the bun at the nape of her neck. She noted Shanna's approach with a lift of her perfectly arched brows.

Roman turned. "Shanna, this is Gregori's mother and my personal assistant, Radinka Holstein."

"How do you do?" Shanna extended a hand.

Radinka looked her over for a moment. Just when Shanna thought the woman was going to refuse to shake hands, she suddenly smiled and gave Shanna's hand a tight squeeze. "At last, you have come."

Shanna blinked, not sure how to respond.

Radinka's smile widened, and she switched her gaze to Roman, then to Shanna, then back to Roman. "I'm so happy for you both."

Roman crossed his arms and scowled at the woman.

She touched Shanna on the shoulder. "If there is anything you need, you let me know. I'm either here or at Romatech every night."

"You work at night?" Shanna asked.

"The facility is open 24/7, but I prefer the night shift." Radinka waved a hand in the air, her perfect fingernails painted a glossy, dark red. "The day shift is far too noisy, all those trucks coming and going. You can hardly hear yourself think."

"Oh."

Radinka adjusted her purse in the crook of her elbow and looked at Roman. "Was there anything else you needed?"

"No. I'll see you tomorrow." He turned to go up the stairs. "Come, Shanna."

Sit. Bark. Roll over. She glared at his back.

Radinka chuckled, and even that sounded exotic and foreign. "Do not worry, dear. All will be fine. We will talk again soon."

"Thanks. It was nice to meet you." Shanna went up a few steps. Where was Roman taking her? Hopefully, he was just showing her to a guest room. But if Laszlo had his tooth, she should try to implant it as soon as possible. "Roman?" He was too far ahead of her, already out of sight.

At the first landing, between floors, Shanna paused to look down at the beautiful entryway. Radinka was headed for a pair of closed doors on the right of the foyer. Her gray leather pumps clicked on the polished marble floor. She seemed sort of odd, but then Shanna figured everyone in this house was a little on the strange side. Radinka opened the doors, and the faint sound of a television spilled into the entryway.

"Radinka!" a female voice squealed. "Where is ze master? I zought he would be wiz you." As she continued to speak, her French accent became more apparent.

Another accent? Good God, she was trapped inside the International House of Nutcakes.

"Tell him to come," the French accent continued. "We want to play."

Other female voices joined in, all urging Radinka to fetch the master at once. Shanna snorted. *The master.* Who the hell was that? He sounded like a male Playmate of the Month.

"Hush, Simone." Radinka sounded angry as she entered the room. "He is busy."

"But I came all ze way from Paris—" The plaintive voice was cut off when Radinka shut the doors.

Weird. Which guy were these ladies wanting? One of the Scotsmen? Yum. She wouldn't mind a peek under a kilt herself.

"Are you coming?" Roman stood on the second floor, glowering down at her.

"Yes." She ascended the stairs, taking her time. "You

know, I really appreciate all you've done to ensure my safety."

His frown cleared. "You are welcome."

"So I hope you won't mind that I have a few concerns about your security team."

His brows lifted. He glanced behind him, then gazed at her calmly. "They are the finest security force in the world."

"Well, maybe so, but—" Shanna reached the second floor and there, on the landing behind Roman, was another kilted Highlander.

The Scotsman folded his brawny arms across his broad chest and regarded her sternly. Behind him, on the wall, a series of oil paintings hung, all portraits of richly dressed people who appeared to be glaring at her.

"Would you care to elaborate?" Roman asked quietly, a glint of amusement in his golden-brown eyes.

Damn him. "Well." Shanna cleared her throat. It was a good thing she was a dentist. Every now and then, she had to extract her foot from her mouth. "I must admit that the Scotsmen are all extremely handsome men. Any woman would think so." She noted the Highlander's face softening a bit. "They're very sharp dressers. Gorgeous legs. And I just adore the way they talk."

Now the Scotsman was starting to smile. "Good save, lass."

"Thank you." She smiled back.

Roman, however, was frowning once again. "Since you obviously consider the guards to be perfect specimens of manhood, then what, pray tell, is your objection?"

Shanna leaned toward him. "It's the weapons. All they have is a little sword at their waist—"

"A Highland dirk," Roman interrupted.

"Yeah, that, and a knife in their sock."

"The *sgian dubh*," he interrupted once again.

"Whatever." She glared at him. "I mean, look at that little knife. It's made of wood! We're talking pre–Bronze Age here, and the Russians have freaking machine guns! Need I elaborate?"

The Scotsman chuckled. "Ye have a clever one there, sir. Shall I give her a wee demonstration?"

Roman sighed. "Fine."

The Scotsman instantly spun about, opening a portrait on the wall to disclose a hidden compartment, while he kept turning till he was facing Shanna once again. It all happened so fast, she barely had time to admire the swirl of his kilt when she realized he was now pointing a machine gun at her.

"Wow," she breathed.

The Scotsman put the weapon back and shut the portrait that was hinged along one side. "Are ye happy now, lass?"

"Oh yeah. You were magnificent."

He grinned. "Anytime."

"There are armaments stashed throughout the house," Roman growled. "When I say you are safe, I mean it. Need I elaborate?"

She pursed her lips. "Nope."

"Then come." He headed up another flight of stairs.

Shanna heaved a sigh. There was no need to be rude. She turned once more to the Scotsman. "I love your plaid. It's different from the others."

"Shanna!" Roman waited on the next landing.

"I'm coming!" She stomped up the steps with the sound of the Scotsman chuckling behind her. Jeez, why was Roman in such a foul mood all of the sudden? "While we're on the subject of security, there's one more problem I'd like to discuss."

He closed his eyes momentarily and took a deep breath. "And what would that be?" He ascended the next flight of steps.

"It's about Ian. He's too young for such dangerous work."

"He's older than he looks."

"He's not a day over sixteen. The boy should be in school."

"I assure you, Ian completed his schooling." Roman reached the third floor and nodded at the kilted guard posted there.

Shanna waved at the guard and wondered if one of the paintings was hiding a thermonuclear device. Somehow she doubted that a house loaded with armaments was all that safe. "The point is, I object to a child being used to guard me."

Roman continued up the next flight of stairs. "Your objection is noted."

Was that it? Objection noted and dismissed? "I'm serious about this. You're the boss here, so I'm sure you can do something about it."

Roman halted. "How did you find out I'm the owner of Romatech?"

"I guessed it, but Connor confirmed it."

Roman sighed, then resumed his climb up the stairs. "I need to have a little talk with Connor."

Shanna followed him. "And if you won't do anything about Ian, I'll have to talk to his boss, Angus MacKay."

"What?" Roman halted once again. He glanced back at her, his eyes wide with shock. "How did you hear about him?"

"Connor told me he was the owner of MacKay Security and Investigation."

"God's blood," Roman whispered. "I need to have a *long* talk with Connor." He trudged up more steps to the fourth floor.

"Which floor are we going to?"

"The fifth."

Shanna kept climbing. "What's on the fifth floor?"

"My private rooms."

Her heart skipped a beat. Oh, Lordy. She reached the fourth floor and stopped to catch her breath. A kilted guard stood in the shadows. "Where are the guest rooms?"

"Yours will be on the fourth floor. I'll take you there later." He continued up the stairs. "Come."

"Why are we going to your office?"

"We need to discuss something important."

"We can't discuss it now?"

"No."

What a stubborn man. With a sigh, she tried to think of something he would discuss. "Have you ever considered installing an elevator?"

"No."

She tried another topic. "Where is Radinka from?"

"I believe it is called the Czech Republic now."

"What did she mean—'at last, you have come.'" Shanna started up the last flight of stairs.

Roman shrugged. "Radinka believes she has psychic powers."

"Really? Do you think she does?"

He reached the top of the stairs. "I don't care what she believes as long as she does her job."

"Right." The man had obviously flunked sensitivity training. "So you trust her with your work, but you don't believe her when she says she's psychic."

He frowned. "Some of her predictions are wrong."

"How do you know?" Shanna hefted herself up the last step.

His frown deepened. "She has predicted that I will find great joy in my life."

"What's wrong with that?"

"Do I look particularly joyful?"

"No." What an exasperating man! "So you're making yourself miserable just to prove her wrong?"

His eyes flashed. "I am not. I was miserable for years before I met Radinka. She has nothing to do with it."

"Well, hurray for you. You've made a lifelong commitment to misery."

"I have not."

"Have too."

He crossed his arms. "This is childish."

She crossed hers. "Is not." She bit her lip to stop from laughing. It was just too much fun to goad this man.

He eyed her carefully, then the corner of his mouth twitched. "You're trying to torment me, aren't you?"

"You like misery, don't you?"

He laughed. "How do you do this to me?"

"Make you laugh?" She grinned. "Is it a new experience for you?"

"No, but I've been out of practice." He regarded her with wonder. "You do realize how close you came to being killed tonight?"

"Yeah, I do. Life can really stink sometimes. You can either laugh about it or cry, and sometimes I'd just rather laugh." She'd cried enough already. "Besides, I was very lucky tonight. Just when I needed one, I found a guardian angel."

His body stiffened. "Do not think that of me. I am far from . . . I am hopeless."

Remorse simmered like molten gold in his eyes. "Roman." She touched his face. "There is always hope."

He stepped back. "Not for me."

Shanna waited, hoping he would say something, confide in her just a little, but he remained silent. She pivoted, looking around her. Another guard stood in a dark corner. There were two doors along the hallway, and between them, a large painting. She moved closer to study the landscape. It portrayed a sunset over a green, hilly land. Down in the valley, a mist hovered among the ruins of stone buildings, fashioned in the Romanesque style.

"It's beautiful," she murmured.

"It's . . . it was a monastery in Romania. There is nothing left of it now."

Nothing but memories, Shanna suspected, and not very good ones judging from the harsh expression on Roman's face. Why would he keep a painting of Romania here if it disturbed him? Oh, right. Duh. The man liked misery. She took a closer look at the painting. Romania? That would explain his slight accent. Perhaps the buildings had been destroyed during World War II or the Soviet occupation, but somehow, the destruction looked much, much older than that. Strange. What could the ruins of an old monastery have to do with Roman?

He moved toward the door on the right. "This is my office." He opened the door and waited for her to enter.

A sudden impulse streaked through her, urging her to bolt down the stairs. Why? The man had saved her life tonight. Why would he harm her now? Besides, she still had her Beretta. She removed her purse from her shoulder and held it against her chest. Damn, after all she'd been through the last few months, she was incapable of completely trusting another person.

And that was the worst part of all. She would have to be a loner for the rest of her life. All she had ever wanted was a normal life—a husband, children, good job, a nice house in a nice neighborhood, maybe a white picket fence. Just a normal life, dammit. And it would never happen. The Russians might not have killed her like they did Karen, but they had still managed to steal her life.

She squared her shoulders and walked into the large room. She looked around, curious about Roman's taste in furniture, when a movement across the room caught her eye. Out of the shadows emerged two men. Connor and Gregori. She should have felt relieved, but their stern expressions worried her. The room felt suddenly cold. Too cold, with icy air swirling around her head.

With a shiver, she turned toward the door. "Roman?"

He locked the door and slipped the key into his pocket.

She gulped. "What's going on?"

Roman stared at her, his eyes wavering like golden flames. Then he stepped toward her and whispered, "It is time."

Seven

Vampires had been using mind control for centuries. It was the only way to seduce mortals into being a willing food source. And it was the only way to erase their memory afterward. Before inventing the formula for synthetic blood, Roman had used mind control on a nightly basis. He'd never felt any qualms about it. It was a matter of survival. It was normal.

These were the facts he'd told himself when he'd led Shanna up the stairs to his office. He had nothing to feel guilty about. Once he, Gregori, and Connor took over Shanna's mind, he could command her to implant his fang. Then, when the job was done, he could erase her memory of it. Simple. Normal. Then why did he get more frustrated with each flight of stairs? By the time he reached his office, he had serious doubts about this plan. Three vampires ganging up on one mortal? It might be the only way to break through Shanna's mental defenses. It might be the only way to get his damned tooth fixed. But it was starting to feel like a vicious assault.

Now, as she stood in his office at their mercy, guilt surged inside him. There was no other way, he told himself. He couldn't be honest with her. If she found out he was a demon, she'd never volunteer to help. Without waiting, Gregori and Connor pounced. He could feel their psychic power swoop across the room, zeroing in on Shanna's mind.

Her purse fell to the floor. She moaned and pressed the heels of her palms against her temples.

Roman hovered over her mentally to see if she was all right. She was. She had erected a shield with more speed and energy than he thought humanly possible. Amazing.

Gregori reinforced his attack, blanketing her with icy determination. *Your thoughts will be mine!*

And mine. Connor's mind chiseled at her defenses.

No! Roman shot his friends a warning look. They recoiled, staring at him, stunned. They had expected resistance from Shanna, not him. But the truth was, he wanted her thoughts to himself. And he wanted her safe. That much psychic force might be needed to crack her defenses, but once her shield crumbled, all that power could rip through her mind, leaving it in shreds.

He strode toward her and pulled her against his chest. "Are you all right?"

She leaned against him. "I don't feel good. My head . . . I'm so cold."

"You'll be okay." He wrapped his arms around her, wishing his old carcass could produce more body heat. "You'll be safe with me." He covered the back of her head with his hand as if to protect her mind from further assault.

His two friends exchanged worried looks.

Connor cleared his throat. "Could I have a word with you?"

"In a moment." They expected an explanation, but damned if Roman knew what to say. How could he explain all these strange feelings that were consuming him tonight? Lust, desire, fear, amusement, guilt, remorse. It was as if meeting Shanna had woken his heart from a deep sleep. He hadn't realized how dead he was before meeting her. And how alive he felt now.

A shudder jolted through her body. "Come and rest." He guided her toward the velvet chaise where he had fed on VANNA earlier that night.

She curled up on the chaise, wrapping her arms around herself. "I'm so cold."

He considered dragging in the suede comforter from his king-sized bed in the adjoining room, then he spotted a burgundy chenille blanket draped over one of the wing-back chairs. He never used it, but Radinka had bought it for his office, declaring the room needed more warmth. He grabbed the soft afghan and stretched it out over Shanna.

"Thank you." She pulled the fringed end up to her chin. "I don't know what came over me, but I just had the worst chill."

"You'll warm up soon." He smoothed back her hair and wished he had time to smooth away all her fears. But Connor was pacing back and forth in front of the wet bar, and Gregori was leaning against a wall, glaring at him. "Gregori, would you make sure Dr. Whelan is comfortable? She might want something from the kitchen. Maybe some hot tea."

"Okay." Gregori sauntered toward her. "Hey, sweet-cakes. What's up?"

Sweetcakes? With a grimace, Roman walked across the room to confer with Connor.

The Highlander turned his back to Shanna and spoke very softly. Only a vampire with acute hearing would make out his words. "Laszlo claimed the lass was different. I dinna believe it, but now I do. I havena ever come across a mortal with that much mental fortitude."

"I agree." Roman glanced back at Shanna. Gregori was apparently pouring on the charm because she looked amused.

"Laszlo also told me that if yer tooth isna fixed tonight, it never will be."

"I know."

"We doona have time to be finding another dentist." Connor motioned to the antique clock on the mantelpiece. "Laszlo will be calling in eighteen minutes."

"I realize that."

"Then why did ye stop us? We were verra close."

"Her mind was about to crack. I was worried that once we broke through, that much psychic power would destroy her mind."

"Ah." Connor rubbed his chin with a forefinger. "And if her brain is damaged, she willna be able to fix yer tooth. I see."

Roman frowned. He hadn't even thought about his damned tooth. His concern had been for Shanna. What was she doing to him? He'd committed too many sins in the past to be acquiring a conscience now. He glanced back. Gregori was taking a seat at the end of the chaise. He lifted Shanna's feet and set them in his lap.

"So what can we do, man?" Connor asked, dragging Roman's attention away from Shanna.

"I have to gain her trust. She needs to let me in of her own free will."

"Humph. Since when does a woman ever cooperate? Ye could spend a hundred years at it, but ye have only eighteen minutes." Connor looked at the clock. "Make that seventeen."

"I guess I'll have to be extra charming." As if he knew how. Roman glanced back. Gregori was slipping the shoes off her feet.

"Aye." Connor nodded. "The ladies like charm."

Roman narrowed his eyes. Gregori was massaging

Shanna's feet. Memories zipped through his mind. Gregori playing with VANNA's feet, raking his teeth over her toes. And his eyes had glowed red. Goddammit. "Get your bloody hands off of her!" he shouted loud enough that everyone in the room jumped.

Gregori set Shanna's feet back onto the chaise as he stood. "You told me to make her comfortable."

Shanna yawned and stretched. "And you were doing a great job, Gregori. I was half asleep when Roman started bellowing like a mad cow."

"Mad cow?" Gregori laughed till he caught the look on Roman's face. He cleared his throat and backed away from Shanna.

"Connor, there's some whisky in the cabinet there." Roman gestured toward the wet bar.

The Highlander opened the cabinet. "Talisker from the Isle of Skye. What are ye doing with malt whisky?"

"Angus sent it. He's hoping I'll invent a new drink for him with my Fusion Cuisine."

"Och. That would be grand." Connor held the bottle up to admire it. "I have sorely missed the stuff."

"Pour a glass for Miss Whelan." Roman strode toward the chaise. "Are you feeling better now?"

"Yes." She lifted a hand to her brow. "I had a terrible headache, but it seems to have disappeared. It was so strange. I could have sworn I heard voices in my head." She made a face. "That's gotta sound bad."

"No, not at all." This was good news. She hadn't recognized whose voices she'd heard. And she hadn't connected her headaches to their attempts at mind control.

She rubbed her forehead. "Maybe I'm coming down with a virus." She grimaced. "Or schizophrenia. Sheesh. Next thing, somebody's dog will start telling me what to do."

"I don't think you need to worry about that." He perched on the chaise beside her. "There's a simple explanation for what you're experiencing. Post-traumatic stress."

"Oh yeah, that's probably it." She moved over a little to make room for him. "A shrink from the FBI told me about it. She said I could expect recurring panic attacks for the rest of my life. Doesn't that sound cheerful?"

"The FBI?" Connor asked as he brought the glass of whisky.

Shanna winced. "I'm not supposed to talk about it, but you guys have been great. You deserve to know what's going on."

"Just tell us what you're comfortable with." Roman took the glass from Connor and offered it to Shanna. "This will help warm you up." *And loosen your tongue. And lower your defenses.*

She raised herself up on an elbow. "I don't usually drink anything stronger than beer."

"You've been through hell tonight." Hell with a full cast of demons. Roman pressed the glass into her hand.

She tossed back a portion, then coughed. "Whoa!" Her eyes watered. "Goddang. That was straight up, wasn't it?"

Roman shrugged one shoulder and set the glass on the floor. "What do you expect when a Highlander pours you a drink?"

She lay back on the chaise, narrowing her eyes. "Jeez, Roman, were you trying to make a joke?"

"Maybe. Did it work?" Charming his way into a woman's mind was a new experience for him. Before this, he'd simply taken what he needed.

She slowly smiled. "I think you were wrong before. There *is* hope for you."

God's blood. She had such cheerful optimism. Would he have to crush it someday with cruel reality? There was no hope for a murdering demon. But in the meantime, he'd let her fantasy of hope continue. Especially if it helped him get into her mind. "You were telling us about the FBI?"

"Oh, right. I'm in the Witness Protection Program. I

have a federal marshal I'm supposed to contact if I get in trouble, but he wasn't there when I called."

"Is Shanna your real name?"

She sighed. "My name is supposed to be Jane Wilson. Shanna Whelan is dead."

He touched her shoulder. "You feel very alive to me."

She squeezed her eyes shut. "I lost my family. I can never see them again."

"Tell me about them." Roman glanced at the clock. Twelve minutes to go.

She opened her eyes and gazed, unfocused, into the distance. "I have a sister and brother, both younger than me. We were very close, growing up, 'cause all we had was each other. My dad works for the State Department, so we grew up in a lot of foreign countries."

"Such as?"

"Poland, Ukraine, Latvia, Lithuania, Belarus."

Roman exchanged a glance with Connor. "What exactly does your father do?"

"He was some kind of aide, but he never really said what he was doing. He traveled a lot."

Roman tilted his head toward his desk. Connor nodded and moved quietly to the computer. "Your father's name?"

"Sean Dermot Whelan. Anyway, my mom had been a schoolteacher, so she home-schooled us. That is until . . ." Shanna frowned and tugged the chenille blanket up to her cheek.

"Until what?" Roman heard Connor tapping away on the keyboard. The investigation of Sean Dermot Whelan had begun.

Shanna sighed. "When I was fifteen, my parents sent me to a boarding school in Connecticut. They said it would be better for me to have some formal school records, so I could get into a good university."

"That sounds reasonable."

"I thought so, too, at the time, but . . ."

"Yes?"

She rolled over onto her side, facing him. "They never sent my brother or sister away. Only me."

"I see." She was the one chosen to leave. Roman understood that more than he wanted to admit.

She twisted a chenille fringe around her finger. "I thought I must have done something wrong."

"How could you? You were a child." Memories filled Roman's mind, memories he had thought long dead. "You missed your family."

"Yeah, something terrible at first, but then I met Karen. We became best friends. She's the one who first wanted to be a dentist. I used to tease her about wanting to stick her hands into people's mouths for a living. But when it came time for me to make a decision, I chose to be a dentist, too."

"I see."

"I wanted to help people and be part of a community, you know, the neighborhood dentist who sponsors the local kids' softball team. I wanted to set down roots and have a normal life. No more moving all over the world. And I wanted to treat children. I've always loved children." Her eyes shimmered with moisture. "I don't dare have children now. Those damned Russians." She leaned over, grabbed the whisky off the floor, and downed another gulp.

Roman took the glass from her hand while she coughed and sputtered. Damn. He wanted her relaxed, not drunk. He glanced at the clock. Laszlo would be calling in eight minutes. "Tell me about the Russians."

She settled back down on the chaise. "Karen and I shared an apartment in Boston. We used to go out every Friday night to this deli. We would scarf down pizza and brownies and curse men because we didn't have a date. Then, one night—" She shuddered. "It was like an old gangster movie."

Roman wondered why she didn't have a date. Mortal men had to be blind. He took her hand in his. "Go on. They can't hurt you now."

Her eyes filled with tears again. "They do hurt me. Every day. I can't sleep without seeing Karen dying in front of me. And I can't function as a dentist anymore!" She leaned over to grab the glass of whisky. "Sheesh, I hate self-pity."

"Wait a minute." He moved the whisky out of her reach. "What do you mean, you can't function as a dentist?"

She collapsed back onto the chaise. "I might as well face the facts. I've lost my career, too. How can I possibly work as a dentist when I faint at the sight of b-blood?"

Oh, right. Her fear of blood. He'd forgotten about that. "This fear of yours—it started that night at the deli?"

"Yes." Shanna wiped her eyes. "I was in the bathroom when I heard the awful screams. They were shooting all over the place. I could hear the bullets hitting the walls. And I could hear the screams when they hit . . . people."

"It was the Russians?"

"Yes. The gunfire stopped, so after a while, I sneaked out of the bathroom. I saw Karen lying on the floor. She . . . she'd been shot in the stomach and the chest. She was still alive, and she shook her head at me like she was trying to warn me."

Shanna pressed her hands to her eyes. "That's when I heard them. They were back behind the pizza oven, yelling in Russian." She raised her hands to look at Roman. "I don't really know Russian, but I recognized the cuss words. My brother and I used to have this competition going—who could learn the most cuss words in different languages."

"Did the Russians see you at the deli?"

"No. When I heard their voices, I hid behind a mess station and some big potted plants. I heard more gunshots in the kitchen, then they came out. They stopped by Karen and looked at her. I saw their faces. Then they left."

"Did they stop by the other victims like they did Karen?"

Shanna frowned, trying to remember. "No, they didn't. In fact—"

"What?"

"They opened her purse and looked at her driver's license. Then they got mad, cursed like crazy, and threw the purse down. It was so strange. I mean, they killed ten people in that deli. Why would they bother to check Karen's ID?"

Why indeed? Roman didn't like the conclusions he was drawing, but he didn't want to alarm Shanna until he was more certain. "So you testified against the Russians in court, and you were given a new identity?"

"Yes. I became Jane Wilson and moved to New York about two months ago." Shanna sighed. "I don't really know anyone here. Except Tommy, the pizza guy. It's kinda nice to have someone to talk to. You're a good listener."

He glanced at the clock on the mantel. Only four minutes to go. Maybe now she would trust him enough to let him into her head. "I can do more than listen, Shanna. I . . . I'm an expert in therapeutic hypnosis."

"Hypnosis?" Her eyes widened. "You do past life regressions and stuff like that?"

He smiled. "Actually, I was thinking we could use hypnosis to cure your fear of blood."

"Oh." She blinked, then sat up. "Are you serious? I could be cured that easily?"

"Yes. You would have to trust me—"

"That would be great! I wouldn't have to give up my career."

"Yes. But it would require you to trust me."

"Well, sure." She gave him a suspicious look. "You wouldn't do any of those weird posthypnotic suggestions, would you? Like making me strip naked and crow like a rooster whenever someone yells taxi."

"I have no desire to see you crow. And as for the other—" He leaned closer and whispered, "It sounds most intriguing, but I would prefer any stripping to be totally voluntary."

She ducked her chin, her cheeks blushing. "Right."

"Then you will trust me?"

She lifted her gaze to meet his. "You want to do it right now?"

"Yes." He willed her eyes to stay trapped with his. "It will be so easy. All you have to do is relax."

"Relax?" She continued to stare at him, but her vision dulled.

"Lie back." He gently lowered her into a reclining position. "Keep looking into my eyes."

"Yes," she whispered. Her brow puckered. "You have unusual eyes."

"You have beautiful eyes."

She smiled, then winced as a pained expression crossed her pretty features. "I feel cold again."

"It'll soon pass, and you'll feel fine. Do you want to conquer your fear, Shanna?"

"Yes. Yes, I do."

"Then you will succeed. You will be strong and confident. Nothing will stop you from being an excellent dentist."

"That sounds wonderful."

"You're feeling very relaxed, very sleepy."

"Yes." Her eyelids flickered shut.

He was in. God's blood, it had been so easy. She'd left the door wide open. All it had taken was the proper motivation. He'd have to remember that, in case he ran across other difficult mortals in the future. But as he settled into Shanna's thoughts, he knew there was no one else like her.

On the surface, her intelligent mind was well organized.

But just beneath that well-structured exterior, strong emotions swelled. They surrounded him, pulling him in. Fear. Pain. Grief. Remorse. And beneath the storm, a stubborn will to persevere no matter what. The emotions were all familiar to him, yet so different, coming from Shanna. Her feelings were fresh and raw. His had been dying away for more than five hundred years. God's blood, to feel this way again. It was heady, intoxicating. She had so much passion just waiting to be unleashed. And he could do it. He could open her mind and her heart.

"Roman." Gregori checked his watch. "You've got forty-five seconds."

He shook himself mentally. "Shanna, do you hear me?"

"Yes," she whispered, her eyes still closed.

"You will have a wonderful dream. You'll find yourself in a dentist office. A new and safe dentist office. I'll be your patient and ask you to implant a tooth. An ordinary tooth. Do you understand?"

She nodded her head slowly.

"If there is any blood, you will not flinch. You will not hesitate. You will continue, calm and confident, till the procedure is done. Then you will sleep soundly for ten hours and forget what happened. You will awaken, feeling happy and refreshed. Do you understand?"

"Yes."

He smoothed her hair back from her face. "Sleep for now. The dream will begin soon." Roman stood. She lay, sleeping peacefully, one hand curled beneath her chin and entwined in chenille fringe. She looked so innocent, so trusting.

The phone rang.

Connor answered it. "Hang on a second. I'm putting you on the speaker phone."

"Hello? Can you hear me?" Laszlo's voice sounded nervous. "I hope you're ready. We don't have much time. It's already four-forty-five."

Roman wondered if the little chemist had any buttons left on his lab coat. "We hear you fine, Laszlo. I'll be there soon with the dentist."

"She—she is cooperating?"

"Yes." Roman turned to Gregori. "Find out the exact time of sunrise. Then call us at the dental office five minutes before dawn so we can teleport back."

Gregori winced. "That's cutting it close. I won't have time to go home."

"You can sleep here."

"Me, too?" Laszlo asked over the phone.

"Yes. Don't worry. We have plenty of guest rooms." Roman gathered a sleeping Shanna in his arms.

"Sir." Connor stood. "About her father. 'Tis like the man doesna exist. I'm thinking CIA. I could send Ian to Langley to find out."

"Very well." Roman adjusted his hold on Shanna. "Start talking, Laszlo, and keep talking till we're there."

"Yes, sir. As you say, sir. I—well, everything is ready here. I put your tooth in the Save-a-Tooth system like the dentist recommended. That reminds me, wasn't there a movie about a dentist, an evil dentist who kept asking, 'Is it safe?' What was the name of that actor . . ."

Laszlo's voice rushed on, though Roman didn't focus on individual words. Instead he used the voice as a beacon, reaching out with his mind until he made the connection. For routine trips, like from his home to his office at Romatech, the journey was imbedded in his psychic memory. But if he was unfamiliar with either a destination or point of departure, the safest way to teleport was to use some sort of sensory anchor. If he could see a place, he could go there. If he could lock onto a voice, he could go there. Without an anchor, a vampire could accidentally rematerialize in the wrong place, like inside a brick wall or in blazing sunlight.

Gregori would remain in Roman's home office, then call

them before sunrise, acting as their beacon for the way home. The room faded before his eyes, and Roman followed Laszlo's voice to the dental office. As he materialized once again, he heard Laszlo sigh with relief. The dental office was bland, all in shades of tan. The smell of disinfectant filled the air.

"Thank God you made it, sir. Come, this way." Laszlo headed toward the examining rooms.

Roman checked to make sure Shanna was all right. She was slumbering peacefully in his arms. He followed Laszlo, wondering what information Ian would discover about her father. If the man had tussled with the Russian mafia while overseas, that would explain why the Russians had wanted revenge. And if they couldn't avenge themselves on the father, they could pick on his daughter. It would also explain why they had checked Karen's ID, then gotten angry. Roman's arms tightened around Shanna. He hoped his suspicions were wrong, but his gut was screaming he was right.

The Russian mafia didn't want to kill Shanna just because she'd witnessed their murder spree in Boston. She'd been the reason for that murder spree. Their original target was Shanna. And they wouldn't give up until she was dead.

Eight

Ivan Petrovsky flipped through the unopened mail on his desk. Electric bill. Gas bill. Here was a stack that was postmarked several weeks ago. He shrugged. What was three weeks when you were more than six hundred years old? Besides, he hated being connected to the mundane, mortal world. He ripped open the first envelope. Oh, his lucky day. He was eligible for life insurance. Morons. He tossed it into the trash.

An ivory envelope caught his eye. Return address—Romatech Industries. A growl vibrated low in his throat. He had the envelope and contents almost completely torn in two when he paused. Why would that accursed Roman Draganesti send him mail? They weren't even speaking to each other. Ivan removed the card and laid the two halves side by side on his desk.

He and his coven were cordially invited to the Gala Opening Ball of the 2005 Spring Conference to be held at Romatech Industries in two nights. Oh, it was that time again. Draganesti hosted this big event every year, with vampires from around the world in attendance, and their coven masters met in secret conferences to discuss relevant issues of modern-day vampire life. Whiny little bastards. Didn't they know vampirism was a superior way of life? Problems were caused by mortals, and there was only one way to handle them. Feed and destroy. No discussion necessary. There were billions of mortals crammed onto the planet, and they kept breeding more. It wasn't like the vampires were in danger of running out of food.

Ivan threw the invitation in the trash. He had not attended their inane conference in eighteen years. Not since that traitor Draganesti had introduced his new, synthetic blood to the vampire world. Ivan had walked out in disgust and never gone back.

It surprised him that Draganesti continued to send him an invitation every year. The fool must still be hoping that Ivan and his followers would change their minds and embrace his new, exalted philosophy of the gentle vampire life. Gag.

Frustration and stress gravitated toward Ivan's neck. He massaged the muscles below each ear and closed his eyes. A vision slipped into his mind—Draganesti and his followers at the Gala Opening Ball, dancing in their elegant evening wear, sipping that slimy, fake blood from their crystal flutes, while they patted one another on the back for their heightened, evolved sensibilities. It was enough to make him puke.

Never would he give up fresh human blood, or the thrill of the hunt, or the ecstasy of the bite. Draganesti and his followers were traitors to the very definition of vampirism. An abomination. A disgrace.

And just when Ivan thought it couldn't get any worse, they managed to sink even lower, plummeting from betrayal into the absurd. Two years ago, Draganesti had introduced his latest invention—Vampire Fusion Cuisine. Ivan groaned. Pain throbbed in his neck. To relieve the pressure, he snapped the vertebrae like a mortal would crack his knuckles.

Fusion Cuisine. It was laughable. Shameful. It was insidious and seductive. It was constantly being hawked in commercials on the Digital Vampire Network. He had even discovered two of his own harem girls sneaking in bottles of Chocolood—Draganesti's perverted fusion drink of blood and chocolate. Ivan had ordered the girls whipped. Still, he suspected his harem was managing to drink the nasty stuff when he wasn't there. For the first time in centuries, his lovely, nubile girls were gaining weight.

That damn Draganesti! He was destroying the vampire way of life, turning the men into cowardly weaklings and the women into fat cows. And if that wasn't bad enough, he was getting filthy rich. He and his coven enjoyed the good life while Ivan and his followers were crammed into a duplex in Brooklyn.

Not for long, though. Soon he'd deliver Shanna Whelan's dead body and earn a quarter-million dollars. After a few more well-paid assassinations, he could be as rich as those other snooty coven masters—Roman Draganesti, Angus MacKay, and Jean-Luc Echarpe. They could take their fancy Fusion Cuisine and stick it where the sun did shine.

A knock sounded on Ivan's door, drawing his attention away from the foul thoughts of Roman Draganesti. "Come in."

His trusted friend Alek entered. "There is a mortal here to see you. Calls himself Pavel."

A stocky, blond male ventured into the small room, his gaze darting nervously about. Stesha claimed he was the most intelligent of his thugs, which probably meant the guy could read.

Ivan rose to his feet. He could have risen to the ceiling, but that was a trick he'd reserve for later. "How did Stesha take the news of your abysmal failure?"

Pavel grimaced. "He wasn't very happy. But we do have a solid lead."

"The pizza place? Did she show up there?"

"No. We haven't seen her anywhere."

Ivan perched on the corner of his desk. "Then what is the lead?"

"The car that I saw. The green Honda. I traced the license plate."

Ivan waited. "And?" God, he hated how mortals tried to be so dramatic about everything.

"It belongs to Laszlo Veszto."

"So?" A twinge of pain pinched Ivan's neck. This was taking far too long. "I've never heard of him."

Alek narrowed his eyes. "Neither have I."

Pavel's smile was a little too smug. "I'm not surprised. We didn't know who he was, either, but we definitely have heard of his employer. You'll never guess who it is."

Ivan zipped over to Pavel so fast, the mortal stumbled back, his eyes widening. Ivan grabbed him by the shirt and pulled him forward. "Don't be a smart-ass, Pavel. Tell me what you know and be quick about it."

Pavel gulped. "Laszlo Veszto works at Romatech."

Ivan released him and stepped back. *Crap.* He should have known. Roman Draganesti was behind this. That accursed bastard was always the thorn in his side. A royal pain in the neck. Ivan tilted his head, snapping the vertebrae back into place.

Pavel flinched.

"Does this Laszlo work the day or the night shift?"

"I . . . I believe the night shift, sir."

A vampire. That would explain how Shanna Whelan had managed to disappear so quickly. "You have this Laszlo's address?"

"Yes." Pavel pulled a slip of paper from his pants pocket.

"Fine." Ivan grabbed the paper and studied it. "I want two more places watched during the day—Laszlo Veszto's apartment and Roman Draganesti's townhouse." Ivan gritted his teeth. "He lives on the Upper East Side."

"Yes, sir." Pavel hesitated. "I . . . I'm free to go?"

"If you can get out of here before my girls decide you look like a snack."

Pavel muttered a curse, then ran to the front door.

Ivan passed the paper to Alek. "Take a few men to this address. Bring Mr. Veszto back in one piece before dawn."

"Yes, sir." Alek stuffed the paper in a pocket. "It looks like Draganesti has the girl. What would he want with her?"

"I don't know." Ivan meandered back to his desk. "I can't imagine him killing a mortal for money. He's too big a wimp."

"*Da*. And he doesn't need the money, either."

So what was that stinking Draganesti up to? Did he think he could interfere with Ivan's plans to get rich? The bloody *svoloch*. Ivan's gaze wandered to the torn invitation in the trash. "Tell Vladimir to watch Draganesti's house. The girl is probably there. Go."

"Yes, sir." Alek closed the door as he left.

Ivan leaned over to retrieve the invitation from the trash bin. This would be the easiest way to confront Draganesti. The bastard was impossible to reach otherwise, surrounded constantly by a small army of Scottish vampires.

Roman Draganesti was right to keep so much security. He'd survived a few thwarted assassination attempts in the last few years. And his security team had discovered a few bombs at Romatech Industries—courtesy of a secret society called the True Ones. Unfortunately, the bombs had been discovered before they could detonate.

Ivan rummaged through desk drawers till he found a roll of tape. Carefully, he restored the invitation to its original form. These conferences were by invitation only, and for the first time in eighteen years, Ivan and a few of his trusted friends were going. It was about time Draganesti learned that he couldn't mess with Ivan Petrovsky and live to gloat about it.

Ivan was more than the master of the Russian coven. He was leader of the True Ones, and he would make the Gala Opening Ball a night to remember.

Nine

$\mathcal{I}$t was a shame mortals needed so much blasted light to see. Roman closed his eyes against the glare of the overhead lamp. He was stretched out flat on his back in the dental office with an infantile bib around his neck. At least, so far, the mind control was working. He could hear Shanna moving about with robotlike efficiency. As long as he kept everything calm and controlled, the procedure should be a success. Nothing could be allowed to jolt Shanna out of what she thought was a dream.

"Open." Her voice was quiet and monotone.

He felt a sharp prick in his gums. He opened his eyes. She was removing a syringe from his mouth. "What was that?"

"A local anesthetic, so you won't feel any pain."

Too late. The shot itself had caused pain. But Roman had to admit that dentistry had come a long way since his last encounter with the profession. As a young child, he'd seen the village barber wrenching out people's rotten teeth with his rusty pliers. Roman had done his best to keep his teeth healthy, even though his toothbrush had consisted of a frayed twig. But he'd made it to the age of thirty with a full set of teeth.

That was when his new life, or death, began. After the transformation, his body remained unchanged for the next five hundred and fourteen years. Not that his life as a vampire had been peaceful, quite the contrary. He'd suffered cuts, slashes, broken bones, even an occasional gunshot, but nothing that he couldn't heal himself with a good day's sleep. Until now.

Now he was at the mercy of a female dentist, and the extent of his control over her was unknown.

Shanna snapped latex gloves onto her hands. "It will be a few minutes before the anesthetic takes effect."

Laszlo cleared his throat to get Roman's attention, then pointed at his watch. He was worried they'd run out of time.

"It's already dead." Roman pointed at his mouth. Hell, technically his whole body was dead. He'd certainly felt dead for a long time. But tonight it had hurt like the devil when she'd kneed him in the groin. And he'd almost blown a fuse in the car. Now that Shanna was in his life, he appeared to be coming back to life. Particularly below the belt. "Can we get started now?"

"Yes." She perched on a little chair with wheels and rolled over to him. As she leaned over him, her breasts pressed against his arm. He stifled a groan.

"Open." She stuck a finger in his mouth and probed along his upper gum line. "Do you feel anything?"

God, yes. He fought an urge to clamp his mouth around her and suck the damned latex off her finger. *Take that glove off, sweetness, and I'll show you what I feel.*

Frowning, she removed her finger from his mouth. She looked at her hand, then started to pull the glove off.

"No!" He touched her arm. *Damn.* She was more connected to him than he had thought. "I didn't feel anything. Let's continue with the procedure."

"All right." She tugged the glove back on.

God's blood, he couldn't believe it. Mind control with mortals was always a one-way street. He planted his instructions into their heads and read their minds. They couldn't read his. A mortal couldn't possibly read a vampire's mind. Roman watched Shanna warily. How much could she actually pick up from him?

He would have to be very careful with his thoughts. Only think about safe subjects. No more thoughts about his mouth and which of her body parts would fit inside. No. None of that. He'd think about something completely different. Like *her* mouth and which of *his* body parts would fit inside. His groin stiffened. No! No sex. Not now. He needed his damned tooth fixed.

"Do you want me to implant your tooth now?" She tilted her head, frowning a bit. "Or shall we have oral sex?"

Roman stared at Shanna. Good God. Not only had she read him like a book, but she was apparently willing to have sex with him. Amazing.

Laszlo was gasping for air. "My God, how did she come up with such a—an outrageous—" He narrowed his eyes, switching his gaze to Roman. "Mr. Draganesti! How could you?"

How could he not, if Shanna was willing. Oral sex with a mortal? Interesting. Mortal sex in an examining chair. Very interesting.

"Sir!" Laszlo's voice rose an octave. He twirled a button with his fingers. "There isn't enough time for—for two treatments. You must decide between your—your tooth or your . . ." With a grimace, he glanced at Roman's swollen jeans.

My fang or my yang? The latter strained against his zipper, as if it wanted to leap out and shoot its mouth off. *Pick me, pick me!*

"Sir?" Laszlo's eyes were wide with panic.

"I'm thinking," Roman growled. Damn. He looked at Shanna. She was standing nearby, her eyes dull, her face deadpan, her body exuding all the vitality of a mannequin. Shit. This wasn't even real to her. It would be like having sex with VANNA. But even worse, for Shanna would hate him afterward. He couldn't do this. As much as he wanted Shanna, he would have to wait. And make certain that she came to him of her own free will.

He took a deep breath. "I want my tooth fixed. Will you do that for me, Shanna?"

She gazed at him, her eyes unfocused. "I am to implant a tooth. An ordinary tooth," she repeated his directions from earlier.

"Yes. Exactly."

"A good decision, sir, if I might say so, myself." Laszlo kept his eyes downcast, apparently embarrassed by the recently proposed change of plans. He inched toward Shanna and handed her a jar. "The tooth is inside."

She unscrewed the top and removed an inner sieve. In the sieve lay his fang. Roman held his breath as she removed the tooth. Would the sight of his fang snap her out of his control?

"It is in excellent condition," she announced.

Good. In her mind, it was an ordinary tooth.

Laszlo glanced at his watch. "Five-fifteen, sir." With a final tug, the button came off in his hand. "Oh dear. We'll never make it."

"Call Gregori and find out the exact time of sunrise."

"All right." The chemist dropped the loose button in his coat pocket and removed a cell phone. He paced across the office as he dialed.

At least it gave Laszlo something to do. The man was out of coat buttons, and that left only his shirt or his pants. Roman shuddered at the thought.

Shanna leaned over him. Once again her breasts pressed against his arm. His pants grew tighter. *Don't think about it.*

"Open."

If only she meant his fly. He opened his mouth. Her breasts were firm, but soft. What size bra? he wondered. Not too big, but not too small, either.

"Thirty-six B," she murmured as she selected an instrument off her tray.

God's blood, could she hear everything he thought? How much could he hear from her? *Testing, testing. What size clothes do we need to buy for you?*

"Ten. No." She grimaced. "Twelve." *Too much pizza. And cheesecake. God, I hate gaining weight. I wish I had a brownie.*

Roman felt like smiling, but his mouth was already stretched to the max. At least she was being painfully honest. *So, what do you think of me?*

Handsome . . . mysterious . . . strange. She went about her work. *Intelligent . . . arrogant . . . strange.* Her thoughts were distant and fuzzy, though she still managed to stay focused on her hands and what she was doing. *Horny . . . hung like a horse . . .*

That's enough, thank you. Hung like a horse? Did that mean she was disgusted or she approved? Damn, he shouldn't have asked. Why should he care what a mortal thought of him, anyway? *Just fix my damned tooth.* And why did she think he was strange?

She sat back suddenly. "This is very strange."

Yeah, strange. That was him.

She peered closer at one of her instruments. It was a long chrome stick with a circular mirror on the end.

Oh no. "It must be broken," he suggested.

"But I can see myself." Frowning, she shook her head. "This doesn't make sense. Why couldn't I see your mouth?"

"The mirror is broken. Proceed without it."

She continued to stare at the mirror. "It's not broken. I can see myself." She lifted a hand to her brow.

Dammit, she was about to snap out of the dream.

Laszlo returned with the cell phone pressed to his ear. He took in the scene. "Oh dear. Is there a problem?"

"Put the mirror down, Shanna," Roman ordered quietly.

"Why doesn't it show your mouth?" She gave Roman a worried look. "I couldn't see you at all."

Laszlo winced. "Oh dear." He whispered into the phone, "Gregori, we have a problem."

That was putting it mildly. If Shanna broke free of his control, Roman knew his fang would never get fixed. She would see the tooth as it really appeared and refuse to implant it. And that was only the beginning.

She might figure out why he had no reflection.

Roman focused on Shanna. "Look at me."

She turned toward him.

He trapped her in his gaze and tightened his grip on her mind. "You are to implant my tooth, remember? You wanted to do this. You wanted to conquer your fear of blood."

"My fear," she whispered. "Yes. I don't want to be afraid anymore. I want to save my career. I want a normal life." She set the mirrored instrument down on the tray and picked up his fang. "I will implant your tooth now."

Roman exhaled with relief. "Good."

"Oh God, that was close," Laszlo whispered into the phone. "*Too* close."

Roman opened his mouth so Shanna could get back to work.

Laszlo cupped a hand around the phone, but he could still be heard. "I'll explain later, but for a while there, it looked like our dentist was going to turn into *Dr. No*." He moved closer so he could watch. "Now it's quiet again. *Too* quiet."

Not quiet enough. Roman groaned inwardly.

"Turn your head a little." Shanna nudged his chin to the left.

"The train is back on track, now," Laszlo whispered. "Full speed ahead."

Roman felt the fang being slipped back into the socket.

"The dentist has the item in her hand," Laszlo continued his play-by-play commentary over the phone. "She's returning the bird to the nest. I repeat, bird is in the nest." There was a pause. "I have to talk like this, Gregori. We have to keep the . . . the fox in the house, but the lights turned off. She came awfully close to flipping a switch a while back."

"Aaargh." Roman glared at Laszlo.

"Mr. Draganesti is unable to speak," Laszlo continued, "which is probably for the best. He was too tempted to abandon the plan when the dentist made an outrageous offer."

"Grrr!" Roman glared at the chemist.

"Oh." Laszlo winced. "I—I better not talk about it." He paused to listen.

A litany of curses careened through Roman's mind. No doubt, Gregori was drilling Laszlo for more information.

"I'll explain later," Laszlo whispered, then raised his voice. "I'll pass the information on to Mr. Draganesti. Thank you." He slipped the phone into his pocket. "Gregori says dawn will break at precisely six-oh-six. He'll call at six o'clock, or we can call earlier if we're finished." Laszlo glanced at his watch. "It's twenty minutes till six now."

"Aaargh." Roman made a sound of acknowledgment. At least Laszlo was off the phone now.

Shanna lifted his upper lip to examine the replaced fang. "Your tooth is back in, but it will need a splint to hold it in place for two weeks." She kept working. It wasn't long before he tasted blood. She gasped, her face growing pale.

Good God, don't faint now. He stared at her, channeling

his strength into her mind. *You will not flinch. You will not hesitate.*

She inched closer to him. "O-open." She took a hoselike tool and sprayed water into his mouth. Then she stuck another hose in his mouth. "Close."

The blood and water mixture was sucked out of his mouth.

This process was repeated several times, and each time Shanna saw blood, she reacted a little less.

Laszlo paced back and forth, constantly checking the time. "Ten minutes till six, sir."

"There," Shanna murmured. "Your tooth is wired into place. You'll need to return in two weeks so we can remove the splint and perform a root canal."

The wire splint felt huge in his mouth, but Roman knew it could be removed the following night. His body would complete the healing process while he slept. "Then we're done?"

"Yes." She slowly stood.

"Yes!" Laszlo punched the air with his fist. "And we beat the deadline by nine minutes!"

Roman sat up. "You did it, Shanna. And you weren't afraid."

She peeled the gloves off her hands. "You should avoid hard, sticky, or crunchy food."

"Not a problem." Roman watched her expressionless face. What a shame she didn't realize this was cause to celebrate. He'd show her his tooth the next evening, and tell her how she'd braved her fear of blood. Then she'd want to celebrate. With him, he hoped. Even if he was strange.

She dropped the gloves on the tray, then closed her eyes. Slowly she swayed to the side.

"Shanna?" Roman stood. He caught her as her legs gave out.

"What's wrong?" Laszlo grabbed for a button, but there was none left. "It was all going so well."

"It's fine. She's sleeping." Roman laid her on the dental chair. He'd done this to her, telling her that once the job was finished, she would sleep soundly for ten hours.

"I'd better call Gregori." Laszlo withdrew his phone from his pocket and headed for the waiting room.

Roman leaned over Shanna. "I'm proud of you, sweetness." He brushed her hair back from her brow. "I shouldn't have told you to fall asleep afterward. What I really wanted was for you to throw your arms around me and give me a passionate kiss. That would have been so much better."

He ran a fingertip along her jaw. Ten hours she would sleep. That would make her wake up around four in the afternoon. No chance of his waking her with a kiss. The sun would still be up.

With a sigh, Roman stretched. What a long night it had been. It felt like a week. He examined the mirrored tool that had caused Shanna so much confusion. Damned mirrors. Even after five hundred and fourteen years, it still unnerved him to stand in front of a mirror and see everything reflected but himself. He'd had all the mirrors removed from his house. Why be reminded that he was long dead?

He watched Shanna sleep. Beautiful, brave Shanna. If he had any honor left in his wretched soul, he'd leave the poor girl alone. Put her somewhere safe and never see her again. But for now, he was almost out of nighttime. The best he could do, before the sun caused him to fall asleep, was to ensconce her safely in one of his guest rooms.

Laszlo rushed in from the waiting room, his cell phone pressed to his ear. "Yes, we're ready to go." He glanced at Roman. "Would you like to go first?"

"No, you go." Roman reached for the phone. "I'm going to need that."

"Oh, right. Of course." Laszlo tilted his head toward the phone that Roman now held. He closed his eyes, concentrated on Gregori's voice, then slowly faded away.

"Gregori, hang on a minute." Roman set the phone down, then gathered Shanna in his arms. After a few seconds of shifting her limp body around, he managed to hold her while putting the phone to his ear. The position was awkward, causing him to slump over and press his face against hers.

Over the phone, he heard the sound of laughter. What the hell? "Gregori, is that you?"

"Oral sex?" Gregori burst into another round of laughter.

Roman gritted his newly fixed teeth. That damned Laszlo. It had taken him only a few seconds to squawk.

"Snap! What a hot babe! Wait till I tell the guys. Or maybe I should tell your harem. Meow!" Gregori hissed in an imitation of a catfight.

"Shut up, Gregori. I have to get back before sunrise."

"Well, you can't if I shut up. You need my voice." He laughed some more.

"You won't have a voice once I wring your neck."

"Oh, come on. Lighten up, bro. So, is it true? You were having trouble deciding which . . . treatment you wanted?" Gregori snickered. "I hear you were *up* for the second one."

"After I strangle you, I'm cutting Laszlo's tongue out and feeding it to a dog."

"You don't have a dog." Gregori's voice sounded fainter. "Can you believe it? He's threatening us with bodily harm."

That last sentence must have been aimed at Laszlo. Roman heard an alarmed squeak in the distance.

"Chicken!" Gregori yelled. "Well, Laszlo just ran off to a guest room. I guess he's heard those rumors about you being some kind of wild, murderous beast in the past."

They weren't rumors. Having been transformed only twelve years earlier, Gregori had no idea the magnitude of sins Roman had committed over the centuries.

"Then there are the other rumors, that you were once a

priest or a monk." Gregori laughed. "But I know that one has to be bogus. I mean, really. Any guy who keeps a harem of ten hot Vamp chicks is not exactly . . ."

Roman let the words fade away as he concentrated on the location of Gregori's voice. The dental office wavered before his eyes, followed by blackness. Then he was home.

"Oh, there you are." Gregori hung up the phone he'd been using. He leaned back in the chair at Roman's desk.

Roman scowled at him silently.

"So the dentist is asleep, huh?" Gregori propped his feet up on Roman's desk and grinned. "Did you wear her out?"

Roman dropped Laszlo's phone on the desk, then wandered over to the chaise. He lowered Shanna onto the blood-red velvet.

"I hear she did a good job on your fang," Gregori continued. "You know, I've been thinking about that exercise program you mentioned, the one where we make sure our fangs stay in good shape, and I had this great idea."

Roman turned toward the desk.

"We could do an exercise video and sell it on the Digital Vampire Network. I asked Simone, and she agreed to be the star of the show. What do you think?"

Roman approached the desk slowly.

Gregori's smile faded. "What's up, bro?"

Roman planted his palms on the desk and leaned forward.

Gregori swung his feet off the desk and gazed at him warily. "Something wrong, boss?"

"You will not repeat anything that happened tonight. Nothing about my fang, and especially nothing about Shanna. Do you understand?"

"Yeah." Gregori cleared his throat. "Nothing happened."

"Good. Now, go."

Gregori headed for the door, muttering beneath his breath. "Grumpy old man." He paused with one hand on the doorknob and glanced at Shanna. "It's none of my business, but I think you should keep her. She'll be good for you." He let himself out.

Maybe she would. But he was definitely not good for Shanna. Roman sat heavily at his desk. The sun must be touching the horizon, for he suddenly felt exhausted. It was a harsh truth that when darkness faded away, so did a vampire's strength. Soon he wouldn't have enough strength to even stay awake.

It was a vampire's greatest weakness, his time of greatest vulnerability, and it happened every damned day. How many times over the centuries had he fallen asleep, worried that his body would be discovered during the daylight hours? A mortal could drive a stake through his heart while he lay there helplessly asleep. It had almost happened in 1862, the last time he'd involved himself with a mortal female. Eliza.

He'd never forgotten the horror of waking after sunset to find his coffin wide open and a wooden stake resting across his chest. This accursed vulnerability had to end. He was working on it in his lab. A formula that would enable a vampire to stay awake and retain his strength during the day. They would still need to avoid the burning rays of direct sunlight, but even so, it would be a momentous achievement. Roman was very close to a breakthrough. If he succeeded, he could change the vampire world forever.

He could almost pretend he was alive.

He looked at Shanna where she slumbered in sweet ignorance. How would she react if she learned the truth about him? Could she pretend he was alive, or would the fact that he was a dead demon drive a stake between them forever? He slumped at his desk, his energy draining away. It could be the sun causing this, but he suspected it was also depression. He dreaded the look of horror that would appear on Shanna's face if she learned the truth.

Shame. Guilt. Remorse. It sucked. He couldn't drag her into it. She deserved joy in her life.

He grabbed a pen and a blank piece of paper. *Radinka,* he wrote at the top. His secretary would see this on his desk when she checked for messages. *Buy everything Shanna will need. Size 12. 36B. I want . . .* His hand dragged slowly across the paper. His eyelids grew heavy. . . . *colors. No black.* Not for Shanna. She was sunshine—sorely missed, but forever beyond his reach. She was like a rainbow, full of color and the sweet promise of hope. He blinked and squinted at the paper. *Get her some brownies.* He dropped the pen and heaved himself to his feet.

With a groan, he lifted Shanna in his arms. He trudged from the office to the top of the stairs. Slowly, he made his way down, one step at a time. At the landing, he rested. His vision grew hazy, as if he were trying to look down a long tunnel.

Someone was coming up the stairs.

"Good morning, sir," a cheerful voice greeted him. It was Phil, one of the daytime mortal guards who worked for MacKay Security and Investigation. "You're not usually up this late."

Roman opened his mouth to answer, but it took every ounce of his remaining strength to keep from dropping Shanna.

The guard's eyes widened. "Is something wrong? Do you need help?" He ran up to the landing.

"Blue room, fourth floor," Roman gasped.

"Here, let me." Phil took Shanna in his arms and headed back down the stairs to the fourth floor.

Roman stumbled after him. Thank God, these daytime guards were trustworthy. Angus MacKay trained them well and paid them a small fortune to keep their mouths shut. They knew exactly what kind of creatures they were protecting. They didn't mind. According to Angus, some of them were creatures, too.

Phil stopped in front of a door on the fourth floor. "Is this the right room?" When Roman nodded, he turned the knob and pushed the door open with his foot.

Sunlight spilled through the open doorway.

Roman jolted to a stop. "The shutters," he whispered.

"I got it." Phil hurried into the room.

Roman waited. He leaned against a wall, out of reach of the strip of sunlight that stretched across the hall carpet. God's blood, he was tired enough to fall asleep standing up. Soon he heard a metallic click, and the strip of light disappeared. Phil had closed the thick aluminum shutters on the window.

Roman staggered forward till he reached the door. There he saw that Phil had deposited Shanna on top of the bed.

"Is there anything else I can do?" Phil headed for the door.

"No. Thank you." Roman lurched into the room and caught himself against an armoire.

"Good morning—or night, then." Phil gave him a doubtful look and closed the door behind him.

Roman weaved toward the bed. He couldn't let Shanna sleep with her shoes on. He pulled the white Nikes off and dropped them on the floor. The stained lab coat needed to go, too. He leaned over and almost collapsed on top of her. He shook his head. *Stay awake!* Just a little bit longer. He unbuttoned the coat, tugged the sleeves down her arms, then rolled her onto her side so he could pull the coat out from beneath her. He dropped it onto the floor beside her shoes. He stumbled around the foot of the queen-sized bed, then pulled back the covers to reveal clean white sheets. With effort, he rolled Shanna onto the exposed sheet. He stuffed her feet under the covers and raised the sheet and bedspread up to her chin. There, she was comfortable.

And he couldn't go any further.

* * *

Shanna woke up feeling wonderfully refreshed and happy. The feeling soon faded, though, when she realized she had no idea where she was. A dark room. A comfortable bed. Unfortunately, she had no memory of entering this room or climbing into this bed. In fact, the last thing she remembered was venturing inside Roman Draganesti's office. Because of a nasty headache, she'd rested on a velvet reclining chaise, and then—nothing.

She closed her eyes, struggling to remember. A dental office flitted through her mind, a strange one, not the place where she worked. Weird. She must have dreamed about working in a new job.

She pushed back the covers and sat up. Her stocking feet brushed against thick carpet. Where were her shoes? Red neon numbers glowed from a clock radio beside the bed. Six minutes after four. Morning or afternoon? The room was so dark, it was hard to tell. She'd gone to Roman's office after four in the morning. So it must be afternoon.

She groped along the bedside table till she felt the base of a lamp. She clicked on the switch and caught her breath.

What a beautiful stained glass lamp. Shades of dusty blue and lavender shone in the dim light. She could see the room now. It was bigger than her entire apartment in SoHo. The carpet was gray, the walls a pale blue. Curtains in muted stripes of blue and lavender framed the window. The window itself was completely covered with shiny metal shutters, clamped shut. No wonder the room was so dark.

The bed was a canopy four-poster of pale white oak. Sheer voile in shades of blue and lavender were draped along the upper frame. A beautiful bed. Shanna looked over her shoulder.

An occupied bed.

With a strangled shriek, she leaped to her feet. Oh my God, Roman Draganesti was in her bed! How dare he sleep in her bed? Or, God help her, maybe she had slept in *his* bed. Maybe this was his room. How could she have no memory of this?

She checked her clothes. Her shoes and lab coat were gone, but otherwise, she appeared intact. And unmolested. He lay flat on his back on top of the bedspread, still fully clothed in his black sweater and jeans. Sheesh, the man's shoes were still on.

Why on earth would he sleep with her? Was he that committed to protecting her? Or did he have other motives? Her gaze gravitated toward his jeans. He hadn't kept his attraction to her a secret. Darn, it would just be her luck if a gorgeous hunk tried to seduce her, and she couldn't even remember it.

She rounded the bed, studying him. He looked very peaceful, almost innocent, though she knew better. Why, it wouldn't surprise her if he was just pretending to be asleep.

On the floor, she spotted her lab coat and shoes. She had no memory of taking them off, so Roman must have done it. Then why didn't he take off his own shoes?

She stepped closer to him. "Hello? Good morning . . . or afternoon."

No response.

She chewed her lip, wondering what to do. He wasn't much of a protector if he slept this soundly. She leaned close to his face. "The Russians are coming!"

His face remained immobile. Sheesh. A lot of help he would be. She scanned the room. Two doors. She cracked the first one and saw a long hallway with many doors on each side. This had to be the fourth floor and a guest room. The fifth floor didn't have a hallway. Roman had that floor all to himself. She spotted a man close to the stairs with his back turned toward her. No kilt, but he wore a gun holster on his belt. A guard, she supposed, though definitely not a Highlander. His khaki pants and navy polo shirt were ordinary.

She closed the door and tried the next one. Great, a bathroom. Everything was there—toilet, bathtub, sink, towels, toothpaste, toothbrush—everything but a mirror. That was weird. She took care of business, then unlocked the door and peeked out. Roman was still asleep in her bed. She flicked the bathroom light switch on and off a few times, creating a strobe effect on his face. Still nothing. What a sound sleeper.

She washed her face and brushed her teeth. Now she felt better equipped for a showdown with the uninvited man in her bed.

She paced toward him, a smile pasted on her face, and in a loud voice, announced, "Good morning, Mr. Draganesti. Would it be too much of an imposition to expect you to sleep in your own bed from now on?"

No answer. Not even a snore. Didn't men snore? Hmm, not if he was pretending.

"It's not that I don't find your company stimulating. You're certainly a laugh a minute." She moved closer and poked him in the shoulder. "Come on, I know you're faking it."

Nothing.

She leaned over and whispered in his ear. "You realize this means war." Still no response. She examined the entire length of him. Long legs, trim waist, broad shoulders, strong jaw, a straight nose, though just a tad too long. It fit him, though, suited his arrogance. A strand of black hair lay across his cheekbone. She brushed the hair back. It was fine and soft.

No reaction whatsoever. He was certainly good at playing possum.

She perched beside him on the bed and placed her hands on his shoulders. "I have come to ravish your body. Resistance is futile."

Nothing. Shoot! Was she that easy to resist? Okay, she'd

resort to torture. She bounced down to the end of the bed and pulled his shoes off. They landed on the floor with loud *clunk*s. Still nothing. She stroked her fingers along his thick black socks, then tickled the soles of his feet. He didn't budge.

She tugged on the big toe of his left foot. "This little piggy went to market." She worked her way down to the little toe. "And this little piggy cried wee, wee, wee . . ." She let her fingers do the walking up his long leg. "All the way home."

She stopped at his hip. His face remained calm, unmoved. Her gaze wandered to his zipper. Now, that would wake him up. If she dared.

She glanced at his face. "I know you're faking it. No red-blooded male could sleep through this."

No response. Damn him. He was waiting to see how far she would go. Okay. She'd give him a wake-up call he'd never forget.

She shoved his black sweater up to reveal the waistband of his jeans. The sight of skin quickened her pulse, and she lifted the sweater a little bit higher. "Don't get out in the sun much, do you?"

His skin was pale, but his waist and stomach were nice and trim. A line of black hair descended from his chest, swirled around his belly button, then continued into the black jeans. Holy moly, he was so gorgeous. So masculine. So sexy.

So unconscious.

"Wake up, dammit!" She leaned over, planted her mouth over his navel, and blew a loud raspberry.

Nothing.

"Sheesh, you sleep like the dead!" She plopped down beside him. Then it struck her. Of course he wasn't snoring. He wasn't breathing. She reached out a shaky hand and touched his stomach. Cold.

She jerked her hand back. No, no, this wasn't happening

to her. The man had been perfectly healthy the night before.

But no one could sleep this soundly. She lifted his arm and let go. It fell down with a thud.

Oh God, it was true! She scrambled off the bed. Terror rose in her throat and erupted in a scream.

Roman Draganesti was dead.

Ten

She'd slept with a corpse. Granted, the few men she'd shared a bed with in the past hadn't exactly set the world on fire. And after a while, they generally walked away, never to return. Shanna had never considered their mobility a plus before.

Even after her earth-shattering screech, Roman was still lying there, peaceful as ever. He had to be dead. *No, dammit!*

She screamed again.

The door slammed open. She jumped and turned all at once.

"What's wrong?" The man she had seen earlier in the hallway was now standing outside the door, a pistol in his hand.

Shanna pointed at the bed. "Roman Draganesti is . . . dead."

"What?" The man slid his gun back into its holster.

"He's dead!" Shanna pointed once more at the bed. "I woke up and found him in my bed. Dead."

With a worried look, the man approached the bed. "Oh." His frown vanished. "No problem, miss. He's not dead."

"I'm sure he's dead."

"No, no. He's just asleep." The guard placed two fingers on Roman's neck. "Pulse is fine. Not to worry. I'm a trained security specialist. I would know a dead person."

"Well, I'm a trained medical professional, and I know a dead body when I see one." And she'd seen way too many of them when Karen had died. Shanna's knees trembled, and she looked around for a chair. None. There was only the bed. And poor Roman.

"He's not dead," the guard insisted. "He's just sleeping."

God, this man was dense. "Look—what's your name?"

"Phil. I'm one of the daytime guards."

"Phil." Shanna leaned against one of the four posters for support. "I know you don't want to admit this. After all, you're a guard, and you're supposed to keep people alive."

"He *is* alive."

"He is not!" Shanna's voice rose higher and higher. "He's dead! Deceased. Snuffed out. *The Roman Empire has fallen!*"

Phil's eyes widened, and he stepped back. "Okay, okay. Calm down." He tugged a walkie-talkie from his pocket. "I need help on the fourth floor. The guest is totally losing it."

"I am not!" Shanna strode toward the window. "Maybe if we open these shutters, it'll shed some light on the matter."

"*No!*" Phil sounded so frantic, Shanna stopped.

Static cackled on the walkie-talkie, then a voice came through. "What's the problem, Phil?" *Beep*.

"We have a situation here," Phil answered. "Miss Whelan woke up to find Mr. Draganesti in her bed, and she thinks he's dead."

Laughter erupted on the other end of the walkie-talkie. Shanna's mouth dropped open. Jeez, these people were cold. She headed back toward Phil and his communication device. "Could I speak with your supervisor, please?"

Phil gave her a sheepish look. "That was my supervisor." He punched a button. "Howard, could you come up here, please?"

"Oh yeah," Howard replied. "I wouldn't miss this." *Beep.*

Phil slipped the walkie-talkie into his pocket. "He'll be right up."

"Fine." Shanna scanned the room, but couldn't see a phone. "Would you please call 911?"

"I . . . I can't. Mr. Draganesti wouldn't like that at all."

"Mr. Draganesti is beyond liking or disliking."

"Please! Trust me, everything will be all right." Phil glanced at his watch. "Just wait about two hours."

Wait? Would he be any less dead in two hours? Shanna paced back and forth across the room. Dammit, how could Roman die like that? He looked so strong and healthy. It must have been a stroke or heart attack. "We need to notify the next of kin."

"They're all dead."

No family? Shanna halted her pacing. Poor Roman. He had been all alone. Like her. A wave of grief poured over her—grief for what might have been. Now she would never look into his beautiful golden-brown eyes again. Or feel his arms around her. She leaned against a bedpost and gazed at his handsome face.

A knock sounded at the door, and a large, middle-aged man strode into the room. He wore khaki pants and a navy polo just like Phil. The utility belt around his waist held an assortment of goodies like a pistol and flashlight. He looked like an ex-football player, complete with a huge neck and a crooked, lumpy nose that had been broken too many times. He would have been quite forbidding if his comb-over didn't look so obvious and his eyes weren't twinkling with humor.

"Miss Whelan?" His voice was nasal, courtesy of his battered nose. He probably snored loud enough to be heard in Jersey. "I'm Howard Barr, head of daytime security. How are you?"

"Alive, which is more than I can say for your employer."

"Hmmm." Howard glanced toward the bed. "Is he dead, Phil?"

Phil's eyes widened. "No. Of course not."

"Good." Howard slapped his hands together and rubbed them against each other. "That clears that up. Would you like to come down to the kitchen for a cup of coffee?"

Shanna blinked. "Excuse me? Are—aren't you going to check the body?"

Howard adjusted his belt and marched over to the bed. "He looks fine to me, though it's damned strange that he'd be sleeping here. I've never known Mr. Draganesti to sleep in someone else's bed."

Shanna gritted her teeth. "He's not asleep."

"I think I know what happened," Phil said. "I saw him this morning, a little after six, coming down the stairs with Miss Whelan in his arms."

Howard frowned. "After six? The sun was already rising."

A terrible thought occurred to Shanna. "He was carrying me?"

"Yeah," Phil replied. "It was a good thing I came along when I did, cause the guy was really struggling."

Shanna caught her breath. *Oh no.*

Phil shrugged. "I guess he was too worn out to get back to his room."

Shanna collapsed on the bed next to Roman's feet. Oh God, she'd been too heavy for him to carry. She'd caused his heart attack. "This is terrible. I—I killed him."

"Miss Whelan." Howard gave her an exasperated look. "That is totally impossible. He's not dead."

"Of course he is." She glanced at his body, only inches away. "I'll never eat pizza again."

Phil and Howard exchanged a worried look. Their walkie-talkies beeped.

Howard whipped his out first. "Yes?"

A scratchy voice came through. "Radinka Holstein just arrived from her shopping trip. She suggests Miss Whelan join her in the parlor."

"Good idea." Howard sighed, visibly relieved. "Phil, will you take Miss Whelan down to the parlor?"

"Sure." Phil looked equally relieved. "This way, miss."

Shanna hesitated, glancing at Roman. "What will you do with him?"

"Don't worry." Howard adjusted his utility belt. "We'll move him to his own bedroom. And in a few hours, when he wakes up, you'll both have a good laugh over this."

"Yeah, right." Shanna trudged down the hall alongside Phil.

Silently they descended the stairs. It was only last night when she had ascended these stairs with Roman. There was something about him—an aloof sadness—that had made her want to pester him and make him laugh. And when he did laugh, he seemed so surprised by it that she felt doubly rewarded.

Shoot, she hardly knew him, but she was going to miss him. He was strong, yet gentle. His intelligence was sharp and challenging. His insistence on protecting her was so macho. And he'd almost kissed her. Twice. Shanna sighed. Now she would never know what it was like to kiss Roman. She'd never get to see his lab or hear about his next brilliant achievement. She'd never get to talk to him again. By the time she reached the ground floor, she was thoroughly depressed. The sympathetic look on Radinka's face was her undoing. Her eyes filled with tears.

"Radinka, I'm so sorry. He's gone."

"There, there." Radinka hugged her and spoke in her deep, accented voice, "Do not worry, my dear. All will be fine." She led Shanna to the room on the right of the foyer.

It was empty. Shanna had expected it to be filled with women, like the night before. Dominating the room were three maroon leather couches, set around three sides of a square coffee table. On the fourth side, the wall was covered with an enormous widescreen television.

Shanna collapsed on a couch. "I can't believe he's gone."

Radinka placed her handbag on the coffee table and sat. "He will wake up, my dear."

"I don't think so." A tear slid down her face.

"These men can be very sound sleepers. My son, Gregori, is the same way. Impossible to wake up once he's asleep."

Shanna wiped the tear away. "No, he's dead."

Radinka brushed imaginary lint off her designer suit. "Perhaps you would feel better if I explain. I was here early in the morning, and Gregori told me what was happening. Roman took you to a dental clinic, and you worked on his teeth."

"That can't be right." Memory of a dental office hung precariously in her thoughts, just out of reach. "I . . . I thought it was a dream."

"It was real. Roman used a form of hypnosis on you."

"What?"

"Gregori assured me that you agreed to it."

Shanna closed her eyes, trying to remember. Yes, she'd been resting on the chaise in Roman's office when he'd suggested hypnosis. And she had agreed. She was desperate to save her career, desperate for a chance at that normal life she wanted so badly. "So he really did hypnotize me?"

"Yes. It was good for both of you. He needed help from a dentist, and you needed help getting over your fear of blood."

"You . . . you know about my fear?"

"Yes. You told Roman all about the terrible incident at the restaurant. Gregori was there, so he heard. I hope you don't mind that he told me."

"No, I suppose it's all right." Shanna leaned back against

the soft leather cushions and rested her head. "I really worked on Roman's teeth last night?"

"Yes. No doubt your memory is somewhat vague, but it will come back to you, eventually."

"I didn't faint or freak out when I saw blood?"

"From what I understand, you did a marvelous job."

Shanna snorted. "I don't know how I managed to do anything if I was under some sort of spell. What exactly did I do?"

"You implanted a tooth he had lost."

Shanna sat up with a jerk. "Not the wolf tooth! Don't tell me I stuck an animal tooth in his mouth. Aw, gee." She collapsed against the cushions. What did it matter? The poor guy was dead.

Radinka smiled. "It was an ordinary tooth."

"Oh, good. I could just see the look on the coroner's face when he examines the body and finds a wolf tooth." Poor Roman. He was so young to die. And so gorgeous.

Radinka sighed. "I wish I could convince you that he's still alive. Hmm." She pressed a forefinger against her closed lips. The dark red nail polish was a perfect match to her lipstick. "Did you give him some sort of anesthesia to lessen the pain?"

"How do I know? I might have sung opera in my underwear. I have no idea what I did last night." Shanna rubbed her forehead, trying to remember.

"I only mention it because it might explain why he is sleeping so soundly."

Shanna gasped and scrambled to her feet. "Oh my God, what if I killed him with anesthesia?"

Radinka's eyes widened. "That is not what I meant."

Shanna grimaced. "I might have overdosed him. Or I was too heavy for him to carry. Either way, I think I killed him."

"Don't be silly, child. Why do you blame yourself?"

"I don't know. It's what I do, I guess." Shanna's eyes

filled with tears once again. "I blame myself for what happened to Karen. I should have helped her somehow. She was still alive when I found her."

"She was your young friend who died in the restaurant?"

Shanna sniffed and nodded her head.

"I am so sorry. I know this is hard for you to believe, but once the anesthesia wears off, Roman will wake up, and you will see for yourself that he is perfectly fine."

With a groan, Shanna sprawled onto the couch.

"You like him very much, don't you?"

Shanna sighed, staring at the ceiling. "Yes, I do, but I don't have much hope for a lasting relationship with a dead guy."

"Mrs. Holstein?" a male voice spoke from the doorway.

Shanna looked over her shoulder and saw yet another guard dressed in khaki and navy blue. What had happened to all the kilts? She missed the Highlanders with their bright plaids and adorable accents.

"The packages have arrived from Bloomingdale's," the guard announced. "Where would you like us to put them?"

Radinka rose gracefully. "Bring a few boxes in here, and put the rest in Miss Whelan's room."

"In my room?" Shanna asked. "Why?"

Radinka smiled. "Because they are for you, my dear."

"But—but I can't accept anything. And you shouldn't put anything in my room when there's a dead body in there."

The guard rolled his eyes. "We moved him to his bedroom."

"Good. Then you may proceed." Radinka sat back down. "I hope you like what I picked out for you."

"I'm serious, Radinka. I can't accept a bunch of presents. It's enough that you gave me sanctuary for one night. I—I need to call the Justice Department and make other arrangements."

"Roman wants you here. And he wants you to have these

things." Radinka turned to the guard as he entered, his arms piled high with boxes. "Put them on the table here, please."

Shanna stared in dismay at the boxes. It was so tempting to take them. She didn't dare go to her apartment now, so she had nothing but the clothes on her back. Still, she couldn't accept all these presents. "I really appreciate your generosity, but—"

"Roman's generosity." Radinka set a package in her lap and opened it. "Ah, yes. These are lovely. Do you like them?" Nestled in white tissue paper was a red lace bra and panties.

"Wow." Shanna picked up the bra. It was a lot fancier than what she usually wore. And a lot more expensive. She checked the tag. Thirty-six B. "It's the right size."

"Yes. Roman left me a note with your sizes."

"What? How did he know my bra size?"

"I suppose you told him while you were hypnotized."

Shanna gulped. Jeez, maybe she *had* sung opera in her underwear.

"Here." Radinka fumbled through her handbag. "I believe I still have the note." She passed the paper to Shanna.

"Oh, my." It had to be the last thing he had written before his death. Shanna scanned the note. *Size 12. 36B.* Roman had indeed known her sizes. Had she told him under hypnosis? What else had she done? *Get her some brownies.* She caught her breath, and tears welled in her eyes.

"What is wrong, my dear?"

"Brownies. He's so sweet." Correction—*was* so sweet. "He didn't think I needed to lose weight?"

Radinka smiled. "Apparently not. I left some brownies in the kitchen, but if you want any, you should hurry. The daytime guards were drooling over them. Those men will eat anything."

"Maybe later, thank you." Shanna was starting to feel hunger pangs, but each time she thought of eating, she was haunted by the image of Roman struggling to carry her down the stairs.

"Let's see what else we have." Radinka whipped open the rest of the boxes.

There were more matching sets of lacy underwear, a blue chenille bathrobe, a salmon-colored tank top and matching blazer, and a blue silk nightgown with matching slippers.

"This is better than Christmas," Shanna murmured. "It's really too much."

"Do you like them?"

"Yes, of course, but—"

"Then it is settled." Radinka stacked the boxes. "I'll take these up to your room and leave a note in Roman's office for him to see you when he wakes up."

"But—"

"No buts." Radinka stood and gathered the boxes in her arms. "I want you to go to the kitchen and eat. I told one of the guards to fix you a sandwich, so they're expecting you. Then I want you to have a nice, hot shower and put on some fresh clothes. By the time you're done, Roman will be awake."

"But—"

"I am too busy to argue. We have a million things to do at Romatech tonight." Radinka marched from the room with the packages. "I will see you later, dear."

Sheesh. Shanna had a feeling Radinka Holstein was a dragon lady at work. But she did have beautiful taste in clothes. It was going to hurt to return most of them, but it was the right thing to do. Did she dare venture out of this house? It would hurt a lot worse if the Russians caught her.

After Shanna ate her sandwich in the kitchen and tried her best to ignore the pastry box of brownies on the table, she went upstairs to her room. She opened the door and peeked inside. The bed was empty. Shopping bags and boxes were piled at the foot of the bed. She took a long, hot shower. Then, dressed in the chenille bathrobe, she went through the bags and boxes. It should have been fun, but she grew increasingly sad, knowing that the man footing the bill had just died.

Guilt needled her. She couldn't accept all these gifts. And she couldn't stay here. She needed to contact the U.S. marshal, Bob Mendoza, and then she needed to start a new life somewhere else. A place where she knew no one, and no one knew her. Again.

God, it was depressing. As part of the Witness Protection Program, she could never contact family or old friends. But she craved companionship. She wanted love. She hadn't realized how much until she had met Roman. Damn. It wasn't like she was asking for too much from life. She only wanted the same thing a jillion other women wanted—a career she was proud of, a husband who would love her, and children. Beautiful children.

Unfortunately, desperate times had altered her goal in life. Now each day was a survival test.

She wandered toward the window and its ugly aluminum shutters. She located a switch behind the curtains and flipped it. The shutters opened and dim sunlight entered the room.

The view was lovely. Below her was a tree-lined street and in the distance, Central Park. The sun was setting in the west, casting purple and pink streaks into wispy clouds. Shanna stood at the window and watched. A feeling of peace descended on her with the night. Perhaps she would live through all this. If only Roman was still alive.

Could Radinka be right, and he was simply sleeping off a large dose of anesthesia? Shanna winced. It was awful that she couldn't remember what she'd done to the poor man. Maybe she should stick around for a little longer. Either Roman would be declared officially dead, or he would miraculously wake up. Either way, she couldn't leave until she knew for sure.

She selected some clothes and dressed. Inside the armoire, she found a television. Good. She could veg out while she waited. She flipped through channels. Whoa, here was a channel she'd never seen before. An animated black bat flew toward her, then it froze into a logo that looked a bit like Batman. Underneath was a message. *Welcome to DVN. On 24/7 because it's always nighttime somewhere.*

DVN? Something Video Network? And what did nighttime have to do with a network being on air? The bat logo disappeared, and another line appeared on the screen. *DVN. If you're not digital, you can't be seen.* That was odd. A knock sounded at the door, interrupting her thoughts. She turned off the television and went to the door. It was probably Phil. He seemed to be in charge of the fourth floor.

"Connor!" She yelped in surprise. "You're back!"

"Aye." He stood there, smiling. "That I am."

She threw her arms around his neck and hugged him. "I'm so glad to see you."

He pulled back, his cheeks blushing. "I hear ye had a wee scare."

"Oh, it's terrible, isn't it? I'm so sorry, Connor."

"Now, why would ye be sorry, lass? 'Tis Mr. Draganesti himself who sent me here. He's wanting to see you."

Her skin chilled with goose bumps. "That . . . that can't be."

"He wants to see you right away. I'll take you up there."

He was alive? "I know the way." Shanna ran for the stairs.

Eleven

Roman Draganesti woke up with no memory of how he had returned to his bed. He was lying on top of the suede comforter with his clothes and shoes still on. He ran his tongue along the inside of his mouth. The wire splint was still there. He felt the fang with his fingers. Solid. Of course, he wasn't sure if the fang could still extend and retract, and it would be impossible to put it to test as long as the tooth was wired in place. He'd have to convince Shanna to remove the splint.

After a quick shower, he threw on a bathrobe and padded into his office to check for messages. Radinka's spidery handwriting caught his eye. She'd completed the shopping for Shanna. *Good.* She was going to Romatech early to make sure everything was ready for the Gala Opening Ball. Since she was now working night and day, she felt she deserved another raise. *Another one? Fine.*

Jean-Luc Echarpe and Angus MacKay, French and British coven masters, were due to arrive at five in the morning. *Good.* The guest rooms on the third floor were ready for them. Roman was planning to introduce two new taste sensations from his line of Fusion Cuisine at the Opening Ball. Five hundred bottles had been prepared for the event. Everything was looking great.

Then he read the last paragraph. Upon waking, Shanna Whelan had discovered him in her bed. *Oh no*. She had decided he was dead and became terribly upset. *Oh shit*. Of course she would think he was dead. During the day, he had no pulse. But on the bright side, this could mean that she actually cared about him.

Radinka had tried to convince Shanna that his heavy sleep was due to the anesthesia he had received at the dental clinic. Unfortunately, that theory only drove her to the conclusion that she'd killed him. *Great*. She was upset not because she felt any affection for him, but because she felt guilty. He could just imagine the scenario—Shanna running about the bedroom, upset, while he lay there like a dumb log. *Shit*.

Roman crushed the paper in his fist and tossed it into the trash. This was the last straw. He had to finish the formula that would allow him to stay awake during the day. He couldn't lie around helpless when Shanna needed him.

He punched a button on his intercom phone.

"Kitchen," a nasal voice answered.

"Howard, is that you?"

"Yes, sir! I'm glad to hear you're up and about. There was a little bit of excitement here while you were sleeping."

Roman could hear stifled laughter in the background. God's blood. You would think being master of the largest coven in North America would entitle him to a little respect.

"Not that we're complaining," Howard continued. "It's usually so boring around here. Oh, Connor just walked in."

"Howard, we have important guests coming in tonight. Your employer, Mr. MacKay, will be here. I expect heightened security during the day and absolute discretion."

"I understand, sir. We'll take good care of everyone. The Highlanders are coming in now, so I'll be going. Good night."

"Good night. Connor, are you there?"

There was a pause, then a beeping noise. "Aye, I'm here."

"Escort Miss Whelan to my office in ten minutes."

"Aye, sir."

Roman strode toward the wet bar, grabbed a bottle of synthetic blood from the mini-fridge, and popped it into the microwave. He headed back to his bedroom. There he pulled on a pair of black slacks and a gray dress shirt—an effort to look a little more formal since he had important guests arriving that night. Angus and his entourage would be dressed to the hilt in their Scottish finery. Jean-Luc would be accompanied by his beautiful vampire models, all wearing his famous haute couture evening wear.

Stuffed in the back of his closet, Roman spotted the black tuxedo and matching cape that Jean-Luc had given him three years ago. Roman groaned. He'd have to wear the damned thing again. Maybe Jean-Luc enjoyed dressing like the Hollywood version of Dracula, but Roman preferred the more relaxed dress code of modern times. He removed the tuxedo from the closet. He'd have to get it pressed before the Gala Opening Ball.

The microwave dinged. His first meal for the evening was ready. He tossed the tuxedo onto his bed. Just then, the outer door to the office slammed open.

"Roman?" Shanna yelled. "Are you there?" There was a definite edge to her voice. Nervous, breathless, near panic.

No way had that been ten minutes. She must have run the entire way. Damn. There went his breakfast.

"I'm in here," he answered and heard a responding gasp as he strode barefoot to the bedroom door.

She was standing close to his desk, her face flushed from running, her pretty mouth agape. Her eyes widened as he moved into the office. "Oh my God," she whispered. Moisture shimmered in her eyes. She covered her mouth with trembling fingers.

God's blood, she'd been through hell. He looked down, embarrassed by the ordeal he'd put her through. Oh, great, he was a sight. His shirt was hanging open. His trousers were unbuttoned and low enough on his hips that his black boxer shorts were showing. He pushed his damp hair back from his face and cleared his throat. "I heard what happened."

She just stood there, staring at him.

Connor rushed through the door. "Sorry, sir. I tried to slow her down, but—" He noted Roman's state of dress. "Och, we should have knocked."

"You're alive." Shanna inched toward him.

The microwave dinged, a reminder bell that his breakfast was still waiting. And would have to wait until Shanna left.

Connor winced. He knew a vampire was always the hungriest when he first awoke. "We should come back later," he suggested to Shanna, "when Mr. Draganesti has finished dressing."

She didn't seem to hear Connor. She moved slowly toward Roman. He inhaled deeply, taking in her scent. She smelled delicious, and that pale orange top made her look as juicy as a ripe peach. What little blood was left in his body surged toward his groin, leaving him doubly starved—for her flesh, and blood.

The intensity of his hunger must have been noticeable. Connor backed toward the door. "I'll be leaving you two alone, then." He eased out, shutting the door behind him.

Shanna was close enough to grab now. He curled his hands into fists, fighting the temptation. "I've been told that I frightened you. I'm sorry."

A tear escaped, but before it could reach her cheek, she brushed it away. "I'm just happy you're all right."

Did she really care that much? Roman watched her

closely. Her gaze traveled the length of him, pausing at his bare chest, slipping lower to his stomach. Damn, he wanted her. He hoped his eyes weren't starting to glow.

"You're really all right." She touched his chest, a light touch with her fingertips, but it jolted him like a lightning bolt. He reacted swiftly, pulling her to him in a tight embrace.

She stiffened at first in surprise, then relaxed, nestling her cheek against the mat of curls on his chest. Her hands rested lightly on his shirt. "I was afraid I had lost you."

"I'm rather hard to get rid of, actually." God's blood, he was hungry. *Control, stay in control.*

"Radinka said I worked on your teeth last night."

"Yes."

"Let me see." She reached up to his mouth and examined the splint. "The tooth looks fine, a little more pointed than usual. It seems to have healed very quickly."

"Yes. You can remove the splint."

"What? No, I can't. These things take time." The microwave dinged again, drawing her attention. "Did you need to get that?"

He took her hand and kissed her fingers. "I just need you."

She snorted softly and removed her hand from his grip. "Is it true, then, that you actually hypnotized me?"

"Yes." It was close to the truth.

She frowned at him. "I didn't do anything strange, did I? I mean, it's awfully disconcerting to know I did stuff and have no memory of it."

"You were very professional." He recaptured her hand and kissed her palm. If only she would suggest oral sex again.

"I didn't freak out at the sight of blood?"

"No." He kissed the inside of her wrist. Type A Positive was pulsing through the vein. "You were very brave."

Her eyes lit up. "You know what this means? My career isn't over. This is great!" She flung her arms around his neck and gave him a kiss on the cheek. "Thank you, Roman."

His arms tightened around her. His heart expanded with a glimpse of hope. Then he recalled his suggestion to her at the dental clinic. *Bloody hell!* This was his doing. She was merely following orders. He wrenched himself out of her embrace.

She gasped, clearly surprised. Then her face seemed to crumble, but only for a second before it settled into a stony, shuttered look. She stepped back. Damn, she must think he had rejected her. And she was trying hard to mask the pain. She really did care about him, and he was fumbling about like an idiot, frightening her during the day, and now hurting her feelings. He had so damned little experience with mortal females.

The microwave dinged once more. He strode toward the machine and yanked the plug from the socket. There, it would stop tempting him with warm blood. Unfortunately, Shanna presented a temptation much harder to resist. She was fresh.

"I'd better be going now." She retreated to the office door. "I . . . I'm happy you're alive, and that your tooth is fine. And I appreciate your protection and all the nice . . . gifts, which I really can't keep."

"Shanna."

She reached for the doorknob. "You're a busy man, so I'll stay out of your way. In fact, I'll be leaving—"

"Shanna, wait." He moved toward her. "I need to explain."

She refused to look at him. "There's no need."

"Yes, there is. Last night, while you were . . . hypnotized, I planted an idea in your mind. I shouldn't have done it, but I made the suggestion that you would throw your arms around me and give me a passionate kiss. And when you did, just now, I realized what I—"

"Wait a minute." She gave him an incredulous look. "You think I was programmed to kiss you?"

"Yes. It was wrong of me, but—"

"That's crazy! First of all, I am *not* under your control. Sheesh, I'm barely under my own."

"Perhaps, but—"

"And secondly, I bet I'm a lot harder to control than you think."

He kept his mouth shut. She was correct, but he didn't want to confirm it.

"And finally, that was *not* a passionate kiss. It was a dinky peck on the cheek. A man your age should know the difference."

He raised his brows. "Should I?" He could hardly explain he'd spent most of his mortal years in a monastery.

"Of course. There's a huge difference between a peck on the cheek and a passionate kiss."

"And you are angry with me for failing to discriminate between the two?"

"I'm not angry! Well, maybe a little." She glared at him. "You pulled away from me like I was some kind of leper."

He stepped toward her. "It won't happen again."

She snorted softly. "You can say that again."

He shrugged one shoulder. "I'm a scientist, Shanna. I can hardly make a comparative analysis of the different types of kisses if I cannot acquire the necessary data."

Her eyes narrowed. "I know what you're up to. You're trying to weasel a free sample out of me."

"You mean they're not normally free?" He smiled. "How much will a passionate kiss cost me?"

"I give them freely when I'm in the mood, which I am *not*." She glowered at him. "It'll be a cold day in hell before I feel like giving you a passionate kiss."

Ouch. He figured that was payback for hurting her feelings earlier. "I actually thought the little peck was very exciting."

"Oh, please. I'm talking real passion here. Hot, sweaty, jungle-fever type stuff. Believe me, if for some strange reason, hell freezes over, and I decide to give you a passionate kiss"—she leaned against the door and crossed her arms—"believe me, you would have no problem recognizing the difference."

"As a scientist, I can't deal with beliefs." He moved closer. "I need proof."

"You won't be getting it from me."

He stopped in front of her. "Maybe you can't deliver."

"Ha! Maybe you can't handle it."

He rested a palm against the door, close to her head. "Is that a challenge?"

"It's a concern. Given the questionable condition of your health, I'm not sure your heart could take it."

"I survived the last kiss."

"That was nothing! A real passionate kiss would have to be on the mouth."

"Are you sure? That definition seems a bit narrow." He planted a palm on the other side of her head, trapping her between his arms. Slowly, he looked her over. "I can think of some other areas I would love to kiss with passion."

Her face turned pink. "Well, I should be going now. I was worried about you being dead and all, but you certainly seem to be—"

"Up?" He leaned toward her. "I certainly am."

She turned, fumbling for the doorknob. "I'll let you finish dressing."

"I am sorry, Shanna. I didn't mean to frighten or hurt you."

She looked at him. Her eyes glistened with unshed tears. "Oh, Roman, you silly man. I thought I had lost you."

Silly? In his total of five hundred and forty-four years, he'd never been called that. "I'll always be here."

She jumped at him, wrapping her arms around his neck. Surprised by the sudden force of her attack, Roman stumbled back a step. The room reeled for a few seconds. He widened his stance to keep from tipping over. Maybe it was hunger that was causing this dizziness. Maybe it was the shock of receiving affection. After all, he was a monster. When was the last time anyone had wanted to hug him?

He closed his eyes and breathed in the scent of her shampoo, her soap, her arteries pumping with blood. Hunger pounded inside him. He kissed the top of her head and then her smooth brow. Blood pulsed at her temples, drawing him there. He kissed her, breathing in the rich aroma. She tilted her face up to look at him, but afraid that his eyes would be glowing, he dove for her neck. He nibbled up to her ear, then nipped at the earlobe.

She moaned, sliding her hands into his hair. "I was afraid I'd never get to kiss you."

"I've wanted to since I first met you." He brushed his lips across her jaw, headed toward her mouth.

Their lips met briefly, then separated. Her breath was warm against his face. Her eyes were closed. Good. He could stop worrying about his own eyes.

He brought his hands up to cradle her face. She looked so innocent and trusting. God's blood, she had no idea what he was capable of. He only hoped he was capable of resisting. Gently, he kissed her. She tightened her grip on his head, pulling him closer. He sucked her bottom lip into his mouth and flicked it with the tip of his tongue. Her body shuddered. Her mouth opened, begging for him.

He invaded. Explored. She matched each move, stroking his tongue with her own. She was so alive, so hot that all his senses burned. He could see her clinging to him, growing more feverish. He could hear her blood pounding. Feel her nerves quivering, the heat simmering. Smell her juices flowing.

That left only taste.

He wrapped his arms around her. With one hand against

her back, he flattened her chest against his. She was breathing quickly, her breasts moving against his skin. His other hand slid down, down and around her rump. God's blood, she was heaven. Firm and round. And she hadn't been kidding about her ability to show passion.

She pressed against his erection. Good God, she was rocking against him. Squirming. Reveling in the glory of being alive and her overriding instinct to create more life.

So sad. His overriding instinct was to destroy life.

He went for her neck. The left fang sprang forth. The right one started to, but jammed against the wire splint. *Ouch!* He pulled away, clamping his lips together. It hurt like hell, but at least the pain had knocked some sense into him.

He couldn't bite Shanna. God's blood, he had sworn never to bite a mortal again. He released her and backed away.

"What's wrong?" she sounded breathless.

He slapped a hand over his mouth. He couldn't even answer her with one of his fangs extended.

"Oh my gosh. Is it the splint? Or your tooth? Did we knock it loose?" She rushed toward him. "Let me see."

He shook his head. His eyes watered from the strain of trying to retract the fangs while he was still so hungry.

"You look like you're in pain." She touched his shoulder. "Please, let me see."

"Mmm." He shook his head, retreating another step. Damn, this was embarrassing. But he probably deserved it, as close as he had come to biting her.

"I shouldn't have kissed you with the splint in your mouth." She grimaced. "Jeez, I shouldn't have kissed you at all."

The left fang finally obeyed and slid back into its hole. He spoke with his hand in front of his mouth. "I'm all right."

"But I broke a very important rule—never, ever date a

client. I shouldn't be involved with you at all."

He lowered his hand. "In that case, you're fired."

"You can't fire me. You still have my splint in your mouth." She moved close to him. "Now open your mouth and let me see."

He did as he was told.

She nudged the splint with her fingers. He tickled her fingers with his tongue.

"Stop that." She jerked her hand from his mouth. "I can't believe this. The splint's loose."

"Well, you're one hell of a kisser."

She blushed. "I don't see how I managed to . . . Don't worry. I won't kiss you again. As your dentist, I'm responsible first and foremost for your dental health—"

"I fired you."

"You can't. Not as long as the splint—"

"I'll rip the thing out myself."

"Don't you dare!"

"I'm not losing you, Shanna."

"You won't lose me. We'll only have to wait a week or so."

"I'm not waiting." He'd waited more than five hundred years to experience something like this. He wasn't waiting another damned week. And he wasn't taking any more chances with his questionable amount of control. He strode toward his bedroom. Black dots swirled around his head. He ignored them, ignored the hunger raging inside him.

"Roman!" She ran after him. "You can't take out the splint."

"I'm not." He yanked open a dresser drawer and dug beneath a pile of underwear. There, on the bottom, was a pouch of red felt. He pulled it out. Even through the felt, he could feel the warmth of the silver inside. Without the felt, his hand would now be covered with burning welts.

He held it out to her. She didn't notice since she was pivoting in a circle, checking out his bedroom. Her gaze lingered on his king-sized bed.

"Shanna?"

She looked at him, then noticed the pouch in his hand.

"I want you to have this." He swayed on his feet. He had to eat soon, one way or another.

"I can't accept more presents."

"Take it!"

She winced. "You should work on your bedside manner."

He leaned on the dresser. "I want you to wear it around your neck. It will protect you."

"Sounds a little superstitious." She took the pouch, loosened the drawstring, and let the contents fall into her hand.

It looked much the same as it had in 1479 when he'd first taken vows. The silver chain was plain but good quality. The crucifix displayed medieval craftsmanship at its best.

"Wow. This is beautiful." Shanna examined it closely. "It looks really old."

"Put it on. It will protect you."

"Protect me from what?"

"I hope you never find out." He eyed the crucifix sadly. He had been so proud when Father Constantine placed it around his neck. Pride. That had been his downfall.

"Help me put it on?" Shanna turned halfway, gathering her hair into a ponytail. She offered the necklace to him.

He stumbled back before the silver could burn him. "I cannot. If you will excuse me, I need to go to work. I have a lot to do tonight."

She eyed him warily. "Fine." She released the ponytail, and her brown hair settled onto her shoulders. "Are you sorry you kissed me?"

"No, not at all." He grabbed the edge of the dresser for support. "The crucifix. Put it on."

She continued to study him.

"Please."

Her eyes widened. "I didn't think that word was in your vocabulary."

"I reserve it for emergencies."

She smiled. "In that case . . ." She looped the crucifix around her neck and flipped her hair over the chain. The cross rested on her breasts like a shield of armor.

"Thank you." He gathered up his strength and escorted her to the door.

"I'll see you again?"

"Yes. Later tonight. When I get back from Romatech." He closed and locked the door. Then he stumbled into the office, grabbed the bottle from the microwave, and chugged it down cold. God's blood, his life had been turned upside down by Shanna. He couldn't wait to kiss her again. He was a demon getting a taste of heaven.

Hell was definitely freezing over.

Twelve

On the way down the stairs, Shanna's thoughts centered on Roman. Thank God he was alive! The question now was should she stay under his protection or make other arrangements with Bob Mendoza? It was very tempting to stay with Roman. She'd never felt so attracted to a man. Or so intrigued.

She sauntered into the kitchen and found Connor at the sink, rinsing out bottles and setting them in the dishwasher.

"Are ye all right, lass?"

"Sure." She noticed a box of Band-Aids that was sitting on the counter. "Did you cut yourself?"

"Nay. I thought ye might be needing one." He peered closely at her neck. "Och, a silver chain. That'll protect you."

"Roman gave it to me." Shanna admired the antique crucifix.

"Aye, he's a good man." Connor swept the box of Band-Aids into a drawer. "I shouldna have doubted him."

Shanna opened a cabinet. "Where do you keep your glasses?"

"Here." Connor opened a different cabinet and retrieved a glass. "What would ye like to drink?"

"Some water." Shanna motioned to the dispenser in the refrigerator door. "I can get it myself."

Connor reluctantly handed over the glass, then followed her to the refrigerator.

"I'm not helpless, you know." She put in some ice and smiled at the Highlander who was leaning against the refrigerator door. "You guys are too sweet. You're going to spoil me rotten." She filled the glass with water.

Connor blushed.

She sat at the table and peered inside the box of brownies. "Yum." She took one out. "Do you think you could find some dental instruments for me? I need to tighten the splint in Roman's mouth."

Connor sat across from her. "Aye. We can take care of that."

"Thanks." Shanna pinched off a corner of the brownie. "Is there anything to do around here?"

"We have a well-stocked library across from the parlor. And there should be a telly in yer bedchamber."

Bedchamber? Shanna loved how archaic the Highlanders could sound. She finished her brownie, then hunted down the library. Wow. Three whole walls were lined with books from the floor to the ceiling. Some looked very old. Some were in languages she didn't recognize.

A wide window, covered with thick draperies, stretched across the fourth wall. She peeked out and saw the dimly lit street with cars parked along each side. It seemed so quiet and peaceful. Hard to believe there were people out there who wanted her dead.

She heard voices in the foyer. Female voices. She moved toward the door. She had to admit, she was curious about these mysterious ladies who watched television in Roman's parlor. She peeked around the doorjamb.

There were two beautiful women approaching the parlor. The first one, dressed in a black spandex catsuit, looked like a model and moved like an anorexic panther. Her hair was long, black, and loose down her back. Sparkling rhinestones studded the black belt around her tiny waist. Black polish gleamed on her long fingernails, and each nail boasted another rhinestone.

The second woman was petite, with her black hair cut into a bob. She wore a tight black sweater to show off her generous cleavage and a black mini-skirt to reveal her pencil legs encased in black fishnet stockings. She was cute and tiny, but her clunky black shoes made her walk like a water buffalo.

The woman in the catsuit was gesturing angrily, her fingernails glittering under the foyer chandelier. "How can he treat me like zis? Does he not know I am a celebrity?"

"He's very busy, Simone," Miss Clunky Shoes replied. "He has a million things to do with the conference starting tomorrow."

Simone flipped her black silky hair over her shoulder. "But I came early so I could see him, zat rat!"

Shanna winced at the way the French catwoman pronounced her *r*'s. It sounded like she had phlegm stuck in her throat and was trying to cough it up.

Simone huffed. "He is so h-rude!"

Shanna gritted her teeth. Definitely something in her throat. Probably a furball.

Simone flung open the double doors to the parlor. The room was filled with women lounging about on the three maroon couches. They were drinking something from crystal wineglasses.

"Good evening, Simone, Maggie," the ladies greeted the two women in the foyer.

"Has our show started yet?" Maggie clunked into the room in her enormous black shoes.

"No," one of the ladies replied. She was sitting on the middle sofa, so Shanna could see only the back of her head. Her short, spiky hair was dyed such a dark red, it was more like purple. "The news is still on."

Shanna took note of the widescreen TV. An ordinary-looking male newscaster was on the air, mouthing words. In the corner of the screen a red mute sign glowed. Obviously, these ladies didn't concern themselves with current events. Beneath the mute sign, the black bat logo was displayed. They were watching DVN.

Shanna counted a total of eleven women, who all appeared to be in their twenties. Well, what the heck. If she was going to pursue a relationship with Roman, she needed to know why these women were here. She stepped into the foyer.

Simone filled a wineglass from a crystal decanter on the coffee table. "Has anyone seen ze master zis evening?" She perched in the far corner of the sofa on the left.

The purple-haired woman was admiring her long, purple fingernails. "I heard he's seeing another woman."

"*What?*" Simone's eyes flashed. Leaning forward, she plunked her glass down on the table. "You are lying, Vanda. He could not possibly want anozher woman when he could have *moi*."

Vanda shrugged. "I'm not lying. Phil told me about it."

"The daytime guard?" Maggie sat beside Simone.

Vanda stood. She was also wearing a black catsuit, but her belt was made of braided leather strips. She shoved a hand through her purple spiky hair. "Phil has a crush on me. He tells me everything I want to know."

Simone sank back into the couch, her gaunt body in danger of being swallowed up entirely. "Zen it is true? Zere is anozher woman?"

"Yes." Vanda turned her head and sniffed. "What is that?" She spotted Shanna in the foyer. "Well, speak of the devil."

All eleven women stared at Shanna.

She smiled and stepped into the room. "Good evening." Shanna looked the women over. Black clothing was normal for New York City, but still, some of these outfits seemed a bit odd. One of the ladies was wearing a gown that looked medieval. Another gown looked Victorian. Was that a hoop skirt?

The one called Vanda circled the coffee table and struck a dramatic pose by the television. Whoa. The neckline of her catsuit plunged all the way to her waist. Shanna was seeing a lot more of Vanda than she really wanted to.

"My name is Shanna Whelan. I'm a dentist."

Vanda narrowed her eyes. "Our teeth are perfect."

"Okay." Shanna wondered what she had done to make these women glare at her. Though there was one, sitting apart from the others, who was giving her a friendly smile. She had blond hair and modern clothes.

The one in the Victorian dress spoke, her accent making her sound like a Southern belle. "A lady dentist? I do declare, I don't know why the master would invite her here."

The one in the medieval gown agreed. "She does not belong here. She should leave."

The friendly blond spoke up. "Hey, it's your master's house. He can invite the pope if he wants."

The other women shot the blond a vicious look.

Vanda shook her head. "Don't make them mad at you, Darcy. They'll make your life miserable."

"Some life." Darcy rolled her eyes. "Oh, I'm so afraid. What could they possibly do to me? Kill me?"

The medieval one lifted her chin. "Do not tempt us. You do not belong here, either."

What a strange group. Shanna retreated a step.

The Southern belle glowered at Shanna. "Is it true, then? You're the master's new lady friend?"

Shanna shook her head. "I don't know who this master is."

The ladies chuckled. Darcy winced.

"Bon." Simone curled up like a contented cat in her corner of the couch. "You will leave him alone, zen. I came all ze way from Paris to be wiz him."

Maggie leaned close to Simone and whispered in her ear.

"Non!" Simone's eyes widened. *"Zut alors!* He did not tell her?" She huffed. "And he is ignoring me. To zink I wanted to have sex wiz him, zat bastard!"

Maggie sighed. "He never has sex with us anymore. I miss the old days."

"Me, too," Vanda said, and all the ladies nodded in agreement.

Jeez. Shanna grimaced. This master character had had sex with all of these women? He was downright creepy.

"He will have sex wiz me," Simone declared. "No man can resist me." She eyed Shanna with disdain. "Why would he want zis woman? She must be size fourteen."

"Excusez-moi?" Shanna glared at the rude Frenchwoman.

"Oh, look!" Maggie pointed at the TV. "The news is over. It's time for our soap."

The ladies forgot about Shanna as they turned to watch the television. Maggie punched the mute button on the remote control to restore the sound. There was a commercial on with a woman praising the yummy, rich flavor of a drink called Chocolood.

Vanda slinked around the couches and headed for Shanna. Upon closer inspection, Shanna realized Vanda's belt was actually a whip. And on the inside curve of one breast, Vanda was sporting a tattoo of a bat. Purple, of course.

Shanna crossed her arms, refusing to be intimidated.

Vanda stopped beside her. "I heard the master fell asleep in someone else's bed."

"No!" The other ladies forgot about the television. They turned to stare at Vanda.

Vanda smiled, enjoying all the attention. She patted her spiky purple hair. "That's what Phil told me."

"Whose bed?" Simone demanded. "I will scratch her eyes out."

Vanda looked at Shanna. The other women stared at her.

Shanna raised her hands. "Look, guys, you've got the wrong bed. I don't know this creepy master of yours."

Vanda chuckled. "Not very smart, is she?"

That was it. "Okay, lady. I'm smart enough not to dye my hair purple. Or to share a man with ten other women."

The ladies reacted—some laughing, some offended.

"Phil told me there was a man in your bed," Vanda sneered. "You woke up and thought he was dead."

The ladies giggled.

Shanna frowned. "That was Roman Draganesti."

Vanda smiled slowly. "Roman *is* the master."

Shanna's mouth dropped open. Could it be true? Could Roman have eleven live-in girlfriends? "No." She shook her head.

The ladies watched her with smug looks. Vanda leaned against the doorjamb, her smile triumphant.

A chill crept across Shanna's skin. No, it wasn't true. These women just wanted to hurt her. "Roman is a good man."

"He is a bastard," Simone declared.

Shanna's head reeled. *Roman* is *a good man.* She had felt it down to her soul. He wanted to protect her, not hurt her. "I don't believe you. Roman cares about me. He gave me this." The crucifix had slid to the side beneath her blazer. She pulled it out.

The women cringed.

Vanda stiffened with a hiss. "We are his women. You do not belong here."

Shanna gulped. Could Roman really have eleven lovers?

How could he kiss her when he already had so many women? Oh God. She pressed the cross against her chest. "I don't believe you."

"Zen you are a fool," Simone said. "We should not have to share Roman wiz someone like you. It is insulting."

Shanna stared at the women. They had to be lying, but why would they? The only logical explanation for their anger was that she was actually seeing their master. Roman.

How could he do this to her? Make her feel so special when he had a house full of women. What a fool she'd been, thinking he wanted to protect her from the bad guys. He only wanted her here so he could add her to his collection and make a full dozen. Simone was right. He was a bastard! Eleven women at his beck and call, and that wasn't enough for him. What a pig!

She ran from the room and hurried up the stairs. By the time Shanna reached the fourth floor, she was seething. No way was she staying here. She didn't care how safe it was from the Russians. She never wanted to see Roman again. She could take care of herself.

What would she need? A few clothes, her purse? She recalled seeing her Marilyn Monroe purse in Roman's office. Roman, the bastard pig's office.

She ran up the last flight of stairs. A Highlander was guarding the fifth floor and moved toward her. "Did ye need something, lass?"

"Just my purse." She motioned toward the office door. "I left it inside."

"Verra well." The guard opened the door for her.

She slipped inside and spotted her purse on the floor next to the velvet chaise. She checked the contents. Her wallet, checkbook, and Beretta were still there. Thank God.

She remembered pointing the gun at Roman the night before. Why had she decided to trust him? The minute she had climbed into a car with him, she had trusted him with her life.

She looked sadly at the velvet chaise. Last night, while lying there, she had let him hypnotize her. She had trusted him again, that time with her career, her dreams, and her fears. And then, over by the door, they had shared their first kiss. One hell of a kiss. And she had trusted him with her heart.

A tear rolled down her cheek. Dammit, no! She wiped her eyes. No tears for that bastard. She was halfway to the door when she stopped.

She wanted him to know. She wanted him to know that she was rejecting him. No one treated her like that. She marched back to the desk, pulled off the crucifix, and dropped it on his desk. There. That was a message he would understand.

When she exited the office, she found the guard hovering by the door. Oh, jeez. How was she going to leave the house? There were guards everywhere. She walked down the stairs to the fourth floor, deep in thought. Earlier, when she had met Roman's women, there had been a Highlander at the front door, one she'd never met. Connor would be at the back door. No way could she get past him. She'd have to give the front door a try. She had no ID card, didn't know the code for the keypad. So she'd have to convince the guard to open the door for her.

Back in her room, she paced back and forth, making her plans. It irked her to accept anything from Roman, King of Pigs, but she was in the midst of a struggle to survive, and she would have to be practical. She grabbed the largest shopping bag and filled it with some clothing and essentials.

Radinka hadn't bought anything black. Darn. She needed black stuff for her plan to work. Aha! The pants she had on last night were black. She put her old clothes back on and packed the new ones into the shopping bag. Then she put on her old white Nikes. They were best for walking.

With her purse and one shopping bag, she headed for the stairs. The guard on the fourth floor nodded at her.

She smiled. "You know, I was going to try these clothes on with . . . Darcy." She lifted the shopping bag to show the guard. "But she forgot to tell me which room is hers."

"Och, the pretty lass with the blond hair." The Highlander smiled. "All the harem sleeps on the second floor."

Shanna's smile froze. *Harem?* Is that what they called them? She gritted her teeth. "Thank you."

She stomped down the stairs. That damned Roman. Master and his harem. How sick! On the second floor, she picked a door and went inside. There were two double beds, both slightly rumpled. It looked like Roman's harem girls had to share rooms. What a pity.

She looked in the closet. Catsuits? She couldn't fit into one of those. There! A black fishnet tunic. She slipped it over her pink T-shirt. No doubt Vanda would wear nothing under it.

She spotted a black beret and stuffed her brown hair into it. Was she disguised enough? She scanned the room. No mirrors. That was hard to believe. How could those women survive without a mirror?

In the bathroom, she located some dark red lipstick. Using a compact mirror from her purse, she put it on. She applied red eye shadow. There, she looked as creepy as they did. She picked up her shopping bag and purse and headed down the stairs.

As she reached the ground floor, she noted the parlor doors were shut. Good. The *harem* was closed up inside. Not that they would try to stop her from leaving. Then she spotted Connor coming from the kitchen. He'd stop her for sure.

She ran behind the grand staircase, looking for a place to hide, then noticed a narrow flight of stairs going down. The basement. Maybe there was another way out of the building from there. She reached the bottom of the stairs. There was a furnace, a washer and dryer, and a door. She opened it.

It was a large room with a pool table in the middle. A stained glass lamp hung over the pool table, its dim light illuminating the room. Exercise equipment was scattered about. Banners decorated the walls, made of plaid material with embroidered mottoes. Between the banners, swords and axes were on display. Against another wall was a leather sofa, flanked by two armchairs upholstered in red and green plaid. This had to be where the Highlanders hung out when they weren't on duty.

Shanna heard footsteps coming down the stairs. Shoot. If she left the room, they would see her. The couch was pushed against the wall—no hiding behind it. She spotted another door.

The footsteps approached. More than one person. Shanna ran for the door and slipped inside. Total darkness enveloped her. Was this a closet? She set her bag and purse on the floor by her feet. She reached out her hands but felt nothing around her.

She leaned against the door. She heard voices in the guardroom, then laughter. Finally the voices faded away. She inched open the door. The guardroom was empty, but they had turned the lights on full blast.

She picked up her bags and tiptoed from her hiding place. She glanced back to close the door and gasped. Light from the guardroom had made her hiding place slightly visible.

It couldn't be. She dropped her bags on the floor, leaned into the other room, and fumbled along the wall for a light switch. *Click.*

She gasped again. Her skin prickled with gooseflesh. The narrow room resembled a ghoulish dormitory with two long rows. But the rows weren't made up of beds. Oh no. These were coffins. More than a dozen coffins. All open. All empty, except for the tartan pillows and blankets inside each one.

She turned the light off and pulled the door shut. My

God! It was sick! She grabbed her bags and stumbled from the guardroom. Her stomach churned. This was too much. First Roman's betrayal with those psycho women; and now *coffins*? Did the Highlanders actually sleep in them? A wave of nausea surged up her throat. She swallowed hard. No, no! She would not give in to fear. Or horror. Her paradise had suddenly turned into hell, but it would not defeat her.

She was outta here.

On the ground floor, she spotted the guard at the front door. Okay, show time. She took a deep breath to calm her shaky nerves. *Don't think about the coffins now. Be tough.*

She squared her shoulders and lifted her chin. "*Bonsoir.*" She marched toward the front door with her bags in hand. She poured on a thick French accent. "I must go out and buy ze hair color. Simone wants ze highlights for her hair."

The guard gave her a confused look.

"You know, ze blond highlights. It is all ze h-rage!"

He frowned. "Who are you?"

"I am Simone's personal hair styliste. I am Angelique of Paris. You have heard of me, *n'est-ce pas*?"

He shook his head.

"*Merde!*" Sometimes her knowledge of foreign curses was a positive boon. And three years of French at her boarding school was a great help, too. "If I do not return wiz ze hair color, Simone will be *furieuse*!"

The Scotsman blanched. He must have witnessed Simone throwing a hissy fit before. "I suppose ye can go out for a while. Ye know the way back, lass?"

Shanna huffed. "Do I look like an *idiote*?"

The Highlander ran his ID card through the machine at the door. The green light came on. He opened the door and surveyed the surroundings. "It looks fine to me, lass. When ye come back, push the button on the intercom so I can let ye back in."

"*Merci bien*." Shanna stepped outside and waited for the Scotsman to close the door. Whew! She waited for her heart to stop racing. She'd done it! She looked right and left. The street was quiet. A few people were strolling down the sidewalk. She hurried down the steps and took a right toward Central Park.

Behind her, a car engine started. Her heart leaped in her chest, but she kept walking. *Don't look back. It's nothing.*

The street lit up when the car behind her turned on its headlights. Sweat popped out on her brow. *Don't look back.*

She couldn't take it. She had to know.

She glanced over her shoulder. A black sedan was pulling away from the curb.

Shit! She jerked her head forward. It looked just like one of the cars the Russians had parked in front of the clinic. *Don't panic.* There were a jillion black cars in the city.

Suddenly she was struck in the face by the glare of headlights. A car that was parked facing her had just turned on its lights. She squinted. It was a black SUV with dark-tinted windows.

Behind her, the sedan revved its engine. The SUV swerved into the street. It headed straight for her, then screeched to a halt, spinning sideways to block the entire street. The black sedan was trapped. The driver jumped out, shouting curses.

Curses in Russian.

Shanna ran. She reached the end of the block, hooked a left, and ran some more. Her heart pounded. Her skin grew sticky with sweat. Still she ran. She reached Central Park and slowed to a walk. She glanced around to make sure no one was following her.

Good God, she had narrowly escaped the Russians. Her skin chilled from her cooling sweat. She shuddered. If it hadn't been for that SUV, she'd probably be a corpse by now. The thought of dead bodies brought back the memory of coffins in the basement. Her stomach twinged.

She stopped and took deep breaths. *Relax.* She couldn't afford to get sick now. *Don't think about the coffins.* Unfortunately, her next thought was just as unnerving.

Who the hell was in the SUV?

Thirteen

Roman wandered across the ballroom, accompanied by Radinka. A small army of janitors was at work. Three men crossed the floor, swinging their buffing machines from side to side, as they polished the black and white checkered linoleum to a glossy finish. Others were cleaning the plate glass windows that looked out onto the garden.

Radinka had her clipboard in hand and was checking off each item on her list. "I called to make sure the ice sculptures would be delivered on time tomorrow. Eight-thirty sharp."

"No gargoyles or bats, please," Roman muttered.

"And what would you have? Swans and unicorns?" Radinka eyed him impatiently. "Need I remind you this is a vampire ball?"

"I know." Roman groaned. Ten years ago, he had insisted on eliminating the ghoulish decorations. It was a spring conference, after all, not a Halloween party. But everyone had thrown such a fit, he was now stuck with the same ridiculous Dracula theme every year. The same gruesome ice sculptures, the same black and white balloons floating along the ceiling. The same guests every year, always dressed in black and white.

Each year, he hosted the event at Romatech. They opened up a dozen conference rooms to make one huge ballroom, and vampires from around the world came to party. He'd started the tradition twenty-three years earlier to please the ladies in his coven. They loved it. He had grown to hate it. It was a waste of time—time that was better spent in his laboratory.

Or with Shanna. She was never black and white. She came in colors. Blue eyes, pink lips, and red-hot kisses. He couldn't wait to see her again, but first he needed to get some work done in his lab. He'd teleported to his office more than forty minutes ago, but he'd been so busy with this nonsense, he hadn't even seen his laboratory. "Did my package from China arrive?"

"What package?" Radinka ran a finger down her list. "I don't see anything here from China."

"It has nothing to do with the damned ball. It's for the formula I'm working on in my lab."

"Oh, well. I wouldn't know about that." She pointed at an item on her clipboard. "We're trying a new band tomorrow. The High Voltage Vamps, and they play everything from minuets to modern rock. Won't that be fun?"

"Hilarious. I'm going to my lab." He headed for the door.

"Roman, wait up!" He heard Gregori's voice behind him and turned around. Gregori and Laszlo were entering the far side of the ballroom.

"About time." Roman strode toward them. "Laszlo, I still have your cell phone." He took the phone from his pocket. "And I need you to remove these wires from my mouth."

Laszlo just stared at him. His eyes were wide and unfocused. His fingers were flexing with jerky spasms as if he wanted to grab a button, but wasn't quite able to master the movement.

"Here, buddy." Gregori escorted him to one of the chairs that lined the walls. "Hi, Mom."

"Good evening, dear." Radinka gave her son a peck on the cheek, then sat beside the chemist. "What's wrong, Laszlo?" When he didn't respond, she looked at Roman. "I think he's in shock."

"We both are." Gregori ran a hand through his thick brown hair. "I've got bad news. Really bad."

Great. Roman called out to the workers to take a thirty-minute break. He waited for them to file out, then faced Gregori. "Explain."

"I offered Laszlo a ride to work this evening, and he wanted to stop by his apartment to change clothes. We went there, and it was a total mess. I mean, destroyed! Furniture broken, cushions shredded. And spray paint on the walls."

"They want to kill me," Laszlo whispered.

"Yeah." Gregori grimaced. "They painted a message on the wall. *Death to Laszlo Veszto. Death to Shanna Whelan.*"

Roman's breath caught. *Bloody hell.* "The Russians know we're harboring Shanna."

"How did they find out?" Radinka asked.

"It must have been Laszlo's car," Roman said. "They traced the plates."

"What will I do?" Laszlo whispered. "I'm just a chemist."

"Don't worry. You're under my protection, and you'll be living in my house for as long as you need."

"There, buddy." Gregori patted the chemist on the shoulder. "I told you it would be all right."

It was far from all right. Roman exchanged a worried look with Gregori. Ivan Petrovsky would take Roman's actions as a personal insult. He might even encourage his coven to attack. By protecting Shanna, Roman had exposed his own coven to the possibility of war.

Radinka squeezed Laszlo's hand. "Everything will be fine. Angus MacKay is coming tonight with more Highlanders. We'll have more security than the White House."

Laszlo took a deep, shaky breath. "All right. I'll be okay."

Roman flipped open Laszlo's cell phone. "If the Russians believe she's in my house, they might attack." He punched in his home number. "Connor, I want security tightened around the house. The Russians—"

"Sir!" Connor interrupted. "Ye called just in time. We canna find her. She's missing."

It felt like a kick in the gut. "You mean Shanna?"

"Aye. She's gone. I was just going to call you."

"Dammit!" Roman shouted. "How could you lose her?"

"What's going on?" Gregori stepped toward him.

"She . . . she's gone," Roman croaked. All of a sudden, his throat didn't seem to work right.

"She fooled the guard at the front door," Connor said.

"How? Couldn't he tell she's mortal?"

"She was dressed like one of yer ladies," Connor explained. "And she pretended she was here with Simone. When she insisted on going out, he let her go."

Why would she leave him? They'd shared a kiss only an hour ago. Unless . . . "Are you saying she met the other women?"

"Aye," Connor said. "They told her they were yer harem."

"Oh shit." Roman walked away a few steps, lowering the phone. He should have known those women couldn't keep their mouths shut. And now Shanna was in so much danger.

"If the Russians get her . . ." Gregori left the sentence unfinished.

Roman lifted the phone back to his ear. "Connor, station someone outside Ivan Petrovsky's house. If he captures her, he'll take her there."

"Aye, sir."

"Send a bulletin out to the coven members. Maybe one of them will see her." He had followers in the five boroughs who worked night jobs. It was possible one of them might see her tonight. Not likely, but it was their best chance at finding her.

"I will. I . . . I'm verra sorry, sir," Connor's voice cracked. "I was fond of the lass."

"I know." Roman hung up. God's blood. His lovely Shanna. Where could she be?

Shanna was waiting in front of the Toys "R" Us in Times Square. The area was always brightly lit and jammed with people, so it had seemed the safest place to go. Tourists snapped pictures and gawked at buildings covered with video screens. Streetcorners were busy with vendors selling handbags.

It had occurred to her while she was walking that she was in desperate need of cash—cash that would not be traceable. She couldn't contact family or old friends without endangering them. Besides, her family was overseas. They'd come to Boston last summer for a short visit, then left again for Lithuania. And her old friends were out of state.

So she'd called some new friends. The guys at Carlo's Deli. Carlo had seen the destruction at the dental clinic and was willing to help. She'd asked Tommy to meet her here.

She was pressed against the building to keep from being mowed over by the constant surge of moving people. When she spotted Tommy, she yelled and waved her arms.

"Hey!" The pizza delivery boy grinned as he dodged pedestrians. In his hands, he carried a zippered pizza case.

"Hi, Tommy."

"Sorry it took me so long." Tommy's jeans slid down his lanky form, revealing boxers with baby Scooby Doos.

She gave him a hug. "Thank you so much. And please thank Carlo for me, too."

"No problem." He leaned close to her ear. "The cash is in a Ziploc bag underneath the pizza. I figured we'd better make this delivery look real."

"Oh. Good idea." She took her checkbook from her purse. "How much do I owe you?"

"For the pizza?" Tommy asked in a booming voice as he looked around. Then, he lowered his voice, "Four enchiladas. It was all we could spare." He seemed to be enjoying the situation, like he'd suddenly joined the cast of a spy movie.

"I'm assuming that's four hundred." She wrote a check out to Carlo's Deli, then handed it to Tommy. "If you can wait a week or so before turning that in, I'd appreciate it."

"What's going on, Doc?" He unzipped the bag and removed a small pizza box. "Some big guys with Russian accents came by the deli, asking questions about you."

"Oh no!" She looked around, suddenly worried they might have followed Tommy.

"Hey, it's cool. We didn't say nothing."

"Oh. Thank you, Tommy."

"Why do those guys want to hurt you?"

Shanna sighed. She hated involving innocent people. "Let's just say that I saw something I shouldn't have."

"The FBI could help. Hey, I bet that's who those guys were."

"What guys?"

"The men in black. They came by asking about you, too."

"Well, I guess I'm very popular lately." She needed to call Bob Mendoza soon. Hopefully, this time he'd answer the phone.

"Anything else we can do?" Tommy's eyes sparkled. "This is kinda fun."

"It's not a game. Don't let them know you've been in contact with me." She fumbled in her purse. "Let me get you a tip."

"No. No way. You need your money."

"Oh, Tommy. How can I ever thank you?" She kissed his cheek.

"Whoa. That'll do. You take it easy, Doc." He wandered off with a grin.

Shanna gathered up her belongings and headed in the opposite direction. In a drugstore, she used the pay phone to call Bob.

"Mendoza here." His voice sounded tired.

"Bob, this is . . . Jane. Jane Wilson."

"What a relief. I was so worried. Where have you been?"

There was something wrong. Shanna couldn't quite put her finger on it. He just didn't sound worried or relieved.

"Tell me where you are."

"I'm on the run, Bob. What do you think? I need to get out of New York."

"You're still in New York? Where, exactly?"

Shanna felt a prick at the back of her neck. Rational thought told her to confide in the federal marshal, but her gut was screaming something was wrong. "I'm in a store. Shall I come to your office?"

"No. I will come for you. Tell me where you are."

Shanna swallowed hard. There was something odd about his voice, something distant and mechanical. "I . . . I'd rather go to your office tomorrow morning."

There was another pause. Shanna thought she heard a voice in the distance. Female.

"I will give you directions to a safe house. Be there to-morrow night at eight-thirty."

"Okay." Shanna wrote down the address. It was some-where in New Rochelle. "I'll see you tomorrow. Good-bye."

"Wait! Tell me, where have you been? How did you escape?"

Was he trying to keep her on the phone? Of course, she was being traced. "Bye." She hung up. Her hand was shaking. Good God, she was getting paranoid. Even a federal marshal seemed suspicious to her. In another week, she'd be blubbering to herself about aliens and wearing aluminum foil on her head.

She gazed at the ceiling as if to communicate with God and let out a long, silent groan of frustration. *Why me? All I ever wanted was a normal life!*

She purchased a box of hair dye and a cheap nylon zippered tote bag for her meager belongings. Then she found a reasonably priced hotel on Seventh Avenue and registered under a false name, paying cash. With a great sigh of relief, she locked herself into her room. She'd done it. Escaped the Russians. Escaped Roman the Pig and his house of horrors. She didn't know which upset her more—Roman's taste in women or the coffins in his basement. Yeech! She shuddered.

Forget them—think of the future and how you will survive.

In the bathroom, she applied the hair color, then settled on the bed to wait thirty minutes. She ate pizza while flipping through TV channels. When a local news channel flashed by, she stopped. Good God, it was the SoHo So-Bright Dental Clinic. Shattered glass littered sidewalks that were partitioned off with yellow crime scene tape.

She turned up the volume. The newscaster explained how the clinic had been destroyed the night before. Police were investigating the matter in connection to a nearby homicide.

Shanna gasped when a picture of a young blond woman flashed on the screen. Her body had been discovered in an alley close to the clinic. Official cause of death was unknown at this time, but the reporter had heard rumors of a bizarre injury. Two punctures in the neck like an animal bite. People in the neighborhood were blaming a secret cult of teenage dropouts who liked to pretend they were vampires.

Vampires? Shanna snorted. She'd heard about the underground societies—bored kids with nothing better to do with their time and money than drink blood and have their canine teeth purposely altered to resemble vampire fangs. It was sick. No reputable dentist would ever do such a thing.

Still, against her will, a series of memories zipped through her mind. A wolf's fang in Roman's hand. His seemingly lifeless body lying in her bed. A basement filled with coffins.

A chill crept up her spine. No, there was no such thing as vampires. She'd been through too much trauma. She was getting paranoid. That was all. People only pretended to be vampires.

And there were rational explanations for everything. She'd checked Roman's tooth, and it had been a normal size. Okay, so it was more pointed than usual. That could be explained, too. It was an unusual genetic trait. A person could be born with webbed fingers or toes without being a mermaid.

And the coffins? Oh God. What possible explanation could there be for that?

She went back to the bathroom to rinse her hair. She toweled it dry and examined herself in the mirror. Platinum blond, like Marilyn Monroe. The comparison was not too comforting. Marilyn had died young. Shanna regarded herself with dismay. She looked a lot like the woman she'd recently seen on television.

The blond woman killed by a vampire.

"This is not my area of expertise, sir." Laszlo twisted a button on his new, bright white lab coat.

"Don't worry." Roman scooted onto a stool in his lab at

Romatech. "Besides, how could you hurt me? I'm already dead."

"Well, not technically, sir. Your brain is still active."

His brain was mush, though Roman didn't care to admit it. Since receiving the news about Shanna's disappearance, he could hardly follow his own train of thought. "You did a good job wiring VANNA to work. I'm sure you'll manage with me."

Laszlo picked up a wire cutter, then changed his mind and selected some needle-nosed pliers. "I'm not quite sure how to go about this."

"Just rip the damn wires out of my mouth."

"Yes, sir." Laszlo advanced toward Roman's open mouth with the pliers. "I apologize in advance for any discomfort."

"Unh." Roman acknowledged the remark.

"I appreciate your confidence in me." Laszlo yanked the wires loose. "And I'm glad to have something to do. Otherwise, I start thinking about . . ." He lowered his hand and frowned.

"Aaargh." Roman had wires poking the inside of his mouth. This was not the time for Laszlo to obsess over death threats.

"Oh, sorry." Laszlo resumed his work. "I still don't have my car. We left it at the dental office last night with VANNA in the trunk. So I don't have anything to work on tonight."

Roman remembered his unfortunate conclusion regarding the Vampire Artificial Nutritional Needs Appliance. That toy had propelled him into a powerful state of bloodlust. She would remind every Vamp how glorious it was to bite. He hated to tell Laszlo his project would have to be scrapped, especially when the guy was going through hell. Maybe after the conference.

"There." Laszlo removed the last of the wires. "All done, sir. How does it feel?"

Roman ran his tongue along his teeth. "Good. Thanks."

Now, he wouldn't have to attend the conference with wires in his mouth. And Shanna wouldn't be able to use the splint excuse to avoid kissing him. Not that he had much hope for future kisses.

He glanced at the clock in his lab. Three-thirty A.M. He'd been calling Connor every thirty minutes for an update, but no one had seen Shanna. She'd pulled a great disappearing act.

Roman knew she was tough and smart. And she had his crucifix to protect her. Still, he worried. He couldn't concentrate on work. His package from China had arrived, but even that couldn't distract him from his growing sense of frustration and anxiety.

"Is there something else I can do?" Laszlo was back to plucking at his buttons.

"Would you like to assist me on my current project?" Roman gathered a pile of papers from his desk.

"I'd be honored, sir."

"I'm working on a formula that would enable us to stay awake during the daylight hours." Roman handed the papers to Laszlo.

His eyes widened. "Fascinating." He examined the papers.

Roman returned to his desk and opened the package. "This is a root from a rare plant that grows in Southern China. It's supposed to have remarkable energizing effects." He dug through a mass of Styrofoam peanuts and pulled out a dried root encased in bubble wrap.

"May I see it?" Laszlo reached for the dried plant.

"Sure." A week ago, the project had fascinated him. But now Roman had lost interest. Why bother to stay awake during the day if he couldn't share the time with Shanna? God's blood, she had affected him more strongly than he had realized. And now that she was gone, there was nothing he could do about it.

Two hours later, Roman returned to his townhouse. His guests from Europe were safely tucked away in guest rooms on the third and fourth floors. His so-called harem had been chastised for their rudeness to Shanna. They were skulking in their rooms on the second floor.

He entered his office and headed to the wet bar for a bedtime snack. While the bottle warmed up in the microwave, he wandered toward his desk. Memories of Shanna filled his mind. He could see her resting on the blood-red velvet chaise. He could see them kissing by the door.

He stopped with a jerk. There on his desk was the silver chain and crucifix. "Shanna, no." He reached for the cross, but it instantly seared his flesh.

"Shit!" He dropped it and examined the burned skin on his fingertips. Just what he needed—a painful reminder that God had abandoned him. Damn. He would heal overnight, but what would become of Shanna? Without the silver cross, she had no protection from the Russian vampires.

This was his fault. He should have been more honest. Now, in her anger, she had rejected the one thing she needed most to survive.

Roman squeezed his eyes shut and concentrated hard. He'd been connected to her mentally just the night before. And it had been an amazingly strong, two-way connection. Perhaps some of it remained.

He reached out for her. *Shanna! Shanna, where are you?* God's blood, he felt so alone and helpless.

Shanna moaned in her sleep, haunted by a strange dream. She was at work, and Tommy was in the examination chair, telling her to chill. Then he transformed into Roman. He raised his hand, palm up. A wolf's fang rested in a pool of blood.

Shanna rolled over. *No, no blood.*

In her dream, she picked up her instruments and looked inside Roman's mouth. She glanced at the dental mirror. What? The mirror showed an empty chair, but Roman was in the chair. Suddenly he caught her hand. He wrenched the dental mirror from her grasp and tossed it onto the tray. "Come with me."

Instantly they were back in Roman's office. He took her in his arms and whispered, "Trust me." Shanna felt herself melting.

Then he kissed her, kisses that she never wanted to end, kisses so hot that she kicked the blanket off the bed. He led her to his bedroom and opened the door. His king-sized bed was gone.

In the middle of the room sat a black coffin. *No.* Shanna stared at it in horror.

Roman held out his hand, beckoning her forward. She retreated to his office, but the harem was there, laughing at her. They had a new member—the dead blond from the television newscast. Blood trickled from two punctures on her neck.

With a jolt, Shanna sat up in bed, gasping for air. Oh God, even in her sleep she was a basket case. She dropped her head forward into her hands and rubbed her temples.

Shanna! Shanna, where are you?

"Roman?"

She looked around the dark room, half expecting one of the dark shadows to move toward her. The clock on the bedside table glowed the time. Five-thirty A.M. She turned on the lamp.

No one there. She took a deep breath. Just as well. Roman couldn't help her. He couldn't be trusted. Tears of frustration threatened to overflow.

Dear God, she had never felt so alone and helpless.

Fourteen

Shanna hid in her hotel room most of the next day, waiting until it was time to meet Bob at the safe house. Her thoughts eventually gravitated back to Roman. How could she have been so wrong about him?

He was a brilliant scientist and a gorgeous-looking man. He'd rescued her without a concern for his own safety. He'd been kind and generous. And there had been something else she'd sensed inside him. A great well of remorse and regret. She'd understood his pain. God knew she lived with guilt and remorse every day of her life. Karen had been alive when she'd first found her, but out of fear, she'd done nothing to help her.

Her gut instinct had told her that Roman suffered from the same kind of torment. She'd felt connected to him in a deep-rooted, elemental way, as if their two souls knew how to comfort each other more than anyone else's ever could. He'd given her hope for the future, and God help her, she had sworn she was giving him hope. It had felt so right with him.

So how could he be a womanizing bastard with a harem? Had her loneliness and fear skewed her perceptions so that she no longer read people correctly? Had she somehow projected her own feelings of guilt and despair on him, making him appear totally different from his real self? Who was the real Roman Draganesti?

She'd been so sure about him. She had thought he was the perfect man. She had thought he was a man she could fall in love with. A tear rolled down her cheek. To be honest, she had already started falling for him. That was why it had hurt so much to discover his harem.

In the afternoon, she visited the hotel's computer room and did a search. She found nothing on Roman, but the website for Romatech Industries came up, complete with a picture of the facility near White Plains, New York. It looked lovely, surrounded by manicured gardens. She printed the page and folded it up in her purse. Why? She didn't want to see him again. He was a womanizing pig. Wasn't he? She sighed. Whatever he was, he was driving her crazy. And she had more important matters to worry about. Like staying alive.

By seven-forty-five that evening, she was ready for her trip to the safe house. The clothes Radinka had purchased were not designed for blending into the woodwork. With her hot-pink pants and camisole, and a big cotton shirt of neon orange and pink plaid, she could be spotted a mile away. Oh well. She would just think of it as a disguise. No one would expect her to look like a hot-pink version of Marilyn Monroe.

She packed up her belongings and took the elevator down to the lobby. She waited a few minutes in the taxi line in front of the hotel. The sun had set, but the city was still bright with lights—bright enough that Shanna spotted a black SUV parked across the street. She caught her breath. A coincidence, that was all. There were hundreds of black SUVs in New York City.

The next cab was hers. She climbed in and was instantly assaulted by the smell of hot pastrami. She leaned forward to give the driver the address and noticed his half-eaten sandwich resting on a sheet of crumpled foil in the front seat. The taxi lurched forward, making her fall back.

"New Rochelle?" the driver asked as he careened onto the avenue, headed north toward Central Park.

Shanna glanced back. The SUV was pulling away from the curb. Oh, great. Her taxi made a right turn. She took a deep breath, waited, then looked back. The SUV was turning. *Dammit!*

She leaned toward the cab driver. "You see the black SUV behind us? It's following us."

The driver looked in the rearview mirror. "No, no. Is okay."

She couldn't place his accent, but his complexion indicated African or maybe Caribbean. She glanced at his ID card. "Oringo, I'm serious. Take a turn up here and see for yourself."

He shrugged. "If you like." He made a left turn onto Sixth, then flashed her a grin. "See? No black SUV."

The SUV turned onto Sixth Avenue.

Oringo's smile faded. "You in trouble, miss?"

"I could be if they catch me. Can you lose them?"

"You mean, like in movies?"

"Yes, exactly."

"We in a movie?" Oringo looked around as if he expected to see cameras set up on the sidewalk.

"No, but I can give you an extra fifty if you lose them." Shanna mentally counted her cash. Dang, by the time this ride was over, she'd be almost completely tapped.

"You got a deal." Oringo slammed on the accelerator and zoomed across two lanes to make a right-hand turn.

Shanna fell back against the seat. She fumbled about for a seat belt. This was going to be one hell of a ride.

"Ah, damn! It is still behind us." Oringo swerved into

another right turn. They were now going south, the wrong direction. "What kind of trouble you in?"

"It's a long story."

"Ah." Oringo cut through a parking lot and burst out onto a street without slowing down. "I know where you can get a good Rolex. Or Prada bag. Real cheap. Looks like the real thing."

"I appreciate that, but I really don't have time to shop right now." Shanna flinched when the cab ran a red light and narrowly missed getting hit by a delivery van.

"Too bad." Oringo grinned at her in the rearview mirror. "You look like good customer."

"Thanks." Shanna looked behind them. The black SUV was still there, though it had been stopped momentarily by the red light. She glanced at the dashboard clock. It was fifteen past eight. She would arrive at the safe house late.

If she ever arrived at all.

Roman arrived at Romatech at twenty past eight. The Gala Opening Ball was scheduled to begin sharply at nine. He wandered across the ballroom. A swarm of balloons hovered along the ceiling like a colony of black and albino bats. He groaned inwardly. Why did his guests love this ghoulish atmosphere? He certainly didn't feel like partying when everything here reminded him he was dead.

The tables were covered with black tablecloths, topped crosswise with square white tablecloths. Black vases filled with white funeral lilies stood at the ends of each table. The center of each table was left blank for now. That space was reserved for the ice sculptures.

Behind each of the three tables was a black coffin. No satin on the interior. They were actually giant ice chests. Nestled among the ice cubes were bottles of the new taste sensations he was introducing tonight—Bubbly Blood and Blood Lite.

A small stage had been erected on one side of the room,

in front of the glass windows that overlooked the garden. The band was already there, setting up their equipment.

A pair of double doors suddenly swung open. Workers held the doors while others wheeled in the ice sculptures. A flurry of activity buzzed around the sculptures. Everyone was excited.

Roman had never felt more depressed. His tuxedo was uncomfortable. The cape—ridiculous. And there had been no word about Shanna. She'd disappeared, leaving him ragged with worry and his tired old heart withered with loss. He'd asked Connor to watch Petrovsky's house to-night. The Scotsman had agreed, even though it meant he would miss the Opening Ball. At least, as far as Roman could tell, the Russians hadn't found Shanna, either.

Radinka strode toward him, her face flushed. "Doesn't it look wonderful? This will be the best party I've ever planned."

He shrugged. "I guess." He noted the warning glint in Radinka's eyes. "It looks great. You did a wonderful job."

She snorted. "I know when I'm being patronized. Your tie is crooked." She reached up to adjust his bow tie.

"It's hard to do without a mirror. Besides, it wasn't in the dress code at the monastery."

Radinka paused. "Then it is true? You were a monk?"

"Not a very good one. I've broken most of my vows." All but one.

She made a dismissive sound as she finished with his bow tie. "You are still a good man. I will forever be in your debt."

"No regrets?" Roman asked softly.

Her eyes filled with tears. "No. Never. He would have died if you hadn't . . ."

Turned her son into a demon? Roman doubted she wanted to hear the harsh words.

Radinka stepped back and blinked to clear her eyes. "Don't make me feel all mushy. I have too much work to do."

Roman nodded. "We still haven't found her."

"Shanna? Don't worry. She will come back. She must. She is in your future." Radinka touched her forehead. "I have seen it."

Roman sighed. "I want to believe you. Really I do, but I lost my faith many years ago."

"And you turned to science?"

"Yes. It's dependable. It gives me answers." *And it hasn't abandoned me like God. Or betrayed me like Eliza. Or run away like Shanna.*

Radinka shook her head, regarding him sadly. "For a very old man, you have much to learn." She pursed her lips. "You realize, don't you, that in order to have a future with Shanna, you will have to get rid of your harem."

"Shanna's gone. The point is moot."

Radinka narrowed her eyes. "Why do you keep them? As far as I can tell, you ignore them."

"And you're supposed to ignore my personal life, remember?"

"How can I when you are so miserable?"

Roman took a deep breath. One of the ice sculptures was in place. God's blood, it was the most hideous goblin he'd ever seen. "A coven master must have a harem. It's an ancient tradition. The harem is a symbol of his power and prestige."

Radinka stared blandly at him, unimpressed.

"It's a vampire thing, okay?"

She crossed her arms. "In that case, I hope my son never becomes a coven master."

"They have nowhere else to go. They were raised in times when ladies weren't expected to work. They have no skills."

"They're good at freeloading."

Roman lifted a brow. "They needed a place to live and blood to drink. I needed the appearance of a harem. Overall, the arrangement has worked quite well."

"It's only for show, then? You haven't had sex with them?"

Roman shifted his weight from one foot to another. He reached up to loosen the tie that was strangling him.

"Don't mess it up!" Radinka slapped his hand away. She glared at him. "No wonder Shanna is so angry with you."

"They don't mean anything to me."

"And that is meant as an excuse?" Radinka snorted. "Men. Even as vampires, you're all alike." She glanced to the side. "Speaking of vampire men, they have arrived. And I need to get back to work." She headed toward one of the tables.

"Radinka." She glanced back when he called her. "Thank you. You really have outdone yourself."

She smiled wryly. "Not bad for a mortal?"

"The best." He hoped she knew he wasn't patronizing her. He waited as the men approached. Jean-Luc, Gregori, and Laszlo were in front. Bringing up the rear were Angus and his Highlanders.

Angus MacKay was a huge man, a warrior who had mellowed only slightly over the centuries. He was in formal Highland dress—a black jacket over a white jabot shirt with lace at the neck and sleeves. Because of the black and white ball, the Highlanders were wearing kilts that displayed the Scott black and white or the Douglas gray tartan. Their sporrans were made of black muskrat fur. With a nod, Angus dispersed his Highlanders. They spread out to conduct a security check of the building.

In an attempt to look somewhat civilized, Angus had tied his shoulder-length auburn hair into a queue with a strip of black leather. A black-handled dagger was barely visible in one of his black knee socks. Angus never went anywhere without a weapon. In fact, Roman figured his old friend had probably stashed a claymore in one of the potted plants by the entrance.

Jean-Luc was so much the opposite, it was almost laughable to see them side by side. Jean-Luc Echarpe had sophistication down to a fine art. He was more than the grand coven master of Western Europe. He was a world-renowned fashion designer. At first, Jean-Luc had focused on evening wear, since he and his followers were only active during the night. But when movie stars had started wearing his designs, his business had mushroomed. Now he was on the cutting edge of everyday fashion with his line of Chique Gothique.

Jean-Luc was sporting a black tuxedo with a black cape lined in gray silk. He carried a black walking stick he didn't need. He was the most agile vampire Roman had ever met. Tall and slim, he could run up the side of a building without batting an eye. His curly black hair was worn with a disheveled look, and his twinkling blue eyes dared anyone to disagree with his taste.

Jean-Luc might look like a fop, but Roman knew better. The Frenchman could turn deadly in less than a second.

Roman nodded at his friends. "Shall we go to my office?"

"Aye," Angus replied for the group. "Gregori tells me ye have some new drinks for us tonight."

"Yes. They're the latest from my line of Fusion Cuisine." Roman escorted the men down a hall to his office. "The first one, Bubbly Blood, is a combination of blood and champagne. It'll be advertised as the drink of choice for those special vampire occasions."

"*Formidable, mon ami.*" Jean-Luc smiled. "I have sorely missed the taste of champagne."

"Well, it still tastes more like blood, I'm afraid," Roman continued. "But the fizz is there. And the alcoholic content. You can get a definite buzz after a few glasses."

"I can vouch for that," Gregori added. "I volunteered as guinea pig and drank a bunch. Great stuff. At least I think it was." He grinned. "I don't remember much about that night."

Laszlo fiddled with a button on his rental tux. "We rolled you out to the car in an office chair."

The men chuckled. Laszlo blushed. Roman suspected the chemist was nervous at being in the company of three major coven masters. But then, Laszlo always looked nervous.

"Did ye get the whisky I sent ye?" Angus asked.

"Yes." Roman slapped his old friend on the shoulder. "Your fusion drink of whisky and blood is next on our list."

"Och, good," Angus said.

"I tried the Chocolood." Jean-Luc wrinkled his Gallic nose. "It was too sweet for my taste, but the ladies love it."

"They love it too much." Roman opened his office door. "That's why I invented the second drink we're introducing tonight. Blood Lite."

"A diet drink?" Jean-Luc entered his office.

"Yes." Roman remained at the door until all the men had entered. "I was receiving too many complaints from the women in my coven. They were gaining weight and holding me responsible."

"Umph." Angus took a seat in front of Roman's desk. "I've had a wee bit of grousing from my women, too, but it dinna stop them from wanting the stuff."

"They love it." Gregori perched on the corner of Roman's desk. "Sales have tripled in the last quarter."

"Hopefully, Blood Lite will take care of the weight problem. It's low in cholesterol and also has an extremely low blood sugar count." When Roman saw that Laszlo was hovering by the door, he laid a hand on the chemist's shoulder. "Laszlo is my most gifted chemist. Last night he received a death threat."

Laszlo studied his scuffed black loafers and twisted a button on his rental tux.

Angus shifted in his chair, his expression grim as he looked Laszlo over. "Who would threaten this man?"

"We believe it was Ivan Petrovsky." Roman closed the door, then crossed the room to his desk.

"Och." Angus frowned. "The Russian coven master here

in America. According to my intelligence reports, he works as a paid assassin. But who would pay to kill yer wee chemist?"

"The Malcontents would want to kill anyone who is involved in the making of synthetic blood," Jean-Luc said.

"Aye, that's true," Angus agreed. "Is that the case then?"

Roman sat behind his desk. "We haven't heard from them since last October when they left their little Halloween present at my front door."

"You mean the explosives?" Jean-Luc turned toward the Scotsman. "You're the expert. Who do you think is the leader of these True Ones?"

"We have it narrowed down to three suspects." Angus loosened the lace collar around his throat. "I thought we would discuss it during the conference. Something has to be done about them."

"I agree." Jean-Luc tapped his walking stick on the floor as if to accentuate how strongly he felt. He had reason to feel strongly. The Malcontents had tried to kill him, too.

Roman clasped his hands on his desk. "If you don't have Ivan Petrovsky on your list of suspects, then you should add him."

"He's already at the top of the list," Angus said. "Why has he threatened yer chemist? Ye would make a more likely target."

"I'm sure he'll get around to me as soon as he realizes I'm responsible for this latest situation."

Angus narrowed his eyes. "Explain yerself."

Roman shifted his weight in his chair. "It's a long story."

"They always are." Jean-Luc gave him a knowing smile. "And they always involve a woman, *n'est-ce pas*?"

"In this case, yes." Roman took a deep breath. "Her name is Shanna Whelan. She's Ivan Petrovsky's latest mark. The Russian mafia wants her dead, and Ivan's working for them."

"Ye gave the woman yer protection?" Angus asked.

"But of course." Jean-Luc shrugged. "If she is a member of his coven, it is his duty to protect her."

"Laszlo was instrumental in her escape," Gregori explained. "That's why Petrovsky wants to kill him."

With a groan, Laszlo leaned over to pick up a button off the floor.

"So ye must protect the lady and the chemist." Angus drummed his fingers on the arms of his chair. "'Tis a tricky situation, to be sure, but one you couldna help. Our most sacred responsibility as coven masters is to protect our followers."

Roman swallowed hard. The shit was about to hit the fan. "She's not a member of my coven."

Angus and Jean-Luc stared at him a full five seconds.

"She's mortal."

Jean-Luc blinked. Angus's knuckles turned white as he gripped the arms of his chair. They exchanged wary looks.

Finally Angus cleared his throat. "Ye're interfering with the assassination of a mortal?"

"Yes. I gave her sanctuary. I felt it was justified since she's being hunted by one of our kind."

Jean-Luc placed both hands on the gold knob of his walking stick and leaned forward. "It is not like you to involve yourself with the mortal world. Especially when it could result in danger to your coven."

"I . . . was in need of her services at the time."

Jean-Luc shrugged. "We all have needs from time to time. But we have a saying in French—in the dark, all cats are gray. Why risk so much for this one mortal?"

"It's hard to explain. She . . . she's special."

Angus banged a fist on his chair. "There's nothing more important than keeping our existence a secret from the mortals. I hope ye dinna confide in the girl."

"I kept her as ignorant as possible." Roman sighed. "Unfortunately, my . . . harem couldn't keep their mouths shut."

Angus's frown was forbidding. "How much does she know?"

"My name, my business. Where I live and that I keep a group of women. She has no idea we're vampires." So far. Roman knew she was clever enough to figure out the truth.

Angus snorted. "I hope the lass was worth it. If Petrovsky finds out ye're hiding her—"

"He knows," Gregori announced.

"Merde," Jean-Luc whispered.

Angus grimaced. "Was he invited to the ball?"

"Yes." Roman crossed his arms on the desk and leaned forward. "The invitations went out before this problem arose. Petrovsky is invited every year as a gesture of goodwill, but he hasn't attended in eighteen years."

"Since the introduction of synthetic blood," Jean-Luc added. "I remember his reaction. He was furious. Refused to try the stuff and stormed out of the building, yelling curses and threats to all who betrayed his outdated ideology."

While Jean-Luc talked, Angus unbuttoned his jacket and withdrew a pistol from a shoulder holster. He checked to make sure it was fully loaded. "I'm ready for the bastard. Silver bullets."

Roman winced. "Try not to shoot any of my coven, Angus."

The Scotsman lifted a brow. "I'm betting he'll come. After all, he knows ye have the girl. Is she here at Romatech?"

"I don't have her anymore. She escaped."

"What?" Angus jumped to his feet. "Are ye saying she escaped while my Highlanders were on duty?"

Roman exchanged a look with Gregori. "Well, yes. She did."

Jean-Luc chuckled. "She is special, *n'est-ce pas?*"

With a muttered curse, Angus stashed his gun back

into its holster. He paced across the office. "I canna be-lieve it. A wee mortal lass outsmarting my Highlanders? Who was in charge at the time? I'll flay him alive, the bastard."

"Connor was in charge," Roman answered, "but she was smart enough to avoid him. She picked a guard who didn't know her. She used a disguise and pretended she had come with Simone. Apparently, her French accent is very convincing."

"I like her more all the time," Jean-Luc said.

Angus growled and continued to pace.

Gregori's cell phone rang. "I'll take this outside." He went out the door.

"Speaking of Simone—" Roman frowned at Jean-Luc. "Why did you let her come early? She's been nothing but trouble."

The Frenchman shrugged. "There is your answer, *mon ami*. She *is* trouble. I needed a break."

"She destroyed a nightclub the first night she was here. Last night she threatened to murder a few of my . . . women."

"But of course. *La jalousie*. It drives the women mad." Jean-Luc set his cane across his lap. "Luckily, Simone is not in my harem. It is hard enough being her employer. If I were her master, she would drive me to despair. I have enough problems with my harem as it is."

Angus was still pacing back and forth, glowering at the floor. "I'm thinking of getting rid of mine," he grumbled. Slowly he became aware that the other men were staring at him. He stopped and squared his broad shoulders. "'Tis not that I doona enjoy them. Hell, I enjoy them all the time. The lassies canna keep their hands off of me."

"Ah. *Moi, aussi*." Jean-Luc nodded and looked at Roman.

"Me, too," Roman repeated the words in English. He wondered if the other men were lying, too.

Angus scratched his chin. "'Tis hard to keep that many

wenches happy. They think I'm supposed to keep them entertained every night. They doona understand I have a business to run."

"*Oui, exactement*," Jean-Luc murmured. "I wonder sometimes if I am being selfish, keeping so many beautiful women all to myself. There are many lonesome male vampires in the world."

God's blood. Roman couldn't believe it. The other coven masters were just as tired of keeping a harem as he was. Maybe Radinka was right, and it was time to let the old tradition go. After all, he had convinced most of the vampire world to give up biting for the bottle.

Gregori slipped back inside, pocketing his cell phone. "That was Connor. Petrovsky and a few of his followers are on the move. Headed north into New Rochelle. Connor's following them."

"Any sign of Shanna?" Roman asked.

"No, but they're dressed in formal clothing. Black and white." Gregori gave Laszlo a worried look.

God's blood, Roman thought. They were coming to the ball.

"What should I do?" Laszlo asked, his eyes wide. "I can't stay here."

"Doona fret, lad." Angus marched over to Laszlo and gripped his shoulder. "I willna let them harm you. My men will be on red alert."

Roman watched as Angus pulled out his pistol. Jean-Luc twisted the knob on his walking stick and withdrew a long, sharp dagger. Damn. Was this going to be a ball or a bloodbath?

Suddenly the door opened, and Angus pointed his gun at the man entering.

Ian blinked. "Bugger. Not quite the welcome I was expecting."

Angus laughed and slipped the pistol back into his shoulder holster. "Ian, my old friend. How are you?"

"Verra well." Ian exchanged slaps on the shoulder with his boss. "I've just now returned from Washington."

"Well, ye're back in the nick of time. Ivan Petrovsky is on his way. We may have a bit of trouble."

Ian grimaced. "We have a lot more trouble than that." He glanced at Roman. "It's a good thing I went to Langley. At least we have prior warning now."

"What are ye saying, man?" Angus asked.

"I did some investigation on Dr. Whelan's father," Ian explained.

Roman stood. "Is he CIA?"

"Aye." Ian nodded. "Last stationed in Russia, but three months ago he was brought back to Washington to head up a new program. The files were heavily encrypted, but I was able to figure out most of it."

"Go on," Roman urged.

"He's in charge of an operation called Stake-Out."

Angus shrugged. "That's a common term in law enforcement."

"Not in this sense." Ian frowned. "They have a logo to go with the name. A wooden stake struck through a bat."

"Bugger," Angus whispered.

"Aye. They're compiling a list of targets for termination. Petrovsky and a few of his friends are on there." Ian regarded Roman sadly. "Ye're on the list, too."

Roman caught his breath. "Are you saying everyone on the list is a vampire?"

"Aye." Ian grimaced. "I'm sure ye know what this means."

Roman sat heavily in his chair. God's blood, this was terrible. His voice came out as a whisper, "They know about us."

Fifteen

𝓘van Petrovsky checked the address Katya had given him. "This is it, Vlad. Pull over."

Vladimir located a parking space not far from the safe house in New Rochelle. Both sides of the dimly lit street were lined with tall, narrow, wood-framed houses. Covered porches looked out onto tiny front yards. Most of the houses gleamed with light from their windows, but the safe house was dark.

There was no female vampire Ivan respected more than Katya, and once again, she'd proven herself worth her weight in gold. A longtime member of his Russian coven, Katya was every bit as vicious as he. She'd been the one to locate and seduce the U.S. marshal in charge of Shanna Whelan. With the marshal completely under her control, Katya had easily set this trap.

Ivan instructed Vlad to stay with the car, then zipped toward the safe house with vampire speed. He stopped at the back door and waited for Alek and his harem girl Galina to catch up. They slipped inside the house, their superior vision enabling them to see in the dark. They moved across the kitchen and down a narrow hallway. In the front room, Ivan found Katya and her U.S. marshal on the couch. She was straddling the man's lap, her skirt scrunched up to her hips.

"Enjoying yourself?" Ivan asked.

Katya shrugged. "I was bored. It's something to do."

"Do I get a turn?" Galina sat next to the marshal. His eyes were glazed over. Blood trickled from punctures on his neck.

Ivan waved a hand in front of the lawman's face. No reaction. He was tempted to stick a Post-it on the man's forehead. Room for rent. "So, where is the Whelan girl?"

Katya scooted off the marshal's lap and onto her feet. The hem of her slinky black skirt tumbled down to graze the tips of her black sandals. "Do you like?" She struck a pose, designed to highlight the slit that went up one side of her skirt to the square knot on her hip. With this skirt, it was obvious Katya was missing her panties. Her sleeveless white blouse draped in folds down to her waist, exposing much of her breasts.

"I like. Very much. But where is the Whelan girl?" Ivan glanced at his watch. It was eight-forty. They needed to leave in ten minutes. It would only take a few minutes to kill Shanna Whelan, but he had his heart set on playing with her first.

Katya gave Ivan's lieutenant a sympathetic look. "Poor Alek. Always seeing the boss with his women, but never having a taste for himself." She slipped her hand beneath her skirt and outlined the contour of her naked derriere.

Alek turned away, his fists clenched.

"Enough, Katya." Why was she trying to cause trouble between him and Alek? It was hard to find good help these days—strong male vampires who would follow his orders but leave his harem alone. Over the years, Ivan had executed too many vampires for messing with his women. He couldn't afford to lose any more.

He motioned to the zombie marshal. "I assume you have the Whelan girl in a similar state? Where is she? Upstairs?"

Katya stepped back, a wary look in her eyes. "She has not yet arrived."

"What?" Ivan advanced toward her.

Katya flinched, clearly expecting to be slapped.

Ivan fisted his hand. Tension coiled in his neck, the pressure building till it became unbearable. When he snapped the vertebrae, there was a distinct *pop*. Katya blanched. Maybe she feared he'd do the same with her pretty neck.

She bowed her head. "I am devastated to have disappointed you, my lord." She reverted to the old form of address.

"You told me the Whelan girl would be here by eight-thirty. What happened to her?"

"I don't know. Bob told her to come here, and she agreed."

Ivan gritted his teeth. "And yet she is not here."

"No, my lord."

"Has she tried to contact him?"

"No."

"I had planned to feed on her before the damned ball." Ivan paced across the room. His plan had been brilliant. Not only would he make a quarter-million dollars, but he'd have the pleasure of watching Roman Draganesti suffer. First he'd suck the Whelan girl dry, then he'd go to Draganesti's ball and toss the dead girl's body at his feet. While Draganesti and his feeble friends flew into a panic, Alek and Vladimir would sneak off to execute the grand finale for the evening. It was perfect. It should have been perfect. Where the hell was the girl? He hated it when his meals were late.

"Stupid bitch!" Ivan cricked his neck to the side.

Katya winced. "She might come. She could be running late."

"I can't wait all night for her to show up. We have to go to that stinking ball. It's our only chance to get inside Romatech without those Highlanders stopping us." Ivan paced to a wall and punched a fist through it. "Now I'll have to go to that damned ball hungry. And there won't be anything fit to eat there."

"I'm hungry, too." Galina stuck out her bottom lip. A former prostitute from the Ukraine, the sexy redhead knew how to pout and how to please.

"There's plenty of blood left in Bob," Katya offered. "I only had a snack."

"Mmm. Yummy." Galina straddled him, licking her lips.

Ivan glanced at his watch. "We have five minutes." He watched as Galina sank her fangs into the marshal's neck. "Leave some for me." The man had outlived his usefulness.

Gregori checked his watch. "Almost nine o'clock. We'd better get to the ballroom."

Roman rose from the chair behind his desk. He dreaded this ball. How could he party while Shanna was in danger? Just the thought of drinking Bubbly Blood made his stomach churn. And now this latest news—Shanna's father was the head of a group who wanted to kill him.

God's blood. Was history doomed to repeat itself? This was too much like the debacle he'd experienced in London in 1862. He'd met a pretty young lady named Eliza. When her father uncovered Roman's secret, he demanded Roman leave the country. Roman agreed, but he hoped Eliza would understand his dilemma and elope with him to America. So he confided in her. The next evening, he woke up with his casket open and a wooden stake resting on his chest.

He went to confront the father, but discovered it was Eliza who had left the stake. Her father had stopped her from killing him out of fear that other demonic creatures would wreak vengeance upon his family. Sickened by the whole affair, Roman erased their memories of him. Too bad he could not erase his own. He started a new life in America, but the sad affair haunted him. Never, he swore, would he risk another involvement with a mortal female. And yet Shanna had entered his life and filled the dark recesses of his heart with hope.

How would she react if she learned the truth? Would she, too, try to kill him while he lay sleeping? Or would she simply wait for her father to do the job?

How had the CIA learned the truth about vampires? Some fool must have performed a vampire trick in front of mortals without clearing their memory of it afterward. However it had happened, it constituted a serious problem. He, Angus, and Jean-Luc would spend most of the conference deciding how to handle the matter.

Roman walked toward the ballroom, accompanied by the men who had been in his office. "Ian, how much did you find out about the Stake-Out project? How many agents are on the team?"

"There are five of them, including Shanna's father."

"Only five?" Angus asked. "That's not too bad. Do ye have their names? Maybe we can get to them first."

Roman winced. Kill Shanna's father? Now that would certainly boost his chances for a happy romance.

"It doesn't make sense to me." Jean-Luc tapped his walking stick on the floor as he walked. "No mortal can attack us while we are awake. We can instantly take control of their minds."

Roman paused in mid-stride. Was that it? Shanna had shown remarkable resistance to mind control. And her ability to read his mind while they were linked was uncanny. It was very possible she had psychic ability. Inherited psychic ability. God's blood. A team of vampire slayers, sanctioned by the government, who could resist mind control—it was unnerving.

"They must be planning to kill us during the day," Angus said. "I'll have to train more daytime guards."

"Mr. Draganesti is working on a formula that would enable us to stay awake during the day." Laszlo glanced nervously at Roman. "Maybe I shouldn't have mentioned it."

"Is that true?" Angus gripped Roman by the shoulder. "Can ye do it, man?"

"I believe so," Roman replied. "It hasn't been tested yet."

"I'll be your guinea pig," Gregori offered with a grin.

Roman shook his head. "I can't afford to have anything happen to you. I need men like you running the business so I can work in my lab."

Jean-Luc pushed open the swinging double doors to the ballroom, then with a gasp, he retreated back into the hallway. "*Merde*. It's that horrid woman from DVN. I think she saw us."

"A news reporter?" Roman asked.

"Not exactly." Jean-Luc shuddered. "It's Corky Courrant. She hosts the celebrity magazine called *Live with the Undead*."

Angus huffed impatiently. "Why is she here?"

"You guys *are* celebrities." Gregori gave them an incredulous look. "Didn't you know?"

"Yes." Laszlo ducked his head. "You're all famous."

Roman frowned. His inventions might have changed the vampire world, but he still spent long hours every night working in his lab. In fact, he sorely wished he was in his lab right now.

"Doona let her smile fool you," Angus warned. "According to my investigations, she once ran a torture chamber in the Tower of London for Henry VIII. She was called Catherine Courrant back then. They say she's personally responsible for wrenching the confession of incest from Anne Boleyn's brother."

Jean-Luc shrugged it off in his usual way. "And now she works for the media. But of course."

"The lads and I call her Porky Implant." Ian was met with questioning looks. "Ye know, Corky Courrant—Porky Implant. 'Tis a jest."

"I like it." Gregori raised his hands like he was holding two casaba melons. "She has huge tits. They got to be fake."

"Aye," Ian joined in. "They're enormous."

"Okay." Roman gritted his teeth. "Thank you all for sharing. But the fact remains that regardless of the woman's questionable background or her even more questionable . . . foreground, we cannot remain hiding in this hallway all evening."

"Aye." Angus squared his shoulders. "We must face the dragon."

Ian took a deep breath. "We must *be* the dragon."

The double doors burst open.

The men shrank back without emitting a single puff of smoke.

"There you are!" the dragon lady announced, her dark eyes gleaming with victory. "You cannot escape me now."

Corky Courrant motioned for her crew to take their positions. Two men held the doors open. A large crewman wielded the digital camera, while a female crew member performed last-minute touches to Corky's makeup. Each of the crew wore black jeans and T-shirts emblazoned with white letters that read DVN. Guests, dressed formally in black and white, gathered in a crowd behind the reporter, effectively blocking off that means of escape.

We're trapped. The only avenue of retreat that Roman could see was back to his office, and no doubt the voracious reporter would simply follow him there.

"Don't even think about running away." She narrowed her dark eyes on the men. "You *will* talk."

That had probably been her favorite line as mistress of a torture chamber. Roman exchanged a look with Angus.

"Enough!" The reporter waved the makeup person away. She touched a miniature earphone in her right ear and tilted her head to listen to someone's voice. "We're on in thirty seconds. Places everyone." She posed in front of the cameraman, her black dress revealing much of her oversized bosom.

Implants, indeed. She must have gone to Dr. Uberlingen in Zurich. He was the only vampire plastic surgeon in existence, and for a large fee, he could help a vampire spend eternity looking young and beautiful. The reporter's implants had probably helped her nab one of the coveted jobs at DVN. The Digital Vampire Network was still fairly new and flooded each week with hundreds of hopeful vampires, each dreaming of being the next big star.

Catching vampires on film had been impossible until the advent of digital cameras. Now digital technology had opened up a whole new world of possibilities and problems. In fact, Roman wouldn't be surprised if this was how the CIA had learned of their existence. They could have discovered the secret frequency DVN used for broadcasting.

Gregori's phone rang. He flipped it open and stepped away. "Hey, Connor," he spoke softly. "What's up?"

Roman focused on the one-way conversation.

"A house in New Rochelle?" Gregori asked. "What happened?"

The cameraman cued the reporter, and she instantly brightened with a high-wattage smile. "This is Corky Courrant, reporting for *Live with the Undead*. We have a special treat for you tonight. We're live at the biggest vampire bash of the year! I'm sure you'll want to meet our celebrities for the evening."

She motioned to Angus MacKay and gave some facts about him, then did the same for Jean-Luc Echarpe. Roman turned away to catch snatches of Gregori's phone conversation.

"Are you sure?" Gregori whispered. *"Dead?"*

Roman gulped. Were they talking about Shanna? His mind visualized an image of her lifeless body. No! Not his Shanna.

"Roman Draganesti!" The reporter moved in front of him. "I have thousands of viewers who would love to meet you."

"This is not a good time, Miss Implant." Roman felt Jean-Luc jabbing him in the back with his walking stick. "Uh, Porky. No, I mean—" Damn, what the hell was her name?

The reporter's eyes flashed like dragon fire. Her smile tightened into a snarl.

"Mademoiselle Courrant," Jean-Luc cut in. "May I have the pleasure of the first dance?"

"Why, yes, of course." Corky aimed a vicious grin at the camera as she curled her claws around Jean-Luc's arm. "This is every woman's dream—dancing with the grand coven master of Western Europe. Why, he's practically royalty!" She strolled into the ballroom with Jean-Luc.

Roman strode toward Gregori. "What happened? Tell me." Angus joined him, followed by Ian and Laszlo.

Gregori pocketed the cell phone. "Connor followed Ivan Petrovsky to a house in New Rochelle. Ivan and his friends went inside. Connor thought they might be holding Shanna there, so he went around back, levitated to a second floor window and teleported inside."

Roman's nerves tensed. "Was she there?"

"No," Gregori replied. "All the rooms upstairs were empty."

Roman breathed a sigh of relief.

"But they did have a mortal captive on the first floor," Gregori continued. "Connor listened in on them. Ivan was furious that Shanna hadn't shown up. Then they killed the mortal. Connor was sore upset 'cause he could only listen. He knew he couldn't defeat four vampires by himself."

"Bugger," Angus muttered.

"Connor heard them receive a call, and then they all rushed out the front door. He went downstairs and found their victim. A U.S. marshal."

"God's blood." Roman grimaced. "He was probably Shanna's contact."

"Bloody hell," Angus muttered. "No wonder the CIA wants us dead. 'Tis vampires like Petrovsky that give us a bad name."

"I don't want to hurt anyone." Laszlo fiddled with a button on his tux jacket. "Can't we convince the CIA that some of us are peaceful?"

"We'll have to try." Angus folded his arms across his broad chest. "And if they doona believe we're peaceful, then we'll have to kill the bastards."

"Aye." Ian nodded.

Roman frowned. Somehow, their Highlander logic escaped him. "So where is Connor now?"

"He's on his way here," Gregori replied. "So is Petrovsky. Connor heard him talking about something he's planning to do here."

"Och, we must be prepared." Angus strode into the ballroom.

Roman waited by the door. The band was playing a waltz. Vampire couples swirled around the floor. Jean-Luc and the reporter danced by, the French coven master shooting Roman a pained look. Angus was giving his instructions to a regiment of Highlanders in a corner of the ballroom.

Ivan Petrovsky was on his way to cause trouble. At least they knew about it ahead of time. It was the unknown that made Roman sick with worry. Where the hell was Shanna?

* * *

The clock on the taxi's dashboard read eight-fifty. Shanna was running late, but at least she was no longer being followed. Thanks to the driving skills of her taxi driver, Oringo, they had shaken the black SUV off their trail.

"This is the street." Shanna glanced at the piece of paper where she'd written the address. "Fifty-two sixty-seven. Do you see it?"

The street was dimly lit, making it hard to read the numbers on the houses. They passed a house that was completely dark.

Oringo slowed down. "I think that was it."

"The dark one?" Why would Bob wait in the dark? An icy finger of doubt tickled the back of Shanna's neck. Bob had sounded strange on the phone, too.

Oringo pulled over to park. "Here you are. I make fifty dollars extra, right?"

"Yes." Shanna removed her billfold from her purse. She glanced again at the dark house. "Does that look safe to you?"

"Looks empty to me." Oringo took a bite of his pastrami sandwich, then twisted in the seat to look at her. "You want to go somewhere else?"

She swallowed hard. "I don't know where else to go." She scanned the area. There were several parked cars along the street. Was that a black sedan? The tickle on the back of her neck drifted down her spine. "Can you drive by that black car?"

"Okay." Oringo coasted up the street, slowly passing the sedan.

Shanna peeked over the backseat. Seated behind the wheel of the sedan was a man. "Oh my God!" He was the same man who had cursed in Russian in front of Roman's house.

He stared back at her, his eyes narrowed.

Shanna turned her back to him. "Drive! Hurry!"

Oringo stomped on the accelerator. The tires squealed. Shanna glanced back. The Russian was yelling into a cell phone. Oringo reached the end of the street and swerved into a left turn, cutting off her view.

Oh shit. The Russians had found out about the safe house. Where on earth could she go? "Aaargh." She sank down in the seat and covered her face.

"You okay, miss?"

"I—I need to think." A friend, she needed a friend. Someone who could hide her, loan her some cash. *Think!* She tapped the heel of her palm against her brow. She couldn't go far. She was almost out of cash now. A friend, somewhere close.

"Radinka!" Shanna sat up.

"What?" Oringo gave her a worried look in the rearview mirror.

"Can you take me to Romatech Industries?" She fumbled through her purse and pulled out the paper she'd printed earlier. "Here's the address. Just outside White Plains." She leaned forward to show it to Oringo.

"Okay. No problem, miss."

Shanna settled back in her seat. Radinka would help her. She was kind and understanding. And she had said she worked evenings at Romatech. There would also be security at the facility. And lots of people working there. Including Roman Draganesti.

Shanna shuddered. No way would she ask that womanizing creep for help. She'd explain to Radinka that she had no desire to ever see Roman again. She only needed a safe place to hide until she could contact the U.S. marshal's office in the morning.

Poor Bob. She hoped he was okay. Memory of the Russian in the black sedan made her skin crinkle with goose bumps. She peered out the back window. "Are they following us?"

"I don't think so," Oringo said. "We had good head start."

"God, I hope so."

"This reminds me of hunting in the savannah. I love hunting. That is my name, you know? Oringo means 'loves to hunt.'"

Shanna wrapped her arms around herself. "How do you feel about being the prey?"

With a laugh, he veered into a sudden right turn. "Do not worry. If black car comes, I lose them."

Soon they were outside Romatech. A long driveway curved from the front gate to the front entrance of the facility. Then it circled back through the manicured grounds to the front gate. The driveway was completely jammed with black limousines.

"I get in line?" Oringo asked.

Shanna looked in dismay at the line of cars. What the hell was going on? Getting stuck in traffic with no avenue of escape didn't seem like a smart idea. "No, drop me off here."

Oringo pulled to the side of the road. "Must be something big going on inside."

"I guess so." Well, the more, the merrier. A ton of people might be her best security right now. The Russians wouldn't want a bunch of witnesses. "Here." She passed Oringo a wad of money.

"Thank you, miss."

"I wish I could tip you more. I'm so very grateful for your help, but I'm running out of money."

Oringo smiled, his white teeth flashing in the dark. "No problem. I not have this much fun since coming to America."

"Take care." Shanna gathered up her purse and tote bag, then sprinted toward the front gate of Romatech.

"Halt!" A guard strode from the gatehouse. A Highlander.

Shanna froze while the memory of open coffins zipped through her mind. *Don't think about it. Just get to Radinka.*

The Scotsman's kilt was a dark gray and white plaid. He eyed her suspiciously. "Ye're not dressed in black and white."

Duh. Was there a law against hot pink? "I'm here to see Radinka Holstein. Can you tell her Shanna Whelan is here?"

The Scotsman's eyes widened. "Holy Christ! Ye're the one they're looking for. Doona move, lass. Stay right here."

He stepped into the gatehouse and grabbed a phone. Shanna pivoted, looking at the limousines. Since when did research facilities hold fancy parties?

She caught her breath. Out on the street, a black sedan pulled up in line. *Shit*.

She turned and ran for the entrance. She could only hope there was a whole regiment of armed Highlanders inside. Forget the damned coffins. As long as they were on her side, she'd manage to put the coffins out of her mind. Well, not completely.

She made it to the front door, where a limousine was unloading men and women dressed in black and white evening wear. They looked down their noses at her. A few of them sniffed as if she had a strange odor.

What a bunch of snobs, Shanna thought as she slipped inside. The wide foyer was filled with elegant men and women, gathered into groups and chatting. She weaved around them, aware of the haughty stares they angled her way. Sheesh, it was like showing up at the high school prom dressed in her grubbies and without a date.

She spotted a pair of double doors on the right, each door held open by a large potted plant. Music and the hum of voices drifted from the room. She made her way toward the doors.

Suddenly she saw a group of Highlanders marching down the hall. She slipped behind a door and potted plant. They spread out, searching the front entrance.

"Are you looking for the mortal?" a gray-haired man in a tuxedo asked.

Mortal?

"Aye," one of the Highlanders answered. "Did she come in?"

"Yes," the gray-haired man answered. "God-awful clothes."

"Definitely mortal," his female companion added with a sniff. "You can always smell 'em."

Oh, please. While the rich snobs kept the Highlanders occupied, Shanna sneaked through the doors and found herself in a ballroom. Couples dressed in black and white appeared to be doing a minuet straight out of the eighteenth century. Other guests wandered about, chatting and sipping from wineglasses.

She threaded her way through the crowd. People turned to stare. Great. With her hot-pink clothes, she was advertising her uninvited status for all to see. She needed to find Radinka fast. She passed a table with a giant ice sculpture of a bat. A bat? This wasn't October. Who did bats in springtime?

She froze in shock when she spotted the open coffin behind the table. It was being used as a giant ice chest. How sick could you get! She pushed her way through the crowd. Where the hell was Radinka? And was that Roman going up on the stage? He'd see her for sure. She hid behind a broad-chested man wearing a black T-shirt. DVN. He was holding a digital camera.

"You're on." The man cued a woman with huge breasts.

"This is Corky Courrant reporting for *Live with the Undead.* What an exciting evening! As you can see behind me"—the reporter motioned to the stage—"Roman Draganesti is about to welcome us all to the twenty-third annual Gala Opening Ball. As you know, Roman is CEO of Romatech, inventor of Fusion Cuisine, and master of the largest coven in North America."

Coven? Who met in covens? Witches? Shanna looked around. Were these people all witches? It would explain the black clothing and the gory details like coffin coolers.

"Would you like a drink?" A waiter stopped in front of her, holding a black tray filled with glasses.

Was he a witch, too? And Radinka? And Roman? "I . . . uh, do you have something light?"

"Yes! Mr. Draganesti's latest invention." The waiter passed her a wineglass. "Enjoy." He wandered off.

Shanna looked down at her glass. The liquid inside was red. Her attention was distracted by the sound of Roman's voice. God, he sounded sexy. The bastard.

"I'd like to welcome you all to Romatech Industries." His eyes scanned the crowd.

Shanna tried to make herself as small as possible behind the man from DVN, but damn, dressed in hot pink, she might as well be shooting off fireworks.

"And welcome you to the annual Gala—" Roman stopped.

Shanna peeked around the DVN man. Good God, Roman was looking right at her. He motioned with a hand, and Ian ran up onto the stage. The young Highlander turned and spotted her. He hurried down the steps and strode toward her.

"—Opening Ball," Roman finished. "Enjoy." He followed Ian down the stairs.

"Oh, wonderful!" the reporter exclaimed. "Roman Draganesti is coming this way. Let's catch a word with him. Oh, Roman!"

Oh shit. What was she supposed to do now? Trust a Highlander who slept in a coffin? Trust a womanizing Roman who must be some kind of grand warlock?

The DVN man stepped back, bumping into her. "Oh, sorry."

"No problem," she murmured. Suddenly, she remembered the flying bat on the television and the slogan, *DVN. On 24/7 because it's always nighttime somewhere.* Always nighttime? Was this some kind of witch network? "What does DVN stand for?"

The man snorted. "Where have you been the last five years?" His eyes narrowed. "Wait a minute. You're a mortal. What are you doing here?"

Shanna gulped. If she was the only *mortal* around, then what were these people? She retreated a step. "What does DVN stand for?"

The man smiled slowly. "Digital Vampire Network."

She gasped. No, it must be some kind of sick joke. Vampires weren't real.

Ian reached out for her. "Come with me, Miss Whelan. It's not safe for ye here."

She flinched. "Stay away from me. I—I know where you sleep." Coffins, vampires slept in coffins.

He frowned. "Now, give me that glass. I'll take ye to the kitchen for some real food."

Real food? Then, what was this? Shanna lifted her wineglass and sniffed. *Blood!* With a yelp, she threw the glass to the side. It shattered on the floor, splattering blood everywhere.

A woman screeched. "Look what you did! Bloodstains on my new white gown. Why, you—" She glared at Shanna and hissed.

Shanna stepped back. She looked around. Everywhere, people were drinking from the wineglasses. Drinking blood. She hugged her bags against her chest. *Vampires.*

"Shanna, please." Roman approached her slowly. "Come with me. I can protect you."

She pressed a trembling hand against her mouth. "You . . . you're one, too." He even had a black cape like Dracula.

The DVN man shouted, "Corky, you've got to get this!"

The reporter shoved her way through the crowd. "We've had an exciting new development. A mortal has crashed the vampire ball!" She shoved a microphone into Shanna's face. "Tell me. How does it feel to find yourself surrounded by hungry vampires?"

"Go to hell!" Shanna turned, but there at the door stood the Russians.

"You're coming with me." Roman seized her in an iron grip and swirled his cape around them both.

Everything went black.

Sixteen

For a moment of sheer terror, Shanna couldn't feel her feet upon the ground. She was floating, confused, dizzy, but always aware that she was in the clutches of Roman Draganesti. Darkness enveloped her, disorienting and scary. A sudden bump and she was standing. No, stumbling.

"Steady." He kept a grip on her arm. When he lowered the cape, a cool breeze feathered her cheeks and surrounded her with the earthy scent of pine mulch and flowers.

Outside. She was in the garden that surrounded Romatech. Dim landscape lighting illuminated the shapes of bushes and trees and cast eerie shadows across the lawn. How did she get here? And she was alone with Roman Draganesti. Roman, the . . . the . . . Oh God, she didn't want to think it. It couldn't be true.

She jerked away from him, her Nikes skidding in the gravel of the garden path. Not far away, she could see the brightly lit ballroom through plate glass windows. "How? How did we . . . ?"

"Teleportation," he replied softly. "It was the quickest way to get you out."

It must be a vampire trick, which meant only a real vampire could do it. Someone like . . . Roman. Shanna shivered. It couldn't be true. She'd never bought into the modern notion of a romantic vampire. A demonic creature, by its very nature, had to be revolting. Surely, vampires were hideous creatures with green, rotting flesh, and fingernails a mile long. Not to mention a case of bad breath that could flatten a herd of buffalo. They couldn't look gorgeous and sexy like Roman. They couldn't kiss like him.

Oh my God, she'd kissed him! She'd stuck her tongue inside a creature from hell. Oh jeez, this would sound great in confession. Say two Hail Marys and avoid further contact with the spawn of the devil.

She stepped onto the grass into the dark shadow of a shade tree. She could see only a silhouette of him in the dark. His black cape stirred in the cool breeze.

Without another thought, she took off in a mad dash, heading for the lights of the front gate. She ran as hard as she could, not allowing the encumbrance of a tote bag and purse to slow her down. Her adrenaline was skyrocketing, her hopes of escape rising, rising. A few more yards and—

There was a whir of movement that shot past her, a blur in the dark that suddenly stopped in front of her. *Roman*. Shanna skidded to a stop to avoid crashing into him. She gasped for air. He didn't even look winded.

She bent over to catch her breath.

"You cannot possibly outrun me."

"I noticed." She eyed him warily. "My mistake. I just realized I shouldn't do anything that'll give you an appetite."

"You needn't worry about that. I don't—"

"Bite? Isn't that exactly what you do?" An image of a wolf's fang flitted through her mind. "Oh, jeez. That tooth I implanted in you—it really was a fang?"

"Yes. Thank you for helping me."

She snorted. "I'll send you a bill." She dropped her head back to gaze at the stars. "This can't be happening to me."

"We cannot stay here." He gestured toward the ballroom. "The Russians might see us. Come." He moved toward her.

She jumped back. "I'm not going anywhere with you."

"You don't have any choice."

"That's what you think." She shifted her tote bag to her shoulder and opened her purse.

His sigh sounded irritated, impatient. "You can't shoot me."

"Of course I can. I won't even get charged with murder. You're already dead." She pulled out the Beretta.

In a flash, he ripped it out of her hand and tossed it into a flowerbed.

"How dare you! I need that for protection."

"It won't protect you. Only I can do that."

"Well, aren't you high and mighty? Problem is, I don't want anything from you. Especially tooth marks." She heard his frustrated groan. So she was trying his patience. Too bad. *He* was trying her sanity.

He jabbed a finger toward the ballroom. "Didn't you see the Russians in there? Their leader is Ivan Petrovsky, and the mafia has hired him to kill you. He's a professional assassin, and a damned good one."

Shanna stepped back, shivering as a cool breeze ruffled her hair. "He came to your party. You know him."

"It's customary to invite all coven masters." Roman advanced toward her. "The Russians have paid a vampire to kill you. Your only hope of survival is with the help of another vampire. Me."

She inhaled sharply. He'd admitted the awful truth about himself. She could no longer deny it, even though she desperately wanted to. The truth was just too scary.

"We must go." He grabbed her quickly. Before Shanna

could object, her vision went black. The swirling disorientation was terrifying. She could no longer feel her body.

When she became aware of her body parts again, she was standing in a dark room. She stumbled, regaining her balance.

"Careful." Roman steadied her. "Teleportation takes a while to get used to."

She shoved his arm away. "Don't ever do that to me again! I don't like it."

"Fine. Then we'll walk." He grasped her elbow.

"Stop it." She pulled her arm away. "I'm not going anywhere with you."

"Didn't you hear what I said? I'm your only hope for escaping Petrovsky."

"I'm not helpless! I've done pretty good on my own. And I can get help from the government."

"Like the federal marshal in New Rochelle? He's dead, Shanna."

She gasped. Bob was dead? "Wait a minute. How do you know?"

"I had Connor watching Petrovsky's house in Brooklyn. He followed the Russians to New Rochelle and found your contact there. The marshal didn't stand a chance against a group of vampires. Neither will you."

She swallowed hard. Poor Bob. Dead. What should she do?

"I've been looking everywhere for you." He touched her arm. "Let me help you."

She shivered at the feel of his fingers gliding down her arm. Not that it repulsed her. It had the opposite effect. It reminded her of how determined he'd been to rescue her, how kind and caring he'd been, how sweet and generous. His desire to help her was genuine. She knew that deep down in her soul, even though she reeled in shock from this latest revelation. How could she accept his help now that she knew the truth? How could she not? Wasn't there a saying about fighting fire with fire? Maybe the same held true for vampires.

Jeez, what was she thinking? Trust a vampire? She was a bloody food source for them. The blue plate special.

"Is that your real hair color?" he asked softly.

"Huh?" Shanna noticed he had moved closer and was looking at her too intently. Like he was hungry.

"I always knew the brown color was false." He touched a lock of hair on her shoulder. "Is this your real color?"

"No." She retreated a step and shoved her hair behind her shoulders. Oh great. She'd just exposed her neck.

"What is your real hair color?"

"Why are we discussing hair color?" Her voice shook and rose in volume. "Do freaking blonds taste better?"

"I thought a safe, mundane subject would calm your nerves."

"Well, it didn't work. I still can't get over the fact that you're a blood-sucking demon from hell!"

He stiffened with a jolt. Oh great. She'd hurt his feelings. But shoot, she had every right to be upset. So why did she feel bad about lashing out at him?

She cleared her throat. "I may have been too harsh."

"Your description is essentially correct. However, since I have never been to hell, it's not appropriate to say I have come from there." His shadow moved slowly across the room. "Though it could be argued that I'm there now."

Ouch. She'd really hurt him. "I—I'm sorry."

There was a long pause. Finally he responded. "I don't need an apology. You're not to blame for this. And I certainly don't need your pity."

Ouch again. She wasn't handling this very well. But then she didn't have much experience talking to demons. "Uh . . . can we turn on a light?"

"No, it would be visible through the window, and Petrovsky would know that we're here."

"Where are we, exactly?"

"My lab. It overlooks the garden."

A curious smell pervaded the room—antiseptic cleanser and something rich and metallic. *Blood.* Shanna's stomach twinged. Of course, he worked with blood. He was the inventor of synthetic blood. And a drinker of it, too. She shuddered.

But if Roman's artificial blood was feeding vampires, then those same vampires were no longer feeding off live people. Roman was saving lives in two different ways. He was still a hero.

And still a blood-drinking demon. How could she deal with this? Part of her was repelled, but another part wanted to reach out to him and tell him he wasn't at all bad for a . . . vampire.

With an inward groan, she realized he didn't need her comfort. He had ten vampire women at home to keep him company on his lonely nights. Eleven women, including Simone.

He opened the door onto a dimly lit hallway. For the first time since leaving the ballroom, she could see his expression. He looked pale. Tense. Angry.

"If you will follow me, please." He stepped into the hall.

Shanna advanced toward him slowly. "Where are you taking me?" She peered out the door. The hallway was empty.

He didn't answer. Didn't look at her. Instead he scanned the hallway as if expecting the bad guys to appear any second. With the power of teleportation, they probably could pop up without warning. Roman was right. Her only hope of surviving the murderous intent of one vampire was to rely on another one. Him.

"Okay. Let's go." She followed him down the hall.

He stalked toward an elevator, his cape fluttering behind him. "There's an underground chamber here at Romatech, completely lined with silver. No vampire can teleport through its walls. You'll be safe there."

"Oh." Shanna stood in front of the elevator, staring at the down button. "I guess silver is like your kryptonite?"

"Yes." The elevator doors opened. Roman held them open and motioned sharply for her to enter. She hesitated.

His jaw clenched. "You have to trust me."

"I know. I'm trying. Is that why you gave me that silver crucifix? To protect me from the Russian vampires?"

"Yes." A pained expression flickered across his pale face. "And from myself."

Her mouth fell open. He had been tempted to bite her?

His eyes narrowed. "Are you coming?"

She swallowed hard. What choice did she have? She stepped inside the elevator.

He let go of the doors, and they swooshed shut. She stood apart from him, staring at the buttons. *He's still the same man you knew before. He's still the same man.*

"You no longer trust me, do you?"

She took a shaky breath. "I'm trying."

He glowered at her. "I could never hurt you."

A spurt of anger burst to the surface. "You have hurt me, Roman. You had the gall to . . . to flirt with me and kiss me when you have ten live-in mistresses. And then, if that's not enough, I find out you're a . . . a . . ."

"Vampire."

"A demonic creature who has actually considered biting me."

He turned toward her. His eyes darkened to a burnished gold. "I knew this would happen. You want to kill me now, don't you?"

Shanna blinked. *Kill?*

"A stake or a silver blade through the heart is the best way to be rid of me." He stepped toward her and pointed to a spot on his chest. "This is my heart, or rather what's left of it."

She stared at his broad chest. Good God, she'd rested her head there. She'd even kissed him, and he'd tasted sweet and so alive. How could he be dead?

He took her hand and pressed it against his chest. "This is the spot right here. Can you remember it? You should wait till I'm asleep. I'll be totally defenseless then."

"Stop it." She jerked her hand away.

"Why?" He leaned close. "Don't you want to kill the blood-sucking demon from hell?"

"Stop it! I could never hurt you."

"Oh, but you have, Shanna."

Her breath hitched. She turned away as hot tears gathered in her eyes. The elevator doors opened. He stalked down a shadowy hallway.

She hesitated. How was she supposed to handle this? Wasn't it enough that her life was in danger? But her heart was aching for a totally different reason. She was trying to understand, trying to accept the truth about Roman. She actually cared about him, but she was just making things worse. She was hurting him when he was trying to help her. But dammit, it was hurting her, too. She had thought he was the perfect man. How could she have any sort of relationship with him now?

And he didn't need her. He had ten females of his own kind at home. They'd probably known him for a hundred years. She'd known him only a few days. How could she compete with that? She trudged into the hallway.

He was standing in front of a massive door, punching in a number on a keypad.

"This is the room lined with silver?"

"Yes." He pressed his forehead against a device. A red beam scanned his eyes. He opened the heavy metal door and motioned for her to enter. "You'll be safe in here."

She stepped inside. It was a miniature apartment complete with a bed and kitchen. Through an open doorway, she spotted a bathroom. She dropped her bags on the kitchen table. Then she noticed that Roman had entered the room and was removing his cape. He draped it over his hands.

"What are you doing?"

"This side of the door is lined with silver. It would burn my skin." Using the cape as insulation, he pushed the door shut. Then he turned the locks and slid a heavy bar into place.

"You're going to stay here with me?"

He looked at her. "Are you afraid I'm going to bite you?"

"Well, maybe. You're bound to get hungry sooner or later."

"I do not feed off mortals," he said through gritted teeth. He marched to the kitchen, grabbed a bottle from the fridge, and stuck it in the microwave.

So he was hungry, Shanna realized with a grimace. Or maybe he ate when he was upset. Like her. Somehow, a lecture on emotional eating didn't seem wise at the moment. She would really rather he be full.

Memories of the kitchen at Roman's house came flooding back. Connor trying to keep her out of the refrigerator. Connor and Ian warming up their "protein drinks" in the microwave. The harem girls drinking red stuff from their wineglasses. Good God, it had been in front of her the whole time. The wolf's fang. The coffins in the basement. Roman sleeping like the dead in her bedroom. He really *had* been dead. Was still dead, even though he walked and talked. And kissed like a . . . a devil.

"I can't believe this is happening to me." She perched on the edge of the bed. But it was happening. It was all true.

The microwave dinged. Roman removed the bottle and filled a glass with warm blood. Shanna shuddered.

He took a sip, then turned to face her. "I'm a coven master. That means I'm personally responsible for the safety of the members of my coven. By protecting you, I have antagonized an old enemy—Ivan Petrovsky, the Russian vampire who wants to kill you. He could declare war on my coven."

He wandered toward an easy chair and set his drink down on the small table beside it. He ran a fingertip along the edge of the glass. "I regret not telling you everything, but at the time, I thought it best to keep you as ignorant as possible."

Shanna didn't know what to say, so she sat there, watching him as he sank into the chair. He yanked at his bow tie till he unraveled the strip of black silk. He seemed so normal and lifelike, talking about people he felt responsible for. Tilting to the side, he rested his forehead on his hand and rubbed his brow. He looked tired. After all, he was responsible for a huge business and apparently a large group of followers.

And now they were in danger because of her. "Protecting me has caused you a lot of trouble."

"No." He shifted in his chair and looked at her. "The animosity between Petrovksy and myself goes back hundreds of years. And protecting you has brought me the most joy I have felt in a very long time."

She swallowed hard as more tears welled in her eyes. God help her, she'd enjoyed their time together, too. She loved making him laugh. She loved being in his arms. She'd loved everything about him until she'd discovered his live-in girlfriends.

With a small gasp, she realized that her chief source of anger and frustration always centered on his harem. She could understand why he hadn't told her he was a vampire. Who would want to admit to being a demon? And besides, he had to protect more than himself. He had a whole coven of followers to protect. His reluctance to confide in her was understandable. And forgivable.

And the fact that he was a demon—well, that seemed open to interpretation. After all, he was saving millions of human lives every day with his synthetic blood. And he was protecting lives by providing other vampires with a different food source. In her heart, she knew there was no evil in Roman. She would have never been so attracted to him, otherwise.

No, the problem was the harem. Good God, she was willing to forgive him for everything but that. Why should the harem stick in her craw? She closed her eyes as the tears threatened to overflow. It was simple jealousy. She wanted him to herself.

But he was a vampire. She could never have him.

She glanced his way. He was still watching her, but now he was doing it while he sipped blood. Oh jeez. What could she possibly say? She blinked away the tears and steeled her nerves. "This is a nice room. Why did you have it built?"

"There have been a few attempts on my life. Angus MacKay designed this room as a sanctuary from the Malcontents."

"Malcontents?"

"That's what we call them. They call themselves the True Ones, but in truth, they're nothing more than terrorists. They're a secret society who believes in their Satangiven right to feed off mortals." Roman lifted his glass. "To them, drinking this synthetic blood is an abomination."

"Oh. And since you invented it, they really don't like you."

He smiled slightly. "No. They don't care for Romatech, either. They've launched several grenades at us in the past few years. That's why I have so much security here and at home."

Vampire security guards who slept in coffin dormitories. Shanna hugged herself while she let this new reality sink in. Roman finished his drink and walked over to the kitchen area. He rinsed the glass out and set it in the sink.

"So you're telling me there are two kinds of vampires— the bad Malcontent guys who feed off mortals, and then the good guys like you."

Roman pressed his palms down on the marble countertop, his back to her. He seemed perfectly still, though she could tell he was breathing rapidly, struggling with some kind of inner demon. Himself.

He slammed a fist against the marble so suddenly, she jumped. He whirled around to face her, his face harsh, his eyes gleaming. He stalked toward her. "Don't ever make the mistake of thinking I'm good. I have committed more crimes than you can imagine. I have murdered in cold blood. I have transformed hundreds of mortals into vampires. I have doomed their immortal souls to an eternity in hell!"

Shanna sat motionless, shaken to the core, frozen by the intensity of his eyes. *Murderer. Maker of vampires.* Good God, if he wanted to scare her, he was doing one hell of a fine job. She leaped to her feet and dashed to the door. She had flipped open two locks before he grabbed her from behind.

"Dammit, no." He shoved her aside and turned the first lock. With a hissing intake of breath, he pulled his hand away.

Shanna saw the welts forming on his fingertips, smelled the terrible odor of burning flesh. "What—?"

Gritting his teeth, he reached for the second lock.

"Stop!" She pushed his hand away and set the lock herself. Sheesh, what was she doing?

He cradled his injured hand against his chest, his face pale with pain.

"You burned yourself," she whispered. Was he that desperate to keep her safe? She reached for his hand. "Let me see."

He stepped back. "It will heal while I sleep." He glared at her. "Don't do that again. Even if you get out the door, you won't get two feet before I catch you."

"You don't have to make me sound like a prisoner."

He walked to the fridge and grabbed a handful of ice. "You're under my protection."

"Why? Why are you so determined to protect me?"

He stood at the sink, rubbing an ice cube over his seared fingers. Shanna finally decided he wasn't going to answer. She trudged back to the bed.

"You're special," he said softly.

She halted by the bed. Special? She closed her eyes. God, this man made her heart ache. Despite everything, she wanted to hold him in her arms and comfort him. "You could kill me yourself, and the Russian mob would probably pay you."

He tossed the ice into the sink. "I could never harm you."

Then, why did he want her to believe the worst of him? He'd described himself as evil. She sat down heavily on the bed. Oh God, was that how he saw himself? As a loathsome, evil creature? No wonder he suffered from so much pain and remorse. "How long have you been a . . . ?"

"A vampire?" He turned to face her. "Say it, Shanna. I'm a vampire."

Her eyes misted. "I don't want to. It doesn't fit you."

He regarded her sadly. "I went through a period of denial, too. Eventually I got over it."

"How?"

His mouth thinned. "I got hungry."

Shanna shivered. "You fed off people."

"Yes. Until I invented synthetic blood. The purpose of Romatech is to make the world safe for vampires and mortals alike."

She knew it. She knew he was a good man, even if he couldn't see it himself. "What else can you do? I mean, other than teleport or sizzle on a silver platter."

His eyes softened. "I have heightened senses. I can hear at a distance and see in the dark. With a good sniff, I can tell you're Type A Positive." The corner of his mouth quirked. "My favorite flavor."

Shanna winced. "In that case, feel free to use the fridge."

He smiled.

Damn, he was too good-looking for a demon. "What else? Oh, right. You can move faster than a speeding bullet."

"Only when I want to. Some things are better done slowly."

She gulped. Was he flirting with her? "Do you turn into a bat and fly around?"

"No. That's an old superstition. We can't change form or fly, but we can levitate."

"Don't you need to go back to your party? And your friends?"

With a shrug, he leaned against the counter. "I'd rather be here with you."

Now for the killer question. "Did you want to become a vampire?"

He stiffened. "No, of course not."

"Then how did it happen? Were you attacked?"

"The details are not important." He wandered toward the easy chair. "You don't want to hear it."

She took a deep breath. "I do. I want to know everything."

He looked uncertain as he unbuttoned his jacket. "It's a long story."

"Go for it." She attempted a wry smile. "I'm a captive audience."

Seventeen

Roman leaned back in the easy chair and stared at the ceiling. He had serious doubts about this. The last time he'd told this story to a woman, she'd wanted to kill him.

He took a deep breath and began. "I was born in a small village in Romania in 1461. I had two brothers and a little sister." He tried to conjure up their faces, but his memory was too vague. He'd had such a short time with them.

"Wow," Shanna breathed. "You're over five hundred years old."

"Thanks for reminding me."

"Go on," she urged. "What happened to your family?"

"We were poor. Times were difficult." The red blinking light in the corner over the bed caught his attention. The digital surveillance camera was working. He sliced the air with a cutting motion, and within seconds, the red light was off.

He continued with his story. "My mother died in child-birth when I was four. Then my sister died. She was only two."

"I'm so sorry."

"When I was five, my father took me to a local monastery and left me there. I kept thinking he would come back. I knew he loved me. He'd hugged me so tightly before he left. I refused to sleep on the pallet the monks gave me. I insisted my father would come back." He rubbed his forehead. "Eventually the monks grew tired of my complaining and told me the truth. My father had sold me to them."

"Oh no. That's terrible."

"I tried to console myself, thinking my father and brothers were doing well, eating like kings off all the money I earned for them. But the truth was I was sold for a sack of flour."

"That's awful! They must have been desperate."

"They were starving." Roman sighed. "I used to wonder why I was the one my father chose to give away."

Shanna leaned forward. "That's how I felt when my family sent me to boarding school. I kept thinking they were mad at me, but I couldn't figure out what I'd done wrong."

"I'm sure you did nothing wrong." Roman met her gaze. "The monks discovered I was eager to learn and easily taught. Father Constantine said that was why my father chose me. He understood I was the best suited of my brothers for intellectual pursuits."

"You mean you were punished for being the smartest."

"I wouldn't call it punishment. The monastery was clean and warm. We never went hungry. By the time I was twelve, my father and brothers were all dead."

"Oh, jeez. I'm sorry." Shanna grabbed a pillow from the head of the bed and dragged it into her lap. "My family is still alive, thank goodness, but I know what it's like to lose them."

"Father Constantine was the healer in the monastery, and he became my mentor. I learned all I could from him.

He said I had a gift for healing." Roman frowned. "A gift from God."

"So you became a doctor, of sorts."

"Yes. There was never any question in my mind what I wanted to do. I took my vows at the age of eighteen and became a monk. I swore to ease the suffering of mankind." Roman's mouth twisted. "And I swore to reject Satan and all his evil guises."

Shanna hugged the pillow to her chest. "What happened then?"

"Father Constantine and I traveled from one village to another, doing all we could to heal the sick and ease suffering. There weren't many educated physicians at the time, especially for the poor, so we were very much in demand. We worked long, hard hours. Eventually Father Constantine grew too old and frail for it. He stayed at the monastery, and I was allowed to go forth on my own. A mistake, perhaps." Roman smiled wryly. "I wasn't nearly as smart as I thought I was. And without Father Constantine to guide me and give wise counsel . . ."

Roman closed his eyes, briefly recalling the wrinkled, weathered face of his adopted father. Sometimes, when he was alone and in the dark, he could almost hear the old man's soft voice. Father Constantine had always given him hope and encouragement, even when he had been a young and frightened child. And Roman had loved him for that.

A picture flashed in his mind. The monastery in ruins. The dead bodies of all the monks strewn about in the rubble. Father Constantine ripped apart. Roman covered his face to try to block out the memory. But how could he? He had brought their death and destruction upon them. God could never forgive him.

"Are you all right?" Shanna asked softly.

Roman dragged his hands down his face and took a shaky breath. "Where was I?"

"You were a traveling doctor."

Shanna's expression of sympathy made it hard to stay in control, so he shifted his gaze to the ceiling. "I traveled far into areas that are now Hungary and Transylvania. In time, I ceased to bother with priestly trappings. My tonsure grew out. My hair grew long. But I kept my vows of poverty and celibacy, so I was convinced that I was good and righteous. God was on my side. News of my healing capabilities preceded me, and I was welcomed into each village as an honored guest. A hero, even."

"That's good."

He shook his head. "No, it was not. I had sworn to reject evil, but I slowly succumbed to a deadly sin. I became proud."

She snorted. "What's wrong with taking pride in your work? You were saving lives, weren't you?"

"No. God was saving them through me. I forgot to see the distinction. Then it was too late, and I was cursed for all eternity."

She gave him a doubtful look as she hugged the pillow.

"I was thirty years old when I heard rumors of a village in Hungary. The people there were dying one by one, and no one knew why. I'd had some success with the plague by enforcing strict quarantines and rules of sanitation. I . . . I thought I could help this village."

"So you went."

"Yes. In my pride, I thought I would be their savior. But when I arrived, I discovered the village wasn't plagued by a disease, but by hideous, murderous creatures."

"Vampires?" she whispered.

"They had taken over a castle and were feeding off the local people. I should have requested help from the Church, but in my vanity, I thought I could defeat them by myself. After all, I was a man of God." He rubbed his brow, trying to erase the shame and horror of his downfall. "I was wrong. On both counts."

She winced. "They attacked you?"

"Yes, but they didn't leave me to die like the others. They transformed me into one of their kind."

"Why?"

Roman scoffed. "Why not? I was their pet project. Turning a man of God into a demon from hell? It was a perverse game for them."

Shanna shuddered. "I'm so sorry."

Roman lifted his hands. "It's done. A pathetic story, really. A priest so immersed in his own pride that God saw fit to abandon him."

She stood, her eyes filled with pain. "You think God abandoned you?"

"Of course. You said it yourself. I'm a blood-sucking demon from hell."

She made a face. "I tend to be a bit dramatic at times. But now I know the truth. You were trying to help people when the bad guys attacked you. You didn't ask for it any more than I asked the Russian mafia to attack me and Karen." Her eyes shimmered with moisture as she slowly approached him. "Karen didn't ask to die. I didn't ask to lose my family or spend my life being hunted. And you didn't ask to become a vampire."

"I got what I deserved. And I became one of the bad guys, as you put it. You can't make me good, Shanna. I've done terrible things."

"I . . . I'm sure you had your reasons."

He shifted forward, resting his elbows on his knees. "Are you trying to exonerate me?"

"Yes." She stopped beside his chair. "The way I see it, you're still the same man. You invented synthetic blood to keep vampires from feeding off people, right?"

"Yes."

"Don't you see?" She knelt beside him so she could see his face. "You're still trying to save lives."

"It hardly makes up for the lives I have destroyed."

She looked at him sadly with tears in her eyes. "I believe there is good in you. Even if you can't believe it."

He swallowed hard and blinked to keep his own eyes from filling from tears. No wonder he needed Shanna. No wonder he cared for her so deeply. After five hundred years of despair, she'd touched his heart and planted a kernel of hope that had never existed before.

He stood and pulled her into his arms. He held her tightly and never wanted to let her go. God's blood, he would do anything to be the man she believed him to be. He would do anything to be worthy of her love.

Ivan smiled at Angus MacKay. The huge Scotsman was pacing back and forth in front of him, glowering at him as if a few ferocious looks could actually scare him. The Highlanders had surrounded them as soon as Ivan and his entourage had entered the ballroom. Ivan, Alek, Katya, and Galina were escorted to a far corner and told to sit. With a nod, Ivan had let his followers know that they would comply. He made himself comfortable in the corner, flanked by his companions. The Scotsmen spread before them, each one fingering the leather hilt of his silver-plated dagger and looking eager to use it.

The threat was clear. A stab through the heart and Ivan's long existence would be over. The threat didn't scare him, though. Ivan knew he and his companions could simply teleport from the building whenever they liked. But for now, he was having too much fun playing with his alleged captors.

Angus MacKay marched back and forth in front of his men. "Tell me, Petrovsky, why are ye here tonight?"

"I was invited." He slipped his hand beneath his cummerbund.

In unison, the Highlanders took a threatening step forward.

Ivan smiled. "I'm just taking out my invitation."

Angus crossed his arms. "Proceed."

"Your boys are a bit high-strung," Ivan observed dryly. "No doubt it has something to do with wearing skirts."

A low growl emanated from the Highlanders. "Let me skewer the bastard," one of them muttered.

Angus held up a hand. "All in good time. For now, we havena finished our wee chat."

Ivan removed the paper from his cummerbund and unfolded it. The cellophane tape connecting the two halves gleamed in the overhead lighting. "This is our invitation. As you can see, we were undecided for a while, but finally my ladies here convinced me that it would be a . . . blast."

"Exactly." Katya twisted to the side in her chair and crossed her legs so everyone could see her bare leg and hip. "I just wanted a bit of fun."

MacKay lifted a brow. "And what is yer idea of fun? Were ye planning to kill someone tonight?"

"Are you always this rude to your invited guests?" Ivan dropped the invitation on the floor and glanced at his watch. They'd been here fifteen minutes. By now, Vladimir should be locating the storage compartments of synthetic blood. The True Ones were about to strike a major victory.

MacKay towered over him. "Ye keep looking at yer watch. Give it to me."

"You've already emptied my pockets. Are you a pack of thieves?" Ivan took his time removing the watch. MacKay knew he was up to something. He just needed to stall for more time. With a resigned sigh, he placed the watch in MacKay's hand. "It's an ordinary watch, you know. I keep looking at it because so far, this party has been a dreadful bore."

"It is." Galina pouted. "No one has even danced with me."

MacKay handed the watch to one of his men. "Examine it."

With a tilt of his head, Ivan spotted the French coven master entering the ballroom with another Highlander.

Most of the guests turned to admire the Frenchman as he strolled across the room. Jean-Luc Echarpe. What a pathetic excuse for a vampire. Instead of feeding off mortals, the silly Frenchman was dressing them. And getting filthy rich in the process.

Ivan jerked his head to the side, causing a loud crack. That got everyone's attention. The guests were now focused on him. Ivan smiled.

Angus MacKay gave him a curious look. "What's the matter, Petrovsky? Is yer head not screwed on properly?"

The Highlanders chuckled.

Ivan's smile faded. *Go ahead and laugh, you fools. When the explosives go off, we'll see who's laughing then.*

Shanna stiffened in Roman's arms. She had wanted to give him comfort, but now that he was taking it, she was a little spooked by the fact that she was hugging a vampire. This was going to take a while to get used to. She pulled back, sliding her hands from his shoulders to his chest.

He kept a loose hold on her and studied her face. "Second thoughts? You haven't decided to kill me, have you?"

"No, of course not." She studied her right hand where it rested against his chest. Over his heart. The thought of a stake piercing him there was too awful to contemplate. "I could never hurt—" She blinked and looked at him in shock. "You have a heartbeat. I can feel it."

"Yes. But when the sun rises, it will stop."

"I—I thought—"

"That nothing in my body worked? I walk and talk, don't I? My body is digesting the blood I consumed. For my brain to function, it must be supplied with blood and oxygen. I need air in order to talk. None of this would be possible without a beating heart to supply blood throughout my body."

"Oh. I just thought vampires were . . ."

"Totally dead? Not at night. You know my body reacts to

you, Shanna. You've known that since the first night we were in the backseat of Laszlo's car."

Her face heated with a blush. His huge erection certainly proved how well his body functioned once the sun went down.

He touched her warm cheek. "I've wanted you since that first night."

She moved out of his reach. "We can't . . ."

"I would never hurt you."

"Can you be sure about that? Do you have complete control over your . . . ?"

His jaw clenched. "My evil impulses?"

"I was going to say your . . . appetite." She wrapped her arms around herself. "I—I care for you, Roman. And I'm not just saying that out of gratitude for you rescuing me. I really do care. And I hate the way you've been suffering for so long—"

"Then be with me." He reached for her.

She stepped back. "How can I? Even if I can deal with the fact that you're a—a vampire, there's still the live-in girlfriends. The harem."

"They don't mean anything to me."

"They mean a lot to me! How can I possibly ignore the fact that you're screwing ten women on the side?"

He winced. "I should have known that would be a problem."

"Well, duh! Why on earth do you need so many of them?" Oh, jeez. Dumb question. Any man would probably jump at the chance.

With a sigh, he turned and paced back to the kitchen area. He tugged at the tie that hung loose around his collar. "It is an ancient tradition for every coven master to keep a harem. I have no choice but to honor that tradition."

"Yeah, right."

He pulled the tie free and tossed it on the kitchen table. "You don't understand vampire culture. The harem is a symbol of a coven master's power and prestige. Without them, I couldn't command any respect. I would be a laughingstock."

"Oh, poor baby! Trapped in an evil custom against your will. Wait a minute, I think my eyes are tearing up." Shanna held up her hands and waited a few seconds. "Oh no. False alarm. Probably allergies."

He scowled at her. "More likely indigestion from your acidic wit."

She glared back at him. "How amusing. Excuse me for not fawning over you like one of your ten harem girls."

"I wouldn't want you to."

She folded her arms across her chest. "That's why I left, you know. I found out you're a womanizing pig."

His eyes flashed. "And you're—" His angry expression slowly cleared into a look of wonder. "You're jealous."

"What?"

"You're jealous." With a grin, he whisked off his jacket with the flair of a victorious matador and draped it over the back of a kitchen chair. "You're so jealous, you can hardly stand it. You know what this means? It means you want me."

"It means I'm *disgusted*!" Shanna turned her back on him and paced toward the door. Damn him. He was far too clever. He knew she was attracted to him. But a vampire with a harem of ten women? If she was going to date a demon, he could at least be a faithful one. Good God. She couldn't believe she was in such a predicament. "Maybe I should contact the Justice Department in the morning."

"No. They cannot protect you like I can. They don't even know what kind of enemy they're facing."

That was true. As far as she could tell, her best chance for survival was with Roman. She leaned against the wall next to the door. "If I stay with you, it can only be temporary. There can't be any sort of relationship between us."

"Ah. You do not wish to kiss me again?" He stared at her so intently, she was ready to squirm.

"No."

"No touching?"

"No." Her heart rate quickened.

"You know I want you."

She swallowed hard. "It won't happen. You have a whole harem to keep you happy. You don't need me."

"I have never touched them. Not intimately."

Who was he fooling? Of all the ridiculous things to say. "Don't take me for an idiot."

"I'm serious. I've never physically shared a bed with any of them."

Anger spiked inside her. "Don't lie to me. I know you've had sex with them. They were talking about it, about how it had been a long time, and how they missed you."

"Exactly. It's been a long time."

"So, you admit it. You've had sex with them."

"Vampire sex."

"What?"

"It's purely a mental exercise. We're not even in the same room." He shrugged. "I simply plant the feelings and sensations into their brains."

"You mean it's some sort of mental telepathy?"

"Mind control. Vampires use it to manipulate mortals or communicate with each other."

Manipulate mortals? "That's how you got me to implant your tooth?" She winced. "I mean your fang. You tricked me."

"I had to make you see it as an ordinary tooth. I regret that I couldn't be completely honest, but under the circumstances, I felt I had no choice."

He had a point. She wouldn't have wanted to help him if she'd known the truth. "So you really didn't show up in the dental mirror."

His eyebrows shot up. "You remember that?"

"Sorta. Do you still have the splint in your mouth?"

"No. I had Laszlo remove it last night. I was so worried about you, Shanna. I could hardly function without you. I was calling to you mentally, hoping we still had a connection."

With a gulp, she recalled hearing his voice in her sleep. "I—I'm not comfortable with you invading my head whenever you feel like it."

"You needn't worry about that. You have an incredibly strong mind. The only way I can get in is if you let me."

"I'm able to block you?" That was good news.

"Yes, but when you let me in, our connection is stronger than any I have ever experienced before." He walked toward her, his eyes gleaming. "We could be so good together."

Oh Lordy. "It's not going to happen. You've already admitted that you're having sex with ten other women."

"Vampire sex. It's an impersonal experience. Each participant is alone in his or her bed."

Participant? Like a team of soccer players, working one ball down the field? "Are you saying you do it with all ten at the same time?"

He shrugged. "It's the most time efficient method of keeping them all satisfied."

"Oh my God." Shanna slapped a hand across her forehead. "Assembly line sex? You'd make Henry Ford proud."

"You may joke, but think about it." He pinned her with an intense gaze. "All sensations of touch and pleasure are registered in your mind. Your brain controls your breathing, your heart rate. It's the most erotic part of your body."

She felt a sudden urge to press her thighs together. "So?"

The corner of his mouth lifted. His eyes gleamed hotter, like molten gold. "It can be extremely satisfying."

Damn him. She locked her knees together. "You've never actually touched any of them?"

"I don't even know what they look like."

She stared at him, then shook her head. "I'm finding this hard to believe."

"Are you calling me a liar?"

"Well, not intentionally. It just seems too weird."

His eyes narrowed. "You do not believe such a thing exists?"

"I'm having a hard time believing you can satisfy ten women without laying a hand on them."

"Then I will prove to you that vampire sex is real."

"Yeah, right. How do you propose to do that?"

He smiled slowly. "By having it with you."

Eighteen

In his corner of the ballroom, Ivan Petrovsky was still biding his time with Angus MacKay and his moronic Highlanders. The French fop Jean-Luc Echarpe was approaching with yet another Scotsman.

MacKay greeted them. "Did ye find them, Connor?"

"Aye," he replied. "We checked the surveillance cameras. They were exactly where ye thought they'd be."

"Are you talking about Shanna Whelan?" Ivan asked. "I saw Draganesti take off with her, you know. Is that his modern Vamp way of doing things? When in danger, run and hide?"

With a growl, Connor stepped toward him. "Let me snap his scrawny neck once and for all."

"*Non.*" Jean-Luc Echarpe blocked the Scotsman with his walking stick. The Frenchman stared at Ivan, his eyes an icy blue. "When the time comes, I want him."

Ivan snorted. "What are you going to do to me, Echarpe? Give me a fashion makeover?"

The Frenchman smiled. "I guarantee no one will recognize you afterward."

"And the chemist?" Angus asked Connor. "Is he safe?"

"Aye. Ian is with him."

"If you're talking about Laszlo Veszto, I have news for you," Ivan said. "The man's days are numbered."

MacKay's bland look said he was unimpressed. He turned to the Highlander with Ivan's watch. "Well?"

The Scotsman shrugged. "It looks like a normal watch, sir. But we canna be sure unless we open it."

"I understand." MacKay took the watch, dropped it on the floor, and stomped his foot on it.

"Hey!" Ivan jumped to his feet.

MacKay picked up the broken watch and examined the crushed innards. "Looks fine to me. A good watch." He handed it back to Ivan with a twinkle in his eye.

"Bastard." Ivan tossed his ruined watch on the floor.

"Wait a minute." Connor stepped back and looked at the Russians. "Ye have four of them."

"Right," MacKay said. "Ye said there were four at the house in New Rochelle."

"Aye, there were," Connor replied. "But there was a driver, too. Where the hell is he?"

Ivan smiled.

"Bugger," MacKay muttered. "Connor, take a dozen men and scour the premises. Call the guards outside and have them search the grounds."

"Aye, sir." Connor motioned for twelve men to follow him. After a few quick words, they divided up and zoomed off at vampire speed.

The gap in the line of Highlanders was quickly taken up by Corky Courrant and her crew from DVN. "About time you let us get a good shot," she snarled. She turned to the camera with a bright smile. "This is Corky Courrant, reporting for *Live with the Undead*. There's been one excit-

240

ing event after another at the Gala Opening Ball. Here you can see that a regiment of Highlanders has taken the Russian-American vampires prisoner. Can you tell me why, Mr. MacKay?" She jammed her microphone under Angus MacKay's nose.

He scowled at her in silence.

Her smile stretched wider and froze. "Surely you don't take prisoners without just cause?" She jabbed the microphone at him once again.

"Go away, lassie," he spoke softly. "This is none of yer business."

"I want to talk." Ivan waved toward the cameraman. "I was invited here, and look how they're treating me."

"We havena harmed you." MacKay drew a pistol and pointed it at Ivan. "Yet. Where is the fifth person of yer group? What is he up to?"

"Still trying to park the car. You know, for a party this big, you really should have valet service."

MacKay arched a brow. "Perhaps I should warn ye these bullets are silver."

"Will you try to kill me in front of so many witnesses?" Ivan sneered. He couldn't have wished for a better situation than this. He not only had the attention of all the guests at the Gala Opening Ball, but everyone watching DVN would also hear his message. He levitated onto his chair and waited for the music to end.

Echarpe slid a sword out of his walking stick. "No one wants to listen to you."

"Will the Gala Opening Ball end in bloodshed?" Corky Courrant whispered in a loud voice. "Don't touch your remote!"

Ivan made a small mocking bow as the music ended. Unfortunately, the bow left his neck misaligned, so he had to pop it back into position.

Corky Courrant faced her camera with a beaming smile.

"Ivan Petrovsky, Russian-American coven master, is about to make a speech. Let's hear what he has to say."

"It has been eighteen years since I attended one of these balls," Ivan began. "Eighteen years that I have been forced to witness the tragic decay of our superior way of life. Our old traditions are laid to waste. Our proud heritage ridiculed. A new politically correct philosophy of the modern-day Vamp has insinuated itself into our midst like a plague."

A murmur began in the crowd. Some didn't like his message, but Ivan suspected there were others who longed to hear him.

"How many of you have grown fat and complacent on this ridiculous Fusion Cuisine? How many of you have forgotten the thrill of the hunt, the ecstasy of the bite? I tell you tonight that this false blood is an abomination!"

"Enough." Angus raised his pistol. "Come down from there."

"Why?" Ivan yelled. "Are you afraid of the truth? The True Ones are not."

Echarpe lifted his sword. "The True Ones are cowards who hide in secret."

"Not anymore!" Ivan looked straight into the camera from DVN. "I am the leader of the True Ones, and tonight we shall have our revenge!"

"Take them!" Angus lunged forward, followed by his men.

Ivan and his followers leaped high into the air, then vanished as they teleported from the building. They landed outside in the garden.

"Hurry!" Ivan yelled. "To the car."

They zipped across the lawn to the parking lot. The car was empty. Vladimir was nowhere in sight.

"Crap," Ivan muttered. "He should have finished by now." He pivoted, scanning their surroundings. "What the hell happened to you?" He stared at Katya.

She glanced down and laughed. "I thought the night air was bit chilly." Her skirt was gone, leaving her naked from the waist down. "When we jumped into the air, the Frenchman tried to grab me. I guess he got a hold of my skirt, and it came off."

"Jean-Luc Echarpe?" Galina asked. "He's so cute. And so are the Scotsmen. Do you think they're naked under those kilts?"

"Enough!" Ivan took off his jacket and tossed it at Katya. "Need I remind you two bitches that you belong to me? Now get in the car."

Katya lifted a brow and instead of wrapping the jacket around her hips as he had intended, she put the jacket on. Her private parts were still on display. Alek gawked at her, his mouth hanging open.

Raw pain stabbed at Ivan's neck. "Do you want to spend the rest of your existence without eyeballs?" he growled.

Alek jerked to attention. "No, sir."

"Then get the ladies in the car and start the damned engine." Ivan gritted his teeth and snapped his neck.

A blur in the dark raced toward them. Vladimir. The vampire stopped beside him.

"Did you find their storage facilities?"

"*Da*." Vladimir nodded. "The explosives are ready."

"Good. Let's go." Ivan spotted Highlanders racing toward them. This was it. He reached for the cuff link on his right sleeve. He had suspected the Highlanders would empty his pockets, so he'd hidden the detonator to the C-4 in his cuff link. One punch of the button and Draganesti's precious stockpile of synthetic blood would be gone.

Shanna was speechless. Vampire sex? She wasn't sure such a bizarre phenomenon even existed. Well, there was certainly one way to find out. Should she even consider it?

Well, she couldn't get pregnant from it. And since he wouldn't even be in the same room with her, it had to be perfectly safe. No bites, no holding, no unnecessary roughness. No little vampire babies flying around the nursery.

She groaned. Was she seriously considering this? She'd have to let Roman into her mind. Who knew what awful things he could do to her? What deliciously wicked sensations he could—oops. That line of defense wasn't working.

He had taken a seat at the kitchen table and was watching her with his gold-tinted eyes, looking infuriatingly amused by the whole situation. As if he knew she would say yes. The rascal. Wasn't it enough for him to confess to being a vampire? But no, he had to propose vampire sex in the same evening. Extremely satisfying vampire sex.

Her skin pebbled with goose bumps. He was so intelligent. And he wanted to concentrate all that mental power on the one task of pleasuring her? Good God. She *was* tempted.

She glanced at his eyes and immediately felt his psychic power encircling her head like a cool breeze. Her heart pounded. Her knees turned to rubber. A loud blast deafened her ears. The floor shook beneath her feet. She grabbed at the wall to steady herself. My God, did he do that to her?

Roman jumped to his feet and dashed to the phone. The room trembled again, and Shanna stumbled toward the easy chair.

"Ian! What the hell is going on?" Roman yelled into the phone. He paused to listen. "Where was the explosion? Was anyone hurt?"

Explosion? Shanna sank into the chair. Oh jeez. She should have known when the Earth moved, it wasn't related to sex. They were under attack.

"Did they catch him?" Roman cursed softly.

"What's going on?" Shanna asked.

"Petrovsky got away," Roman grumbled. "It's all right, Ian. We know where he lives. We can retaliate whenever we wish."

Shanna gulped. It looked like a vampire war had started.

"Ian," Roman spoke into the phone. "I want you and Connor to take Shanna back to the house. And Laszlo and Radinka, too." He hung up. "I have to go. Connor will be here soon."

"Where was the explosion?" She followed him to the door.

He picked up his cape and used it as insulation to turn the locks. "Petrovsky blew up a storeroom of synthetic blood."

"Oh no."

"It could have been worse." He slid back the bar. "The storeroom was far enough away from the ballroom that no one was hurt. But it'll put a dent in our supply."

"Why destroy synthetic blood? Oh." Shanna winced as the answer dawned on her. "He wants to force vampires into biting people again."

"Don't worry." Roman touched her shoulder. "What Petrovsky doesn't know is that I have other plants in Illinois, Texas, and California. We can make up for the shortage on the East Coast if we have to. He hasn't hurt me nearly as bad as he may think."

Shanna smiled with relief. "You're too smart for him."

"I'm sorry I have to go, but I need to check the damage."

"I understand." She pulled open the silver door so he could leave.

He grazed his knuckles down her cheek. "I can be with you later tonight. Will you wait for me?"

"Yes. Be careful." She wanted to hear more about the upcoming war. Roman zoomed down the hall at lightning speed.

As Shanna shut the door, she realized her mistake. He meant he would come to her tonight for vampire sex. And without realizing it, she had agreed.

Thirty minutes later, Shanna was riding in the back of a limousine with Radinka and Laszlo. In the front seat, Connor sat next to Ian, who was driving. Shanna realized now that Ian was much, much older than fifteen. She eyed her companions, trying to figure out if they were all vampires. Ian and Connor definitely were, and they slept in those coffins in the basement. Laszlo was such a sweet, little, cherub-faced man. It was hard to think of him as a demon, though she supposed he was.

Now, Radinka was harder to figure. "You . . . you went shopping for me during the daytime, didn't you?"

"Yes, dear." Radinka poured herself a drink from the small wet bar. "I'm mortal, in case you were wondering."

"But Gregori—"

"—is a vampire, yes." Radinka tilted her head to look at Shanna. "Would you like to hear how it happened?"

"Well, it's none of my business."

"Nonsense. It involves Roman, so you should know." Radinka sipped her Scotch and gazed out the tinted window. "Fifteen years ago, my husband, God rest his soul, died of cancer and left us with some horrendous medical bills. Gregori had to leave Yale and come home. He transferred to NYU and got a part-time job. I needed a job, too, but I was inexperienced. Luckily, I found a job at Roma-tech. The hours were atrocious, of course."

"The night shift?" Shanna asked.

"Yes. After a few months, I adjusted and found I was very capable. And I was never intimidated by Roman. I think he likes that. Eventually I became his personal assistant, and that was when I began to notice things. Especially in Roman's lab. Half-empty bottles of blood, still warm." Radinka smiled. "He's like an absent-minded professor when he's hard at work. He would forget to give himself time to drive home before sunrise. So he'd have to teleport home at the last minute. One second he would be in his lab, and the next, he was gone."

"You knew something was weird."

"Yes. I'm from Eastern Europe originally, and we grow

up with tales of vampires. It wasn't difficult to figure it out."

"Didn't it bother you? You didn't want to quit?"

"No." Radinka waved a hand elegantly in the air. "Roman was always very good to me. Then one night, twelve years ago, Gregori came to pick me up from work. We only had one car. He was in the parking lot, waiting for me, when he was attacked."

Connor twisted in his seat. "Was it Petrovsky?"

"I never saw the attacker. He was gone by the time I found my poor son, dying in the parking lot." Radinka shuddered. "But Gregori says it was Petrovksy, and I'm sure he's right. How could you forget the face of the monster who tries to kill you?"

Connor nodded. "We'll get him."

"Why would he attack Gregori?" Shanna asked.

Laszlo fiddled with a button on his tuxedo jacket. "Most likely, he thought Gregori was a mortal employee at Romatech. He made an easy target."

"Yes." Radinka gulped down some Scotch. "My poor Gregori. He'd lost so much blood. I knew he would never survive a trip to the hospital. I asked Roman to save him, but he refused."

A chill crept over Shanna's skin. "You asked Roman to turn your son into a vampire?"

"It was the only way to save him. Roman insisted he would be condemning the boy's soul to hell, but I wouldn't listen to him. I know Roman is good." Radinka gestured to all the vampires in the car. "These were all good, honorable men before death. Why would death change them? I refuse to believe they're condemned to hell. And I refused to give up on my son and let him die!"

Radinka's hand shook as she set her glass down. "I begged him. I got down on my knees and begged him till he couldn't stand it anymore. He took my son in his arms and transformed him." She wiped a tear from her cheek.

With a shiver, Shanna hugged herself. Radinka believed there was good in Roman, too. Why couldn't he see it in himself? Why was he torturing himself for hundreds of years? "How—how does someone get transformed?"

"A mortal must be drained dry by one or more vampires," Laszlo explained. "At that point, the mortal enters a coma. Left alone, he will die a normal death. But if a vampire feeds his own blood to the victim, the mortal will awaken as a vampire."

"Oh." Shanna swallowed hard. "I don't suppose many people get transformed anymore?"

"Nay," Connor answered. "We doona bite anymore. Of course, Petrovksy and his damned Malcontents do. But we'll take care of them."

"I hope so." Laszlo jerked at a button. "He wants to kill me, too."

"Why?" Shanna asked.

Laszlo fidgeted in his seat. "No good reason."

"Because he helped you escape." Radinka sipped some more Scotch.

Because of her? Shanna's throat tightened, making it hard to breathe. "I . . . I'm so sorry, Laszlo. I had no idea."

"It's not your fault." Laszlo scrunched down in his seat. "I was watching Petrovsky on the surveillance camera with Ian. That man is not . . . normal."

Shanna wondered what was normal for a vampire. "You mean he's crazy?"

"He's cruel," Connor said from the front seat. "I've known the bastard for centuries. He hates mortals with a passion."

"And he does that creepy thing with his neck." Ian turned the limo to the right. "Verra strange."

"You havena heard that story?" Connor asked.

"No." Ian glanced at him. "What happened?"

Connor twisted in the seat so he could see everyone. "About two hundred years ago, Ivan was still in Russia. He was attacking a village, not only feeding off the people, but torturing them. Some of the villagers found his coffin in the cellar of an old mill. They waited till he was asleep so they could kill him."

Laszlo leaned forward. "They tried to stake him?"

"Nay, they were an ignorant lot, the poor sops. They thought burying the coffin would do the trick, so they took it to a consecrated graveyard and buried Ivan under a large statue of an avenging angel. That night, Ivan awoke and tried to dig his way out. He upset the earth so much, the statue tipped over and clobbered him on the head. Broke his bloody neck."

"You're kidding." Shanna grimaced. "Yuk."

"Doona feel sorry for the bastard," Connor continued. "Instead of fixing his neck, he flew into a rage and murdered the entire village. The next day, when his body tried to heal itself, his neck wasna lined up properly, and he's suffered for it ever since."

"He should suffer," Ian said. "He needs to die."

Even if they managed to kill the Russian vampire, Shanna didn't know if her problems would be over. The Russian mafia could hire someone else. And a vampire war was erupting around her. She sank down in her seat. The situation seemed hopeless.

Back in her bedroom at Roman's townhouse, Shanna had no choice but to face the truth: She was seriously attracted to a vampire.

She glanced at the pillow where Roman had rested his head. No wonder she had thought he was dead. During the day, he really was dead. But at night, he walked and talked and digested blood. He worked in his lab, using his brilliant brain to produce amazing scientific achievements. He protected his followers. And whenever he felt like it, he had vampire sex. With his harem. All at the same time. And now he wanted to do it with her?

She groaned. What a strange dilemma. She had locked the door after Connor had brought up a tray of food, but it wouldn't stop Roman from trying to enter her brain. A very satisfying experience, he had said.

She put the empty tray on the floor and grabbed the remote control. She didn't want to think about sex anymore. Or his harem. On the DVN channel, she saw Corky Courrant standing in front of a blown-up section of Romatech and reporting on the latest details. Shanna hardly heard her, for she spotted Roman by the crater. He looked tired and strained. His clothes were gray with dust and grime.

The poor man. She longed to touch his handsome face and offer words of encouragement. Just then, the DVN reporter started a series of flashbacks, chronicling the highlights of the Gala Opening Ball. Shanna gasped when her own picture filled the screen. There she was, discovering vampires for the first time. My God, the horror on her face. *My face.*

She watched herself throwing the glass of blood to the floor. Then Roman grabbed her, flung his cape around her, and she disappeared. The whole thing was digitally recorded so vampires could enjoy watching it over and over.

With trembling fingers, Shanna turned the television off. The full weight of her situation bore down on her. A vampire assassin wanted to kill her. Another vampire wanted to protect her. Roman. She wished he were with her now. He didn't frighten her. He was kind and caring. A good man. Radinka, Connor, and the others agreed. Roman was a wonderful man. He just couldn't see it. He was too haunted by awful memories, memories too atrocious for one person to bear.

If only she could help him see himself as she did. She lay back on the bed. How could a relationship with him ever work? She ought to avoid further contact with him, but she knew in her heart she couldn't resist. She was falling in love with him.

Hours later, in the deep, dreamy moments before sunrise, she felt a sudden chill and snuggled deeper under the covers.

Shanna.

The cold seeped away, and she felt warm and cozy. Desired.

Shanna, darling.

She blinked her eyes open. "Roman? Is that you?"

A soft breath tickled her left ear. A low voice.

Let me love you.

Nineteen

Shanna sat up and peered about the dark bedroom. "Roman? Are you here?"

I'm upstairs. Thank you for letting me inside.

Inside? Inside her head? It must have happened while she was asleep. An icy jab of pain shot from one temple to another.

Shanna, please. Don't push me out. His voice faded till it sounded like an echo coming from the far end of a cave.

She rubbed her aching temples. "Am I doing this?"

You're trying to block me. Why?

"I don't know. When I feel something coming at me, I just push back. It's a reflex."

Relax, sweetness. I won't hurt you.

She took a few deep breaths, and the pain lessened.

That's better. His voice sounded closer. Clearer.

Shanna's heart raced. She wasn't at all sure she wanted Roman in her head. How many of her thoughts could he read?

Why are you worried? Are you keeping secrets from me?

Oh God, he *could* hear her thoughts. "No big secrets, but there are some things I'd rather keep private." Like how incredibly handsome and sexy he—*You're an ugly old toad!*

Sexy?

Darn. She wasn't good at this telepathy stuff. The fact that he could read her mind made her want to produce strange thoughts just to throw him off track.

An air of amusement surrounded her like a warm cocoon. *Then don't think so much. Relax.*

"How can I relax if you're in my head? You wouldn't make me do something against my will, would you?"

Of course not, sweetness. I won't control your thoughts. I'll only give you the sensations of me making love to you. And as soon as the sun rises, I'll have to go.

She felt something warm and moist against her brow. A kiss. Then, soft fingers caressing her face. They rubbed at her temples till the last vestige of pain slipped away. She closed her eyes and felt the fingers tracing her cheekbones, her jaw, her ears. She wasn't sure how he managed it, but it felt so real. So wonderful.

What are you wearing?

"Hmm? Does it matter?"

I want you naked when I touch you. I want to feel every lush curve, every deep hollow. I want your breath shuddering in my ear, your muscles tensing with passion, tighter and tighter—

"Enough! You had me on the first sentence." She pulled off her nightgown and dropped it into a silken puddle on the floor. Then she nestled into the warm sheets and waited.

And waited. "Hello?" She gazed at the ceiling overhead, wondering what was happening on the fifth floor. "Hello? Earth to Roman—your bedmate is naked and ready for launch."

Nothing. Maybe he was so tired, he fell asleep. Great. She'd never been good at holding a man's interest for very long. And Roman—he could be around forever. How could she be more than a passing fancy to him? Even if their relationship lasted a few years, it would be like a blink of an eye to him. With a groan, Shanna rolled onto her stomach. How could this ever work? They were polar opposites, as in alive and dead. When people said opposites attract, they didn't mean it in such an extreme way.

Shanna?

She raised her head. "You're back? I thought you'd left."

Sorry. Business. His fingers gently kneaded her shoulders.

With a sigh, she lowered her head onto the pillow. Business? "Where are you exactly? You're not at your desk, are you?" The thought that he might be doing paperwork on the side really irked her. The man was so brilliant, he could probably give her a mental orgasm while answering his email.

He chuckled. *I'm sitting in bed, having a bedtime snack.*

He was drinking blood while he mentally massaged her shoulders? Ugh. How romantic. Not.

I'm naked. Does that help?

Oh Lordy. She visualized his gorgeous body—*ugly old toad.*

He stroked her back with feather-light caresses. She shivered. This was wonderful. He applied pressure with the heel of his hand, burrowing into her with slow, sweet circles. Correction—this was heaven.

Can you hear other vampires?

"No. One is quite enough, thank you." She felt his presence looming larger, swelling with emotion. Pride. No, fiercer than that. More like . . . possessiveness.

You are mine.

Right. Just because she could hear him, it gave him ownership rights? Alive for more than five hundred years, and he still thought like a caveman. Though his hands did feel absolutely delightful.

Thank you. I aim to please. His hands roamed her back, his long fingers seeking out knots of tension. *Caveman, huh?*

Damn, he could hear too much. She could almost see him smiling. It was a good thing he didn't know she was falling in—*ugly old toad, ugly old toad.*

You're still not comfortable with me in your head.

Bingo. Two points for the mind-controlling demon. She felt a light smack on her rump. "Hey!" She lifted her shoulders, only to be pushed back down. "You're manhandling me." Her voice was muffled by the pillow.

Yes, I am. He had the gall to sound pleased with himself.

"Caveman," she muttered. With a whole harem of women. "You said before this was impersonal. It seems very personal to me."

It is right now, because it's only you and me. I'm thinking only of you. His presence felt heavy around her, heavy and hot with desire. Her skin tingled in response. He skimmed his fingers up her spine to her neck. There he brushed her hair to the side.

She felt something hot and moist on her neck. A kiss. She shivered. It was so weird, getting kissed by an invisible face. His breath warmed her ear. Then something tickled her toes.

She started. "There's something in the bed."

Me.

"But—" It was impossible for him to kiss her ear and reach her toes at the same time. Unless his arms were six feet long. Or he wasn't quite human.

Bingo. Two points for you, sweetness. Roman nuzzled her neck and tweaked her toes. On both feet. And he continued to rub the skin between her shoulder blades.

"Wait a minute. How many hands do you have?"

As many as I want. It's all in my mind. Our mind. His thumbs dug into the arches of her feet. He massaged her back with the heel of his palm, dragging the circles down her spine. And still he continued to kiss her neck.

She sighed dreamily. "Oh, this is nice."

Nice? His hands stopped.

"Yeah. Very nice, very—" Shanna tensed, aware of a simmering irritation inside her head. It was coming from him.

Nice? Sparks sizzled around him.

Oh dear. "I'm enjoying it. Really, I am."

His voice hissed through her head. *No more Mr. Nice Guy.*

He seized her ankles and pulled her legs apart. More hands curled around her wrists. She wiggled, trying to get loose, but he was too strong, with too many damned hands. She was pinned down and helpless, her legs spread wide open.

Cool air wafted against her most tender flesh. She waited, tense and exposed. Her heart pounded loud in her ears.

She waited. The room was quiet, except for the labored sound of her breathing. Her nerves coiled, sensing an imminent attack. Where would he strike first? There was no way to tell. He wasn't visible to the eye. This was terrible. This was . . . exciting.

She waited. Four hands still gripped her wrists and ankles. But he had an infinite number of hands and fingers, as many as he could imagine. Her heart raced faster. The muscles in her buttocks contracted in an attempt to squeeze her legs together. She was so exposed. So open to him. Her skin began to tingle. He was doing this to her. Making her wait. Making her ache with anticipation. Longing. Desire.

And then he was gone.

Shanna raised her head. "Hello? Roman?" Where did he go? She sat up and glanced at the clock radio beside the bed. It would be just her luck if the sun was rising and he was officially dead for the day. But it was too early for sunrise. Had he just run out on her in the middle of a date? Minutes ticked by.

She rose onto her knees. "Dammit, Roman, you can't leave me like this." She considered throwing something at the ceiling.

Suddenly she felt hands encircle her waist. She gasped. "Roman? That better be you." She reached behind her where she thought he should be, but felt nothing but air.

It's me. He skimmed his hands over her ribs, then cupped her breasts. His mouth nibbled at her shoulder.

"Where—where were you?" It was hard to carry on a conversation while he was stroking her with his thumbs.

I'm sorry. It won't happen again. He played with her nipples, gently tweaking the hardened buds between his thumb and forefinger. Each tug seemed to pull at an invisible cord connected to her soul.

She crumpled onto the bed and stared at the ceiling. "Oh, Roman, please." She wished she could see him. Or touch him.

Shanna, sweet Shanna. His voice whispered in her head. *How can I tell you what you mean to me? When I saw you at the ball, it was as if my heart started beating again. You lit up the room, bright in an ocean of black and white. And I thought—my life has been nothing but a dark, endless night. Then, you came like a rainbow and filled my black soul with color.*

"Oh, Roman. Don't make me cry." She rolled onto her stomach and wiped her moist eyes with the sheet.

I'll make you cry with pleasure. His hands trailed slowly up her legs, while two more of his imaginary hands skimmed down her back. He reached her thighs and the small of her back. Soon, soon all hands would converge on her sex. Her buttock muscles tensed. Moisture pooled between her legs. The hunger grew sweeter, hotter, more desperate.

She felt his mouth on her bottom, kissing her. The tip of his tongue slipped across one cheek, dipped into the crevice, and continued across the other cheek.

"You're driving me crazy, Roman. I can't stand it."

Is this what you want? His fingers brushed against the curly hair guarding her sex.

She jolted. "Yes."

How wet are you?

The question alone elicited another warm gush of liquid. "I'm dripping. Soaked. See for yourself." She rolled onto her back, expecting to see him. It was disconcerting to lie there, her legs open to welcome him, and no one was there. "Roman?"

I want to kiss you. His breath wandered over her breast, then he sucked the nipple into his mouth. His tongue swirled around, then flicked the hard tip.

She reached for him, but there was nothing there.

He moved to her other breast.

"I want to touch you, too. I want to hold you." She jolted when he cupped her between the legs.

His fingers began to explore. *You're drenched. You're beautiful.*

"Roman." She reached for him again, but found nothing to hold. This was more than disconcerting. It was downright aggravating. With nothing to hold, she clenched the sheet in her fists.

He skimmed along the slick folds, then gently parted them. He dipped a finger inside and stroked the inner walls. *Do you like that? Or do you prefer this?* He circled her clitoris, then teased the tip.

She cried out. She twisted the sheet in her hands. She longed to hold him, run her hands through his hair, feel the muscles on his back and buttocks. This was so one-sided. But so damned good.

He inserted two fingers inside her. At least, she thought it was two fingers. Maybe three. Oh God, he was torturing her from the inside out. His fingers circled and stroked, plunged and withdrew. She had no idea how many thousands of nerve endings she possessed down there, but he seemed determined to set each one on fire. He rubbed the hard, swollen nub of her sex faster and faster. She dug her heels into the mattress, tensing her legs and pressing her hips into the air. *More. More.*

He gave her more.

She panted, gasping for air. Tension mounted, sweet and strained. She burned with need. *Harder. Harder*. She pushed her sex into his hands, writhing against him. He grabbed her buttocks and took her with his mouth.

One flick of his tongue and she shattered. Her inner muscles clenched his fingers. She cried out. Spasms throbbed from her inner core, shooting ripples of sheer pleasure to her fingers and toes. With each wave of release, her breath caught in her throat, her fingers twitched at the sheets. The tremors went on and on. She pulled her legs up, pressing her thighs together, reveling in the glorious aftershocks.

You were beautiful. He kissed her brow.

"You were fantastic." She pressed a hand against her chest. Her heart was still beating rapidly, her skin still hot.

I must go now, sweetness. Sleep well.

"What? You can't leave now."

I must. Sleep well, my love.

"You can't just leave. I want to hold you." A jab of cold pain pinched the bridge of her nose, then disappeared. "Roman?"

Silence.

She searched for his presence within her. He was gone.

"Hey, caveman!" she yelled at the ceiling. "You can't just love me and leave!"

No answer. She struggled to sit up. The bedside clock glowed with the time. Six-ten. Oh, that was it. She collapsed onto her back. The sun was rising. Time for all good little vampires to go sleepy-bye. That certainly sounded nicer than the truth. For the next twelve hours, Roman was dead to the world.

Shit. For a corpse, he made one hell of a lover. With a moan, she covered her eyes. What was she doing, having sex with a vampire? It wasn't like there was any future in this. He was stuck forever at the age of thirty. Condemned to be young, sexy, and gorgeous for all eternity, while she would grow old.

Shanna groaned. Their relationship was doomed from the start. He would stay the beautiful, young prince.

And she would be the ugly old toad.

Early in the afternoon, Shanna woke and had lunch with Howard Barr and a few of the daytime guards. Although trained in security, the guys were also paid to clean house during the day. After all, the sound of vacuum cleaners wasn't going to disturb the dead. Shanna spent a boring afternoon washing her new clothes and watching television. The Digital Vampire Network was on, but most everything was in French or Italian. It was nighttime in Europe. The slogans still appeared in English. *On 24/7 because it's always nighttime somewhere. DVN—if you're not digital, you can't be seen.* Now the words made a lot more sense.

She took a hot shower before sunset, eager to look her best for Roman. Back in the kitchen, she ate supper and witnessed the changing of the guard. The Highlanders arrived. Each one gave her a smile before heading to the refrigerator for a bottle of blood. They waited their turn at the microwave, while they smiled at her and exchanged knowing looks.

Did she have a piece of lettuce stuck in her teeth? Finally the Scotsmen left to take up their posts for the evening. Connor remained behind, rinsing out bottles in the sink. She recalled seeing him do that before, but at the time, the significance hadn't registered.

"Why is everyone so happy?" Shanna asked from her seat at the kitchen table. "After the bombing last night, I thought a war was about to break out."

"Oh, aye, it will," Connor answered. "But when ye live as long as we have, ye lose a sense of urgency about it. We'll take care of Petrovsky soon enough. 'Tis a shame we didn't kill him in the Great War."

Shanna leaned forward. "There was a Great Vampire War?"

"Aye, in 1710." Connor closed the dishwasher, then leaned against the counter. His eyes grew hazy with memories. "I was there. So was Petrovsky, though not on the same side, ye ken."

"How did it happen?"

"Roman dinna tell you?"

"No. Was he involved?"

Connor snorted. "He started it."

Was that what Roman meant when he said he'd committed terrible crimes? "Will you tell me about it?"

"I suppose there's no harm in it." Connor wandered toward the kitchen table and took a seat. "The vampire who changed Roman was a verra nasty character named Casimir. He had a pack of vampires at his command, and together they were destroying whole villages, raping and murdering, torturing for the pleasure of it. Petrovsky was one of Casimir's favorite minions."

Shanna winced. Roman had been a gentle monk, dedicated to healing the poor. It was appalling to think of him thrust into the midst of such evil. "What happened to Roman?"

"Casimir was fascinated with him. He wanted to wrench every bit of goodness out of Roman, and turn him into pure evil. He . . . he did cruel things to Roman. Gave him terrible choices." Connor shook his head in disgust. "One time, Casimir captured two children and threatened to kill them both. He said Roman could save one of them if he would only kill the other one himself."

"Oh God." A wave of nausea swept through Shanna. No wonder Roman thought God had abandoned him.

"When Roman refused to partake in such perversity, Casimir flew into a rage. He and his pack of devils descended on Roman's monastery and murdered all the monks. Then they destroyed the buildings."

"Oh, no! All the monks? Even Roman's adopted father?" Shanna's heart ached at the thought.

"Aye. Ye ken, it wasna Roman's fault, but he still felt responsible."

No wonder Roman suffered so much from self-loathing. It wasn't his fault, but she could see why he would feel guilty. Karen's death hadn't been her fault, but she still blamed herself. "The ruined monastery—that's the painting on the fifth floor, isn't it?"

"Aye. Roman keeps it there to remind himself—"

"You mean torture himself." Shanna's eyes misted with tears. For how many centuries did he intend to whip himself over this?

"Aye." Connor nodded sadly. "It was the sight of the monastery and his dead brothers that instilled in Roman a purpose for his new and awful existence. He made a vow then to destroy Casimir and his evil followers. But he knew he couldna do it alone. So he sneaked away, traveling to the west, seeking out battlefields where the wounded lay dying in the dark. In 1513 he found Jean-Luc at the Battle of the Spurs in France and Angus at Flodden Field in Scotland. He transformed them, and they became his first allies."

"When did they find you?"

"At the battle of Solway Moss." Connor sighed. "There was never peace for long in my bonnie Scotland. It made a prime hunting ground for dying warriors. I had crawled under a tree to die. Roman found me and asked if I was willing to fight again for a noble cause. I was in so much pain, I doona remember much. I must have said yes, for Roman transformed me that night."

Shanna swallowed hard. "Do you resent what happened to you?"

Connor looked surprised. "Nay, lass. I was dying. Roman gave me a reason to exist. Angus was there, too. He changed over Ian. By 1710, Roman had acquired a large

army of vampires. Angus was his general. I was a captain."
Connor smiled proudly.

"And then you marched on Casimir?"

"Aye, it was a bloody war and raged on for three nights. Those who were wounded and too weak to move would fry when the sun rose. On the third night, shortly before sunrise, Casimir fell. His followers fled."

"And Petrovsky was one of them?"

"Aye. But we'll be getting him soon. Doona worry about that." Connor stood and stretched. "I'd best get to my rounds."

"I suppose Roman is up by now."

Connor grinned. "Aye. I'm sure he is." He strode from the kitchen, his red and green kilt swinging about his knees.

Shanna heaved a big sigh. So Roman had told the truth about his crimes. He had killed and transformed mortals into vampires. But he had transformed those who were already dying, and his purpose had been a noble one. He defeated Casimir, the evil vampire who enjoyed torturing innocent people.

It was a violent past Roman had, but it was one that she could accept. In spite of Casimir's attempts to vilify him, Roman had remained a good man. He'd always sought to protect the innocent and save mortals. Yet he was so filled with remorse, he believed God had abandoned him. She needed to get through to him somehow and ease his pain. Their personal relationship might be doomed, but she still cared about Roman, and she couldn't stand for him to suffer anymore. She wandered into the hall and headed for the stairs.

"Oh, Shanna!" Maggie stood at the opening to the parlor.

The double doors were open, and Shanna could see the harem inside. Aw, jeez. She really didn't want to see these women.

"Shanna, come on." Maggie grabbed her by the arm and tugged her toward the parlor. "Look, everybody! It's Shanna."

The harem girls all gave her glowing smiles.

What the hell were they up to? Shanna didn't trust their newfound friendliness one bit.

Vanda came forward with an apologetic smile. "I'm so sorry I was rude to you." She touched a lock of Shanna's hair. "This color suits you."

"Thank you." Shanna took a step back.

"Don't go." Maggie grabbed her arm. "Come in and join us."

"Yes," Vanda agreed. "We'd like to welcome you to the harem."

Shanna gasped. "Excuse me? I'm not joining your harem."

"But you and Roman—you are lovers now, *non?*" Simone curled up in the corner of the couch.

"I—I really don't think it's any of your business." How on earth did they know what had happened?

"Don't be so touchy," Vanda said. "We all like Roman."

"*Oui.*" Simone sipped from a wineglass. "I have come all ze way from Paris to be wiz him."

Anger sizzled in Shanna. Anger at Roman and these ladies, but mostly anger at herself. She shouldn't have gotten so involved with him while he still had all these women on the side. "What happens between Roman and myself is private."

Maggie shook her head. "It's very hard to be private amongst vampires. I overheard Roman when he asked to make love to you."

"What?" Shanna's heart lurched toward her throat.

"Maggie's very good at picking up thoughts," Vanda explained. "When she heard Roman, she alerted the rest of us, and we all asked Roman to let us join in on the fun."

"What?" Sparks of fire shot off in Shanna's head.

"Relax." Darcy gave her a worried look. "He didn't let them in."

"He was so h-rude!" Simone huffed.

"It was awful." Maggie crossed her arms, frowning. "We've waited so long for Roman to take an interest in sex again. And then, when he finally does, he wouldn't let us play."

"It was terrible." Vanda sighed. "We're his harem. We have a right to share vampire sex with him, but he blocked us out."

Shanna stared at them, agape, with her heart pounding in her chest.

"I do declare," the Southern belle said, "I have never felt so rejected in all my life."

"You—" Shanna struggled to breathe. "All of you tried to join us?"

Vanda shrugged. "Once someone initiates vampire sex, anyone can join in."

"That's how it's supposed to be," Maggie agreed. "We asked twice to participate, but Roman kept blocking us out."

"He even fussed at us." Simone pouted on the couch.

"There was so much arguing and mental shouting going on," Maggie continued, "that even the Highlanders got into the fight and told us to leave Roman alone."

Shanna groaned inwardly. No wonder the Scotsmen had been smiling at her. Did everyone in the house know what she and Roman had been doing? Her face heated up.

"You will have sex again tonight, *non*?" Simone asked.

"That's why we want you to join the harem," Maggie said with a friendly smile.

"Yes." Vanda smiled, too. "Then, Roman can make love to all of us."

"No, no." Shanna shook her head and backed away. "Never!" She ran before the harem could see any tears on her face. Damn! Now she knew why Roman had disappeared twice last night. He'd put her on hold in order to answer the deluge of mental calls from his harem. The whole time he'd been making psychic love to her, he'd been forced to expend mental energy to block the harem out. It was like they were making love with a bunch of peeping Toms trying to see in the window.

She ran up the stairs to the first floor. Shock turned to horror, then to raw pain. How could she have gotten herself into such a horrid mess?

By the time she reached the second floor, tears were streaming down her face. How could she have been so stupid? She should have never let Roman into her head. Or into her bed. And certainly not into her heart. When she reached the third floor, the pain morphed into anger. That damned harem! And damned Roman. How dare he keep a harem while claiming to care about her? On the fourth floor, she headed to her room, then stopped. The anger was burning at full blaze, too hot to be controlled. She stormed up to the fifth floor.

The guard there gave her a knowing smile.

She wanted to slap that smile off his face. She gritted her teeth. "I'd like to see Roman."

"Aye, lass." The Highlander opened Roman's office door.

She strode inside and shut the door. Roman might have survived the Great Vampire War of 1710, but he was about to face an even worse terror.

A mortal female in full rage.

Twenty

Roman lay in bed thinking, and foremost in his thoughts was Shanna. Last night had been wonderful, but at the same time aggravating. He'd had to expend too much energy blocking out those women downstairs. God's blood, he hated being stuck with them. He didn't even know all their names. He'd never spent any real time with them. During vampire sex, he'd simply imagined making love to a woman's body. It might have felt good to the harem ladies, but the body he imagined might as well have belonged to VANNA. It wasn't real. It wasn't any of them.

It wasn't even Shanna. That, too, had annoyed him. He had imagined Shanna in his mind, but he knew it wasn't really her. He didn't know what she looked like naked, and now his imagination wasn't enough. He wanted the real thing. And he believed she did, too. Last night she had complained about not being able to touch him or hold him.

He had to complete that formula he was working on. If he could stay awake during the day, he could protect Shanna around the clock. He could also be alone with her at a time when other vampires couldn't interfere. And if he could convince Shanna to live with him, then his ability to be awake during the day would allow her to maintain a more normal lifestyle.

He jumped out of bed and took a hot shower. He wanted to see her tonight, but he also needed to go to Romatech. The rest of the week would be filled with the conference. He, Angus, and Jean-Luc needed a plan of action for dealing with the Malcontents, particularly now that they knew Petrovsky was their leader. And getting rid of Petrovsky would not only make the world safer for law-abiding, modern Vamps, but safer for Shanna.

Roman smiled to himself. Even with a vampire war imminent, he couldn't keep his mind off her. She was so different. So raw and honest with her emotions. While in her mind, he'd tried to detect her feelings for him. She was adjusting fairly well to the reality of his being a vampire, mostly because she had such a kind, compassionate heart. When he called her *sweetness*, he meant it. She had a true, sweet nature that he loved.

He chuckled as he toweled himself dry. She could also be fearless and feisty when upset. He loved that about her, too. He hoped with all his heart that she could fall in love with him. That would be perfect, since he was already in love with her.

He'd realized it the moment he saw her at the ball, hot pink in a sea of black and white. She was life, she was color, she was his true love. Somehow, he sensed that if she could love him and accept him, even with his soul blackened with sin, then all was not lost. If there was something remotely lovable about him, he could hope for forgiveness. He'd wanted to tell her last night that he loved her, but had refrained. He needed to be with her in person to make such a confession.

He leaned over to tug on some boxer shorts. Black dots circled his head. Damn, he was hungry. He should have eaten before showering, but thoughts about Shanna had distracted him. Wearing only his underwear, he padded into his office and retrieved a bottle of blood from the mini-fridge. God's blood, he was starving so much, he was ready to drink it cold.

He heard the office door shut and glanced back. *Shanna.* Smiling, he unscrewed the top from his bottle. "Good evening."

No answer.

He glanced back again. She was stalking toward him, her cheeks glistening with tears, her eyes swollen, red, and . . . furious. "What's wrong, darling?"

"Everything!" She was breathing heavily, and rage was practically seething from her pores. "I'm not putting up with this anymore."

"Okay." He put the bottle down. "It appears I did something wrong, though I'm not sure what."

"Everything is wrong! It's wrong for you to have a harem. It's sick that you left me in bed on hold while you talked to them. And it's really disgusting that they wanted to join us in some kind of mental orgy!"

He winced. "I wouldn't have allowed that. What we had together was totally private."

"It was *not*! They knew we were making love. And they kept banging on the door wanting in."

He groaned inwardly. Those damned women. "I gather you've been talking to the other women again."

"*Your* other women. Your *harem*." Her eyes narrowed with seething anger. "Do you know they invited me to join them?"

God's blood.

"And do you know why? They want me in the harem so they can join us next time in bed! Like one giant psychic love fest. Ooh, talk about your multiple orgasms. I can't wait!"

"You're being sarcastic, right?"

"Aaargh!" She raised clenched fists in the air.

He gritted his teeth. "Look, Shanna, I expended a huge amount of energy to keep what happened between us private." And all that spent energy had left him starving.

"It wasn't private! Even the Highlanders knew what we were doing. You knew that everyone knew, but you still made love to me."

He stepped toward her, his anger spiking. "No one heard what happened between us. It *was* private. Only I heard you moan and cry out. Only I felt your body shuddering when—"

"Stop it. I shouldn't have done it. Not when you have a harem wanting to join us."

Roman balled his fists, fighting for control, but it was damned hard when he was starving. "There is nothing I can do about them. They wouldn't know how to survive on their own."

"You're kidding me! How many centuries old do they need to be before they can grow up?"

"They were raised in times when women weren't taught any job skills. They're helpless, and I'm responsible for them."

"Do you really want them?"

"No! I inherited them when I became coven master in 1950. I can't even remember all their names. I've spent all my time building Romatech and working in my lab."

"Well, if you don't want them, pass them on to someone else. There must be plenty of lonely vampire men around just dying for a good, *dead* woman to keep them company."

Roman's anger started to sizzle again. "I happen to be one of those *dead* people, too."

She crossed her arms over her chest. "You and I are . . . different. I don't think this is going to work out."

"I thought we did very well last night." God's blood, she wasn't going to leave him. He wouldn't let her. And they *were* alike. She understood him like no one else.

"I can't—I won't make love to you again when there's a bunch of women trying to join us. I won't stand for it."

Anger sliced into him fresh and raw. "You can't convince me you didn't enjoy it. I *know* you did. I was in your head."

"That was last night. Now all I can feel is embarrassment."

Roman swallowed hard. "Are you ashamed of what you did? Are you ashamed of me?"

"No! I'm angry that those women have a claim to you, that they think they have every right to join us in the bedroom."

"I won't let them! They don't matter, Shanna. I'll block them out."

"You shouldn't have to block them out, because they shouldn't be here at all! Don't you get it? I refuse to share you with *them*. They have to go!"

Roman's breath caught in his throat. God's blood, *that* was the real problem. Not that she was ashamed or didn't care. She did care. She did want him. She wanted him all to herself.

She stepped back, her eyes wide. "I . . . I shouldn't have said that."

"But it's true."

"No." She backed toward his desk. "I . . . I don't have any claim to you. And I shouldn't expect you to totally change your lifestyle for me. I mean, this relationship probably can't work anyway."

"Yes, it can." He strode toward her. "You want me. You want all my love, all my passion just for you."

She retreated another step and bumped into the velvet chaise. "I should be going."

"You don't want to share me, do you, Shanna? You want me all to yourself."

Her eyes flashed. "Well, I don't always get what I want, do I?"

He grabbed her by the shoulders. "This time, you will."

He lifted her and set her bottom on the high curved end of the red velvet chaise.

"What—?"

He gave her a little push, and she fell back.

"What are you doing?" She struggled to sit up and managed to prop herself on her elbows. Her hips were still elevated on the higher end of the chaise.

He pulled off her white Nikes and dropped them on the floor. "Just you and me, Shanna. No one will know what we're doing."

"But—"

"Complete privacy." He unzipped her pants and dragged them down her legs. "Just like you wanted."

"Wait a minute! This is different. This is . . . *real.*"

"You're damned right it is. And I'm ready for it." He noted her red lace panties. God's blood. Real sex.

"We have to think about this."

"Think fast." He took a hold of the red lace. " 'Cause these are coming off."

She looked at him, her eyes wide, her chest heaving with quick breaths. "You—your eyes are red. They're glowing."

"It means I'm ready to make love."

She gulped. Her gaze drifted down to his bare chest. "It would be an important step forward."

"I know." He rubbed the pad of his thumb over the lace. Actual, physical sex with a mortal. "If you tell me to stop, I will. I've never wanted to hurt you, Shanna."

She collapsed back. "Oh God." She covered her face.

"Well? Shall we make it real?"

She lowered her hands and looked him in the face. A light shiver ran down her body. She whispered, "Lock the door."

A storm of strong emotions surged through Roman—excitement, desire, and most of all, relief. She hadn't given up on him. In a swoosh, he zoomed to the door, locked it, and returned to her.

As he came to a standstill, black dots circled his head. Using vampire speed had drained too much of his energy, and he needed what little energy he had left for Shanna. He lifted a foot and peeled off her sock. One foot at a time now. This was real, so he was confined to only two hands. No mind tricks.

Her feet were a little different from what he had imagined. Longer and slimmer. Her second toe was as long as her big toe. These little details hadn't entered his imagination last night, but now, now they seemed paramount. This was the real Shanna, not an erotic dream. And no dream could ever compare to her in real life.

He clasped an ankle and lifted her leg. It was long and beautifully shaped. He ran an appreciative hand over her calf. Her skin was as soft as he had imagined, but once again, there were details he hadn't expected. A few freckles above her knee, and on the inside of her thigh, a small, flat mole.

It drew him like a magnet. He pressed his lips against it. The warmth of Shanna's skin surprised him. This was new. Different. Vampires didn't generate much heat, so during all his years of vampire sex, he had never imagined body heat. Or smell. Her skin smelled of clean, fresh woman and . . . life. Life-giving blood. A large vein throbbed just under her skin. Type A Positive. He rubbed his nose against her inner thigh, enjoying the rich, metallic scent.

Stop! He turned his head to rest his cheek against her thigh. He had to stop before instinct took over and his fangs sprang out. In fact, just to be safe, he should drink a quick bottle of blood before continuing.

But then his nostrils flared with another scent. Not blood, but equally intoxicating. It was coming from beneath her panties. *Arousal.* God's blood, it was sweet. He could have never imagined such a potent fragrance. His groin swelled, straining against his cotton boxers. Her scent lured him in until his nose was pressed against the lace.

Shanna gasped. Her body shuddered.

Roman straightened, standing between her legs. He grasped the top edge of her underwear and drew the fabric down a few inches. His knuckles were nestled in a mass of curly hair.

He stared. God's blood, he should have known. After all, she came in color. His gaze met hers. "You're a redhead?"

"I . . . guess." She licked her lips. "Some call it strawberry blond."

"Reddish gold." He rubbed his knuckles against the springy hair. The texture was different—coarse, curly, exciting. He smiled at her. "I should have realized. You have the temper of a redhead."

She gave him a wry look. "I had every right to be furious."

He shrugged. "Vampire sex is overrated. This . . ." He glanced down at his fingers entwined in her curls. "This is much better." He slipped a finger into the moist cleft.

With a gasp, she started. "Oh God, what you do to me." She pressed a hand to her chest as if to ease her breathing. "You don't . . . make me react like this, do you? I mean, last night, when you were in my head . . ."

"I planted the sensations in your mind. Your reactions were your own." He burrowed his finger deeper into the wet heat until he was rubbing against the slick nubbin.

She let out a long moan.

"Your reactions are so beautiful." His finger was drenched. The scent wafted up to him, heady and rich. His groin hardened, urging him to get on with it. He eased her underwear over her hips and down her legs, then dropped it on the floor.

She welcomed him between her legs, spreading them for him, then wrapping them around his waist. His erection was damned uncomfortable, but before he did anything, he wanted to see her. He bent over and brushed back the damp curls. There, there was the sweet flesh, swollen and glistening with the dew of her own desire. Desire for him. It was almost too much to bear. He clamped down on his own raging need. Not yet.

He wanted to taste her first.

He slipped his hands under her rump and lifted her to his mouth. She cried out. Her legs wrapped tighter about him, then trembled with each slow lick. He began a tender exploration, but soon, Shanna's little cries incited him to push it harder and faster. She dug her heels into him and writhed against him. He held on to her hips and applied vampire speed to his tongue.

With a jolt, she screamed. A gush of her sweet fragrance covered his face. She was quivering in her release, panting for breath. Her swollen sex was pressed against him. Engorged, red, and pulsating with blood. He turned his head, trying to escape the inevitable reaction. But her thigh squeezed against his nose, the blood in her vein throbbing against his skin.

The instinct to survive roared through him. His fangs sprang forth, and he sank them into the rich vein of her inner thigh. Her blood filled his mouth. Her scream filled his ears, but he couldn't stop. The hunger-lust was upon him, and he couldn't remember ever tasting such rich, delicious blood. She yelled and struggled to pull away. He clasped her leg to his mouth and drew a long, succulent gulp.

"Roman, stop!" She kicked him with her free leg.

He froze. God's blood. What had he done? He had sworn never to bite a mortal again. He ripped his fangs out. Blood dripped from the punctures on her leg.

She squirmed on the chaise to put distance between them. "Get away from me!"

"Sha—" He realized his fangs were still extended. With the last, dying remnants of his strength, he forced his fangs to recede. They didn't want to. He was so hungry. So damned weak. He needed to get to the counter where he'd left a bottle of blood.

Something trickled down his chin. *Her blood.* Goddammit, no wonder she was watching him with such a stricken look of horror. He must look like a monster.

He *was* a monster. And he'd bitten the woman he loved.

Twenty-one

He'd bitten her.

Shanna saw him wandering toward the wet bar as if nothing was wrong. Nothing? That was *her* blood on his face. She stared at the punctures on her left thigh. Thank God, he'd stopped before draining her dry. Otherwise, she'd be in a coma right now, waiting to be transformed.

Oh God. She lowered her head into her hands. What did she expect? Dance with the devil, and you're going to get burned. Surprisingly enough, it didn't burn, didn't even sting. The pain had been short-lived. It was the shock that had terrified her. The shock of seeing his fangs spring out, of feeling them pop through her skin. And then she'd seen his fangs dripping with her own blood. At least she hadn't fainted. Her instinct for survival had kicked in.

He had lost complete control. Normally she would love the notion that she could totally unhinge a man during sex. Who wouldn't want that kind of sexual power? But unhinging Roman meant unleashing a vampire who thought she was breakfast.

Oh God, how could such a relationship work? As much as her heart longed for Roman, the only safe way to deal with him was at a distance. She could accept his protection for the time being, but not his passion.

And that hurt. It hurt a lot more than the damn pricks in her leg. Why did he have to be a vampire? He was such a wonderful man. He would be perfect for her if he weren't dead. She gazed at the ceiling. *Why? All I wanted was a normal life, and You give me a vampire? What kind of divine justice is that?*

A loud *thud* was her response. Shanna twisted on the chaise to look behind her. Roman had collapsed on the floor a few feet from the wet bar.

"Roman?" She stood. He lay still, facedown on the carpet.

"Roman?" She approached him slowly.

With a moan, he rolled onto his back. "I . . . need . . . blood."

Good God, he looked terrible. He must be starving. He couldn't have taken much from her. She spotted the bottle on the counter. *Blood.* A full bottle. Yeech. She didn't want to do this. She could dress and bring in the guard from outside. She glanced at Roman. His eyes were shut, his skin pale as death. He couldn't wait. She had to take action. Now.

She stood there frozen, her heart hammering in her chest. For a second, she felt as if she were back behind the potted plants, watching Karen die. And she had done nothing. She'd let fear keep her from helping Karen. She couldn't do that again.

She swallowed hard and walked toward the bottle of blood. When she reached the counter, the smell of it brought back wretched memories. Her best friend lying in a puddle of blood. She turned her head, trying not to breathe in the aroma. She had another friend now, and he needed this. She closed her hand around the bottle. It was cold. Should she warm it up so it would taste fresh? Her stomach churned at the thought.

"Shanna."

She glanced toward him. Roman was struggling to sit up. Good God, the man was so weak. So vulnerable. Maybe it wasn't surprising that he'd bitten her when he needed blood so badly. It was more surprising that he'd managed to pull away from her. He'd put himself at risk.

"I'm coming." She knelt beside him. With one arm, she supported his shoulders, and with the other, she lifted the bottle to his mouth. *Blood.* Bile rose in her throat. Her hand trembled, and a few drops rolled down his chin. A memory flashed of blood oozing from Karen's mouth. "Oh God." Her hand shook.

Roman reached up to steady her hand, but his was shaking, too. He drank long and deep, his throat moving with each gulp.

"Are you helping me do this? Mentally?" He'd used mind control at the dentist office to help her overcome her fear.

He lowered the bottle. "No. I wouldn't have the strength." He raised the bottle back to his mouth.

So she was overcoming her fear on her own. She still felt a little nauseated, watching him guzzle down cold blood, but she hadn't fainted.

"I'm better now. Thank you." He raised the bottle one more time and finished the last of the contents.

"Okay." She straightened. "I guess I'll be going then."

"Wait." He rose slowly to his feet. "Let me . . ." He took her arm. "I want to take care of you."

"I'm all right." She didn't know whether to laugh or cry. She was standing there half-naked with holes in her thigh. Maybe it was shock. It felt more like grief. Like a heavy, black stone, crushing her heart and constantly reminding her that a relationship with a vampire could never work.

"Come." He led her into his bedroom.

She glanced sadly at his king-sized bed. If only he were

mortal. By the looks of his bedroom, he was neat and orderly. He drew her into the bathroom. And look, he even kept the toilet seat down. Who could ask for more? If only he were alive.

He turned on the water faucet above the sink. There were no mirrors, just an oil painting of a pretty landscape. Green hills, red flowers, and a brilliant sun. Maybe he missed seeing the sun. It would be hard to live without the sun.

He dampened a washcloth and leaned over to clean her thigh. The warm cloth felt soothing. She had a sudden urge to simply fold up and collapse on the floor.

"I'm so sorry, Shanna. This won't happen again."

No, it wouldn't. Her eyes filled with tears. No more loving, no more passion. She couldn't afford to love a vampire.

"Does it hurt?"

She looked away so he couldn't see the gathering tears.

"I guess it does." He straightened. "It should have never happened. I haven't bitten anyone in eighteen years, not since the introduction of synthetic blood. Well, that's not quite true. There was one emergency transformation. Gregori."

"Radinka told me about it. You didn't want to do it."

"No." Roman dug through a drawer and removed two Band-Aids. "I didn't want to condemn his immortal soul."

Spoken like a true medieval monk. Shanna's heart ached for him. He obviously thought his own soul was damned.

He tore open the wrappers. "A vampire is always the hungriest when he first awakes in the evening. I was just about to eat when you came in. I should have had a bottle before making love." He attached the Band-Aids over her wounds. "From now on, we make sure I eat first."

There was no *from now on*. "I . . . I can't."

"Can't what?"

He looked so worried. And so damned beautiful. Color had seeped back into his skin. His shoulders were broad.

His chest was bare with a mat of black hair that looked so soft and touchable. His golden-brown eyes watched her steadily.

Shanna blinked back the tears. "I can't . . . believe you have a toilet." Chicken, she chided herself. But she hated to hurt him. She hated to hurt herself.

He looked surprised. "Oh, well, I use it."

"You use a toilet?"

"Yes. Our bodies only require red blood cells. Stuff like plasma and the added ingredients from Fusion Cuisine are all unnecessary and become waste."

"Oh." That was really more than she needed to know.

He tilted his head. "Are you all right?"

"Sure." She turned and left the bathroom, aware that he was watching her naked rump. So much for a graceful exit. She crossed his office to the pile of clothes on the floor.

She was dressed and sitting on the chaise, tying her shoes, when he came into the office. He removed another bottle from the mini-fridge and popped it into the microwave. He was fully dressed now—black jeans and a gray polo shirt. His face was washed, his hair brushed. He was absolutely beautiful and apparently still hungry.

The microwave dinged and he poured the warmed blood into a glass. "I owe you my thanks." Sipping from the glass, he strode toward the desk. "I shouldn't have allowed myself to get so hungry. You were very kind to help me after . . . what I did."

"You mean after biting me?"

"Yes." He looked irritated as he sat behind his desk. "I prefer to look at the positive side of this."

"You're kidding, right?"

"No. A few nights ago, you fainted at the mere sight of blood. I had to help you through the dental procedure, or you would have fainted again. But tonight you fed me blood. You're conquering your fear, Shanna. That's something to be proud of."

Well, yes. She was making definite progress.

"And we have proof of what an excellent dentist you are."

"How's that?"

"You implanted my fang, and it's working perfectly."

She snorted. "Right. I have the marks to prove it."

"That was an unfortunate mistake, but it's good to know the tooth is fixed. You did a great job."

"Oh yeah. It would be terrible for you to have only one working fang. Your friends might want to call you Lefty."

He raised his eyebrows. "I suppose you're angry." He took a deep breath. "I suppose I deserve it."

She wasn't angry. She was hurt, sad, and tired. Tired of trying to adjust to every shocking event that had occurred in the last few days. A part of her just wanted to crawl into bed and never come out. How could she even begin to explain how she felt? "I—" She was saved by a sudden rattling of the doorknob.

"Roman?" Gregori knocked on the door. "What's the deal with locking the door? We have an appointment."

"Damn, I forgot," Roman muttered. "Excuse me." He zipped to the door, turned the lock, then zipped back to the desk.

Shanna's mouth fell open. Vampire speed was so disconcerting to watch. Though it certainly came in handy during sex. She blushed. She couldn't afford to think about sex. Not when it was followed by sharp fangs and loss of blood.

"Hey, bro." Gregori strolled into the office with a portfolio under his arm. He was dressed in formal evening wear, complete with a dashing cape. "I have the presentation ready for our solution to the poor problem. Hey, sweetcakes." He nodded in Shanna's direction.

"Hi." She stood. "I should be going."

"I don't mind. In fact, I'd like your opinion." Gregori removed some large cards from his portfolio and propped the bottom edge of the stack on Roman's desk.

Shanna sat as she read the first one. *How to encourage poor Vamps to drink synthetic blood.*

Roman glanced at Shanna. "It's been difficult to persuade the poor to buy synthetic blood when they can get all they want fresh. And for free."

"You mean they can go straight to the food source—mortals." She frowned at him. "Like me."

He returned her gaze with a look that said, *Get over it.*

Gregori looked from one to the other. "Am I interrupting something?"

"No." Shanna motioned toward the posters. "Please continue."

With a smile, Gregori started his pitch. "The mission at Romatech Industries is to make the world safer for mortals and vampires alike. I know I speak for all of us at Romatech when I say I would never want to harm a mortal." He turned the first card facedown, so that the second card was revealed.

There were two words. *Cheap. Convenient.* Shanna could only hope they weren't referring to her.

"I believe these two factors are the solution to our poor problem," Gregori continued. "I've discussed the cheap factor with Laszlo, and he's had a brilliant idea. Since we only need red blood cells in order to survive, Laszlo plans to formulate a mixture of red blood cells and water. It would be much cheaper to produce than the normal synthetic blood or one of your Fusion Cuisine drinks."

Roman nodded. "It's also likely to taste like swill."

"We'll work on the taste. Now, for the convenience factor." Gregori revealed the next poster in his presentation. It showed a building with a drive-through window.

"This is a Vamp restaurant," he explained. "The menu will include Fusion Cuisine favorites like Chocolood and Blood Lite, but it will also have the new, cheaper mixture. The meals will be warmed up and served quickly."

Shanna blinked. "A fast-food restaurant?"

"Exactly!" Gregori nodded at her. "And with our new mixture of red blood cells and water, it'll be very cheap."

"A vampire value meal! What will you call the place? Bat in a Box? Vampire King?" To Shanna's surprise, a giggle escaped.

Gregori chuckled. "You're good at this."

Roman wasn't laughing. He was watching Shanna curiously.

She ignored him and pointed at the drive-through window. "Won't it be dangerous to have a drive-through? I mean, a normal human could get in line, thinking it's a real restaurant, and then see that the menu has nothing but blood. That would sorta blow your big secret, wouldn't it?"

"She has a valid point," Roman said.

"I know what to do." She raised her hands, imagining the restaurant. "You rent an upper floor, like ten floors up, and put the drive-through up there. That way, you couldn't have real people getting in line."

Gregori looked confused. "Ten floors up?"

"Yes! It would be a fly-through window." Shanna burst into laughter.

Gregori exchanged a look with Roman. "But we don't fly."

Roman stood. "I think you have some good ideas, Gregori. Have Laszlo start on the formula for the . . . value meal."

Shanna covered her mouth, but more giggles escaped.

Roman gave her a worried look. "And begin research on a suitable rental property."

"You got it, boss." Gregori slid the posters back into his portfolio. "I'm going out clubbing with Simone tonight. For research purposes, of course. I'll be investigating the most popular vampire hangouts to see what works best."

"That's fine. Try to keep Simone out of trouble."

Gregori nodded. "Will do. You know, she's only going out with me because she's trying to make you jealous."

Suddenly Shanna didn't feel so giggly. She glared at Roman.

He had the grace to look embarrassed. "I made it clear to her that I'm not interested."

"Yeah, I know." Gregori started toward the door, then stopped. "Oh, I thought I'd arrange for a market survey tomorrow night at Romatech. Have a focus group of poor Vamps come in and fill out a questionnaire about the new restaurant. I'll spread the news tonight at the Vamp clubs."

"Sounds good." Roman walked toward the door.

Gregori glanced at Shanna. "Hey, you're good at this stuff. Would you like to help with the research study tomorrow night?"

"Me?"

"Yeah. It would be at Romatech, so you'd be safe." Gregori shrugged. "Just an idea. It would give you something to do."

Shanna considered the alternative, which was hanging around Roman's house with the harem. "Yeah. I'd like that. Thank you."

"Sure." Gregori tucked his portfolio under his arm. "Well, I'm off for a night on the town. This cape is cool, huh? Jean-Luc loaned it to me."

She smiled. "You're looking hot, dude."

Gregori strutted toward the door. "I'm too sexy for my cape, too sexy for my fangs. Too sexy." He whirled in a circle, then struck a disco pose with a hand pointing at the ceiling. "Too sexy!" He left with a flourish of his cape.

Shanna grinned. "I think he enjoys being a vampire."

Roman closed the door and returned to his desk. "He's a true modern-day Vamp. He's never had to bite in order to survive."

She snorted. "You mean he's so young, he's completely bottle-fed?"

Roman smiled as he sat behind his desk. "If you ever want to upset him, just tell him disco is dead."

Shanna laughed, but when she looked at Roman, the tragedy of their situation jolted through her and abruptly cut off her laughter. How could their relationship ever work? She would grow old while he stayed young. She doubted she could ever have children with him or the normal life she wanted. And he couldn't make love to her without wanting to bite her. It was impossible.

Roman leaned forward. "Are you all right?"

"Sure," it came out a bit high-pitched and squeaky. Tears clouded her eyes, and she looked away.

"You've been through an awful lot the last few days. Your life has been threatened. Your reality has been . . ."

"Destroyed?"

He winced. "I was going to say altered. You know about the vampire world now, but the mortal world is much the same as it always was."

It would never be the same. Shanna sniffed, trying to hold back the tears. "All I ever wanted was a normal life. I wanted to set down roots in a community and feel like I belonged there. I wanted a normal, steady job. A normal, steady husband." A tear rolled down her cheek, and she quickly brushed it away. "I wanted a big house, with a big yard, and a picket fence, and a big dog. And . . ." Another tear escaped. "I wanted children."

"Those are good things to want," Roman whispered.

"Yes." She wiped her cheeks and avoided looking at him.

"You don't think we have a future, do you?"

She shook her head. She heard his chair squeak and ventured a quick glance. He was leaning back, staring at the ceiling. He seemed calm on the surface, but she could see the muscles rippling in his jaw as he ground his teeth.

"Maybe I should go now." She stood on shaky legs.

"A normal, steady husband," he muttered. He leaned forward, pinning her with a pair of angry eyes. "You have too

much life, too much intelligence in you for a boring husband. You need passion in your life. You need someone
who challenges your mind, who makes you scream in bed."
He rose to his feet. "You need *me*."

"Like a hole in my head. Or in my case, a hole in my
leg."

"I'm not going to bite you again!"

"You can't help it!" Tears streamed down her face. "It's
in your nature."

He sat in his chair, his face pale. "You believe it is my
nature to be evil?"

"No!" She wiped her cheeks angrily. "I think you're
good and honorable and . . . almost perfect. I know normally you would never want to hurt anyone. But when
we're making love, there will come a point where you'll
lose control. I've seen it. Your eyes glow red, and your
teeth—"

"It won't happen again. I'll drink a full bottle before
making love to you."

"You can't help it. You . . . you have too much passion."

He clenched his fists. "There's a good reason for that."

"You can't guarantee you won't bite me again. It's
just . . . who you are."

"I give you my word. Here." Using a pencil, he dragged
the silver cross and chain across his desk. "Put this on. I
won't even be able to embrace you, much less bite you."

With a sigh, Shanna looped the chain around her neck.
"I guess I need silver ring toes and a pair of silver garters.
Oh, and a silver belly ring and nipple rings."

"Don't you dare pierce your beautiful body."

"Why not? You did."

He flinched.

Jeez. Now she was hurting him. "I'm sorry. I'm not handling this well."

"You're doing fine, but you've been through too much

lately. All that giggling with Gregori—I think you're feeling a bit . . . shaky right now. You should get some rest."

"Maybe so." Shanna lifted the crucifix to examine it. "How old is this cross?"

"Father Constantine gave it to me when I was ordained."

"It's lovely." She pressed it against her chest and took a deep breath. "Connor told me what happened to the monks. I'm so very sorry. You have to know it wasn't your fault."

He closed his eyes and rubbed his brow. "You said we were different, but we're not. We're so much alike. You feel the same way about your friend who was murdered. We have an emotional connection and a strong psychic one, too. You can't ignore that."

The tears threatened to overflow again. "I'm sorry. I do want you to be happy. After all you've been through, you deserve happiness."

"So do you. I'm not giving up on us, Shanna."

A tear slipped down her cheek. "It would never work. You'll be young and beautiful forever. And I'll grow old and gray."

"I don't care. It doesn't matter."

She sniffed. "Of course it matters."

"Shanna." He stood and rounded the desk. "You will still be you. And I love you."

Twenty-two

Ten minutes later, Roman teleported to Radinka's office at Romatech.

She looked up from her work. "There you are. You're running late. Angus and Jean-Luc are waiting in your office."

"Fine. Radinka, I need you to research something for me."

"Sure." She leaned forward, resting her elbows on her desk. "What is it?"

"I think I should buy some new property."

"For another facility? That's a good idea, what with these Malcontents going around, blowing things up. By the way, I went ahead and ordered a transfer of synthetic blood from your Illinois plant."

"Thank you."

Radinka picked up a pen and legal pad. "So, where do you want the new plant?"

Frowning, Roman shifted his weight. "It's not a plant. I need a . . . house. A big house."

Radinka's brows lifted, but she scribbled his request on the pad. "Any specifications, other than *big*?"

"It needs to be in a nice community, not too far from here. Picket fence, big yard, big dog."

She tapped the tip of the pen on the pad. "I don't believe dogs are normally included in the purchase of a house."

"I'm aware of that." He crossed his arms, irritated by the amusement on Radinka's face. "But I'll need to know where to buy a big dog, or maybe a puppy that will grow into a big dog."

"What kind of dog, may I ask?"

"A *big* one." He gritted his teeth. "Get me some pictures of different breeds. And different houses for sale. I won't be the one making the final selection."

"Ah." Radinka's smile widened. "Does this mean things are going well between you and Shanna?"

"No, they're not. I'll probably end up using the house as a rental property."

Radinka's smile withered. "Then perhaps this idea is premature. If you push her too fast, she might run."

She might run anyway, Roman thought with a groan. "More than anything she wants a normal life and a normal husband." With a grimace, he shrugged one shoulder. "I'm not exactly normal."

Radinka's mouth twitched. "I suppose not, but after fifteen years at Romatech, I'm not sure what normal is anymore."

"I can give her a normal house and a normal dog."

"You're trying to buy normalcy? She'll see through that."

"I'm hoping she'll see that I'm trying to make her dreams come true. I'll try to give her as normal a life as I can."

Radinka frowned, considering. "I think what any woman really wants is to be loved."

"She has that. I just told her that I love her."

"Wonderful!" Radinka's smile faded once again. "You don't look very happy."

"That could be because she ran from my room, crying."

"Oh dear. I'm not usually wrong about these things."

Roman sighed. He'd often wondered if Radinka was truly a psychic, why the hell didn't she foresee the attack on her son? Unless she'd also foreseen that Gregori would become a vampire.

Radinka tapped her pen on the legal pad. "I am certain she is the one for you."

"I'm convinced of that, too. I know she cares for me very deeply, or she wouldn't have—"

Radinka raised her eyebrows, waiting for him to finish the sentence.

He shifted his weight. "If you could look for a house, I'd appreciate it. I'm late for a meeting."

Radinka's mouth twitched once again. "She'll come around. It'll work out just fine." She swiveled her chair to face her computer. "I'll start house hunting right away."

"Thank you." He headed out the door.

"And you'll need to fire your harem!" Radinka called after him.

Roman winced. They were a big problem. He'd have to give them financial support until they could make it on their own.

He strode into his office. "Good evening, Angus, Jean-Luc."

Angus jumped to his feet. He was back to wearing his usual green and blue MacKay tartan. "Ye took yer time getting here, man. We have to deal with these bloody Malcontents right away."

Jean-Luc remained seated, but raised a hand in greeting. *"Bonsoir, mon ami."*

"Have you decided anything?" Roman skirted his desk and sat.

"The time for discussion is over." Angus paced across the room. "With the explosion last night, the Malcontents have declared war. My Highlanders are ready to strike. I say we do it tonight."

"I disagree," Jean-Luc cut in. "Petrovsky is, no doubt, prepared for such a retaliation. We would be attacking his house in Brooklyn, leaving us in the open while they can take cover. Why should we give those bastards the advantage?"

"My men are no' afraid," Angus growled.

"Neither am I." Jean-Luc's blue eyes flashed. "This is not about fear. It's about being practical. If you and your Highlanders weren't always so hotheaded, you wouldn't have lost so many battles in the past."

"I am not hotheaded!" Angus thundered.

Roman held up his hands. "Can we take this down a notch? The explosion last night didn't hurt anyone. And though I agree that Petrovsky must be dealt with, I am reluctant to engage in an all-out war in front of mortal witnesses."

"*Exactement.*" Jean-Luc shifted in his chair. "I say we watch Petrovsky and his men, and when we find one or two of them alone, then we kill them."

Angus snorted. "'Tis no' an honorable way for a warrior to behave."

Jean-Luc stood slowly. "If you're insinuating that *I* have no honor, I'll have to challenge you to a duel."

Roman groaned. Five hundred years of listening to these two argue was enough to strain the best of friendships. "Can we kill Petrovsky first, before you two kill each other?"

Angus and Jean-Luc laughed.

"Since we are in disagreement, as usual," Jean-Luc said as he sat back down, "you will cast the deciding vote."

Roman nodded. "I'm with Jean-Luc on this one. A full attack on a house in Brooklyn is going to draw too much attention. And it puts too many of the Highlanders at risk."

"We doona mind," Angus grumbled as he returned to his chair.

"I mind," Roman said. "I've known you all for a long time."

"We are also limited in number," Jean-Luc added. "I

haven't transformed a vampire since the French Revolution. And you?"

"Not since Culloden," Angus answered. "But vampires like Petrovsky are still transforming men with evil hearts."

"And thus, making more evil vampires." Jean-Luc sighed. "For once, *mon ami*, we are *en accord*. Their numbers are growing while ours are not."

Angus nodded. "We need to make more vampires."

"Absolutely not!" Roman was alarmed by the turn of the conversation. "I will not condemn more souls to hell."

"I'll do it." Angus brushed back a strand of auburn hair. "I'm sure there are honorable soldiers dying somewhere in this world who would welcome the chance to continue fighting evil."

Roman leaned forward. "It's not the same as it was three hundred years ago. Modern armies keep up with their soldiers. Even the dead ones. They would notice if some went missing."

"Missing in action." Jean-Luc shrugged. "It happens. I'm with Angus on this one."

Roman rubbed his brow, dismayed at the thought of growing another vampire army. "Can we table this discussion for the time being? Let's take care of Petrovsky first."

Jean-Luc nodded. "Agreed."

"All right." Angus frowned. "Now, we need to talk about the problem with the CIA and their Stake-Out team. There's only five of them, so we shouldna have trouble handling them."

Roman winced. "I don't want them killed."

Angus snorted. "I doona mean that. We all know ye're involved with the leader's daughter."

Jean-Luc smiled. "Especially after last night."

Roman was surprised to feel his face heat up. Shanna's reaction seemed to be wearing off on him.

Angus cleared his throat. "I think the best way to deal with the Stake-Out team is to erase their memories of us.

Timing would be important. We must do all five on the same night that we break into Langley to erase all their files."

"A clean sweep." Jean-Luc smiled. "I like it."

"I'm not sure it would work." Roman received surprised glances from his friends. "Shanna can resist mind control."

Angus's green eyes widened. "Ye canna be serious."

"I am. And what's more, I suspect she inherited her psychic abilities from her father. I also suspect the Stake-Out team is small because everyone on it possesses similar abilities."

"*Merde*," Jean-Luc whispered.

"Since they're working on an anti-vampire program," Roman added, "it would be obvious who would want to kill them."

"And it would give the American government more incentive to hunt us," Jean-Luc concluded.

"They're a bigger threat than I thought." Angus drummed his fingers on the arm of his chair. "I have to think about this."

"Fine. Let's take a break for now." Roman stood and headed for the door. "I'll be in my lab if you need me." He hurried down the corridor, anxious to get some work done on his formula for staying awake during the day. He spotted a Highlander standing outside Laszlo's lab. Good. Laszlo was still getting the protection he needed.

Roman greeted the Scotsman as he entered the lab. Laszlo was sitting on a stool, gazing into a microscope. "Hi, Laszlo."

The small chemist started and nearly fell off the stool.

Roman rushed over and steadied him. "Are you all right?"

"Yes." Laszlo adjusted his lab coat. All the buttons were missing. "I've been a bit nervous lately."

"I hear you're working on a cheap drink for the poor."

"Yes, sir." Laszlo bobbed his head, enthusiastically. "I'll

have three formulas ready for the survey tomorrow night. I'm experimenting with different proportions of red blood cells to water. And I may try adding some flavors like lemon or vanilla."

"Vanilla blood? I'd like to taste that myself."

"Thank you, sir."

Roman perched on a neighboring stool. "I'd like to run an idea by you. See what you think."

"Of course. I'd be honored to help, if I can."

"It's theoretical at this point, but I was thinking about sperm. Live sperm."

Laszlo's eyes widened. "Our sperm is dead, sir."

"I know. But what if we took a sample of live human sperm, erased the genetic code, and planted someone else's DNA in it."

Laszlo's mouth fell open. He blinked several times. "Who would want their DNA inserted into live sperm?"

"I would."

"Oh. Then you . . . you want to father children?"

Only with Shanna. "I want to know if it's possible."

The chemist nodded slowly. "I believe it would be."

"Good." Roman strode toward the door, then paused. "I'd appreciate it if you kept this conversation between us."

"Of course, sir." Laszlo plucked at the strings that had once held a button in place. "I won't say a word."

Roman hurried to his own lab to work on his daytime formula. He turned on his CD player. Gregorian chants filled the room, helping him to concentrate. He was so close.

Before he knew it, the chants stopped and Roman glanced at the time. Five-thirty. Time always flew by when he was involved in a new project. He called Connor and teleported to the kitchen. "How's everything?"

"Fine," Connor answered. "No sign of Petrovsky's men."

"And Shanna?"

"She's in her room. I left some diet cola and brownies by her door. They disappeared, so she must be all right."

"I see. Thank you." Roman headed for the staircase and stood in the center of the spiral. With a glance at the top landing, he teleported there in a second. He went in his office and stopped short when he saw the blood-red velvet chaise. What a fool he'd been to bite her. And a bigger fool to blurt out that he loved her.

He trudged toward the wet bar for his bedtime snack. Should he go to her room to check on her? Would she even speak to him? He unscrewed a bottle and popped it into the microwave. Maybe he should leave her alone. Her reaction to his confession of love had not been good. He'd give her time. And he wouldn't give up.

"Damn it to hell!" Ivan paced back and forth in his small office. He'd watched the news on DVN, and even though the explosion at Romatech was the top story, it hadn't accomplished much more than blowing up one lousy storeroom. Not a single Highlander had been blown to tiny bits or burned to a crisp. And as far as Ivan could tell, the city was not experiencing a sudden increase in hungry vampires on the prowl. After blowing up Draganesti's supply of fake blood, he had hoped to see a difference.

"Maybe the Vamps keep a supply of synthetic blood in their homes," Alek suggested. "They just haven't run out yet."

Galina curled up in one of the wingback chairs. "I agree. It's too soon to see a shortage. Besides, Draganesti probably has supplies we don't know about."

Ivan stopped pacing. "What do you mean?"

"He's supplying synthetic blood around the world. He could have plants we don't know about."

Alek nodded at her. "That would make sense."

Galina raised an eyebrow. "I'm not as stupid as you think."

"Enough." Ivan resumed his pacing. "I need a plan. I haven't hurt Draganesti enough."

"Why do you hate him so much?" Galina asked.

Ivan ignored the harem girl. He needed to get back into Romatech. But how? Tension grew in his neck, pinching the nerves.

"Draganesti is the one who built an army to defeat Casimir," Alek whispered to Galina.

"Oh. Thanks for telling me." She gave Alek a sly smile.

Alek, damn him, smiled back. With a growl, Ivan popped his neck. That got their attention. "Any sign of Highlanders?"

"No, sir," Alek answered, keeping his eyes off Galina. "If they're out there, they're staying hidden."

"I don't think they're attacking tonight." Ivan resumed his pacing. The door to his office opened and Katya entered. "Where the hell have you been?"

"Hunting." Katya licked her lips. "A girl has to eat. Besides, I heard some good news at one of the Vamp clubs."

"What? Our bomb killed one of those stupid Highlanders?"

"No." Katya smoothed back her long hair. "Actually, I heard the damage was minimal."

"Crap!" Ivan grabbed a glass paperweight off his desk and smashed it against the wall.

"Now, now. Throwing a tantrum won't help, will it?"

Ivan zoomed over to Katya and grasped her by the neck. "Neither will a show of disrespect, bitch."

Her eyes flashed. "I have good news if you care to hear it."

"Fine." Ivan released her. "Out with it."

She rubbed her neck while she gave Ivan an irritated look. "You want back into Romatech, don't you?"

"Of course. I said I would kill that little chemist, and I mean to keep my word. But the place is crawling with those stinking Highlanders now. We can't get in."

"I believe we can," Katya countered. "At least one of us can. Romatech's vice president of marketing has invited poor Vamps to the facility tomorrow night for a market survey."

"A what?" Ivan asked.

Katya shrugged. "Does it matter? One of us could go, disguised as one of the poor."

"Ah, excellent." Ivan patted her on the cheek. "Very good."

"I will go, sir," Alek announced.

Ivan shook his head. "They saw you at the ball. And they would recognize me, too. Maybe Vladimir?"

"I'll go," Galina offered.

Ivan snorted. "Don't be ridiculous."

"I'm not. They wouldn't be expecting a woman."

"True." Katya sat in the chair next to Galina. "I know a makeup artist at DVN. And we could use their wardrobe room."

"Great!" Galina smiled. "I could be a fat old Vamp tramp."

"A bag lady," Katya agreed. "No one would ever suspect you."

"Since when do either of you make decisions around here?" Ivan glared at them both. They lowered their heads, looking properly submissive. "How could Galina capture Laszlo Veszto? And if a Highlander is guarding him, how would she subdue him?"

"Nightshade," Katya whispered. "You have some, don't you?"

"Yes." Ivan rubbed at a knot of tension in his neck. "In my safe. How did you know about it?"

"I used some once. Not yours, of course. But you could let Galina use it."

"What is nightshade?" Galina asked.

"A poison for vampires," Katya explained. "You prick

the vampire with a dart, and the poison goes into his bloodstream and paralyzes him. He's still conscious, but unable to move."

"Cool." Galina's eyes lit up. "I want to do it."

"All right. You can go." Ivan perched on the edge of his desk. "Once you locate Laszlo Veszto, call and teleport back here with the little bastard."

"Is that all you want me to do?" Galina asked quietly.

Ivan considered. "I want another explosion. A bigger one. One that will really hurt Draganesti."

"In that case," Katya suggested, "I think you should kill some of the people he most cares about."

Ivan nodded. "Those bloody Highlanders."

"Oh, he cares about them, I'm sure." Katya ran a finger over her red-painted lips. "But his real weakness is the mortals."

"Exactly," Galina agreed. "He has plenty of mortal employees. We could put a timer on the bomb so it will go off at sunrise."

"That's it!" Ivan jumped to his feet. "Draganesti's precious mortals will be dying, while he and his Highlanders are forced to return to their coffins. There won't be a bloody thing they can do about it. It's perfect! Tomorrow night, Galina will plant the C-4 in an area where the mortals gather."

"Their cafeteria, perhaps?" Galina exchanged a wry look with Katya.

"I know where," Ivan announced. "Their cafeteria."

Twenty-three

"Can they see me?" Shanna watched the scroungy assortment of vampires through the window.

"No." Gregori stood next to her in the viewing room. "Not as long as you keep the lights off. It's one-way glass."

Shanna didn't know anything about market research, but she figured it had to be more interesting than watching television all night. "I'm surprised there's such a thing as poor vampires. Can't they use mind control to wheedle money out of people?"

"I suppose," Gregori answered, "but most of these people were already broken before they became vampires. They only think about their next meal, like a junkie and his next fix."

"That's so sad." Shanna observed the ten vampires who had come to Romatech for a free meal and the fifty-dollar incentive. "Vampirism doesn't change a person very much, does it?"

"Nay." Connor stood at the door. He had insisted on

coming along as her personal bodyguard. "A man will stay true to his heart even after death."

So Roman was still trying to save people, and the Scottish warriors were still fighting for a just cause. Shanna wondered what Roman was doing now. He hadn't even tried to see her since his declaration of love. Maybe he'd realized their situation was hopeless. "So how does this work?"

"We've divided them into two groups." Gregori motioned to the group on the left. "That group will be watching a power-point presentation and filling out a questionnaire about the new restaurant. The second group will be testing different formulas and rating them according to taste. When they're done, the two groups switch places and start over."

"What do you want me to do?"

"They'll be testing the drinks here in front of the window. They'll rate each drink themselves, but I'd like you to watch their expressions and jot down their reactions."

Shanna noted five legal pads. "Are there five drinks?"

"Yes. Three new formulas that Laszlo put together, and then, Blood Lite and Chocolood. Just put a mark under the headings *Like*, *Neutral*, or *Dislike*. Okay?"

"Sure." Shanna picked up a pencil. "Bring on the Vamps."

Gregori grinned. "Thanks for your help, Shanna." He opened the connecting door and entered the participant room.

Shanna heard him go into a lengthy dissertation regarding the new restaurant. Then the first vampire came to taste the drinks. He was an old man in a stained raincoat. A scar ran down his face, zigzagging through the gray whiskers. He finished the first drink, then burped.

"Was that a dislike?" Shanna asked.

"Neutral," Connor replied.

"Ah." She marked the notepad and followed the old vampire to the next drink. He took a big gulp, then spewed the contents all over the window.

"Yeech!" Shanna jumped back. Blood everywhere.

"I would say that was a dislike," Connor said.

Shanna snorted. "Brilliant observation, Connor."

He smiled. " 'Tis a gift."

At least all that blood wasn't making her nauseous. She really was improving. Gregori wiped the window clean before the next vampire's turn. This one was a plump, elderly woman with gray, tangled hair. She worked her way down the line of drinks, clutching her big bag to her chest. At the end of the line, she put her bag on the table. She looked around, then grabbed a bottle off the table and stuffed it into her purse.

"Oh, my gosh." Shanna looked at Connor. "She just stole a bottle of Chocolood."

He shrugged. "The puir woman is hungry. She can have it."

"I guess so." Shanna had finished with the first group when the bag lady doubled over and moaned.

Gregori rushed over to her. "Are you all right, ma'am?"

"I . . . Do you have any restrooms here, young man?" she asked in a gruff voice.

"Yes, of course." Gregori escorted her to the door. "This man will take you." He motioned to one of the Highlander guards who stood by the door.

The bag lady left in the company of a Highlander. It was the second group's turn to test the new formulas. Two hours later, Shanna was relieved when the whole process had finally finished. The back door to their room opened and Radinka peeked inside.

"Are you done yet?" she asked.

"Yes, finally." Shanna stretched. "I had no idea these things were so tiring."

"Well, come with me for a bite to eat. That'll perk you up."

"Thanks." Shanna picked up her purse. "I have a feeling Connor will want to come, too."

"Aye, I have sworn to keep you safe, lass."

"You're a sweetie." Shanna smiled at him. "Is there a little lady vampire waiting for you somewhere?"

He blushed and followed the women into the hall.

"Where are we going?" Shanna asked.

"The employee cafeteria." Radinka walked briskly down the hall. "They have fabulous cheesecake."

"Sounds wonderful."

"Yes." Radinka sighed. "It's to die for."

As soon as the phone rang, Ivan Petrovsky grabbed it. "Yes?"

"I'm in Veszto's lab," Galina spoke quietly. "I need help."

"I knew I shouldn't have sent a female." Ivan motioned to Alek. "Keep this line open till we get back."

"Yes, sir." Alek reached for the receiver.

"Okay, Galina. Talk." Ivan focused on her voice and teleported to Veszto's lab at Romatech. The small chemist lay on the floor, watching them. He was still conscious, terror making his eyes large and glassy like a deer caught in headlights.

Ivan inspected Galina. She looked like a frumpy old hag. "Excellent. I would have never known that was you."

She smiled, displaying a blackened tooth. "It's been fun. I acted like I needed to go the restroom. A Highlander escorted me, and when he opened the door, I pricked him with a dart."

"Where is he?"

"He fell into the restroom. I wasn't so lucky with this one." She opened the door to reveal a Highlander on the floor.

"Shit! You can't leave him out there in the hallway."

"He's huge. I couldn't budge him."

Ivan took hold of the Scotsman under the arms and dragged him into Veszto's lab. "How long was he out there?"

"Not long. I pricked him, then ran in here and pricked Veszto. When I couldn't move the guard, I called you."

Ivan dropped the Highlander on the floor, then shut and locked the door. "Did you set the explosives?"

"Yes. The guards at the door checked my bag, so it was a good thing we hid the C-4 in my clothes. I stuck it under a table in the cafeteria. It'll go off in about forty minutes."

"Excellent." Ivan noticed the Highlander watching them, listening to their plans. "I've always wanted to do this." He knelt and withdrew a wooden stake from his jacket.

The Scotsman's eyes widened. A strangled sound vibrated in his throat as he struggled in vain to move.

"He can't defend himself," Galina whispered.

"You think I give a shit?" Ivan leaned over the Highlander. "Look into the face of your murderer. It's the last thing you'll ever see." He plunged the stake into the Highlander's heart.

The Scotsman arched. Pain registered on his face, then his body crumbled into dust.

Ivan brushed the stake against his thigh to clean off the dust. "This will make a good keepsake." He slipped it into a jacket pocket. "Now for the little chemist."

He walked over to Laszlo Veszto. "Your weakling of a coven master couldn't protect you, could he?"

Veszto's face had paled to a deathly white.

"You shouldn't have helped that Whelan bitch escape. Do you know what I do to people who get in my way?"

"Come on." Galina rushed to the phone. "We need to go."

Ivan hefted the chemist up in his arms. "Hold the phone for me." He listened to Alek's voice, then teleported back to his house in Brooklyn. Galina followed.

Ivan dropped Veszto on the floor and kicked him in the ribs. "Welcome to my humble home."

*   *   *

Shanna enjoyed another bite of cheesecake as she looked around the dimly lit cafeteria. She and Radinka had taken a table by the window. Connor roamed about for a few minutes, then found a newspaper to read. They were the only customers there.

"I like working at night. It's so peaceful." Radinka emptied a packet of artificial sweetener into her tea. "In another thirty minutes, this place will be crammed full of people."

Shanna nodded and looked out the window. Across the garden, she could see the lights of another wing of Roma-tech. Roman's lab was over there.

"Did you see Roman tonight?" Radinka asked.

"No." Shanna took another bite of cheesecake. She wasn't sure she wanted to. Or that he wanted to see her. It had to hurt when a guy confessed to loving a girl, and she ran away, crying.

Radinka sipped her tea. "For the last two nights I've been doing some research for Roman. I left the information in his lab, but he says the final decision will be yours."

"I don't know what you're talking about."

"I know that, dear. So, you should discuss the matter with him. Connor can take you to his lab."

Jeez. As a matchmaker, Radinka was relentless. Shanna glanced at the large clock on the cafeteria wall. It was already five-ten. "I don't have time. I came here with Gregori and Connor, and they said we were leaving by five-fifteen, right?" She looked at Connor for support.

"Aye, but we came in a car." Connor folded the newspaper. "Ye can teleport back later with Roman, if ye like."

Shanna made a face at him. Some help he was. "We'd better find Gregori. I hope he's done with all those poor Vamps."

"Did the research study go well?" Radinka drizzled some dressing over her grilled chicken salad.

"I guess. It was sad, seeing people that downtrodden.

There was this one bag lady who—" Shanna stopped. She searched her memory. "Oh my gosh. She never came back."

"What?" Connor leaned forward. "Who was this?"

"The old lady who stole a bottle of Chocolood. She left with a guard to go the restroom and never came back."

"Och, this is bad." Connor stood and removed a cell phone from his sporran.

"Perhaps she was ill and went home," Radinka suggested.

Shanna doubted that. "Can vampires even get sick?"

"Yes, if they drink infected blood." Radinka stabbed at her salad with a fork. "And the new Fusion Cuisine doesn't set well with all of them."

Connor punched in a number. "Angus? There may be a member of Gregori's focus group loose in the facility. An elderly woman."

"Maybe she's lost." Radinka took a bite of salad.

Shanna watched Connor pacing about. He seemed worried.

He dropped the phone into his sporran and strode toward them. "Angus has ordered a complete sweep of the building and a lockdown. They'll be starting at the storerooms where the last explosion occurred. Each room will be searched, then sealed, until the whole facility has been checked."

"You expect foul play?" Radinka asked.

"We're not taking any chances." Connor glanced at the clock and winced. "We havena much time before the sun rises."

He was anxious to help with the search, Shanna could tell, but the poor man was stuck babysitting her. "Go on, Connor. I'll be all right with Radinka."

"Nay. I canna leave you, lass."

Radinka stabbed a tomato wedge with her fork. "Connor, take her to Roman's lab. He can watch her while you join the search."

Shanna winced. Radinka just never gave up. Unfortunately, Connor was giving her such a hopeful look, she hated to disappoint him. "I guess my ride back home has been canceled?"

"For now, aye."

"Okay." She grabbed her purse. "I'll go."

Radinka smiled. "I'll see you later, dear."

Shanna had to jog to keep up with Connor's long-legged stride. As they rounded the corner to the wing where Roman's lab was located, a loud, beeping alarm went off. "What's that?"

"Red alert." Connor started running. "Something's happened."

He stopped in front of Roman's lab and knocked. He opened the door and waited for Shanna to catch up. Gasping for air, she followed him inside.

Roman was on the phone, but looked up when she came in. His worried expression immediately cleared, and the smile he gave her took away what little air she had left. "She's all right. She's here with Connor." He listened on the phone, but his gaze never left Shanna.

Her heart was pounding, her mouth dry. It was from the running, though. It had nothing to do with the way Roman was looking at her.

She set her purse on a black-topped table. There was some music playing quietly. No instruments, just male voices singing. The soothing sound was in sharp contrast to the insistent beep of the alarm coming from speakers in the hallway. She peered through the open window blinds. She could see the cafeteria across the garden.

"Keep me updated." Roman hung up the receiver.

"What happened?" Connor asked.

"Angus found a guard in a restroom close to where the research study took place. The man was conscious, but paralyzed."

Connor paled. "Petrovsky is behind this."

"What about the bag lady?" Shanna asked.

"They're looking for her," Roman admitted. "We know you're all right, so our main concern now is Laszlo."

Connor paused halfway out the door. "I need to go."

"Go. Shanna will be safe with me." Roman closed the door and locked it. "How are you?"

"I'm okay." She seemed to be developing a healthy tolerance level for dealing with shock. Or maybe she was so past her limit, she was just numb. She looked around the room. She'd been here once before, but it had been too dark to see. A wall of diplomas caught her attention. She wandered over.

Roman had acquired advanced degrees in microbiology, chemistry, and pharmacology. After all this time, he was still a healer. Like Connor had said, death didn't change a man's heart. And Roman's heart was good. She glanced over her shoulder. "I didn't realize you were such a nerd."

He raised an eyebrow. "Excuse me?"

"You have a lot of degrees."

"I've had a lot of time," he said dryly.

She bit her lip to keep from smiling. "Night school?"

The corner of his mouth lifted. "How did you guess?" A printer across the room started working with a clacking noise. He strode toward a computer screen where a tangle of lists and graphs were filling the screen. The data looked incomprehensible to Shanna, but Roman was following it with great interest.

"This is good," he whispered. He grabbed some finished pages from the printer and studied them. "This is really good."

"What?"

He dropped the papers on a black-topped table. "This." He picked up a beaker filled with greenish liquid. "I think I did it." A grin spread across his face. "I think I really did it."

He looked so young and happy. As if the cares of several centuries had suddenly lifted from his shoulders.

Shanna couldn't help but smile. This was the way Roman should be. A healer, hard at work in his lab, delighting in his discoveries.

She approached him. "What is it? A new toilet bowl cleanser?"

With a laugh, he set the beaker down. "It's a formula that will enable vampires to stay awake during the day."

Shanna halted in mid-stride. "You're kidding."

"No. I wouldn't kid about something like this. This is . . ."

"Revolutionary," she whispered. "You could change the world for vampires."

He nodded, a look of wonder crossing his face. "It hasn't been tested, of course, so I can't be sure. But it would be the biggest step forward since the successful manufacture of blood."

And his synthetic blood was saving thousands of lives. She was in the presence of a genius. And he claimed to love her.

He crossed his arms, studying the greenish liquid. "You know, if this formula successfully invigorates a vampire who is clinically dead, it could possibly have applications for certain mortal conditions, like comas or catatonic states."

"Oh my gosh. You're such a genius, Roman."

He winced. "I've had a lot more years to study than most scientists. Or nerds, as you call us." He smiled.

"Hey, nerds rule. Congratulations." She reached out to hug him, then reconsidered and patted his arm before stepping back.

His smile waned. "Are you afraid of me?"

"No. I just think it's better for us not to . . ."

"Touch? Or make love?" His eyes darkened with a glint of hunger. "You know we have unfinished business between us."

She gulped and moved back. It was not a problem of

trusting him. She knew he'd do anything to protect her from harm. The truth was, she couldn't trust herself. When he looked at her like that, her resistance melted. Twice she'd let him make love to her, and twice she should have refused. Logically, she knew a relationship with a vampire could never work. Unfortunately, knowing that fact did little to ease the longing in her heart. It sure didn't stop the physical attraction that flooded her senses and made her body ache for him.

She attempted to change the subject. "What is that music you're listening to?"

"Gregorian chants. They help me concentrate." He went to a small fridge and removed a bottle of blood. "We'll make sure I'm not hungry." He unscrewed the top and started drinking it cold.

Whoa. Did this mean he intended to seduce her? Surely not. The sun would be rising soon. Another fifteen minutes or so and he would be out cold. Of course, vampires could move really fast when they wanted to. She wandered about his lab while he stood there, drinking and following her every move. "This looks old." She examined an old stone mortar and pestle.

"It *is* old. I rescued it from the ruins of the monastery where I grew up. That and the cross you're wearing are all I have left of that life."

Shanna touched the crucifix. "Once I'm safe, I need to give this back. It must be precious to you."

"It is yours. And nothing is more precious to me than you."

She had no idea how to respond to that. *I like you, too*, seemed a little lame. "Radinka said she was doing some research for you and I should discuss it with you."

"Radinka talks too much." He took another sip of blood. "The red folder." He pointed to the lab table nearest her.

Shanna approached the folder slowly, wondering what on earth this research could be. She opened it and found herself staring at an eight-by-ten glossy of a golden retriever. "Oh. It's a . . . dog." She turned to the next photo and the next. A black Labrador, a German shepherd. "Why am I looking at dogs?"

"You said you wanted a big dog."

"Not now. I'm on the run." She lifted a photo of an Alaskan malamute and gasped. Underneath it lay a picture of a house. A large, two-story, white-framed house with a big front porch and a white picket fence. Prominently displayed in the front yard was a *For Sale* sign. Her dream house.

But more than a dream house. It was a proposal of a dream life that Roman wanted to share with her. Shanna's throat constricted, leaving her speechless and short of air. She'd been wrong. Her tolerance level for shock was not nearly as tough as she thought. Her eyes filled with tears. Her hand trembled as she turned the photo over. There was another house with another picket fence. This one was an old Victorian with an adorable tower. It was also for sale.

She'd told him what she wanted most in life, and he was trying to give it to her. By the time she reached the eighth and last picture, she could hardly see. Her vision was blurred with tears.

"We could see them at night." Roman set down his empty bottle and walked toward her. "You can pick out which one you like. If you don't like any of them, we'll keep looking."

"Roman." Her hands shook when she closed the folder. "You are the dearest man. But—"

"You don't have to answer right away. The sun will be up soon, so we need to be going. We could teleport back to my bedroom. Will you come with me?"

And be alone with him. Even if he attempted a seduction, once the sun came up, he would have to stop. He wouldn't be able to raise a finger, much less his . . .

The door burst open and a huge Scotsman entered. He

was breathing heavily. His green eyes glittered with unshed tears.

"Angus?" Roman turned toward him. "What happened?"

"Yer wee chemist is gone. The bastards have kidnapped him."

"Oh no." Shanna covered her mouth. Poor little Laszlo.

"The phone in his lab was off the hook," Angus continued. "We traced the call to Petrovsky's house in Brooklyn."

"I see." Roman's face paled.

"And Ewan. Ewan Grant was guarding him." Angus's expression hardened. "They killed him."

Roman stepped back with a stunned look. "Are you sure? They might have kidnapped him."

"No." Angus shook his head. "We found his dust. The bloody bastards staked him."

"God's blood." Roman grabbed the edge of a table. "Ewan. He was so strong. How could he . . . ?"

Angus's breath hissed between his gritted teeth. He clenched his fists. "We believe they may have used nightshade on him like the guard in the restroom. He . . . he would have been defenseless."

"Goddammit!" Roman hit the table with his fist. "Those bastards." He paced across the room. "When does the sun rise? Do we have enough time to retaliate?"

"Nay. The bastards timed it this way on purpose. The sun is rising in about five minutes, so it is too late."

Roman muttered another curse. "You were right, Angus. We should have attacked tonight."

"Doona blame yerself." Angus looked at Shanna and frowned.

My God. Goose bumps spread across her skin. He thought *she* was at fault. Petrovsky wouldn't have targeted Laszlo if he hadn't helped her escape. And without Laszlo as a target, their Scottish friend would still exist.

Roman continued to pace. "At least they won't be able to torture him for long."

"Aye, the sun will put a stop to their evildoings." Angus paused with a hand on the doorknob. "Then ye agree. Tomorrow night, we go to war."

Roman nodded, his eyes blazing with anger. "Yes."

Shanna gulped. Then more Vamps would die. Maybe even Roman.

"The lads and I are taking refuge in the cellar. We'll be making our plans till the sun rises. Ye should find a place to sleep while ye still can."

"I understand." Roman stopped at a table.

As Angus closed the door, Roman propped his forehead onto his hand and closed his eyes. Shanna wasn't sure if it was grief or fatigue. Probably both. He must have known the dead Highlander for a long time.

"Roman? Maybe we should go the silver room."

"It's my fault," he whispered.

Ah, so he was feeling guilt, too. Her eyes welled with tears. She knew all about feeling guilty for a friend's death. "It's not your fault. It's mine."

"No." He looked surprised. "I was the one who made the decision to protect you. I called Laszlo on the phone and told him to come back. He was following my orders. How can you be at fault? You were unconscious at the time."

"But if it wasn't for me—"

"No. The trouble between Petrovsky and myself goes way back." Roman swayed on his feet.

She grabbed his arm. "You're worn out. Let's go to the silver room."

"Not enough time." He looked around the lab. "I'll be all right in the closet."

"No. I don't want you sleeping on the floor."

He gave her a tired smile. "Sweetness, I won't notice any discomfort."

"I'll have the daytime staff move you to the bed in the silver room."

"No. They don't know about me. I'll be fine." He stumbled toward the closet. "Close the blinds, please."

She rushed to the window. The sky was lightening to gray with a pink tint in the east. Just as she closed the blinds, a ray of golden sun shot over the rooftop of Romatech.

Roman had made it to the closet and was opening the door.

Suddenly a loud blast deafened her. The ground shook. She grabbed at the blinds to steady herself, but they swayed, causing her to stumble. Alarms rang out. And another sound that Shanna realized was people screaming.

"Oh my God." She peeked out the window. In the glare of the morning sun, she spotted a plume of smoke.

"An explosion?" Roman whispered. "Where?"

"I'm not sure. All I see is smoke." Shanna glanced back. He was sagging against the closet door, deathly pale.

"They timed it this way, so I couldn't do anything."

Shanna peered through the blinds again. "It's the wing across from us. The cafeteria! Radinka was there." She ran to the phone and dialed 911.

"There . . . will be many people there." Roman pushed away from the door, stumbled forward a few steps, and fell to his knees.

When an operator answered, Shanna yelled into the phone, "There's been an explosion at Romatech Industries."

"What is the nature of your emergency?" the woman asked.

"It's an explosion! We need ambulances and a fire truck."

"Calm down. And your name is?"

"Will you hurry it up? There are injured people here!" She hung up and rushed toward Roman. The poor man was crawling across the floor. "There's nothing you can do. Go and rest."

"No. I have to help them."

"I called the paramedics. And I'll go over there myself, just as soon as I know you're all right." She pointed to the closet and tried to look authoritative. "Go to your room."

"I can't bear to be helpless when people need me."

With tears in her eyes, she knelt beside him. "I understand. Believe me. I've been there. But there's nothing you can do."

"Yes, there is." He grabbed the lab table and pulled himself to his feet. He reached for the beaker of greenish liquid.

"You can't! It hasn't been tested yet."

He gave her a wry look. "What could it do to me? Kill me?"

"That's not funny. Roman, please. Don't."

His hand shook as he raised the beaker to his mouth. He swallowed down several large gulps before setting the beaker back down.

Shanna curled her fingers around the crucifix he'd given her. "Do you even know what a normal dose is?"

"No." He stepped back and swayed on his feet. "I feel . . . strange." He collapsed on the floor.

Twenty-four

Shanna fell to her knees beside him. "Roman?" She touched his cheek. He was cold. Lifeless. Was this his normal deadish behavior for daytime, or had he actually killed himself with an experimental drug?

"What have you done?" She laid her head against his chest, listening for a heartbeat. Nothing. But then normally he only had a heartbeat at night. What if it never started up again? What if he was gone forever?

"Don't leave me," she whispered. She sat back, pressing her fingers to her face. She'd tried so hard to convince herself their relationship wouldn't work. But now he looked so . . . dead. And it was killing her.

"*Roman.*" His name seemed to wrench itself from her soul. She bent over, strained with emotion. She couldn't bear to lose him.

There were people in the cafeteria who needed her help. She needed to go. Now. But she couldn't budge. She couldn't leave him. It had been so hard to lose Karen, but this—this was like her own heart was being crushed. And with the pain came a searing realization.

She could no longer pretend that a relationship with Roman was impossible. It already existed. She was in love with him. She'd trusted him with her life. She'd allowed him inside her head. She'd fought her fear of blood for him. She'd always believed he was a good and honorable man. Because she loved him.

And he was right. She understood his guilt and remorse like no one else. They were connected emotionally and mentally. Cruel twists of fate had hurt them in the past, but now they could rise above the pain and despair by facing the world together.

Something grabbed her wrist.

He was alive! His chest suddenly heaved with an intake of air. His eyes opened. Bright red.

Shanna gasped. She tried to move back, but his grip tightened. Oh God, what if he'd turned into a Mr. Hyde?

He turned his head to look at her. He blinked once, twice, then his eyes slowly returned to their normal golden-brown.

"Roman? Are you okay?"

"I believe so." He released her and sat up. "How long was I out?"

"I—I don't know. It seemed like forever."

He glanced at the clock on the wall. "It's only been a few minutes." He looked at her. "I scared you. I'm sorry."

She scrambled to her feet. "I was afraid you'd done yourself serious harm. That was a crazy thing to do."

"Yes, but it worked. I'm awake with the sun." He stood and headed for the closet. "There should be a medical kit in here." He grabbed a white plastic box. "Let's go."

They rushed down the hallway. The alarm was still blaring. People scurried about with frightened faces. Some stared at Roman, while others did a double-take.

"Do they know who you are?" Shanna asked.

"I guess. My picture's in the employee handbook." Roman looked about curiously. "I've never seen the place so crowded."

They rounded the corner to the corridor that connected the laboratory wing to the cafeteria. It was jammed with people and bright with sunlight from three east-facing windows. As Shanna passed by the first window, she heard Roman wince. An angry, red burn mark had sliced a path across his cheek.

She grabbed his arm. "The sun's burning you."

"Only my face burned. You must have blocked the sun from the rest of me. Stay by my side."

As they rushed through the second shaft of sunlight, Roman lifted the medical kit to the side of his injured face. The sun burned a red streak across his exposed hand.

"Damn." He flexed his burned fingers.

"Let me hold the box." Shanna took the medical kit and perched it on top of her head to give her added height. People looked at them strangely, but they made it through the last shaft of sunlight without Roman receiving more burns.

As they entered the cafeteria, Roman gestured toward a man. "That's Todd Spencer. Vice president of production."

Shanna hardly noticed. She was too shocked by the scene before her. Injured people were lying on the floor. People rushed about. Some were sweeping away debris. Others hunched over the injured, wrapping them with gauze bandages.

A large hole gaped in the wall where concrete columns and glass windows had once stood. Overturned tables, mangled chairs, and food trays were scattered about. The hissing spray of fire extinguishers masked the moans of the injured. And Radinka was nowhere in sight.

"Spencer." Roman approached the vice president. "What's the situation?"

Todd Spencer's eyes widened. "Mr. Draganesti, I didn't know you were here. Uh, we have the fires under control. We're seeing to the injured. Paramedics are on their way. But I don't understand this. Who would do such a thing?"

Roman surveyed the scene. "Is everyone alive?"

Spencer grimaced. "I don't know. We haven't found everyone."

Roman headed to a spot where the walls and ceiling had caved in. "There could be someone under there."

Spencer accompanied him. "We tried lifting that mess, but it's too heavy. I sent for some special equipment."

A concrete column had fallen and crushed a table beneath it. Roman seized a huge hunk of concrete, lifted it over his head, and heaved it into the garden.

"Oh my God," Spencer whispered. "How could he—?"

Shanna winced. Roman wasn't bothering to conceal his super vampire strength. "Maybe it's trauma-induced. I've heard of people lifting cars after an accident."

"Maybe so." Spencer frowned. "Are you all right, sir?"

Roman was bent over. Slowly he straightened and turned.

Shanna gasped. His proximity to the garden had exposed him to more sunlight. His shirt was smoldering, black and scorched. Smoke drifted from his wounded chest, carrying the smell of roasted flesh.

Spencer winced. "Sir, I didn't realize you were injured, too. You shouldn't be doing this."

"I'm fine." Roman leaned over to grasp another chunk of concrete. "Help me clear this."

Spencer tackled some smaller chunks of concrete. Shanna gathered up ceiling tiles and tossed them in a heap. Soon the crushed table was exposed. Luckily, chairs beneath the table had kept it from being completely flattened. There was a small pocket of air beneath the table. And a body.

Radinka.

Roman seized the table and flipped it over. He shoved the mangled chairs out of the way. "Radinka, can you hear me?"

Her eyelids flickered.

"She's alive," Shanna whispered.

Roman knelt beside Radinka. "We'll need more bandages."

"I'll see to it." Spencer rushed off.

Shanna opened the small medical kit and passed Roman a bandage.

"Radinka, can you hear me?" He pressed the bandage against a cut on her temple.

She moaned and opened her eyes. "Hurts," she whispered.

"I know," Roman replied. "An ambulance is on its way."

"How can you be here? I must be dreaming."

"You're going to be fine. You're too young to die."

She gave a weak snort. "Everyone is young to you."

"Oh God." Shanna's stomach rippled with queasiness.

"What's wrong?" Roman asked.

She pointed. There, stabbed into Radinka's side was a dinner knife. A pool of blood was forming. Shanna covered her mouth and swallowed hard at the bile in her throat.

Roman glanced at her. "You'll be all right. You can do this."

She took a few deep breaths. She had to do this. She would not fail another friend.

A young man came toward them with an armload of linen strips cut from tablecloths. "Mr. Spencer said you needed thesc."

"Yes." With trembling hands, Shanna set the bandages in her lap. She folded one into a thick pad.

"Ready?" Roman grasped the knife. "As soon as this comes out, press hard." He pulled the knife out.

She pressed the pad against the wound. Blood seeped onto her fingers. Her stomach churned.

Roman grabbed a bandage and made a pad. "My turn." He pressed against the wound. "You're doing fine, Shanna."

She dropped her bloodied pad to the side and folded up a new one. "Are you helping me? Mentally, I mean."

"No. You're on your own."

"Good." She pressed the new pad against the wound. "I *can* do this."

Paramedics rushed in, pushing gurneys.

"Over here!" Roman yelled.

Two paramedics wheeled a gurney over. "We'll take it from here," one of them said.

Roman helped them lift Radinka onto the gurney.

Shanna walked alongside her, holding her hand. "We'll tell Gregori. He'll come see you tonight."

Radinka nodded, her face pale. "Roman, will there be a war? Don't let Gregori fight, please. He's not trained for it."

"She's delirious," a paramedic muttered.

"Don't worry." Roman touched Radinka's shoulder. "I won't let anything happen to him."

"You're a good man, Roman," she whispered. She squeezed Shanna's hand. "Don't let him get away. He needs you."

The paramedics wheeled her away. Police officers arrived. Flashes lit the room as the crime scene investigators snapped pictures.

"Damn." Roman moved back. "I have to leave."

"Why?" Shanna asked.

"I don't think those are digital cameras." Roman grabbed Shanna's hand and headed for the door.

A paramedic stopped beside him. "Sir, you have severe burns. You should come with us."

"No, I'm fine."

"We'll take you in an ambulance. This way."

"I'm not going."

"I'm Dr. Whelan." Shanna smiled at the paramedic. "This man is my patient. I'll look after him. Thank you."

"Fine. Suit yourself." The paramedic rushed off to join the others.

"Thank you." Roman led her out of the cafeteria. "We'll go to the silver room." He opened a door to the stairwell, and they descended the steps. "This is so aggravating. I really want to see what kind of evidence the police uncover, but I don't dare stick around with all those cameras."

"You don't show up in a regular camera?"

"No." Roman opened the door to the basement. They walked down the hallway to the entrance of the silver room.

"I tell you what," Shanna suggested as he punched a number into the keypad. "I'll help clean up your wounds. Then I'll go back upstairs, see what I can find out, and report back to you."

"Okay." He peered into the retinal scanner. "I don't like to leave you unguarded, but I suppose you'd be safe up there with the police." He opened the door and ushered her inside.

She suddenly felt irritated. He was worried about her safety when he totally disregarded his own? "Look, I'm fine. The question is, how are you doing? You're the one with a strange, untested drug in your system."

"It's not untested anymore." He looked around for something to insulate his hands from the silver door.

"I'll get it." She shoved the door shut, flipped the silver locks, and scraped the bar into place. "We still don't know if that formula is completely safe. It sure isn't safe for you to be out during the day. You look awful."

"Why, thank you."

She frowned at the burn on his chest. "You're injured. You'd better have some blood." She marched over to the fridge and pulled out a bottle.

He lifted his eyebrows. "Are you ordering me around?"

"Yes." She put the bottle into the microwave. "Someone has to look after you. You take too many risks."

"People needed my help. Radinka needed us."

Shanna nodded, her eyes misting at the memory. "You're a heroic man," she whispered. And she loved him so much.

"You were very brave, too." Roman stepped toward her.

Her eyes met his. She wanted to wrap her arms around him and never let go.

The microwave dinged, startling her. She removed the bottle of blood. "I don't know if this is warm enough for you."

"It'll be fine." He took a long gulp. "There's other food here in the cabinets if you're hungry."

"I'm all right. We need to take care of your wounds. Finish up that drink, and then take off your clothes."

He smiled. "I'm beginning to like bossy women."

"And get in the shower. We need to clean you up." She strode into the bathroom. No mirrored medicine chest. That figured. She dug through drawers until she found some antibiotic cream. "Here. Once you're cleaned up, we'll put this on." She straightened and turned.

"Aagh!" She jumped and dropped the tube of ointment.

"You told me to undress." He stood naked in the doorway, sipping from his bottle of blood.

She bent over to retrieve the tube of medicine. Her cheeks flamed with heat. "I didn't expect you to do it so fast. Or to stand in front of me." She approached the doorway. He didn't move. "Excuse me."

He turned slightly to the side so she could squeeze through. Barely. Her cheeks were now on fire. She was all too aware of what her hip was brushing against.

"Shanna?"

"Enjoy your shower." She strode to the kitchen and began opening cabinets. "I'm hungry."

"So am I." He closed the bathroom door partway.

Soon she could hear the sound of rushing water. Poor guy. Those burns were going to sting. She poured herself a glass of water and drank. She wasn't really hungry, just stressed out. Roman had said she was brave, and she was overcoming her fear of blood. But what about her other fear—the fear that their relationship couldn't work.

She paced across the floor. How many relationships did work? About half? There was never any guarantee. Was she just afraid of losing him? She'd lost Karen. She'd lost her family. Should she ruin her chance for happiness today because she was afraid Roman might leave her years from now? Should she let doubt destroy this beautiful, overpowering feeling inside her?

She loved him with all her heart. And he loved her. The fact that they'd found each other was a miracle. Roman needed her. He'd suffered for hundreds of years. How could she deny him a taste at happiness? She should be delighted to bring him joy, even if it couldn't last forever.

She stopped in the middle of the room, her heart pounding. If she was truly brave, as he believed, she would march right in there and show him how much she loved him.

She went to the kitchen counter and gulped down some water. Well, she had guts. She could do this. She kicked off her shoes. She glanced toward the bed. The comforter was thick and boasted an Oriental design in red and gold. The sheets looked like gold silk, very fancy for a hiding place.

She looked up. A surveillance camera. That had to go. She grabbed Roman's shirt off the floor and climbed onto the bed. After a few tosses, she managed to completely cover the camera. She jumped down from the bed and pulled back the comforter.

Her pulse quickened as she finished undressing. Naked, she eased through the bathroom doorway. Steam obscured her view, but she could still see Roman in the shower stall. His eyes were shut as he rinsed off his shoulder-length black hair. His chest hair was flattened against his wet skin.

The wound sliced across his chest. She wanted to kiss it and make it better. Her gaze lowered. His manhood was relaxed and nestled in the midst of black curls. She wanted to kiss it and make it . . . bigger.

She opened the shower door with a *click*. His eyes opened. She stepped inside, and spray misted her body and hair.

His gaze swept down her body and back to her face. His eyes took on a reddish tint. "Are you sure?"

She slid her arms around his neck. "I'm very sure."

He enveloped her in his arms and planted his mouth on hers. The kiss was wild and hungry. No introductory pecks, no sweet build-up, just passion flaring out of control. He explored her mouth. His hands cupped her buttocks to press her against his swelling manhood.

Shanna stroked his tongue with her own. His hair was slick and wet as she pulled his head closer. She broke the kiss and scattered small kisses along the burn mark on his cheek.

He slipped a hand between them and caressed her breast. "You're so beautiful."

"Oh yeah?" Her hand glided down his flat stomach till her fingers reached the tangle of rough hair. She curled her fingers around him. "I think *you're* beautiful."

His breath hissed with a swift intake of air. "Oh God." He leaned against the tile wall. "Shanna."

"Yes?" She slid her hand up and down the shaft. He was hard, but the skin was soft and pliant. Especially on the tip.

"I don't know how much of this I can bear."

"You'll manage. You're a tough guy." She squatted down and took him into her mouth.

His body stiffened. He groaned. He was so big by now, she could hardly take in the whole length. She wrapped one hand around the base of the shaft, squeezing and tugging as she worked him with her mouth. He grew harder and thicker.

"Shanna." He grabbed her by the shoulders. "Stop. I can't—"

She straightened and rubbed her body against him. He held her tight with his eyes squeezed shut.

Relentless, she tugged on his stiff manhood. She stretched up on her toes to reach his ear. "Roman, I love you."

His eyes opened, bright red. With a gasp, his body convulsed. She felt the hot gush against her hip.

She hugged him, reveling in the shudders that racked his body. Yes, he would have no doubt that she loved him.

His breathing slowed. "God's blood." He leaned into the spray of hot water. With water running down his face and hair, he drew back and shook his head. "Wow."

Shanna laughed. "Not bad, huh?"

He looked down at her hip. "I made a mess on you."

"So? I'm washable, you know." She stepped under the spray and wet her hair. "Pass me the shampoo, will you?"

He did. "Did you mean what you said about loving me?"

She lathered up her hair. "Of course. I do love you."

He pulled her against him and kissed her mouth.

"Aagh. Shampoo in my face."

"Sorry." He eased her back under the spray. She arched her back to rinse her hair. Soon she felt his mouth on her breasts. She held on to his shoulders. He grabbed her under the buttocks and lifted her. She wrapped her legs around his waist.

Holding her, he turned and pressed her back against the tiles. He nuzzled her neck. "You love me?"

"Yes."

He lifted her higher so he could kiss her breasts. She enjoyed every kiss, every swirl of his tongue, every little tug at her nipples. Even so, she was painfully aware that her sex was pressed against his stomach. His flat stomach. She wanted more. She needed him inside.

"Roman," she gasped. "I need you."

He propped her up with one arm and eased a hand between them. When his fingers touched her, she moaned and pushed against him. He slid a finger inside her. She rocked against him. Their wet skin skidded and smacked against each other.

His hand stilled. "This is not entirely comfortable, is it?"

She opened her eyes. His were glowing red. She smiled. The fact that his eyes could change no longer frightened her. On the contrary, she loved it. It was so blatantly honest. He could never hide his hunger for her. "Take me to bed."

He smiled back. "As you wish." He turned the water off and opened the shower stall.

Shanna held on to his shoulders and kept her legs wrapped around his hips. As he walked across the bathroom, he grabbed a towel and rubbed it along her wet back and hair.

He approached the bed and laughed. "I see you found a good use for my shirt." He lowered her onto the bed. She started to close her legs, but he grabbed her knees to stop her.

"I like the view." He knelt beside the bed and pulled her hips to the edge. He kissed the inside of her thigh, then kissed her most intimate flesh.

Shanna was already too excited, too much in need, to last for very long. With the first swirl of his tongue, she was spiraling upward. Luckily he understood her need, for he was wonderfully aggressive. The ascent was quick. She hovered on a glorious plateau, then burst into long shudders of release.

She cried out.

He climbed into bed and gathered her in his arms. "I love you, Shanna." He kissed her brow. "I will always love you." He kissed her cheek. "I'll be a good husband." He kissed her neck.

"Yes." She wrapped her legs around him. Her sweet, old-fashioned, medieval man. He felt the need to commit himself to her before entering her, and it touched her heart. Her eyes blurred with tears. "I love you so much."

He reached down to position himself against her. "The last vow," he whispered.

"Hmm?"

He raised his red-hot gaze to her eyes. "I've waited a long time for you." He plunged inside.

She gasped, immediately tightening at the sudden assault.

He was breathing heavily, his head against her shoulder. "Shanna," he whispered.

At the sound of his voice, she felt her muscles relax. He slid in all the way, filling her. His voice continued to echo inside her head. *Shanna, Shanna.*

"Roman." She looked into his eyes. There was more than passion in the red glow of his gaze. There was love and wonder, warmth and joy. Everything she'd ever wanted.

He withdrew slowly, then eased back in. *I don't know how long I can last. This is so . . .*

"I know. I feel it, too." She pulled him forward till his forehead rested against hers. He was inside her head, inside her body. A part of her heart. *I love you, Roman.*

Their minds mingled so that Shanna could hardly tell the difference between her own pleasure and his. It was all the same, shared by them both. Soon they were grasping at each other and quickening the pace. He climaxed first. His release exploded through her body and mind, igniting her own shattering response.

They lay in each other's arms, catching their breath.

Finally Roman rolled away. "Am I smushing you?"

"No." She curled up beside him.

He gazed at the ceiling. "You . . . you're the only woman I've ever loved. In person, that is."

"What do you mean?"

"I took vows when I became a monk. I vowed I would do no harm. I broke that. I took a vow of poverty. I broke that, too."

"But you've done so much good. You shouldn't feel bad."

He turned onto his side and looked at her. "I took a vow of celibacy. I broke that just now."

She recalled his odd words before entering her. "The last vow?"

"Yes."

She propped herself up on her elbow. "Are you saying you were a virgin?"

"In the physical sense, yes. Mentally, I've been engaging in vampire sex for centuries."

"You've got to be kidding me. You never . . . ?"

He frowned. "I kept my vows while I was alive. Would you expect less of me?"

"No. I'm just amazed. I mean, you're incredibly hand-some. Weren't the village girls swooning over you?"

"They were swooning, all right. They were dying. All the women I saw were sick, covered with sores and growths and—"

"Okay. I get the picture. Not exactly attractive."

He smiled. "The first time I overheard vampire sex, it was by accident. I thought the lady was in trouble and needed help."

Shanna snorted. "Yeah, she needed something, all right."

He rolled onto his back and yawned. "I think the for-mula is wearing off. Before I fall asleep, I want to ask you something."

He was going to pop the question. Shanna sat up. "Yes?"

"If you're attacked, not that I would allow such a thing to happen, but—" He looked at her. "If you're attacked and dying, do you want me to transform you?"

Her mouth fell open. That wasn't a marriage proposal. "You want to turn me into a vampire?"

"No, I wouldn't want to condemn your immortal soul."

Jeez, he was stuck in such a medieval mindset. "Roman, I don't think God has abandoned you. Your synthetic blood saves lives every day. You could still be part of God's master plan."

"I wish I could believe that, but—" He sighed. "If things get bad with Petrovsky, I want to know where you stand."

"I don't want to be a vampire." She winced. "Please don't take that in a bad way. I love you just as you are."

He yawned again. "You're all that is good and pure and innocent in this world. No wonder I love you so much."

She stretched out beside him. "I'm not that good. I'm down here enjoying myself while people upstairs deal with the mess."

Roman frowned, gazing at the ceiling. Suddenly he sat up. "Laszlo!"

"He's asleep right now."

"Exactly." Roman touched his forehead. "I'm seeing spots."

"You're worn out." Shanna sat up. "You need to sleep now so your wounds can heal."

"No. Don't you see? All the vampires are dead right now. It's the perfect time to rescue Laszlo."

"But you're about to fall asleep."

He grabbed her hand. "Do you remember how to get to my lab? You can bring back the rest of the formula—"

"No! You're not taking another dose. We don't know what kind of damage it might do."

"I would heal during my sleep. I have to do this, Shanna. As soon as Petrovsky wakes up, he could kill Laszlo. And if we attack his house, he'll kill Laszlo for sure. Come on." He gave a nudge. "Quickly, before I pass out."

She crawled out of bed and began to dress. "We have to think this out. How will you get to Petrovsky's house?"

"I'll teleport in, find Laszlo, and teleport back home. It'll be easy. I should have thought of this before."

"Well, you were a bit distracted." Shanna tied her shoelaces.

"Hurry." Roman sat on the edge of the bed.

"I will." She unlocked the door. "I'll leave this open slightly so I can get back in."

He nodded. "Good."

She ran to the nearest stairwell and darted up the stairs. She wasn't sure she approved of this idea. Who knew what another dose of that formula might do to Roman? The ground floor was crowded with people, and she weaved around them as quickly as she could. And what if there were guards in Petrovsky's house? Roman shouldn't go in there alone. In the lab, she found the beaker of green liquid on the table. She picked it up, then noted her purse. What a shame her Beretta was gone.

She grabbed her purse and headed back to the silver room. Maybe she could borrow another gun. One thing was for sure. Roman was not doing this mission alone.

Twenty-five

"Are you sure you want to go in there alone?" Phil asked as he parked down the street from Petrovsky's house.

"I won't be alone for long." Shanna checked her purse. It was stuffed with lengths of rope for tying up prisoners. She pulled out the cell phone she'd borrowed from Howard Barr and punched in the newly memorized phone number for Roman's house.

"Barr," the head of Roman's daytime security answered.

"We're in place. I'm going in."

"Good. Keep the line open," Howard warned her in his nasal voice. "Here. Roman wants to talk to you."

"Be careful," Roman warned her.

"I'll be fine. Phil's here if I need him." Shanna opened the car door. "I'm setting the phone in my purse now. See you soon." She propped the open phone on top of everything in her purse.

Phil gave her an encouraging nod. She climbed from the car and walked toward Petrovsky's house.

At Romatech, she'd given Roman another dose of the formula before they teleported to his house. There, with Howard Barr's advice, they'd made their plan for Laszlo's rescue. She'd been opposed to Roman's theory that he could simply call Petrovsky's house and teleport there. He might accidentally arrive in a room full of sunlight. So, with Howard's support, she'd talked Roman into letting her participate.

She stopped in front of Petrovsky's duplex and glanced back. Phil was still in the black sedan, watching. Another vehicle caught her eye, a black SUV parked across the street. It looked just like the one that had followed her before. But they all looked alike. The city was full of them.

She hugged her purse to her chest. The phone was close by, with Roman listening in. She climbed the steps to the front door and rang the bell.

The door opened. A heavy-set man with a shaved head and graying goatee glared at her. "What do you want?"

"I'm Shanna Whelan. I believe you've been looking for me?"

His eyes widened. He grabbed her arm and pulled her in the house. "You must be one stupid bitch," he growled with a thick accent as he shut the door.

She backed away. There was too much light coming in from a window above the door. She saw an open doorway to the side and slipped inside a small parlor. The carpet was threadbare, the furniture old and sagging. Light filtered in through dusty, yellowed blinds.

The Russian followed her into the room. "This is too strange. You either have a death wish or this is some kind of trick." He opened his jacket to reveal a shoulder holster.

She moved toward the window. "No trick. I'm just tired of running."

The man removed his pistol. "You know Petrovksy will kill you."

"I was hoping to make a deal with him." She inched

closer to the window. "You see, I've been in Draganesti's house, and I know a lot about his security."

The Russian narrowed his eyes. "You wish to trade your life for information."

"That's the plan." Shanna eased back the curtains.

"Give me your purse. I must check it."

She set it down in a nearby chair. While the Russian moved forward, she quickly closed the blinds. "There," she announced in a loud voice. "It's nice and dark in here now."

The Russian peered inside her purse and pulled out her cell phone. "What is this?" He closed the phone, breaking the connection.

But Roman had heard her cue and was already materializing in the room. With vampire speed, he wrenched the gun from the Russian's hand and punched the man in the jaw. The Russian crumpled to the floor.

Shanna removed the rope from her purse and handed it to Roman. Quickly he tied the Russian's hands and feet.

"So far, so good," she whispered. "How are you feeling?"

"I'm fine." Roman handed her the Russian's gun. "Use this if you have to."

She nodded.

"I'll be back as soon as I can." Roman sped away in a blur.

Shanna knew if there were any more guards in the house, they'd never see him coming. He'd knock them flat, tie them up, then continue his search until he found Laszlo.

She picked up the phone and once again dialed Roman's house. "Howard? Are you still there?"

"Yes. How's it going?"

"Fine. We should be coming back soon." She set the phone down next to her purse.

Suddenly the front door burst open. With a gasp, Shanna raised the Russian's pistol. Footsteps raced across the foyer, then stopped in the doorway to the parlor. Two men in black suits faced her, their pistols drawn.

Shanna's mouth fell open. She blinked. "Dad?"

Sean Dermot Whelan looked much the same as he had a year ago when she'd last seen him. There was a little more gray in his reddish-gold hair, but his blue eyes were as sharp as ever. He lowered his pistol. "Shanna, are you all right?" He entered the parlor, looking about the room. He frowned at the unconscious man on the floor.

"Dad!" Shanna dropped her borrowed gun next to her purse. She ran to him and threw her arms around his neck.

"Sweetheart." He held his gun to the side while he hugged her with his free arm. "You scared me to death when I saw you coming into this house. What the hell are you doing here?"

She pulled back. "I could ask the same thing about you. I thought you were in Lithuania."

"I've been back awhile." He touched her face. "Thank God you're all right. I've been so worried about you."

"I'm fine." She hugged him again. "I thought I'd never see you again. How is Mom and—"

"Later," he cut her off. "We need to get out of here." He nodded toward her purse. "Get your stuff."

The second man in black entered the room. He was young with wavy, dark hair. "The foyer's clear." He inched toward a doorway across the room.

Shanna glanced at her purse. The phone was still sitting beside it on the chair cushion. How could she leave without Roman? How could she explain to her father what she was doing here? She was thrilled to see him again, but she had to wonder why he was here. "You saw me come here?"

"We've been watching Petrovsky's house for weeks. Draganesti's place, too." He tilted his head toward his companion. "This is Garrett."

"Hi," Shanna greeted the other man, then turned back to her father with a sudden realization. "You were in the black SUV I saw across the street."

"Yes." Sean motioned impatiently. "Come on. There could be a dozen mafia goons in this house. We can't stay and chat."

"I—I'm not here alone."

Sean narrowed his blue eyes. "You were alone when you came into this house. But you did have a driver—"

"Drop it!" Phil jumped into the parlor entryway, pointing his gun at Sean and Garrett.

They swung around, aiming their pistols at Phil.

Shanna gasped. "Don't shoot."

Phil held his gun steady while he glared at the men in black. "Are you all right, Shanna? You can come with me now."

Sean stepped in front of her. "She's not going anywhere with you. Who the hell are you?"

"Security," Phil answered. "I'm responsible for her safety. Now step aside and let her go."

"I'm her father. She's coming with me."

"Oh, I know who you are." Phil gave them a look of disgust. "You're CIA. The Stake-Out team."

"What?" Garrett exchanged a worried look with Shanna's father. "How do they know?"

CIA? Shanna glanced from one man to another, trying to figure out what was going on. Her dad had always said he worked for the State Department, but he sure wasn't behaving like a diplomat. And what was the Stake-Out team?

"So you must be one of Draganesti's daytime guards." Sean's voice was heavy with disapproval. "You're a traitor to humanity. A human working to protect vampires."

Shanna gasped. Her father knew about vampires?

"Drop it," a new voice warned. Another man in black appeared behind Phil.

Phil glanced back and muttered a curse. He lowered his gun onto the floor.

"Good work, Austin," Sean said. He strode toward Phil and retrieved his gun. "You're a human, so I'm going to let you go. Go back to that monster you serve and tell him his days, or rather his nights, are numbered. We're taking the vampires out, one by one, and there's nothing they can do about it."

Phil gave Shanna a worried look.

"I'll be all right. Go on." She watched him run from the house. Dear God, what a mess. Her father and these men were vampire slayers?

As if to confirm her conclusion, Garrett pulled a wooden stake from his jacket. "Since we're here, why don't we take care of a few vampires while they're sleeping?"

"They'll be heavily guarded." The man named Austin entered the parlor. He was young, with shaggy, blond hair. He noted the Russian on the floor. "There are usually ten to twelve armed men in this house during the day. I never saw them leave. So where are they?"

Sean nodded. "The place is too quiet." He looked at Shanna. "You said you weren't here alone?"

She swallowed hard. That was before she knew her father was a vampire killer. If he and his men went roaming about the house, killing vampires, they might kill Laszlo or even Roman.

"I was wrong. I think we'd better leave." She leaned over the chair to pick up her purse. The phone was still open, so she raised her voice, hoping Howard Barr would hear. "I'm ready to go with you, Dad."

Sean grabbed the phone, examined the number, then raised the phone to his cheek. "Who is this?" He frowned at his daughter. "They hung up." He closed the phone and dropped it in his pocket. "What's going on, Shanna?"

"Nothing." She swung her purse onto her shoulder in a nonchalant gesture. "I'm ready to go." It didn't matter if her dad had the phone. Roman could use any phone in the house to teleport home. And when he got home, Howard

Barr and Phil would be able to explain what had happened to her. Right now, she needed to get these vampire slayers out of the house and away from Roman.

"Shall we?" She moved toward the foyer.

"Wait." Sean reached out to stop her. "You didn't seem very surprised about vampires." He studied her carefully. "You spent a lot of time at Draganesti's house. You know what kind of evil creature he is, don't you?"

"I think we'd better leave before the mafia guys find us."

Sean shoved her hair back and examined each side of her neck. "Did that monster bite you?"

"He's not a monster." Shanna stepped back. "If you've been watching him and Petrovsky, you should know they're completely different. Roman is a good man."

Sean's mouth twisted with disgust. "Draganesti is a hideous creature from hell."

"He is not! He risked his life to protect me."

"Stockholm syndrome," Garrett muttered.

Sean nodded, his eyes narrowed. "Did you let him in, Shanna?"

In her mind? Yes, and in her body and in her heart. But there was no way she could admit that to her father. He already wanted to kill Roman. If he knew the truth, he'd move Roman to the top of his list. She needed to warn Roman of this new danger. But then he might already know about the Stake-Out team. Phil had known.

"Everything I did was of my own free will."

Sean cocked his head, studying her. "We shall see."

A blur of motion shot into the room. Roman came to a stop with Laszlo slung over his shoulder. "I heard voices. What's going on here?"

Sean, Garrett, and Austin gaped at him.

He noted their weapons and gave Shanna a questioning look. "You know these men?"

She motioned toward her father. "My dad thought I needed rescuing."

Sean blinked. "This can't be. A vampire moving about during the day?"

"And so fast," Austin whispered. "I never saw him coming."

Roman frowned at Shanna's father. "You're Sean Whelan."

Sean nodded. "And you're Draganesti, the disgusting creature who's been holding my daughter prisoner."

Roman's mouth thinned. "She has a different opinion. Don't you, Shanna?"

She saw Garrett behind Roman, moving slowly toward him with a wooden stake. "I think you need to leave."

"I'm not going without you."

"You bastard." Sean removed a wooden stake from his jacket. "I don't know what you've done to my daughter, but you'll pay for it."

Shanna ran to her father, hoping her embrace would keep him from jumping at Roman. The poor man was just standing there, staring at her, making himself an easy target. "Go!"

"You see?" Sean wrapped an arm around Shanna. "She's staying with me. In fact, she's going to become one of my team."

Roman looked ill. "Is this true, Shanna? Do you want to kill me now?"

Her eyes filled with tears. *There's a man with a stake behind you.*

Roman glanced back and saw Garrett. He gave Shanna one more tortured look, then zoomed into the foyer and up the stairs.

"After him!" Sean yelled. Garrett and Austin ran up the stairs.

Sean released Shanna and gave her a disappointed look. "You warned him, didn't you? You're sympathizing with the creature that held you prisoner."

"He's not a creature! And I was never his prisoner. I left when I wanted to."

"And then you ran back to him the very next night. Face it, Shanna. He's controlling you. That's what vampires do. They mentally manipulate their victims until you can no longer see the truth."

A tear ran down her cheek. "That's not what happened. The truth is that death cannot change a man's heart. Evil men, like Ivan Petrovsky, will become evil vampires. But men like Roman Draganesti remain good and honorable."

Sean's jaw tightened. "There's nothing good or honorable about vampires. They're serial killers. They've gotten away with murder for centuries." He leaned toward her. "But not anymore."

Her skin chilled. "You can't kill them all."

"That's exactly what we're going to do—stake them through the heart one by one till the world is free from their evil existence."

Austin and Garrett came back downstairs.

"He's gone," Austin reported. "Disappeared. All we found was a phone off the hook."

Shanna heaved a sigh of relief. Roman was safe. Safe at home, but tortured with the belief that she'd betrayed him. Somehow she had to get back to him.

Sean grabbed her arm. "You're coming with us."

Fifteen minutes later, Shanna was riding in the back of a black SUV with her father. Austin was driving, and Garrett was riding shotgun. She gazed out the window and noted they were headed for Manhattan by way of the Brooklyn Bridge.

Roman would be home, probably upstairs in his bedroom. She hoped the formula was wearing off. He wouldn't suffer if he was asleep. And at least, Laszlo would wake up this evening in a safe place. Her eyes continued to well with tears, and she blinked them away, not wanting to cry in front of her father.

"I know you've been through a tough couple of months," her father spoke softly. "But it's all over now. You're safe."

Safe, but heartbroken if she could never see Roman again. She cleared her throat. "How's Mom?"

"Fine. She's here in the States. Your brother and sister, too. I'm afraid you can't see them."

Shanna nodded.

"I'm very sorry about your friend who was killed," Sean said. "I asked the Justice Department about you, but they couldn't tell me anything. I've been worried sick about you."

"I'm fine. It's been hard, but I'm okay." She'd been so lonesome until she'd entered Roman's world. She missed him already. And she missed Radinka, Gregori, and Connor. They'd become her first real friends since losing Karen.

"I discovered your whereabouts by accident," Sean continued. "My team's been watching Petrovsky for weeks. We have his house bugged, his phone tapped. We heard him make that call to the SoHo SoBright Dental Clinic. I recognized your voice and realized they were coming to kill you."

Shanna shuddered, remembering the terror she'd felt.

"We rushed to the clinic, but you'd already disappeared. We knew Petrovsky didn't have you. I was in a panic, trying to find you. I had Garrett watching Draganesti's house, and he spotted you leaving. Unfortunately, he lost you."

"I was afraid that Russian would kill her," Garrett mumbled.

"Luckily you called that pizza place. We had a tap on their phone, so we found you. We waited outside your hotel, then followed you." Sean glared at Garrett. "But we lost you again."

Garrett's face turned pink.

Shanna almost felt sorry for the young man. It was never good to disappoint her dad. "You work for the CIA now?"

"I always have."

"Oh." Shanna winced inwardly. So her dad had been lying to them for years.

"I was recently given a new assignment—to create a special team for the purpose of eliminating the most dangerous threat mankind has ever faced."

She swallowed hard. "Vampires?"

"Yes." Sean leaned back in his seat. "Five months ago, I was in St. Petersburg when I spotted a man attacking a woman. I drew my weapon. Told him to release her and back away. When he let go, she collapsed in the snow. I fired my weapon, but it didn't faze him. Then this chill came over my mind, and I heard a voice telling me to forget. And then he vanished. I checked the woman. She was dead with two punctures on her neck."

Sean shrugged. "They've probably been spotted many times over the centuries, but they always used mind control to keep humans from remembering what they'd seen. In my case, it didn't work."

"You can resist mind control."

"Yes. We all can. That's why my team is so small. There's only a handful of people in the world with enough psychic power to resist their mind control. We're the only ones who can defeat those demons."

She breathed deeply, letting this new revelation sink in. "How . . . how long have you known about your psychic power?"

Sean shrugged. "Thirty years or so. When I joined the CIA, they discovered my talent and trained me to read and manipulate minds. It came in handy when dealing with scum."

"All those years you were working as a spy, you told us you were a diplomat."

"I couldn't let your mother know. It was hard enough on

her as it was, with us always moving from one place to another, always living in foreign countries."

Shanna remembered how her mom always seemed cheerful and optimistic. She'd been a pillar of strength for the children, always making the upheavals in their lives seem like grand adventures. "I thought Mom handled everything really well."

Sean frowned. "Not at first. She was a nervous wreck. But in time, I learned how to manage it, and things got much better."

Manage it? A queasy feeling settled in Shanna's stomach. "How did you manage it?"

"I bolstered her mental strength with my own. She was much more capable after that."

The queasy feeling twisted in her gut. "You used mind control on *Mom*?"

The two guys in the front seat exchanged glances.

Sean shot her an irritated look. "You don't need to make it sound so bad. I merely helped your mother maintain a healthy mental balance. Otherwise the poor woman would have had a breakdown."

Shanna gritted her teeth. "It was for her own good?"

"Exactly. And you kids, too. It was much easier to concentrate on my job when there was peace at home."

Anger boiled inside Shanna. "You . . . you controlled all of us? Like a freaking Stepford family?"

"Calm down. You're too old for a temper tantrum."

She clenched her fists and took a deep breath. She couldn't believe it. All these years, she had missed her family so much. But was her family, her entire childhood, all a lie? Was none of it real?

Suddenly a burst of warm air swept across Shanna's brow, encircling her head and pricking at her mental defenses. She closed her eyes and pushed back.

"That's my girl," Sean whispered.

She opened her eyes and stared at her father. The mental assault melted away. "That was you?"

He shrugged. "Just testing your defenses. You always were the strong one. And the more you fought me mentally, the stronger you got."

Her breath hitched. "That's why you sent me away. You sent me to boarding school because I was too hard to control."

"Hey." He pointed a finger at her. "I spent a fortune on you. And you got the best education in the family. You have no reason to complain."

Tears stung her eyes. "I missed my family."

He patted her hand. "We missed you, too. I was always proud of you, Shanna. I knew your abilities could be as strong as mine someday."

She pulled her hand away. Good God. Had she ever known her real mother or brother or sister? Or were they just peaceful robots her father had controlled? All these years, she'd felt bad about being sent away. Now she realized she was the lucky one. She'd been allowed to grow up free and develop her own sense of right and wrong.

And what her father was doing was wrong. Eliminating all vampires was akin to racial purging. It was a crime of hate.

She gazed out the window. What could she do?

"So, tell me," her father continued. "How can Draganesti stay awake and mobile during the day?"

"He's a brilliant scientist. He was testing a formula, at the risk of his own life, in order to rescue a friend."

Sean snorted. "He has you thinking he's some kind of noble superhero. Believe me, if he got hungry, you'd be just another warm meal to him."

She gritted her teeth. "He's the inventor of synthetic blood. He's responsible for saving millions of human lives."

"He probably invented the stuff to give his buddies more food."

Shanna turned to face him. "If you knew him, you would know he was good. But you won't even try. You're just determined to hate them all."

Sean frowned at her. "You're forgetting a very important fact, Shanna. They're no longer human. They feed off humans."

"They *are* human. Roman and his followers don't bite people anymore. They want to protect mortals. Petrovsky and the Malcontents are the ones who want to attack us."

Sean shook his head. "This synthetic blood is new. Before Draganesti invented it, he was feeding off humans just like the other vampires. They're monsters, Shanna. You can't turn them into saints."

She sighed. Her father had always been so stubborn. "There are two different kinds of vampires out there—the modern-day Vamps and the Malcontents."

"And it's our job to kill them all," Sean concluded.

"There may be some truth to what she says," Austin said as he steered the SUV into a right turn. "I've been listening in on Petrovsky's phone. He hates Draganesti with a passion. There's been some talk about the two factions duking it out."

"A vampire war?" Garrett asked. "That would be cool."

Sean turned to Shanna. "Those explosions at Romatech—do you know who was behind it?"

"It was Petrovsky and the Malcontents. They want to destroy all the synthetic blood in order to force vampires everywhere to go back to biting people."

Sean nodded. "What else do you know?"

"Roman and his followers are opposed to biting mortals. They're willing to fight in order to protect us."

Sean narrowed his eyes. "I find that hard to believe."

"Hey, let 'em fight," Garrett said. "Maybe they'll kill each other off. It would sure make our job easier."

Shanna groaned inwardly. Roman, Connor, Ian, and all the Highlanders risking their lives in battle? It made her sick. If only there was some way she could stop the war from happening.

The SUV pulled into a line at the entrance of nice hotel.

"Are we staying here?" she asked.

"You will," Sean answered. "Austin will remain with you for protection. Garrett and I have some business to attend to."

So her dad was going to leave her with a watchdog. That would make it hard to contact Roman.

"Like I said before," her father continued, "our team is small. I've been searching for people with enough psychic power to resist vampire mind control. Any American with that ability has a duty to his country to put that ability to proper use."

Shanna swallowed hard. Was her dad referring to her?

"What I'm saying, Shanna, is—I want you to join my team."

Yep, he meant her. "You want me to kill vampires?"

"I want you to protect the world from demonic creatures. We're terribly outnumbered, Shanna. We need you. I can get you into the CIA immediately, and we'll begin your training."

"I already have a career. I'm a dentist."

Sean waved a hand in dismissal. "That's not your true calling. God has given you a gift, a gift to fight this curse on mankind. It would be unforgivable not to use it."

Work for her domineering father? Talk about feeling cursed. Shanna's gut reaction was to tell her father to leave her the hell alone. She wanted more than anything to be with Roman. But what if living with Roman made her father move him to the top of his hit list? In that case, it would be better for her to stay with her father.

What if she knew all about her father's plans? Then she could keep Roman alerted to any trouble coming his way.

And maybe, in time, she could convince her dad that good Vamps really did exist. Maybe, in time, she could be with Roman again.

If she refused to join her dad's team, and her dad went on a killing spree, staking her friends, how could she live with herself? Roman had done his best to protect her. Now it was her turn to protect him.

The SUV pulled up in front of the hotel's revolving door.

She took a deep breath. "All right. I'll consider joining your team."

Twenty-six

Roman woke with his usual sharp and sudden intake of air. His heart lurched in his chest, then settled down to a steady beat. He opened his eyes.

"Thank God," a voice muttered. "We dinna think ye'd ever wake up."

Roman blinked and turned his head toward the voice. Angus was standing next to his bed, frowning at him. In fact, there were several people crowded around his bed. Jean-Luc, Connor, Howard Barr, Phil, Gregori, and Laszlo.

"Hey, bro." Gregori smiled. "We were worried about you."

Roman glanced at Laszlo. "Are you all right?"

"Yes, sir." The small chemist nodded. "Thanks to you. You can't imagine how relieved I was to wake up in your house."

Angus crossed his arms over his broad chest. "The question is, how are you? I hear ye were up and about during the daytime."

"Yes." Roman sat up and glanced at his bedside clock.

God's blood. The sun must have set over an hour ago. "I overslept."

"I havena ever heard of that happening before," Connor said.

"Possibly a side effect of the drug you took." Laszlo leaned forward. "Do you mind if I check your pulse, sir?"

"Go ahead." Roman stretched his arm out. Laszlo studied his watch while he gripped Roman's wrist.

"Congratulations, *mon ami*," Jean-Luc said. "Your formula is a great success. Awake during the day—it is amazing."

"I was still burned by sunlight." Roman glanced down at his chest where the sun had slashed a wound across his skin. The rip in his shirt was still there, but the skin had healed. Now, the wound was inside, tearing at his heart. Eliza had caused the wound a hundred years ago when she'd wanted to kill him. Now, because of Shanna, it was sliced open once again.

"Pulse is normal." Laszlo let go of Roman's wrist.

How could it be normal when his heart was ripped to shreds? Roman swallowed hard. "Did Shanna come back?"

"Nay," Connor whispered. "We havena heard from her."

"I tried to save her," Phil said, frowning. "But they had me outnumbered."

"That bloody Stake-Out team," Angus muttered. "Phil and Howard told us all about yer daytime adventure while we were waiting for ye to wake up."

Roman's heart squeezed in his chest. "She's joining her father's team. He'll train her to kill us."

Connor scoffed angrily. "I doona believe it."

Gregori shook his head. "It doesn't sound like her."

Angus sighed. "Mortals canna be trusted. I learned that the hard way." He regarded Roman sadly. "I thought ye did, too."

He had, but Shanna had filled him with hope once again. Roman had fallen asleep totally confused, and now it still didn't make sense. It seemed clear that Shanna had wanted to stay with her father. And staying with her father meant she would become a vampire killer. But why had she warned him of the slayer behind him? Why try to save his life if she wanted him dead? Did she think somehow she was protecting him by staying with her father? Did she actually love him after all?

"We've been busy while ye were sleeping," Angus announced. "When we woke, there was still an hour or so of nighttime in London and Edinburgh. So we've had every phone in this house busy while we teleported more of my men here. The good news is we now have an army downstairs of two hundred warriors. We're ready to go to war."

"I see." Roman climbed out of bed. Many of the men downstairs would be ones he had personally transformed. If they died in battle tonight, what would happen to their immortal souls? He knew they were good men, but still, they'd existed for centuries by feeding off mortals. God would never allow such creatures into heaven. And if the only alternative was hell, then Roman had doomed their immortal souls the minute he had transformed them. It was a burden of guilt too heavy to bear. "I'll be with you in a minute. Please wait in my office."

The men filed out. Roman dressed, then went into his office to warm up a bottle of blood. "How's your mother, Gregori?"

"Fine. I just came from the hospital." Gregori slouched in a wingback chair, frowning. "She says she made you swear to keep me safe during the upcoming war. I'm not a coward, you know."

"I know." The microwave dinged, and Roman removed his bottle of blood. "But you haven't been trained to fight."

"Big deal," Gregori muttered. "I'm not staying behind."

Roman sipped straight from the bottle. "Do we have enough weapons?"

"We're bringing stakes and our silver-plated swords." Angus paced about the room, his kilt swinging about his knees. "And we're bringing guns in case Petrovsky has mortals helping him."

The phone on Roman's desk rang.

"Speak of the devil," Jean-Luc whispered.

Roman strode to his desk and picked up the receiver. "Draganesti here."

"This is Petrovsky. I don't know how you managed to get in my house during the day, but don't ever try it again. From now on, I'll have thirty armed guards here, and they'll be shooting silver bullets."

Roman sat behind his desk. "I see my new formula has you worried. Are you afraid we'll come and stake you while you're sleeping?"

"You won't find us, you bloody *svoloch*! We have other places to sleep during the day. You'll never find us."

"I found my chemist. I can find you."

"You can have the stupid chemist. The little weasel ripped all the buttons off my couch. Now, here's the deal, Draganesti. You deliver Shanna Whelan to me tonight, or I keep bombing your plants and kidnapping your employees. And the next time I take one of your people, he'll be a pile of dust by the time you find him. Just like that Highlander I staked last night."

Roman's grip on the receiver tightened. He wouldn't risk any more Highlanders. And he'd never betray Shanna, even if she betrayed him. "I don't have Dr. Whelan."

"Of course you do. I heard she was in my house with you. You turn her over, and I'll stop bombing Romatech."

Ridiculous. Petrovsky would never stop causing trouble. Roman knew that without a doubt. And he knew he would protect Shanna with his dying breath. "Listen, Petrovsky. You won't be bombing Romatech, or kidnapping my employees, or harming a hair on Shanna Whelan's head, because you're not going to live through the night."

Ivan snorted. "That drug you took has messed up your head."

"We have an army of two hundred warriors, and we're coming after you tonight. How many men do you have, Petrovsky?" There was a pause. Roman knew from Angus's latest reports that the Russian-American coven could muster about fifty warriors at the most.

"I'll be generous," Roman continued, "and say you have a hundred men. That still leaves you outnumbered two to one. Would you care to wager on who's going to win tonight's battle?"

"You stinking *svoloch*. You can't have two hundred men."

"We teleported some in from the United Kingdom. But don't take my word for it. You'll see us soon enough."

Petrovsky cursed in Russian. "We can do that, too, you know. I'll bring in hundreds from Russia."

"Too late. The sun's already up in Russia. You can call, but they won't be answering the phone." Roman heard his friends chuckling. They wouldn't find his next comment very amusing. "But since you're in a bind, I'm willing to make a deal."

"What kind of deal?" Petrovsky asked.

Angus, Connor, and Jean-Luc approached Roman's desk with wary expressions on their faces.

"What do you want more than anything?" Roman asked. "More than killing Shanna Whelan or a few Scotsmen?"

Petrovsky snorted. "I'd like to rip your heart out and roast it over an open fire."

"Okay, I'll give you the chance. We'll settle this dispute once and for all. Just you and me."

Angus leaned over the desk, whispering, "What are ye saying, man? We canna allow ye to fight alone."

"Let our warriors fight," Jean-Luc said. "It's a sure win."

Roman covered the receiver with his hand. "This is the best way. We won't have to risk anyone's life."

Connor frowned. "Ye're risking yer own. We willna have it."

"What exactly are you saying, Draganesti?" Petrovsky asked on the phone. "Are you giving yourself up?"

"No," Roman answered. "I'm proposing a duel. Silver swords, and we don't stop till one of us is dust."

"What do I get for winning, other than the pleasure of killing your ass?"

"You will accept my death as payment for the safety of all my employees, my coven, the Highlanders, and Shanna Whelan. You will not harm any of them."

"Nay!" Angus thumped the desk with his fist. "Ye willna do this."

Roman held up a hand to stop further objections from his friends.

"How noble of you," Petrovsky sneered on the phone. "But that wouldn't be much fun for me, would it? I want a victory for the True Ones."

Roman considered. "All right. If I die this evening, all manufacture of Vampire Fusion Cuisine will end." After all, he wouldn't be around to invent the formulas.

"Does that include your synthetic blood?" Petrovsky asked.

"No. Synthetic blood saves human lives. Don't you want healthy mortals roaming about?"

Petrovsky snorted. "Fine. I get to skewer your ass, and I put a stop to your crappy Fusion Cuisine. Two A.M., Central Park, East Green. See you there."

"Wait a minute," Roman interrupted. "We haven't established what I get when I win."

"Ha! You're not winning."

"When I win, your people must swear never to harm any of mine again. That includes all my employees, both vampire and mortal, the Highlanders, and Shanna Whelan."

"What? Then your people remain safe whether you live or die. That sucks."

"It's my only condition," Roman said. "If you want a chance to kill me and end Fusion Cuisine, you'll take it."

While Petrovsky thought this over, Angus and Jean-Luc fussed at Roman.

"This is foolish, *mon ami*," Jean-Luc whispered. "When is the last time you practiced with a sword?"

Roman couldn't remember. "You trained me for over a hundred years. I can do this."

"But ye're out of practice, man." Angus glowered at him. "Ye've been closed up in yer wee lab for too long."

"*Exactement*," Jean-Luc announced. "I will go in your stead."

"No," Roman answered. "I transformed you, and I will not risk your immortal soul."

Jean-Luc's eyes narrowed. "That is the problem. You still feel guilty for transforming us."

"Dammit to hell," Angus growled. "It is *our* choice if we want to risk our souls. Who the hell do ye think ye are?"

Roman ignored them and spoke into the phone, "We come alone, Petrovsky. Just you and me, and only one survives. Are we in agreement?"

"Yes. But only because I've wanted to kill you for over five hundred years. Say your prayers, priest. Tonight, you die." Petrovsky hung up.

Roman dropped the receiver into place and stood.

"Ye canna do this," Angus shouted. "I willna have it."

Roman placed a hand on his old friend's shoulder. "This is my choice, Angus. It will save the lives of my friends."

"I am the best swordsman among us." Jean-Luc's eyes flashed an icy blue. "I demand to go in your stead. It is my right."

"Don't worry, Jean-Luc." Roman gripped the Frenchman's shoulder. "You taught me well. Wasn't I the one who delivered the fatal blow to Casimir?"

Jean-Luc scowled at him. "Only because I was watching your back."

"Ye're no' thinking straight," Angus insisted. "Ye're too distraught over that Whelan lass leaving you."

Roman swallowed hard. Was there any truth to Angus's claim? If Shanna were here, would he be so willing to risk himself? Still, he wasn't trying to kill himself. He certainly planned on winning. Killing Petrovsky might damage the Malcontent movement, but it wouldn't put an end to it. He needed to survive so he could continue to protect his people. "My decision is made."

"I'll be yer second," Connor announced.

"No. Petrovsky and I agreed to meet alone."

"He willna honor the agreement," Angus declared. "He canna be trusted. Ye know that."

"I will not break the agreement. And neither will any of you." Roman looked each of his friends in the eye. "You don't know where we are meeting. And you will not follow me."

They gave him looks full of despair. Angus opened his mouth to argue.

"Promise me," Roman broke in before they could object. "You will not follow me."

"All right." Angus glanced at the others with a pained expression. "Ye have our word."

Roman headed for the door.

"Ye once thought ye could save an entire village, and in yer pride, ye fell prey to Casimir. Now ye think to save us all."

Roman paused halfway through the door and looked back at Angus. "This isn't the same."

"Are ye sure?" Angus whispered. "Beware, my old friend. Ye've fallen to pride once before."

Shanna sat up in bed. She looked around, momentarily disoriented.

"Are you okay?" Austin asked.

"I—yes. I must have fallen asleep." She was in a hotel

room with two watchdogs. Austin had been joined by a young, brunette woman shortly after they arrived. The clock radio beside the bed glowed 8:20. Darn. She'd slept for too long. But after staying up all night, she'd been exhausted. "Is it dark outside?"

"Sure." Austin pointed to a pizza on the table next to him and the woman. "You want to eat?"

"In a little while." So Roman would be awake now. Was he preparing for war with the Russians? If only she could talk to him to see if he was all right. Her dad had confiscated her cell phone. She glanced at the phone on the bedside table. Still disconnected. Austin had pulled the plug on it when they'd first arrived. She was obviously not to be trusted. She could hardly complain, since they were right. The first chance she got, she intended to go back to Roman.

"Hi, I'm Alyssa," the brunette introduced herself. "Your dad asked me to bring some of your clothes from your apartment." She motioned to a suitcase at the base of Shanna's bed.

Shanna recognized her old luggage. "Thank you."

"We rigged the television to show DVN." Austin picked up the remote and turned up the volume. "The explosion at Romatech was the big story on their news. They're wondering if Draganesti is going to retaliate tonight."

"This vampire television is amazing." Alyssa sipped from a canned cola. "They have soap operas just like we do. And what on earth is Chocolood?"

"A drink made of chocolate and blood," Shanna explained. "It's popular with the ladies, though I heard it's making them gain weight."

Alyssa laughed. "You're kidding me."

"No. In fact, Roman made a new drink to help solve the problem. It's called Blood Lite."

This time, both her watchdogs laughed.

Austin shook his head. "They're not at all what I expected."

"Me, neither." Alyssa bit into a piece of pizza. "I thought they'd be white and slimy, but they look so normal."

"Yeah," Austin agreed. "And they have this whole culture that's different, but it still seems so . . . human."

"They *are* human. They feel pain and fear and . . . love." Shanna wondered what Roman was feeling right now.

"Well, don't let your dad hear that," Alyssa warned her. "He thinks they're a bunch of vicious psychopaths."

"Where is my dad?" Shanna asked.

"Watching Petrovsky's house, as usual," Austin replied. "He hates the Russians with a passion, especially since they targeted you at that restaurant."

Shanna blinked. "Excuse me?"

"Way to go, Austin," Alyssa muttered.

"I thought she knew." Austin turned to Shanna. "Didn't the FBI tell you?"

"Tell me what?" Shanna's heart rate quickened. "Are you saying my friend's murder wasn't an accident?"

Austin frowned. "It was payback. Your dad sent some of the top mafia guys in Russia to jail. Your family was flown out of Russia in secret. No one knows where they are. When the remaining mafia guys wanted revenge, you were the only family member they could find."

Shanna shook off a wave of dizziness. "They were trying to kill me? Karen died because of *me*?"

"It's not your fault," Alyssa insisted. "You only became a target because you're Sean Whelan's daughter."

"Given the circumstances," Austin continued, "working on our team will be the best life for you. You'll be under the radar, untraceable, and well trained in self-defense."

Shanna collapsed onto her back and stared at the ceiling. All this time, she'd thought that night at the restaurant was a terrible fluke. They'd been at the wrong place at the wrong time. But all along, she'd been the target. She was supposed to die, not Karen.

"Are you okay?" Alyssa asked.

"I feel terrible about Karen dying instead of me."

"Well." Austin popped open a can of soda. "If it helps, the mafia would have killed you both if they'd seen you. They wouldn't have left any witnesses."

Somehow, that didn't really help. Shanna closed her eyes.

Shanna? Where are you?

She gasped and sat up. Austin and Alyssa stared at her. "I, uh, need to go." She hurried to the restroom. My God, was Roman trying to contact her? Could their connection be strong enough to work long distance? She turned on the water faucets to mask her voice. "Roman, can you hear me?"

Yes. I'm here. His voice grew louder in her head as if he were tightening the connection. *Where are you?*

"I'm in a hotel with some of my father's team members."

Are you a prisoner? Or is that where you want to be?

"I'm fine for now. Don't worry about me. How are you? Are you going to war tonight?"

The dispute will be finished tonight. Why—why did you call your father? I thought you were going to stay with me.

"I didn't call him. He was outside, watching Petrovsky's house, and saw me go in. He thought I was in danger, so he came in to rescue me."

You intend to stay with him?

"I'd rather be with you, but if staying here helps me to protect you—"

I don't need your protection!

His angry voice reverberated in her head for a few seconds. "Roman, I will always love you. I would never betray you."

The connection crackled with tension.

"Roman? Are you there?"

A new emotion sifted into the connection. Despair. He was hurting. Shanna pressed his silver crucifix against her heart.

If I survive this night, will you come back to me?

If he survived the night? "Roman, what are you saying? Are you going to war?"

Will you come back to me?

"Yes! Yes, I will. But Roman, don't do anything dangerous. Please." Her grip on the crucifix tightened.

There was no response.

"Roman! Don't go!" She jumped when there was a banging on the bathroom door.

"Shanna!" Austin shouted. "Are you okay in there?"

"I'm fine," she yelled. She concentrated on sending a mental message. *Roman. Roman, can you hear me?*

No response. The connection was gone. And so was Roman.

It couldn't be a matter of pride. Angus had to be wrong. Roman knew Jean-Luc was a better swordsman. Angus was a better soldier. So how could it be pride that was hurtling him down this chosen path? He didn't know. All he knew for certain was he would do anything to save his people and Shanna. He'd changed many of the Highlanders himself. He'd even transformed Jean-Luc and Angus. He'd condemned all their souls to an eternity in hell should they perish. He couldn't allow that to happen, even if it meant his own death and eternal damnation.

It was shortly after eleven when Roman climbed the stone steps and opened the heavy wooden door of a church. His steps echoed in the empty foyer. Flames flickered in row upon row of red glass votives. Statues of saints and the Holy Mother stared down at him, questioning his presence in a house of God. He wondered about it, too. What did he think to gain here?

He crossed himself, then reached for the holy water. He paused, his hand hovering over the font. The water swirled, then began to boil. Steam drifted upward, heating his skin.

He snatched his hand away. He needed it in good shape

for the swordfight. As the water ceased to boil, his heart sank into despair. Surely he had received the answer to his question. His soul was doomed.

The door banged shut behind him. Roman whipped around, then relaxed when he saw who had entered.

Connor, Gregori, and Laszlo gave him sheepish looks.

"I thought I made myself clear. I was not to be followed."

Connor shrugged. "We knew we could follow ye here. Ye wouldna be fighting a duel in a kirk, now would ye?"

"Besides," Gregori added. "We were coming here, anyway. We wanted to pray for you."

"Yes." Laszlo crossed himself. "We've come to pray."

Roman snorted. "Pray all you like, for all the good it will do." He strode down the aisle to the confessional booths. He entered a booth and took a seat.

A small door slid open. On the other side of the screen, Roman could barely make out the shape of the priest in the dark. He seemed old and hunched over.

"Bless me, Father, for I have sinned." Roman turned away and mumbled the first half of the next sentence. "It's been five hundred and fourteen years since my last confession."

"What was that?" an old voice rasped. The priest cleared his throat. "Fourteen years?"

"It's been a long time. I have broken my vows before God. I've committed many sins. And tonight, I may cease to exist."

"Are you ill, my son?"

"No. Tonight, I will risk my life to save my people." Roman rested his head on the wooden wall. "But I'm not sure good can triumph over evil, or that I am even good. God has abandoned me, so surely I am also evil."

"Why do you believe God has abandoned you?"

"Once, long ago, I believed I could save a village, but I succumbed to the sin of pride and fell into darkness. I have been there ever since."

The priest cleared his throat once again and shifted in his chair. Roman figured his story sounded too strange. He'd wasted his time coming here. What had he hoped to find?

"Let me see if I understand," the priest said. "The first time you tried to save people, you were certain of victory?"

"Yes. In my pride, I knew I could not fail."

"Then, in your mind, you were risking nothing. Are you certain of victory tonight?"

Roman stared into the darkness of the booth. "No, I am not."

"Then why are you risking your life?"

Tears filled his eyes. "I cannot bear for them to risk their own. I . . . love them."

The priest took a deep breath. "Then you have your answer. You do this not out of pride, but out of love. And since love comes from the Father, He has not abandoned you."

Roman scoffed. "You do not understand the magnitude of my sins."

"Perhaps you do not understand the magnitude of God's forgiveness."

A tear rolled down Roman's face. "I wish I could believe you, Father. But I have done such evil. I fear it is too late for me."

The priest leaned close to the screen. "My son, for the truly repentant, it is never too late. I will pray for you tonight."

Twenty-seven

It was after midnight when Austin's cell phone buzzed. By his respectful tone and the way he kept glancing at her, Shanna suspected he was talking to her father. She'd been worried all evening about the possibility of a vampire war. Her attempts to contact Roman mentally had failed.

"I understand, sir." Austin handed his phone to Shanna. "Your father wants to talk to you."

She lifted the phone to her ear. "Dad?"

"Shanna, I thought I'd let you know what was going on. We have a tap on Petrovsky's phone, so we heard him talking to Draganesti."

"What's happening? Are they going to war?"

"Well, it appears Draganesti was ready for one. He claims to have two hundred warriors. Petrovsky's been on the phone all evening, ordering his followers to show up. We think he has about fifty at the most."

Shanna exhaled with relief. "Roman has him outnumbered."

"Well, not exactly. You see, Draganesti made a deal with

Petrovksy. They're meeting in Central Park. Instead of a war, the two of them are supposed to duel to the death."

Shanna's knees buckled and she collapsed on the bed. *"What?"*

"Yeah, they're supposed to meet alone on the East Green at two in the morning. Silver swords and only one left standing."

Shanna struggled for air. Roman was fighting to the death? "This—this can't be true. We have to stop this."

"Don't think we can, sweetheart. But I'm a bit concerned about your friend. You see, we heard Petrovsky order his men to show up this evening. As far as we know, Draganesti will be coming alone. But Petrovsky, he's bringing his whole army."

Shanna gasped. "Oh my God."

"When we listened in, we could tell Draganesti's people don't know where the duel's taking place. So there's no way they can help him. Kinda sad. Looks like a slaughter to me."

Shanna thought back over the conversation. Two A.M., East Green, Central Park. She had to let the Highlanders know.

"Gotta go, sweetheart. Just wanted to give you an update. Bye."

"Bye." Shanna gripped the phone tightly and glanced at Austin and Alyssa. "I have to make a call."

Alyssa stood. "We can't allow that, Shanna."

Austin lounged on the second bed. "What's the harm in it? Even prisoners are allowed one call."

Alyssa pivoted toward Austin. "Are you crazy?"

"No." Austin gave her a pointed look.

Shanna quickly punched in the number to Roman's house. She knew this was too strange. Too convenient. First her dad told her the information, and now Austin was letting her use his phone. But it made no difference. She still had to save Roman.

"Hello?"

"Connor, is that you?"

"Aye. Shanna? We've been worried about you."

"Can you, uh, do that phone thing?"

"Teleport? Aye. Where are you?"

"A hotel room. Hurry. I'll keep talking." Shanna glanced at Austin and Alyssa. "There are two other people here, but I don't think it should be a—"

Connor materialized beside her.

"Holy shit!" Austin scrambled out of bed.

Alyssa's mouth dropped open.

"Sorry for the intrusion." Connor took the phone from Shanna. "Ian, are ye there?"

"He—he's wearing a kilt," Alyssa whispered.

"Aye, that I am." Connor's gaze drifted over the female CIA agent. "And ye're a bonnie lass."

Alyssa sputtered.

"How the hell did you do that?" Austin asked.

"Och, about the same way I do this." Connor wrapped an arm around Shanna. She grabbed him just as everything went black.

When the darkness faded away, she found herself in the foyer at Roman's house. The first floor was jammed with Highlanders, all armed to the teeth. An air of frustration hung over them as they paced about.

Angus MacKay strode toward her. "Connor, why have ye brought her here?"

Before Connor could answer, Shanna broke in. "I have news. Roman and Petrovsky are fighting a duel tonight."

"That is no' news, lass." Connor regarded her sadly.

"But Petrovsky is bringing an army! You have to help Roman."

"Bugger," Angus muttered. "I knew that bastard wouldna keep his word."

"How do ye know this, Shanna?" Connor asked.

"My father bugged Petrovsky's house. He heard their

plans and told me. I had to warn you. Roman is meeting Petrovsky on the East Green in Central Park at two A.M."

The Scotsmen exchanged desperate glances.

Angus shook his head. " 'Tis no use, lass. We promised we wouldna follow him."

"I'm not leaving him alone!" Shanna reached for Connor's sword. "I made no promise, so I'm going."

"Wait," Connor shouted. "If Shanna goes, we can follow her. We never promised we wouldna do that."

"Aye." Angus grinned. "And the lass will need our protection. Roman would want us to follow her."

"Great." Shanna faced the Highlanders and lifted her sword in the air. "Follow me!"

The small kernel of hope Roman had garnered from his confession quickly withered away when he arrived at the East Green. Petrovsky had broken his agreement. He was not alone.

His coven spread out in a semicircle. Roman estimated fifty vampires, mostly male. About two dozen carried torches.

Petrovsky stepped forward. "It will be a pleasure killing you."

Roman gripped the hilt of his sword. "I see you were too afraid to come alone. You even brought a few women with you to wipe your nose."

"I'm not afraid. I gave my word I wouldn't harm any of your people, but I never promised that my followers wouldn't attack you if I'm killed. So you see, Draganesti, one way or another, tonight you will die."

Roman swallowed hard. He'd already figured as much. The prayers of one priest and three friends were not enough. God had abandoned him long ago.

"Are you ready?" Petrovsky drew his sword.

Roman drew his own sword. A gift from Jean-Luc, it was razor sharp, the steel blade plated with pure silver. The hilt was steel and leather and fit perfectly in his hand. He swished the blade through the air and saluted Petrovsky. He allowed himself one last thought of Shanna, then focused his mind on one thing only—survival.

As Shanna ran to the East Green, she could hear the clash of swords. The sound was terrifying, yet reassuring. If Roman was fighting, he was still alive.

"Halt!" Angus stopped beside her. "I know we're supposed to be following you, lass, but we need to do it faster." He swung her up into his arms.

Trees zoomed by, and Shanna held on tight. The Highlanders moved with vampire speed until they reached the edge of the clearing.

Angus set her down on her feet. "I'm sorry I misjudged you. Here." He handed her a sword. "Now we will follow you."

"Thank you." She stepped into the clearing.

The warriors spread out behind her, led by Angus MacKay and Jean-Luc Echarpe. Roman and Ivan Petrovsky were in the middle of the clearing, circling each other. As far as Shanna could tell, Roman was untouched. Ivan's clothes were slashed in a few places. Blood oozed from a wound on his left arm.

Petrovsky glanced her way and cursed. "You bastard, you had her all along. And you brought your bloody army."

Roman eased back and glanced quickly at Shanna and the Highlanders. He focused once more on Petrovksy, but yelled, "Angus, you gave me your word you would not follow me."

"We dinna follow you," Angus shouted back. "We dinna know where ye were. It was the lass we followed."

Roman leaped to the right as Petrovsky charged. He spun about and jabbed the Russian in his hip. Ivan cried out and pressed a hand against the wound.

"Shanna!" Roman yelled. "Get out of here."

"I'm not leaving you." She stepped forward. "And I'm not letting you die."

Ivan looked at the blood on his hand. "You think you're winning, don't you, Draganesti? But you're wrong. Just like you were wrong about Casimir."

Roman circled him. "Casimir is dead."

"Is he now?" Ivan pivoted to keep Roman in view. "Did you see him die?"

"He fell just moments before sunrise."

"And you and your friends fled to shelter. So you didn't see what happened next. I took Casimir to my secret lair."

A gasp echoed among the Highlanders.

"You lie," Roman whispered, his face pale. "Casimir is dead."

"He lives. And he's growing his army for revenge!" Ivan lunged forward and slashed his sword across Roman's stomach.

Roman leaped back, but the slice still found its mark. Blood seeped from the wound. He stumbled back.

Shanna gasped at the sight of Roman bleeding. Then, behind him, she spotted two Russians drawing their weapons. "Roman! Watch out!" She ran toward him.

With lightning speed, Angus caught her. "Nay, lass."

Roman spun around to defend himself from the two Russians.

Ivan glared at Shanna. "I'm sick of you, bitch!" He zipped over to her, slicing the air with his sword.

Angus shoved her behind him and drew his weapon, but Jean-Luc leaped forward first, his sword raised. He brought it down with a loud clash. Ivan stumbled back. Jean-Luc lunged forward, thrusting and sending Ivan back in retreat.

Shanna gasped when she saw Roman skewer one of his Russian attackers through the heart. The man collapsed to the ground and crumbled into dust. The other Russian dropped his sword and backed away.

Roman moved toward Shanna. "Angus, take her back

home where she'll be safe." He pressed a hand to the wound across his mid-section.

Shanna tried to run toward him, but Angus held her back. "Roman, come with us. You're wounded."

He gritted his teeth. "I have unfinished business." He charged toward Petrovsky.

Jean-Luc jumped back just as Roman's sword clashed against Ivan's. Petrovsky was caught by surprise. With a quick maneuver, Roman whisked Ivan's sword from his grasp. The sword flew through the air and landed close to one of the Russians.

Ivan ran toward his sword. Roman sliced him across the back of the legs, and he stumbled to the ground. He rolled over, but Roman was already there, pointing his sword at Ivan's heart. "You lose," Roman whispered.

Ivan looked frantically about.

Roman pressed the tip of his sword against Ivan's chest. "Swear that you and your coven will never harm any of my people."

Ivan gulped. "I swear."

"And you will cease your terrorist activities against my factories."

Ivan nodded. "If I promise, you won't kill me?"

Jean-Luc eased forward. "He has to die, Roman."

"Aye." Angus let go of Shanna and strode toward them. "You canna trust him."

Roman took a deep breath. "If he dies, someone else will take over his coven and leadership of the Malcontents. And the new leader will continue to terrorize us. But if we let Petrovsky live, he'll have to keep his word. Right?"

"Right." Ivan nodded. "I'll keep my word."

"Of course you will." Roman smiled grimly. "Or I will find you during the day while you are defenseless. Understand?"

"Yes." Ivan slowly stood.

Roman backed away. "Then we're finished here."

One of the Russians dashed forward and picked up Ivan's sword. "I believe this belongs to you." He stabbed Ivan through the stomach.

Ivan stumbled back. "Alek? Why do you betray me?" He fell to his knees. "You, you bastard. You want my power, my coven."

"No." Alek glared at him. "I want your women."

Ivan collapsed on the ground, clutching his stomach.

"You fool." A female vampire walked toward him and pulled a wooden stake from her belt. "You treated me like a whore."

Ivan gasped for air. "Galina. You stupid bitch. You are a whore."

Another female pulled a stake from her belt. "You won't ever call us bitches again. We're taking over your coven."

"What?" Ivan scooted across the grass as the two female vampires approached. "Katya, Galina, stop. You can't run a coven. You're too stupid."

"We were never stupid." Galina knelt beside him. "I'll have all the men I want."

Katya knelt on the other side. "And I'll be like Catherine the Great." She glanced at Galina. "Shall we?"

The two women plunged their stakes into Ivan's heart.

"No!" His cry faded as he crumbled away to dust.

The women rose and faced the Highlanders.

"A truce, for now?" Katya suggested.

"Agreed," Angus said.

The Russians zipped away, disappearing into the night. It was over.

Shanna gave Roman a shaky smile. "That was strange. Here. Raise your arms so we can bind your wound."

Connor wrapped a bandage around Roman's middle and tied it off. Then he removed a bottle of blood from his sporran and passed it to Roman.

"Thank you." Roman took a drink, then reached for Shanna. "We need to talk."

"We sure do. Don't you ever agree to a stupid duel again. I'll lock you up in the silver room and lose the key."

He smiled as he wrapped his arms around her. "I love it when you're bossy."

"Release her!" a voice shouted.

Shanna turned to see her father approaching with a flashlight. Behind him, Garrett, Austin, and Alyssa were carrying flashlights and silver pistols. Their belts were lined with wooden stakes. They stopped a distance from them and surveyed the scene, their lights moving here and there.

Her father shone a light on a pile of dust. "I'm hoping that's Petrovsky?"

"Aye," Angus answered. "And ye're Sean Whelan?"

"Yes." Sean located the second pile of dust. "Another Russian?"

"Yes," Roman answered. "I killed him."

With a sigh, Sean gazed about the East Green. "Not exactly the result I was looking for. Only two dead."

"What are you talking about?" Shanna asked.

"You did your part well, sweetheart. I know you're under the influence of that filthy creature who has his paws on you right now. I told Austin to let you use his phone. I knew you would warn Draganesti's friends."

"You were hoping for a war." Roman tightened his arms around Shanna. "You hoped most of us would die."

"Less work for us if you kill each other off." Sean shrugged. "But we'll get you. Mark my word."

Jean-Luc lifted his sword. "Foolish words when we have you outnumbered."

"Aye." Angus moved toward them. "What ye doona realize is that ye need us. There's an evil vampire amassing an army as we speak. Ye'll not be able to defeat Casimir without our help."

Sean's eyes narrowed. "I haven't heard of this Casimir. And why should I believe anything a demon tells me?"

"It's true, Dad," Shanna yelled. "You need these men."

"They're not men!" Sean shouted. "Now, step away from that monster and come with me."

Roman cleared his throat. "I don't suppose this would be a good time to ask for your daughter's hand in marriage?"

Sean whipped a wooden stake from his belt. "I'll see you in hell first!"

Roman winced. "Yeah, bad timing."

Shanna touched his face and smiled. "I think your timing's perfect."

"Shanna, I'll try to give you everything you ever wanted. The house with the picket fence—"

She laughed and hugged him close. "All I really need is you."

"Even children," Roman continued. "We'll figure out a way to insert my DNA into live sperm."

"What?" Shanna looked at him. "You want to be a father?"

"Only if you're the mother."

She grinned. "You do realize the harem has to go?"

"Already taken care of. Gregori's taking them to his house until they can manage on their own."

"Oh, how kind of him." Shanna laughed. "His mother will have a fit."

"I love you, Shanna." Roman kissed her mouth.

"Get away from her!" Sean advanced with the wooden stake.

"No!" Shanna turned to face her father.

"Shanna, come with me. That creature has a hold on your mind."

"No. The hold is on my heart." She pressed a hand to her chest. "I love him." She realized her hand was on the silver cross. "Oh, my gosh." She swiveled to face Roman. "Hug me again."

He pulled her close.

"It doesn't hurt you?" She stepped back and lifted the crucifix. "It didn't burn you."

Roman's eyes widened as he gently touched the cross.

"It must be a sign." Shanna's eyes misted with tears. "God has not abandoned you."

Roman's hand curled around the cross. " 'Perhaps you do not understand the magnitude of God's forgiveness.' A wise man told me that tonight. I couldn't believe it until now."

Shanna blinked back the tears. "God never abandoned you. And neither will I."

Roman touched her face. "I will always love you."

Shanna laughed as a tear escaped. "You realize if God can forgive you, you'll have to forgive yourself. You can't get away with hating yourself anymore. None of us can."

"Aye," Connor muttered. "We'll have to like the bugger."

Roman shoved the Scotsman away with a grin, then wrapped his arms around Shanna.

"This is not over!" Sean yelled. "We'll hunt you down, one by one." He stalked off, followed by his team.

"Don't worry about my dad." Shanna rested her head on Roman's shoulder. "He'll get used to you."

"Then you really will marry me?" Roman asked.

"Yes." As Roman's mouth came down on hers, she heard the cheers of Highlanders. She snuggled close. Life was good, even with the Undead.